DREAMSPY

By the same author:

Fiction

House of Zeor
Unto Zeor, Forever
First Channel (with Jean Lorrah)
Mahogany Trinrose
Channel's Destiny (with Jean Lorrah)
Molt Brother
RenSime
City of a Million Legends
Dushau
Farfetch
Outreach
Zelerod's Doom (with Jean Lorrah)
Those of My Blood

Non-Fiction

Star Trek Lives! (with Sondra Marshak and Joan Winston)

DREAMSPY

Jacqueline

Lichtenberg

ST. MARTIN'S PRESS
New York

Library of Congress Cataloging-in-Publication Data

Lichtenberg, Jacqueline.
    Dreamspy / Jacqueline Lichtenberg.
        p.   cm.
    ISBN 0-312-03327-3
    I. Title.
PS3562.I3D74 1989
813'.54—dc20   89-34854
                                                             CIP

First Edition

10 9 8 7 6 5 4 3 2 1

To Robert Anson Heinlein
May he rest in peace

To Sophie Herbert
May she rest in peace

Acknowledgments

The list of acknowledgments for this book is substantially the same as that for the companion volume in this universe, *Those of My Blood*, with the following additions.

It is unfortunate that the dedication of this novel to Robert Heinlein had to be made after his death. My first novel, *House of Zeor*, was also dedicated to him, but for different reasons. In this one, I have tried to pay tribute to something I learned from him during my teens, namely that it isn't necessary to wait for someone to teach you something before you try to do it. The great leaps forward in human history have come from people doing things that have never been done (never mind taught) before. People who live by that creed tend to irritate those who don't.

Secondly, I have to acknowledge the unwitting contribution of Katherine Kurtz to this universe. Nothing could be farther from her Deryni universe than this novel, yet the basic premise, the Pools and the mathematics behind them, is connected to a burst of inspiration triggered by the rereading of nine Deryni novels (and an anthology) and the fevered creation of an alternate-universe Deryni story outline revealing the Qabalistic origin of the Deryni Portals. Since that story can never be written, I have incorporated a few of my postulates in the Pools.

Thirdly, I have to thank Katie Filipowicz, Roberta Klein-Mendelson, and Marge Robbins for test reading the manuscript of *Dreamspy*. Marge in particular has been very busy preparing to turn the Sime/Gen Welcommittee over to Linda Whitten while she takes up editing ZEOR FORUM, a Sime/Gen fanzine. The activities of the Sime/Gen fans have become particularly complex since the fanzines have been opened to discussion of all my universes.

Lastly, we come to the map that Stuart Moore, my editor at St. Martin's, wanted to include in this volume. The artwork was inspired by and loosely based on the map of the Milky Way galaxy in the article "Coming Home" by Marcia Bartusiak published in *Discover* magazine, September 1988, which pinpointed the position of Earth—the Planet of the Dreamers. But I have added many star clusters to create the typography for the Teleod/Metaji war.

The map was prepared by Michael Poe and Kier Neustaedter, using the Apple Scanner and a Macintosh II.

For further information on the fan activities, contact with other s/f fandoms, current availability of all my novels, or just to comment on this book or *Those of My Blood*, send a Self-Addressed Stamped Envelope (SASE) with your request to: P.O.B. 290, Monsey, N.Y., 10952. If that fails to reach me, I can always be reached through my publishers, or through the Scott Meredith Agency (845 Third Avenue, New York, NY 10022).

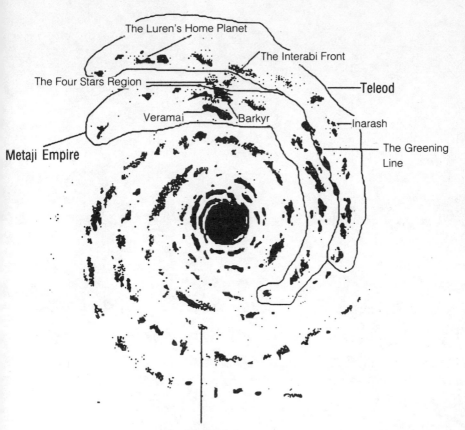

The Luren's Home Planet

The Interabi Front

The Four Stars Region

Teleod

Veramai

Barkyr

Inarash

Metaji Empire

The Greening
Line

Planet of the Dreamers

DREAMSPY

chapter **one**

● ●

It was just an overheard comment, a non-human voice floating on the echoes trapped in the ship's corridor: ". . . that woman Kyllikki! She thinks she's so much better than the rest of us." But the comment stung. *I'm not like Zimor! I'm not!*

Kyllikki focused on the red of the lift doors ahead of her and kept walking toward them, breathing deeply to suppress the unbidden tears, trying not to hear the echo of a voice answering the bitter comment.

"How do you know what she thinks? *She's* the telepath, not you."

"Look at how she wears her uniform, how she walks, how she holds her hands away from contamination, how she speaks in that distant voice, never meeting your eyes. You don't have to be a telepath to tell what someone thinks of you."

The nonhuman voices faded, but the thoughts didn't. //She used to be some kind of Teleod princess. You can't fault her if she has Imperial manners—*human* manners!//

Kyllikki's face flushed and her heart sped faster. She could not blot out the searing reply. //I can fault anything Teleod. In the Teleod I'd be considered little better than an animal because I haven't a single human gene in me.//

A hatch clanged shut, reducing the amplitude of the thoughts, and at last she gained control. She hadn't even been able to guess what species the two were. *Too arrogant to learn the voices and accents of the* people *I live among?*

The lift doors whipped aside and Kyllikki flung herself into the empty compartment, hitting the controls. As the lift moved, she let herself sob out loud, once, and then marshaled the tattered remnants of her mental barriers and fought down guilt for the accidental intrusion.

She'd known defecting to the Metaji Empire wouldn't be easy. *If Zimor ever saw me like this, she'd laugh so hard the servants and guards would think she'd been drugged!*

The vision of her ruthless cousin laughing at her in triumph stiffened Kyllikki's spine. It had been nearly a year since she'd given the woman a single thought. Now, three times in one day, she'd reacted as if she were still in Zimor's household, having to face Zimor over the dinner table each evening. *Is there to be no escape, anywhere?*

She told herself that anyone would react to overhearing such scathing comments. It didn't mean Zimor had reached through space and across stellar empires to corrupt her mind.

But if she could, she would!

The lift opened onto a crowded passenger corridor. In her panic, she'd misdirected it. *Some ship's officer I am!* Politely, she yielded the compartment to the passengers and pushed her way into the streams of moving people.

The passenger liner *Prosperity* was carrying more than a capacity load. Since the Teleod had begun to attack Metaji civilians, the Metaji Emperor had assigned a fighter escort to every passenger liner. This meant cutting passenger service and filling every ship on every trip.

Kyllikki defiantly let herself be jammed against a Paitsmun, who was waddling along on powerful hind legs that were designed for leaping or running, not gliding under low ceilings. His hard armor plating was polished smooth as glass, the sections rubbing musically as he moved. He darted a glance at her, recognized her uniform and murmured an apology as he shied away, embarrassed by his own thoughts, worried she'd pick them up.

She refused to react. He meant no offense. He was trying to control his reaction to her uniform. She had to get hold of herself. She'd be on duty soon.

Her destination, the Window Room, was the one place insulated from the mental noise in the ship, yet where a telepathically transparent bubble allowed a telepath to scan space outside the ship. Once past the main dining saloon, she'd be there. Within the hour, *Prosperity* would be passing close to a courier ship. By reporting for duty early, she'd have time to gossip with the courier's telepath.

The mere thought made her tremble. In the Teleod, she'd never starved for deep contact, but here they'd exacted a dire oath from her, shackling her mind into their protocols. *And that's why I can't keep my barriers in place,* she told herself, *not Zimor's mockery but simple sensory deprivation.* Her barriers slipped again, and the whirling mind-mutter of the people around her roared through her skull.

Suddenly, warm breath rushed into her ear and arms came around her shoulders from behind. "What's the matter? You look like you're about to faint."

She started so hard she nearly screamed out loud, then realized it was only Zuchmul, his luren Influence encasing her in a shell of his presence. She could feel the fine chain mesh worn under his clothes to protect his radiation-sensitive skin. Only his pasty-white face was exposed, the mask draped to one side, jingling against his shoulder. As he held her close, she felt his Influence despite the inhibiting device he wore at the base of his throat. A hand's breadth from his body, she'd have felt nothing.

"Zuchmul, you're not supposed to do that!" she hissed. He had oaths to obey, too. A luren's Influence—a kind of mind power unknown to any other human race—could make a person see and believe anything. The effect was stronger when he was hungry, as now. One of her duties was to monitor the luren aboard to be sure they didn't use their power illicitly. But he was shielding her from the mental roar, his touch so mild she felt no reflexive aversion.

Half supporting her, he guided her into the dining saloon. Tables, round, square and oblong, dotted the thick carpet, many draped with white cloths and set with gleaming utensils. Those were meant for the human passengers. Among them were tables for various nonhumans, which gave Kyllikki the feeling of dining in a zoo. Zuchmul positioned her over a gold-upholstered chair and let go. Her knees collapsed.

As her weight came onto the chair, an air curtain surrounded the table, controlling sound and odor.

Zuchmul took a place beside her and poured a hot drink from the pitcher on the table, shoving it under her nose. She leaned back, objecting, "This is passengers' mess!"

"The Captain ordered us to mingle."

"Not us, the officers."

He fingered the brocaded sleeve of her uniform. "Don't look if it will scare you, but you've been an officer since you signed onto the ship. Communications Third Officer."

She wrapped her shaking hands around the cup and managed to get it to her mouth without spilling any.

"Kyllikki, are you going to tell me about it? Or are you just going to wander around mentally screaming for help?"

"I didn't know luren were telepaths."

"Empaths," he corrected. "You're hurting. And—you're, well—hungry. I don't know for what."

She gripped the cup. *Hungry. But there's no chance. Not now. Not ever. Because I ran from Zimor.*

A deeper male voice cut across the table. "Zuchmul, what are you doing here?"

"Idom. I could ask you the same. Aren't you on duty?"

"Finished. We make planetfall late next shift—Barkyr, the Paitsmun colony." The big white-bearded man was the ship's Guide, responsible for interstellar astrogation. He wore the typical Guide's uniform, dark-purple silk cape over a white cassock

4

that parted to show a black robe, ship's insignia on the collar, Guide's medallion around his neck.

He sat down on Kyllikki's other side. "Are you hungry, Zuchmul? I think you've disturbed the lady."

The luren sighed and fastened the sheer mesh mask across his face, obscuring the limpid black eyes, made brighter by their light shielding inserts. "She was worse than this when I found her in the hall."

"I'm not a stray pet, you know." But the two friendly presences close around her had helped. All three of them were exiles of a sort, Zuchmul because the power of luren Influence was so feared, Idom because the Guide's Guild kept their practices secret, and Kyllikki because she could invade the most private places of mind and soul. "I'm sorry," she said. "I know you were just trying to help, and you did. But I need some time alone before I go on duty."

Zuchmul refilled her cup and rose as a human waiter came to the table, all white coat, clean black accessories, and professional smile. Zuchmul bowed courteously to the waiter. "I will seek my refreshment elsewhere." And he departed on silent feet, presumably to feed on the blood of the livestock they carried for him and the luren passengers.

Kyllikki ordered thrixal-root pudding and Idom asked for a pastry, settling in as if to stay awhile. When the waiter had left, Kyllikki said, "You can have my pudding, too," and started to rise.

Idom caught her wrist, fingers closing around her sleeve and pulling her back down. She sat, not daring to make a scene. "Idom, I meant it. I have to get away."

"It's not isolation you need. It's *contact*."

She started as if he'd scalded her. Then she took a schooled breath, relaxed, and concentrated on building her barriers. In the Metaji, she wasn't allowed to project thoughts to a non-telepath—not even worded thoughts.

When she raised her attention to him again, Idom was saying, ". . . do I have to do to get through to you?"

"Don't be so sure you haven't," she replied, keeping her

eyes on her drink. The surface was mirror-smooth. At least her hands had stopped shaking. *He can't possibly know.*

"You've been like this all day," he insisted. "If something has upset you, you should talk about it, and of all the people on this ship, I'm the most likely to understand."

"Talk!" She heard the scorn in her voice and clamped her mouth shut. Too late.

He leaned close, making sure no one would overhear. "Even if I'm mute in your medium, at least I can 'listen.'"

Wouldn't it be legal if he volunteered? But he was only offering to open himself to voice-analogue, worded thoughts, not to any real contact. The temptation was so intense she knew she'd abuse his trust if she permitted herself to accept. She lurched to her feet and started for the door.

She'd gone only two steps when his sympathy overwhelmed her. She turned. His hands were folded neatly on the table, his eyes closed, and out of him beat wave upon wave of pure feeling—not images, not verbalized thoughts, just sympathy. Not pity. Sympathy. He knew what she hungered for.

His Guild training, whatever it was, had fostered his ability to concentrate and to focus emotion to such a fine degree that he might as well have been luren. The air around him throbbed with power.

All at once, it was too much for her. //If you're so brave, then come to my quarters tonight and listen!//

She wrenched herself around and plunged out into the corridor. Behind her, the throbbing waves of sympathy cut off. *He didn't mean it. He'll report me.* As it was her job to watch the luren, so there were those who watched her. If he'd been testing her, she'd failed. *No. He's my friend. He wouldn't trap me like that.*

She flung herself against the hatch of the Window Room, set her palm against the AUTHORIZED PERSONNEL sign, and waited for the hatch to yield. It took its time identifying her, but then she was inside, sealed off from the mental chaos of hundreds of minds. She paused in the lounge to catch her breath, hardly aware of the subdued lighting, the bland decor, or the standard chairs, racks, and perches.

"You're early." A voice came from a speaker. There was no glad welcome in it, but no rejection either.

"Oh. Lee. I wanted to work the courier traffic. We're approaching range now, right?"

"Yes. I was just about to Search. Come on out."

She pushed through an airlock and into the Window itself. It was a huge, visually and telepathically transparent bubble set into the skin of the ship, so that they seemed to be working in a waist-high pit with nothing over them but space and stars. Their fighter escort wasn't visible, and the solar system they were approaching was barely distinguishable from the more distant stars.

Three communications work stations were set into a circular rim. Ship's intercom, transmitters, recorders, and screens for all manner of data displays surrounded each work station. Lee, Com Second, was alone.

He turned to look up at her. Lee was a slightly built human with a dark complexion and the most beautiful black eyes she'd ever seen. But they were neutral, not friendly. //The courier is the *Otroub*. My record shows their Com Officer is Etha Ckam. Do you know her?//

Adopting the formal, businesslike manner she'd been taught, she slid into the place at his right and brought up her screens. //We've met. She seems competent.// Actually, Ckam was one of the few Kyllikki seriously hoped would become a friend one day. *Otroub*, according to the records she had before her, would be in traffic range for two hours. //I'm showing a long list of messages for *Otroub*. Apparently their owners have been trying to get in touch with them by relay.//

//Yeah. Something about Sa'ar Stock needing transport— you know, orl, the experimental animals the luren make.//

//I know about orl. We carry some to feed luren.//

//Sa'ar designs special laboratory animals, one of the few things we still import from the Teleod despite the war.//

//The luren citadels are officially neutral. What they import—or export—is strictly legal. Zuchmul was telling me yesterday how careful they are about that.//

//Yeah,// answered Lee, //but Zuchmul hasn't heard the

latest. Now that the scion of the Sa'ar family, the richest luren family in Metaji or Teleod, is missing with a shipload of expensive orl, the Teleod is saying that we—the Duke of Fotel, actually—captured the Sa'ar and his orl as hostages.//

//Why would a Duke want to antagonize the luren?//

//Who knows? But *Otroub* is owned by D'sillin Service, which is luren-owned and based on one of Fotel's fiefs. If Sa'ar is dealing with Fotel, willing or not, it could affect the outcome of the war. Deny that, if you can.//

//Can't. But if Fotel wanted *Otroub* to transport hostages, they wouldn't be filling space with the message. No, the Sa'ar was lost, just like hundreds of others. Luren in the Teleod use their own ships, a design that can't be relied on anymore, from the days when they didn't even carry life pods. Sa'ar runs a fleet of them. Or used to.//

Prosperity was older yet, and carried a full complement of life pods, which let them charge extra for passage now.

//Well, maybe he was just lost, then,// he allowed. He glanced at her, and she picked up an unworded idea. *Unless the Sa'ar heir is defecting, like she did, and bringing the luren with him. In which case, I'll bet she knows.*

She bent over her station, poking things at random, struggling to discipline her mind. But it was too late. She felt Lee's thoughts recede as if stung. Her heart stopped. Metaji protocols demanded working telepaths stay out of each others' minds. *Shog! I hate this place!*

"What's the matter, Kyllikki?" His barriers were so tight she might have been hearing a voice transmission.

At least he's not crying traitor. Her heart slammed into action again. She bent to repair the damage she'd done to her displays. "I'm sorry. I've been nervous all day."

"I guess I can understand how hard it must be here for you. I just do this kind of work because I'm not much good at anything else. You were bred for it."

Not for this kind of work, she wanted to say. She had been bred for the total immersion of the Dreambond, the unique linkage that could form only between a member of the Eight

Families, like Kyllikki, and a Dreamer. That linkage was illegal in both Teleod and Metaji, the Dreamers confined to their planet. In the Teleod, Bonders like Kyllikki had to survive on an occasional deep contact, and when it got particularly bad, there were drugs to blunt the need. But not here. Her Metaji retraining had supposedly conditioned her to block out even that need. Until today, it had. She met Lee's eyes. "You're right. The work will steady my coordination so I won't make any more . . . mistakes."

"That's what it was, ill-coordination?" She assented and he got to his feet, shutting down his station. //All yours, then, Com Third.// His mental voice was disciplined, distant, perfectly modulated.

But even so, the surface touch was such a tremendous relief that she looked up at him with a grin of pure joy. //Thank you, Lee.// She turned to log onto the bridge stations and accept the hails from the bridge officers who were surprised to find her on duty already. As Lee departed, she sealed herself into the Window, making sure she wouldn't be disturbed when her mental barriers were down, and at the same time she readied a file for incoming traffic and began the mental Search Lee had been about to do for *Otroub* and the courier's Com Officer, Ckam.

In moments, she had forgotten herself in the routine of tracking the approach to the Barkyr system, exchanging relayed greetings, and coordinating with *Prosperity*'s three matched escort ships, Gita One, Gita Two, and Gita Three.

Each escort fighter carried a crew of three, one of whom was a marginal telepath with minimal training and range. Such talent was plentiful enough to be expendable, or so the military thought.

The three fighters escorting the liner *Prosperity* had split up. One had gone out to check on *Otroub*, one was behind them, and the other was ahead of them clearing their way into Barkyr space. *Otroub* would bypass the system, not even coming within coherent spectral transmission range of either the system or *Prosperity*. Kyllikki would send *Otroub* the mail bound for a military base, which was *Otroub*'s next stop, and pick up any messages bound for Barkyr or Station Prime, the free-orbiting habitat that housed Barkyr Defense.

When she finally made contact with *Otroub*'s Etha Ckam, Kyllikki wasted no time pushing her traffic. Each message was read, then read back as the ships neared closest approach, then began to separate again.

As she had expected, Kyllikki's nerves steadied down once the routine was established and she had contact with a friendly, open mind, however formal. They worked quickly and smoothly together and finished before contact faded.

//Kyllikki, what do you make of this business with the Sa'ar livestock?// added Ckam. //Do you think it could be important enough to keep us from delivering our passenger?//

//Passenger? Couriers don't carry passengers.// To compensate for the fading contact, Kyllikki lowered her barriers, suddenly very interested.

//We've got one this trip. He's some kind of exotic entertainer bound for a court functionary's reception, or that's the story. He *is* gorgeous enough, but—//

Without warning, a whole-sensory image exploded into Kyllikki's mind, filtered and embroidered by Ckam's libido, and fraught with fulsome overtones. She learned more from that one instant than she could have from an hour of words. But it was illicit knowledge. She'd invaded another mind, and again broken out of audio-analogue. Unaware of what Kyllikki sensed, Ckam added, //—you're right, no mere entertainer would be on a courier—what's the matter?//

The image throbbed through Kyllikki's whole being.

//—Kyllikki?// Ckam had withdrawn to a cool professional distance. The image was no longer coming from her, but Kyllikki couldn't let it go.

//Etha, do you know what race he is?// *Can't be. Just simply can't be. There are no Dreamers in the Metaji. None.*

//Oh—well . . .//

It was rude to ask about race here. //Never mind. It's just that he—uh—sounded familiar.//

//You recognized his voice from my memory! Who is he? Come on, you can trust me. I won't—// Suddenly, her mental voice escalated into a gasp.

//Etha?//

//Six ships! Your Gita One is under attack.// Ckam's attention went to close focus. Kyllikki strained to follow what was happening on the retreating ship. Meanwhile, her hands flew over her own board, alerting *Prosperity*'s bridge crew and the Captain minutes before lightspeed transmissions could reach them. A moment later, without any volition, she received another image from Ckam's mind, the illicit contact suddenly wide open between them, showing her Ckam's displays.

Six fighters were streaking by *Otroub* on a heading that would intersect *Prosperity* at the edge of the Barkyr system, outside local defenses. Two of them were laying down fire at the rapidly maneuvering Gita One, and two more were firing directly on *Otroub*.

Gita One's Com Officer yelled a telepathic warning that pierced through Ckam's mind and lanced into Kyllikki's awareness like an electric shock. Suddenly, Kyllikki was deadly calm, her mental voice firm as she announced, //Gita Two, Gita Three, this is *Prosperity*. Gita One and *Otroub* are under attack by six incoming ships which will intercept *Prosperity*.// She added speed and course figures. //Barkyr Defense, I have relay from Gita One. Bogeys on trajectory intercept your Station Prime, one-oh-two-mark-six-seven. Advisement; use all force. Shall I repeat.//

//Alert acknowledged, *Prosperity*. One-oh-two-mark-six-seven. All force. Advise Gita One—//

White pain smashed through Kyllikki's eyes, a stark searing heat so hot it made death welcome. *No. That's Etha's pain. She's closer.* The relayed pain hardly touched the icy core of calm within Kyllikki. //Barkyr Defense. Gita One is destroyed.// She made sure the escorters heard also as she tapped the data into *Prosperity*'s bridge display.

The two remaining escorters near *Prosperity* were struggling to maneuver around the wallowing liner to meet the incoming ships. The attackers were small, but moving so fast they must have materialized at full velocity somewhere nearby, planning to nail Barkyr's Station Prime without slowing, then head directly into their next dive point. They were going too fast to change direction, and so were simply taking advantage of the chance to destroy two Metaji ships that happened to be in their path.

In the back of Kyllikki's mind, Ckam's awareness of the evacuation sirens on *Otroub* blatting away mixed with Gita Two's Captain snarling, "I don't care if we have to ram them. We're going to stop them! Override!" Barkyr Defense cut across it all: //Stand clear, Gita Two and Three. We got 'em.// And, from the very distant colony planet, a nonhuman mentality added, //It's a diversion. Give me a full scan.//

That must be a Paitsmun telepath. Inanely, Kyllikki recognized the mental tones of her overheard critic, who had no human gene in his body, and who must also be Paitsmun.

And then, for the second time, the world was wiped out in heat, pain, and an unbearable white light that illuminated her bones and sizzled through her guts. She hadn't realized how deep into Ckam she'd been until she died with her. The darkness was so welcome.

Kyllikki came to draped over her screen's housing, unbidden tears of pain leaking from her eyes, her own gasping sounding in her ears. Then her mind cleared.

"—llikki, you all right? This is Captain Brev. Answer or I'll override your seals!" His voice faded. "Lee! Where is Lee? Get him in there!" Then louder: "Com Third!"

"Here, Captain." Aloud and mentally, she sent to all points. //"*Otroub* has been destroyed. Com Officer Etha Ckam is dead with all hands . . . correction. There is one survivor. In a pod. Unconscious. The passenger. I presume."//

There was no harm broadcasting that. The attaackers couldn't very well turn around and finish the job. They were now bearing down on *Prosperity*.

Kyllikki had never been so close to death before and was surprised that her hands were more steady than they'd been all day, despite the real pain that burned through her whole body. She tapped into the helm screens and brought up the spectrum display. Minutes out of date, it had just begun to show Gita One and *Otroub* as expanding clouds of debris. *I was out that long? No wonder the Captain was upset.* There was no life-pod distress beacon out there. *Defective pod?*

Nearby, the six attackers showed as streaks of light surrounded by a flashing array of arcane military symbols.

Six Teleod ships. And someone coordinating their attack. *Has to be a master telepath coordinating. Not Family, though, a middling-good coordinator. Expendable.*

All at once, she knew what she had to do and did it.

Mentally, she summoned the proper key image, swallowed the exquisite nostalgia, and ventured through the image into the working realm, a "place" none of the Metaji had the keys or the training to reach.

In a nearby segment of the working realm, the master telepath had created a large cave, a comfortable private space. His presence filled it with multisensory gestalts, his orders. To enter his space was to know his plans. Kyllikki lurked in the "shadows," striving to grasp his tactical thinking without revealing the presence of a Laila Family telepath.

Her ears registered a voice from her console, jarring her partially away from the realm. She groped for the balance of bilocation—*It's been so long!* But in seconds, the skill came back and she was hearing with her ears and apperceiving the working realm simultaneously.

". . . knowledge, Com Third, this is the Captain. Abandon that Window. You have ninety seconds. Acknowledge."

She knew the Window's radiation shielding wasn't meant to absorb weapons fire, but then neither was the ship's. Inside, she'd be virtually blind and hardly any safer. "With all respect, Captain, I've a job to do here."

"That was an order, Com Third!"

Then the Teleod telepath caught her attention with a command image. //On my mark, execute.//

As the six ships acknowledged the order, she retreated from

the working realm, fumbling for the way to speak to her allies again. //Gita Two, Gita Three, Station Prime, Barkyr, this is *Prosperity*. I've broken their code. The two lead ships will be firing jump-cannon, the next two lightspeed projectors, and the trailing two will lay down a field of proximity devices.//

The jump-cannon was a particularly nasty weapon. The energy knot it fired dived through a space-warp and appeared inside the defenses of the target.

//This is Gita Three. Thanks, *Prosperity*.//

The two fighters fired maneuvering jets in unison, altering trajectory by the tiniest increment. *They're going to ram!* Kyllikki didn't have a tactical display, just the helm tracker with gross estimates on an overlay, but she knew the escort intended to take out the jump-cannons.

Determined to distract the enemy coordinator until it was too late, she retraced her steps into the working realm. The key image she had dismissed still lurked, clean and precise, in her foreconscious, as if she'd never missed a daily exercise at these skills.

She moved into the periphery of the Teleod coordinator's working awareness, feigning clumsy stealth. He started, and turned on her. //Who—Korachi!// he swore. //A spy! They've broken into the realm!//

She retreated, darkening her key image by an act of trained will, simultaneously building a wall of silver bricks around herself, tensing for the mental blow she knew he'd launched at her. Simultaneously, she flung herself under her work station and curled into a ball.

Before the coordinator's attack connected, the two escorters smashed into the two lead ships.

Four telepaths died simultaneously, inadvertently amplifying the deathscreams of the others who died with them. The four remaining telepaths on the other Teleod ships filled the working realm with magnified pain.

The working realm's key image floating in Kyllikki's consciousness, so dark she was not even aware of the outlines, suddenly flared, limned with intense light. It burned itself into her, leaving an afterimage. The echo of the two Metaji telepaths' deathscreams deafened her. Her body was outlined in pain, shaken by sound, burned by light.

Still, she was aware of the artificial gravity rippling under her. She felt the bulkhead shudder against her back. The air throbbed with alarms. The lights failed, and dim emergency lights flickered on. An acrid tang diffused from the air registers. Curled in fetal position, her muscles locked in spasm, she endured somewhere outside of time.

Eventually, it was over. Her body went limp. She was still breathing, so the Window had to be intact. Smoke had fogged the transparent bubble above her and swirled in the air, though near the floor, she could breathe. She might be radiation-fried, but she wasn't bleeding. And to her complete shock, she discovered she could move.

Got to go help find the injured. She scrabbled to get her knees under her.

A sign she'd never seen before flashed over the exit hatch. BRIDGE OVERRIDE! The sealed lock clicked open.

//Kyllikki?// Lee peeped around the cowling. Then he was on his knees beside her, one arm over her shoulders. //Don't move. Understand? I'll get you to sick bay.//

She humped up against the pressure of his arm. "Don't shout at me, all right?" Her voice was husky, and her throat felt as if she'd been screaming.

"Shout?" he whispered. *What's the matter with her?*

She pulled away, clamping her hands to her head. The key image to the working realm was burned into the back of her mind and would not darken and disappear. Lee's mind was washing through her, uncontrolled. *Barriers. Come on. Image. Make the image.* She found the wall of silver bricks, mirror-bright on the outside, half-transparent from the inside, showing the outer world dim but undistorted.

"Kyllikki? What are you doing?"

The edge of panic in Lee's voice, reinforced by a vibrant mental bleed-through of fear, went right through her.

She wanted to turn on him, to shove him out the hatch, get away from him. "Barriers," she gasped.

He withdrew his hands and she apperceived the thick felt damper he folded around himself. *Sound analogue. They do everything with sound analogues.* He was not using an image, yet she apperceived his effort as an image.

With supreme determination, she pulled herself to her feet, coughed and rubbed tears from her eyes. "Thanks. I've got it now. We've got to go help—"

"Abandon ship. Captain ordered." He coughed. "Fires. Damage control in the hold inoperative. We've got weapons in that hold as cargo. The Captain was informed by Main Data only after damage control failed." He urged her toward the lock. "The ship is going to go up in a matter of minutes."

And he came to pry me out of here.

She squeezed through the lock, which had jammed half-way open. The lounge was a tumbled mess, filled with smoke. They found breathing masks and emergency gear, fastened the belts around them, and forged out into the corridor.

People were moving swiftly, with determination. There was no panic, but the babble of voices that filled the air was edged with terror. In moments, the ship's uniforms made Kyllikki and Lee the target for the helpless and confused.

They split up, trying to help everyone, beating their way toward their assigned evacuation stations.

Using an emergency lantern, Kyllikki ushered people down dark side corridors and into life pods, stacking them in by the numbers, preventing fatal overcrowding, disregarding species preferences for speed. "That's all for this one!" she shouted more than once. "The rest of you follow me!" And she forged back through the press to another pod slip.

Even after the three mandatory drills and five extra ones the Captain had required, the passengers couldn't find their way around through the dim smoke.

Occasionally, she encountered another crew member, exchanged a quick "See you on Barkyr!" or traded power cells or breathing packs. Not all of *Prosperity's* emergency equipment worked. At one point, she provided a bandage pack to a Paitsmun, the very one who had criticized her arrogant manners. He was very grateful for her help in dealing with the wound of a soft-fleshed Zund.

Gradually, the noise diminished, the thump-whump of launching pods ceased, and Kyllikki began to wonder how she herself might get off. The standard launch pattern had not been followed. Her assigned pod had probably been launched.

She made her way aft, considering that passengers who couldn't find their own pods wouldn't have located the crew's pods or the extra ones. People who knew where the explosives were probably wouldn't head toward them. Most of the unused pods would be in the crew's quarters or behind Cargo and Stores.

She passed a lounge where the ceiling had fallen. There were body parts protruding from the rubble, no sign of movement. But, despite her own pain, she had to stop and scan for life. There was none. Beyond that, she came to a pressure barrier slammed across a corridor. Crew's quarters.

The hold, then. She turned and shimmied down an access tube, crawled through a smoke-filled duct, and battered her way out the duct's register into the cargo area. Here she could barely hear the beat of the emergency announcements and alarms. Her light carved a tunnel through the smoke, and she scanned for signs of life as she went, glad that she had the map of the ship engraved in her memory.

And then she felt them. Familiar. Desperate. *Which way?* She wasted precious seconds trying to listen mentally, then remembered she could still speak. "Idom! Zuchmul!" Her worn voice was husky and muffled by the breathing mask.

She advanced, flashing her light this way and that, certain they had to be at one of the pod hatches in the bulkhead in front of her. "Zuchmul! Idom! *Zuchmul!*"

"Kyllikki?" It was the luren's voice. "This way!"

His Influence grew to a beacon, then cut off with a guilty start. *He's not wearing his Inhibitor!* Then she remembered. Zuchmul had been on his way to feed. The only time he was

JACQUELINE LICHTENBERG

permitted to set the inhibiting device aside was when he was using his Influence on his food animals, a physiological imperative.

A dim glow emerged from the smoke and gradually became a pair of emergency lanterns. Two shadows developed into Idom and Zuchmul struggling with a tumbled pile of crates that blocked a pod hatch with glowing ready lights. Together, they heaved, and the last of the crates crashed aside. Idom smacked the control and the hatch swung open.

Zuchmul grabbed Kyllikki's elbow and propelled her toward the opening ahead of him. Knees sagging, she took one last look around and suddenly realized which pod ejector she was entering. It would throw the pod straight aft.

"No!" She pulled back, breaking the luren's hold.

"We're the last aboard," said Idom. "Come on!"

"No!" She pointed. "We've got to get down to that pod! This one will hit a flight of proximity mines! Come on!"

They followed as she beat her way aft and starboard, in one place crawling over containers that might well be the weapons no passenger liner should ·be carrying. *No. If they were here, they could have been jettisoned manually.*

They found another pod hatch with ready lights showing but the controls didn't open the portal. "Here, let me!" Zuchmul shouldered her aside and ripped the panel open, studying the circuitry. "Stand back." He snatched a tool from his belt and rammed it into the mechanism.

The door flicked open faster than it was supposed to. "What if it doesn't close?" she asked.

Idom said, "Decompression will stop the fire. In this hold, anyway. Go!"

They piled in, and the pod's own hatch closed. The launch was rougher than she remembered from the drills, but they were away and safe.

In unison, they lifted their breathing masks and took huge breaths.

Zuchmul went to the control board and glanced over the displays. "Anyone trained to fly this thing?"

"Not me," said Idom. "I thought you—"

"Not me," asserted Zuchmul. The two looked at Kyllikki. "I was trained as pod medic."

They looked at each other. The pods didn't really need pilots. The distress beacon was automatic. All they had to do was wait. But a young colony like Barkyr wouldn't have unlimited resources to chase stray life pods. The closer they could get, the better their chances of survival. She had launched only one other pod without a certified pilot, and that one had had a boy who held an insystem yacht license.

Idom laughed first. Zuchmul joined and Kyllikki found her own hoarse voice wheezing along with them. "The last three ship's officers, so careful in their duty to see the passengers safe—and what do we do? Pack ourselves into a pod without a pilot!"

chapter **two**

∙∙∙∙∙∙∙∙∙∙∙∙∙∙∙∙∙∙∙∙∙∙∙∙∙∙∙∙∙∙∙∙∙∙∙∙∙∙

"Only one thing to do," announced Idom, turning toward the control console. "Find the instruction manuals."

"In that compartment." Zuchmul pointed.

"No, this one," said Kyllikki. "That's blueprints."

Neither contained the manuals. "Well, has to be this one, then," said Kyllikki and opened the slim door placed symmetrically to the one she'd just opened. And there were the three gleaming manuals, each able to display data in the three main languages of the Metaji. Idom grabbed one and Kyllikki took another, set the display language, and settled into the only chair. The manual had its own power and memory, so it could be consulted no matter how ignorant the user was. "Pod pilot," she muttered, "is only a two-day course. We probably have that long before pickup. Maybe longer."

But in a few moments, she abandoned the instructions, finding that the display controls were familiar enough. The pilot's station was designed for one person to manage helm, environmental, communications, and basic course plotting.

Kyllikki's head was pounding, her body felt pulverized, and

her vision was blurring, but she had to know what was going on out there in the space around them.

The detectors on the pod produced displays that were like caricatures of the real thing, but she did locate the four remaining attackers on course for the Station. "I think those little blips there are Barkyr Defense ships," she told Zuchmul, who was hanging over her shoulder, mesh mask fastened over his face. She filled in her companions on what she'd seen from the Window. "Defense may be able to handle those four now they've been warned and now that the jump-cannons are gone." *At the price of six lives, but they're gone.*

"How close are we to *Prosperity*?" asked Zuchmul.

She shifted the display and read the figures, feeling Zuchmul's apprehension. He knew the pod's hull wasn't able to protect luren from all the sorts of radiation they were sensitive to. "But I've no idea what that means for you."

Idom leaned over her other shoulder and poked at the helm controls. "I've figured out how to steer. Move."

She traded places with him and leaned over his shoulder so she could see while he played with helm controls. "There they are!" she cried as the screen filled with tiny green flags. It was the cloud of pods ejected from *Prosperity*. A few had jockeyed clear and were driving toward Barkyr, but most were drifting, moving with the ship toward Barkyr while drifting away on ejection momentum. Not far enough away.

Zuchmul pulled out the third manual, muttering, "We must have a com-projector to reach other pods." He broke off and clamped a hand onto Kyllikki's shoulder. "*You're* the Com Officer! Get Wiprin and get this mob organized! Wiprin's probably with the Captain's pod because he's Com First—"

"Wiprin's dead, I think. Crew's quarters were holed and he was on sleep shift. Lee went off to pack the passengers into pods, and I never saw him again."

"Well, find out where he is."

She suppressed a convulsive shudder.

"Kyllikki?" The air around the luren throbbed with low-level Influence. Zuchmul was perhaps her oldest friend in the

Metaji, close enough that they'd discussed their common resentment of the strictures placed on them by law, as well as their mutual fear and distrust of each other. "Kyllikki, if he's dead, you won't get anything. If he's injured, he'll be drugged, and you won't feel his pain. But most likely he's fine and as bewildered as the rest of us."

His power carried his conviction through her defensive wall of silver bricks, setting them humming tunes of responsibility and duty. She felt her own perceptions aligning with his. Her uncontrolled reflex struck his hand from her shoulder and slapped his power from her mind.

Zuchmul gasped. Idom spun to stare up at her, then at Zuchmul, whose mesh-shrouded hands covered his masked face. She pulled his hands down and held them. "Did I hurt you?" Her eyes went to the base of his throat, where the mandatory Inhibitor was missing. "Zuchmul, are you all right?"

He pulled one hand free to finger the empty spot. His naturally chalk-white complexion paled. Even in the Metaji, use of luren Influence on others carried a death penalty, which wasn't fair because, after all, it was a natural reflex.

"Listen, Zuchmul, living here in the Metaji, there're things you might not know about the Eight Families. Don't ever use Influence on me the way you just did. It triggers a defensive reflex as natural as yours. Understand?"

He licked dry lips. "Yes. I know. I'd forgotten I'd lost the— I was with the orl when the alarms—"

She nodded and broke eye contact. Yet even while feeding, he should have had the device secured on his person, not set aside to be lost in an emergency. Still, she really did understand how he felt soiled and unable to feed properly with the thing anywhere near him. Now that emotion might ultimately cost him his life. "You'll just have to control yourself carefully, so that later we can testify for you."

And if he can't, it's partly my doing. With the Inhibitor attenuating his power, she had tolerated his covert communication simply because she hungered so for more than the mental speech she was allowed. But that was one thing. Influencing her mind was something else.

His hands clutched themselves at his waist, and she could feel his power retreating into himself, leaving the space around her empty, almost as if he were telepathically barriered. *Good. He has the discipline.* She flashed him a smile and, turning back to the screens, she schooled herself to audio-analogue. //Lee? Are you clear?//

Her mental voice didn't project beyond her silver brick wall. It should have gone right through it—or around it in another dimension—or however it worked.

She buried her face in her hands and scrubbed at the tension. *It's not possible. The two levels don't mix like this!* They were as incompatible as the Teleod and Metaji methods of using a space drive.

"Kyllikki?" It was Idom. *Doesn't she realize the ship's going to blow up any minute now? Or is she hurt?*

She flinched from his private thoughts. "I'm all right. I can do it." She had to reach Lee, so she had to dismiss her barrier image and approach him in the pure audio analogue. *I can do it.* But the key image to the working realm glowed persistently, burned into her mind by the deaths of the linked telepaths. It seemed to have destroyed her selective barrier control, but Lee must not see that.

"Hey, look!" said Zuchmul, thrusting a display of directions under her nose and pointing with one long finger at a control, taking great care not to crowd her. "There! That should give us a channel to address all the other pods."

She touched the switch. Sound roared through the pod. Idom, startled, dropped his manual and then swore.

Kyllikki thought she heard Captain Brev's voice shredded among all the others babbling at each other. *They'll never get anywhere!* Lips compressed, she vanquished the silver wall. //Lee? Are you clear?//

//Kyllikki? You made it.//

//You with the Captain?//

//No. And—Wiprin's dead.//

//I figured. Any telepaths among the passengers?//

There was a pause, and he answered, //Clerk here says no. Not registered, anyway.//

Hesitantly, she suggested, //You know I could reach the Captain, address his mind directly, relay for him to everyone else. None of the pods are yet out of my range for that.//

//No! Kyllikki, no! Your oath. The Captain will have us organized shortly. Listen, I can't get anyone at Barkyr. They're not Searching. And I can't raise Station Prime for relay, either. You have better range than I do. You try.//

//Yes, sir.// She lifted her attention to her mental horizon. There was a new Com Officer on duty, a different Paitsmun. She listened to the traffic for a few minutes, then attracted the attention of the Paitsmun at Barkyr because the Station was busy organizing for battle. //This is *Prosperity* life pods, Kyllikki, Com Third.// She outlined their problem. //Do you have an estimate on pickup for us?//

//Pickup? Life pods? *Prosperity* blew? I don't have light-speed scan yet. What is your exact position?//

She gave him the numbers from the pod's instruments. //Our Captain needs to know about a pickup point and time.//

//Depends how the Station does in the next skirmish. Could be a couple days. Head in-system.// He provided orbital data to facilitate pickup and she copied it.

//Thank you, Barkyr.// The Paitsmun turned away to talk to ships on the other side of the system, ships deployed in case the six attackers were just a diversion. Kyllikki brought her attention in closer. //Get that, Lee?//

//Get what?//

Not taking time to puzzle out what she'd done wrong that had kept Lee from following the exchange, she told him while repeating it all aloud for Idom and Zuchmul. *At least Lee didn't catch me invading his mind again!*

But now she was struggling to sort out the internal mentation of her companions from what they were saying aloud and what Lee was projecting. In the background, she was getting the rhythmic traffic handling of Barkyr planetside, and the military cadences from Station Prime where Barkyr Defense was located. It made an insuperable babble against the backdrop of the Captain's voice coming from the speakers, outshouting everyone else. Under, over, and around it all like a roaming ghost image, the key to the working realm pulsed lurid colors in time to the throbbing of her head.

It was as if her brain had been riddled with holes, letting data mix into a senseless jumble. She'd never experienced any-thing like it, never heard of anyone enduring anything like it.

She was about to tell Lee she was going down for the dura-tion when she felt something very strange. But it was also famil-iar. Chasing it around the edge of her mind, she found she was staring at the monitor, which now showed the outer area where *Otroub* had blown apart. The bits of debris didn't show on the toylike display, but she knew that by now the cloud would be very large. There was a shimmering image on the screen, though—no, it wasn't there. Or was it?

She pointed. "What's that?"

"What?" asked Zuchmul, leaning closer, his voice sound-ing like six of him speaking in near unison.

Idom chorused with himself, "There's nothing there."

"There's something . . ." And then she knew. The life pod from *Otroub*. "He's conscious. He's terrified." She knew. She didn't know how she knew. She just knew.

"Who's terrified?"

"The passenger!" She recounted what she knew of *Otroub's* passenger without mentioning her impression that he could be a Dreamer. That, of course, was nonsense. "And Barkyr says it will probably be days until help can reach us, never mind him. He's hurt. He can't pilot that pod."

Idom pivoted in the seat and took her hands. "Kyllikki, it's at least six times as far from here to that pod as it is from here to Barkyr, and the distance is increasing rapidly. Child, there's no way you could be getting anything from a nontelepath you don't even know who's that far—"

She pulled her hands away. Idom was old enough to have the right to "child" anyone on *Prosperity*—even the Captain. But fighting the smearing echoes in her brain left her no pa-tience. "Idom, when I tell you how to count a ship into a dive, then you can tell me what I can and can't do!"

Their eyes locked.

He's right. It's not possible. Admitting that she'd been injured in some strange way, she doubted her sanity. Like the light-etched key image that still burned behind her consciousness, the vision of the passenger as Ckam had seen him possessed her mind's eye. It all whirled and mixed and beat at her, and she couldn't think straight.

But—"Regardless of what I do or don't know now, I knew when *Otroub* blew, that one pod had escaped. Lightspeed scanners never showed the beacon ignite. It's a defective pod. Are we going to let him die? Out there? Alone?"

Idom sighed. "I do think I can move this thing now, but I programmed Barkyr as our destination. We are being carried in that general direction by momentum—"

"Recalculate," she said implacably.

He stared at his readouts, nibbling his lip as a strange expression crept over his face. "*This* pod ejected with a momentum component toward *Otroub's* last-known position."

"So? That just makes it easier."

He twisted to scrutinize her. "This pod has only jets, sails, and gravitics. It's a pathetic little toy. And we can't use that pod's beacon to get a fix. We can't just wander out and look around until we find it."

The babble in her head was driving her crazy. She closed her eyes and struggled to reconstruct her silver wall, taking care with every detail of every brick as she had learned to do almost before she could talk. Gradually, the insane babble retreated. To her dismay, it was still very perceptible, but at least it was reduced. *I'll make it.*

"Move," she snapped at Idom. "I think I've got the figures." She had seen *Prosperity's* helm display, and had tracked that single life pod. If there was one skill that Teleod training developed, it was visual memory.

With a touch here and a stroke there, she recreated the helm displays. "There. Is that enough, Idom?"

"For me, yes. For the Captain, maybe not."

They traded places as the Captain's voice burst from the

speaker against a backdrop of silence. Lee must have relayed the message from Barkyr the moment the voice channel cleared, for the Captain was ordering the pods in-system. "Pod Twelve, take course parallel to Pod Six. Pod Eight, deploy sails as soon as Pod Fifteen is clear, and Pod Fifteen—"

Kyllikki searched the controls, trying to find out which pod she was in and discovered it was Fifteen. "Captain Brev, this is Com Third in Pod Fifteen. We need a decision."

"Go ahead, Com Third, but keep in mind *Prosperity* may blow at any moment."

"Pod Fifteen contains only crew—Idom, Zuchmul, and myself. There was a defective pod ejected from *Otroub* with their passenger aboard unconscious. A passenger on a courier is likely to be important to the war effort, sir. Request permission to go after that pod. Idom says we can do it."

She twisted to catch Zuchmul's gaze with a silent interrogative. "Yes, we can do it," he agreed.

Brev said, "Idom and you are not exactly expendable."

"I understand, sir. If you have a pod better situated, I'll relay my course data to them." It was a bluff. She intended to argue each pod he elected right out of the job.

After discussion the Captain decided that Pod Fifteen's ejection velocity was the most favorable for matching course with *Otroub's* pod and they were the only one not carrying passengers. They got the job. But Kyllikki didn't like the look Idom turned on her. Analysis of the random processes of the universe was his field, so he often saw significance where others saw only chaos. And that was the look in his eye, Kyllikki realized—as if she were an element of chaos suddenly imbued with significance. She shivered.

The Captain went on assigning courses to the mob of tiny ships while Idom followed orders and switched frequencies to consult a Helm Officer in another pod, plotting their course correction, avoiding the mines spreading in the wake of the attackers. Within minutes they had a course with a return roughly calculated and had begun to accelerate away from *Prosperity* at a more reassuring rate.

The Captain came onto their frequency. "Pod Fifteen! Idom, what do you think you're doing? You'll have no fuel for the return. Go out on a slow, economic orbit!"

Idom glanced back at Kyllikki, swallowed visibly, then said in the hard, level tone of one delivering indisputable fact, "The man's injured. Time could be critical. We'll return on gravitics or tack in using the sails."

"I've got my log dump from *Prosperity* now, and I'm not showing any such skills among the three of you."

"That's right, sir," answered Idom. "We don't have those skills *yet*, sir."

It was an old argument. The Captain trusted people to do only what they'd been taught and drilled in. He expected his crew to do the same job always in the same way. Idom, however, never did anything the same way twice if he could help it, and it never occurred to him that anyone had to teach him a thing before he could do it. Kyllikki was definitely of Idom's persuasion in this matter and knew it added to the Captain's distrust of her competence as a ship's officer. Brev cleared his throat. "You haven't thought this through! Idom, you're supposed to be in command there. How do you expect to get that passenger out of that pod?"

Kyllikki leaned over Idom and spoke into the pickup. "Whichever way you order us to, Captain, of course." She, herself, had no concrete ideas. She knew only that it was possible to do pod-pod transfers in space. "Since I'm aboard, you can have Lee relay your orders even after we lose voice-com and coherent spectral transmission. We'll be out of touch only for a short while. Don't worry. We can handle it." *If I can just get my head back in proper working order!*

The Captain's pod was accelerating in-system now, and already the voice channel was crackling with noise. It was too late for the Captain to order a turnaround, so when he came back, he said, "Pod Fifteen, you are to proceed with the rescue, but use both the docking tube and pressure suits. There have been too many pod-equipment failures. Don't trust anything. We'll send you a pickup as soon as we can."

Watching the green flags representing the pods moving away, Kyllikki said, "Yes, sir. Docking tube and suits. Now, I suggest you check with Lee. He should be picking up Barkyr. And the Defense ships from the Station are now engaging the attackers—"

Just then *Prosperity* turned into a fiery energy ball. Zuchmul recoiled, cried out, and reeled away from the bulkhead back toward an inner compartment.

Kyllikki searched the overhead for a sign that the radiation alarms had been activated, but they were silent. The hull had stopped most of the sleeting rain of particles, just not enough for a luren. *If the detectors are working!*

She hunkered down before the one cabinet she knew, then came up with a brightly painted case. "I doubt we've taken a dangerous exposure, but it's better to be cautious. Here." She handed Idom an injection ampoule and selected one for herself. Its code bands indicated it ought to be safe, but in the Metaji, she was never sure. The genetics of the Eight Families weren't normally considered by Metaji physicians writing the codes. Still, it wasn't likely to do any real harm. She pressed the ampoule to her skin.

Idom asked, "Is there one for luren?"

"I'm looking." The pod-medic training hadn't included luren. Luren were a race of human stock, but a splinter branch more different from the norm than the Dreamers. The luren and the Dreamers were the last two remnants of an era when humanity had experimented with its own genetic material and produced some very dangerous and disruptive variants. Tradition had it that the Eight Families were the descendants of those who had done the experimenting.

"Here," she said, selecting two ampoules. "I'll take these to Zuchmul and see what he says."

Zuchmul was curled into a storage closet behind an insulated stretcher. Knowing how he preferred the dark, even while wearing his protective eye inserts as he always did under normal ship's lighting, she didn't turn on the light, but just offered the ampoules and some encouragement. When she convinced him

JACQUELINE LICHTENBERG

that the sheeting blizzard of particles had abated, he crawled
out of the closet and examined the ampoules, selecting one but
commenting that it probably wasn't necessary. "Luren tend to
heal fast."

She chuckled at the understatement, but his skin looked
raw and there were pain lines graven about his mouth. His
power was still clenched tightly to himself, not a thrum of Influence pervading the space between them. She admired his control, wondering if she'd have done as well under the
circumstances. "Maybe you don't need it, but it could help you
feel better even faster. We may yet need your skills."

Zuchmul had been *Prosperity's* number-two environmental
technician, but he'd worked on many sorts of ships in various
capacities. He was a hardware expert, as overqualified for his
job as Idom was for his.

For the first time, Kyllikki added it up, and began to understand the meaning of war. The government had wanted to
transport dangerous weaponry unknown to Teleod spies. They'd
arranged to use one of the few passenger liners that carried life
pods. They'd picked a military Captain who was just a bit too
old for combat and an astrogator who was one of a handful in
the Metaji who really understood astrogational theory well
enough to take any ship anywhere and get back again, even if
they got lost on the way. They had added to that a Com Third
who had a greater range than most Metaji telepaths, and overqualified technicians who could improvise anything. The weapons would arrive safely.

*Was it just an accident that we were in the way of those
Teleod ships? Or had Zimor's spies known where the courier and
Prosperity would be, so they could cut an incoming orbit to hit
three targets with one run?*

Three targets. "Come on, Zuchmul." She headed back for
the controls. She realized that for the last several minutes she'd
been internally tensed against the onslaught of distant deaths.
The voice-com now emitted nothing but white noise.

Checking with Lee, she found that he could now raise Barkyr as well as the Station, and though their instruments couldn't

30

penetrate the cloud of particles to reveal the battle, he told her the battle was over and the Station was out of communication. //Defense got a couple of the Teleod ships, but a lot of people died. I think the Station's gone. Be glad you're moving away so you didn't feel any of that.//

//You have my sympathy, Lee.//

//The Captain says you should take extra care because if the Station is gone or even badly damaged, it'll be a very long time before they can send you a pickup. He really expected Defense would win this one.//

//So did I,// she told him and repeated everything aloud for her companions.

"We could be in a lot of trouble, Kyllikki," said Idom.

"We'll make it," she predicted grimly.

Satisfied that the course was set, Idom locked down the automatics. It would take several days to close the gap with the retreating pod. They were all too tense to rest, so they sat at the galley table, nursed their headaches, and read the manuals to each other, sketching plans until none of them could see straight anymore. After a sleep period, Kyllikki went to take inventory of their rations and discovered to her horror that there was nothing aboard rated for luren.

She should have expected that. There were only a few million luren scattered among the Metaji's multibillions.

"Don't worry about it." Zuchmul shrugged. "I expected as much when I didn't make it to my assigned pod. I'll be all right for the six or eight days this will take, and there'll be stored supplies I can use on Barkyr."

"Sure you don't want to try some of this digested protein? It's supposed to be good for any race of human."

"No. Really. I'll be fine."

She'd heard stories about luren hunger, about luren becoming like animals that would go for anything with blood flowing in veins. But they were just stories. She didn't really know the facts of luren tolerances and felt it was too personal to ask about—at least at the moment.

There were plenty of supplies for her and Idom, and they

passed the time eating, sleeping, and worrying over the manuals and their contingency plans. Gradually, the riddled-full-of-holes feeling in her head subsided. The key image still glowed darkly in the back of her mind, no matter how stringently she applied the banishing for it. Before she'd lost contact with Lee, she had repaired her barriers and felt secure once more in what she had dubbed the "realm" of audio-analogues. The headaches diminished and she could often hear her companions' spoken words without echoes.

As they drew closer to the disabled pod, she became aware of the passenger's consciousness. He didn't know they were coming, and he alternated between fear and despair. She knew when he started to consider suicide. As soon as they came within range for spectral equipment, she began sending a re-corded-voice message. His receivers might be working even if his transmitters weren't.

And she knew when he heard it.

Her growing sensitivity to the passenger was eclipsed only by her awareness of Zuchmul's hunger. After his third refusal, she stopped pressing him to try the rations, and pointed out that the medical stores held various sorts of blood. He evaded until she pinned him down, then, checking that Idom was in the pilot's seat, he drew her into the rear chamber of the pod, clos-ing the hatch for privacy.

"Kyllikki, I admit that human blood is tempting, but most kinds would make me so ill they'd hardly be worth the bother. Legend has it that there are some kinds that are compatible, but if they exist, *I* don't want to know about them." He squirmed uncomfortably. "You know I have my—disagreements—with parts of the law governing luren. But there's a good reason for the law forbidding us human blood."

"But you're starving." It was her turn to be uncomfortable. "They say . . . I've heard . . ."

He moved closer, bracing one hand on the wall behind her. His powerful field of Influence flowed around him like a cloak, barely caressing her body, conveying a kind of sensuous relaxation rather than any sort of intrusion. He wasn't *using* it on her. It was simply there, part of him, and intensely arousing. "My hunger is no danger to you or Idom or anyone. You have my word on that."

Did her acceptance of that come from some insidious effect of his Influence? "Zuchmul, I've heard there have been times when luren have had to be hunted down by other luren—because they killed for human blood, and the human blood wasn't poisoning them fast enough to stop them."

He inspected his feet, then pushed back and folded his arms as he leaned on the wall next to her. "That could happen only if I died and you ignored the law and let me revive spontaneously. There is a rage to the hunger that comes then. I could kill you, then hunt humans and never know why I was starving. That's the reason for the strict laws governing luren corpses."

"I—I didn't know." Even in the Teleod, near the luren homeworld, this wasn't common knowledge.

"It's not something we're proud of or wish to advertise. If someone were tempted to gain control of a luren to use as a weapon—well, we don't advertise how to go about it."

His eyes, shielded by the filtering inserts, seemed unfocused, as if he were considering other frightening vulnerabilities of his kind that he wasn't ready to reveal to her. "Kyllikki, it wasn't too many generations ago that the galaxy was all set to destroy the Dreamers, the Eight Families, and us, so no one would be tempted to gain control of us and use us as weapons.

"But in the end, they let luren live under a law that is cruel and stupid in spots, but wise in others. And they interdicted the Dreamers, to make sure no member of the Families who carried the Bonding gene could ever get power over both a Dreamer and a luren, or a luren over a Bonder, or a Dreamer over us all, and there would never be another Triumvirate, never another galactic holocaust. Even this war is *nothing* compared to that." He turned his face to her.

She felt him lose interest in history, his Influence becoming a caress that transmuted hunger to passion. He murmured,

"At least you and I are free in the galaxy. If the price is that I must never taste human blood, then I shall not. And the truth is, I don't want to. There are other, more pleasant and less dangerous, ways to taste you."

The need to kiss him burned in her chest. Oddly, something about the raw-edged intensity of that need was actually repellent. She lunged away from the corner, breaking the spell, then turned with a shrug. "I promised Idom I'd go check the instruments. You're supposed to be studying the gravitic manuals."

And how am I supposed to concentrate on that!

It wasn't her thought. It was his. Jolted, she reinforced her mental barriers on all levels, and went to do the superfluous checking.

Some hours later, Zuchmul apologized. "What I said— about tasting you—was inappropriate. Consider it unsaid."

"Without further thought," she replied automatically, but his apology raised all kinds of questions she had no time to consider. They had arrived at the target area.

Without a beacon to home on, they had come only to the approximate position. Now they began searching.

After a time, she began to doubt her reconstruction of the data. Several times she was on the verge of telling them that she must have been wrong, that they'd have to give up, and each time the *sense* of the passenger's mind stopped her. After long, back-straining hours over the display screens, Idom jabbed a finger at a blip. "There! That's it!"

He ran in the data directing the computer to dock them. The other pod lay inert, showing no emissions, apparently unable to link to their guidance computer for easy docking.

"Let's just hope he doesn't discover his maneuvering jets while you're out there doing it manually!" said Zuchmul as he climbed into his vacuum suit to take the pilot's place.

Idom and Kyllikki suited up and went to the rear chamber, where they'd found the oversize air lock with the docking-tube apparatus. The tube was a fabric cylinder reinforced with the same kind of fine mesh particle and magnetic insulation that made up Zuchmul's protective gear. He might even be able to tolerate going outside into the tube, but they'd decided he'd do them the most good at the pilot's station.

The control panel beside the air lock showed ready lights, and Zuchmul's voice came over their suit phones: "Standing by for the grapples?"

"Go!" answered Idom.

"That should do it," said Zuchmul. "Did it?"

They felt a faint thump as some mechanism outside the air lock functioned. Kyllikki said, "This panel now shows grapples deployed, for whatever that's worth." They were all well aware that this particular mechanism may have answered its self-test program for them, but it had never been *used*.

"That's it, then," said Zuchmul. "Docking complete. Go ahead and deploy the tube."

Kyllikki flipped the protector off the proper control panel and entered the command on the brightly glowing touchpads. Nothing happened. She tried it several times, checked to see she had the command right, let Idom try—nothing. With Zuchmul reading them directions, they opened the very stiff safety door and deployed the manual control. It took both of them using all their strength to ram the lever down into its receptor socket, but they were rewarded with a very definite thump-whump-bang.

But then the pressure reading in the tube did not come onto scale. "Something's wrong."

"Didn't I tell you?" said Zuchmul. "That pod is not de-signed to mate with this one. *Otroub* was new, carrying life pods according to the regulations made since ships began disap-pearing. *Prosperity* was ancient, built before we stopped putting life pods on ships that never needed them. Two different sets of specs. Just be glad both ships had pods at all. Most ships in space these days don't."

"So we'll have to go out and attach the cowling to the other pod manually." Kyllikki sighed.

"Yes. And there should be caulking for that stored inside panel number six right over the air lock."

They found it, cycled the air lock, watched the pressure gauges on their suits carefully, deployed safety lines, and then she and Idom went out to explore their dangling tube.

Kyllikki had no trouble with the free-fall maneuvering. She'd always loved free-fall, but she *knew* the passenger would be driven to mindlessness by the disorientation. They needed the tube secured.

"I think I see how it has to go," said Idom. "See, here this pod has a small flange where we have a large groove, and that's why the catch didn't seat properly. We should learn to take Zuchmul's word for things in his field."

"I heard that," commented Zuchmul.

While Idom experimented with the caulking, Kyllikki anchored their safety lines and studied the other pod's air-lock controls. The manual for them was, no doubt, stowed inside the craft. By the time the tube pressurized into a nice, secure corridor, she thought she had the puzzle solved.

On the fifth try, the outer hatch opened. They convinced it to close again, as if there were vacuum outside, just in case the seal didn't hold, then they were facing the inner lock, watching it open on darkness.

She hit the light switch, and before them stood the man Kyllikki had seen through Ckam's eyes. He was taller than she'd expected, with bright gold hair, and sharp features with a peculiar racial cast she'd never seen before. His body was reed-slender, with sculpted muscles showing through his light-blue ship's clothing. *Masculine* musculature.

He leaned casually against the bulkhead, posture and movement giving no clue to the riptide of emotion she could feel tearing him apart. There was a clumsy bandage tied around his head, with a spot of blood soaking through. *Good thing Zuchmul isn't here to smell that!*

He smiled, more in the eyes than with the mouth. "Won't you come in? I've been expecting you." His baritone voice was rough, as if to disguise a tremor.

She fumbled her helmet off and when she finally met his naked gaze, she blurted, "Get dressed and come with us.

Quickly." It wasn't what she'd planned to say. The order came spilling out as if she'd suddenly returned to her Family position and was dealing with an indolent retainer. She hadn't used that tone since she'd left Zimor's household.

But he cocked his head to one side, essayed a crooked grin and answered her banteringly. "Is it a formal affair, then? I must have something appropriate aboard."

Idom had his helmet off now. "Space suit," he said. "Hurry or we'll have to recalculate our return."

"I see." But he remained unmoving, studying them, especially Kyllikki, warily.

His voice and tone held a familiar cadence. Or was it in his mind? She tried to tighten her mental barriers to listen only to his words. "I think we've done this badly," she offered, and introduced them by name, explaining the situation. She was favored with all his attention.

When she'd finished, he breathed, "Kyllikki!" It seemed he hadn't heard a word beyond her name. "Kyllikki."

For one dizzy moment, she thought she heard Zimor spitting her name like a curse. She could almost see Zimor's face superimposed over his features, but she blinked it away.

"Kyllikki must be a common name," he said, and it was just the pleasant velvet voice of a gorgeous man asking an inane question at an inappropriate moment.

"Not very," she answered, "but that's a long story."

"Space suit," insisted Idom. "Hurry."

"Gladly," he answered, unmoving, but she sensed his balance shift as he watched Idom. "My name is Elias."

He doesn't know where it is and is waiting for a clue! Only then did she note the dimness down the open corridor behind him, emergency lighting. Either from injury or ignorance, he had done nothing to normalize the pod's function. She started opening the larger storage lockers at random and found the suits on the third try.

Reminding herself that he was passenger and she crew, she followed the drill for stuffing a groundling into the sacklike, untailored vacuum suit. They had to try three helmets to find one that worked, explaining that they had little confidence in their caulked vacuum seal.

It took both of them to jockey Elias through free-fall into their pod, then she installed him in a bunk and treated his head wound while Zuchmul went to the other pod to see if they could salvage some fuel, and return on jets rather than playing with systems they really didn't know how to use. But the fuel cells were incompatible.

As soon as Kyllikki had adjusted the healing lamps over Elias, he fell into a deep slumber, the strain of meeting them on his feet having drained his last reserves.

Staring at his unconscious form, everything in her wanted to believe he was a Dreamer. If so, and if he was Bonded to Zimor, the subliminal effect of his presence even at that distance would explain why Kyllikki had been so irrational for hours before they'd contacted *Otroub*. But that was the easy way out. Blame him, or Zimor, or call it one of her periodic spells of Bonding need, and she wouldn't feel so guilty over the mental invasions she'd committed.

Gritting her teeth, she went to Idom at the pilot's station and apologized as she should have the moment she'd seen him in *Prosperity*'s hold, finishing, "I should never have done that to you, Idom. Consider it undone."

"Without further thought, Kyllikki."

She felt better, the knot of guilt unraveling. Returning to check the settings on the healing lamp, she considered Elias again. She had of course heard rumors of secret enclaves where the Families bred Dreamers from those captured centuries ago, Dreamers who were given to those Bonders who were loyal. But she, like all reasonable people, discounted that. She couldn't believe her relatives would sink to such depravity. Besides, even Zimor couldn't get away with something like that.

As for Elias, no Dreamer raised as a slave could possibly exhibit such self-possession as Elias had after days alone, days of anxiety and terror. People didn't develop such nerve from living a sheltered life.

So he couldn't be Zimor's Dreamer. But planting a dreamspy in the Metaji was just what Zimor would do—if she could. No. The idea was absurd. Even if Zimor had gone totally insane, kidnapped a Dreamer from their home planet, and sent him to spy, what were the chances Kyllikki would meet up with him? *I've got to get hold of my imagination.*

"Kyllikki! We're ready." It was Zuchmul calling from the aft chamber, where he was sealing the lock and releasing the docking tube. The gravitic drive was also there.

Kyllikki secured restraints over the unconscious man in the bunk, then straightened. The cramped aisle of the pod was lined with bunks. To her left, beyond the facilities and the galley, Idom manned the pilot's station. To her right was the aft chamber.

She joined Zuchmul, ducking under the cargo crane stored overhead on a swing-down arm, ready to serve the oversized rear lock. There was also a jigsaw puzzle of beams, tools, and raw material for use in surface survival, leaving just enough room for her and Zuchmul to stand side by side before the gravitic unit. It was barely as tall as they were and only a bit broader than the two of them. It wouldn't develop much power, so their return would be slow, but still, going down into the gravity well, gravitics would be faster than tacking in against the solar wind. Or so the manual claimed.

She took her place and opened the com to the pilot's station. "Ready, Idom?" *If anything has to fail, let it be the com. I could shout that far.*

"Here come the final figures now. All automated. I never realized how easy a helmsman's job is. Perhaps this is what I'll do when I retire."

"Sure," said Kyllikki, knowing him well enough to know he'd never retire. She read him the figures as they appeared on the screens before her, then they did the whole thing again just to make sure. Finally, Zuchmul engaged the drive.

For a moment, it seemed nothing would happen. Then everything went crazy. The lighted readouts before Kyllikki blinked, turned to pyrotechnic spirals and disappeared. The deck bucked and shook as if the pod were about to tear itself apart. The air beat at them with pure sound.

Clutching the gravitic housing for balance, Kyllikki danced on the unsteady floor and tried to help Zuchmul, who was down on his knees prying away a lower access plate. He shouted, "It's bleeding into the interior gravity plates!"

She squatted down to lend her strength to his and together they popped the cover off the mechanism.

She heard Elias' voice cursing the restraints.

"Hand me that Radikov tuner, the little one with the red handle," demanded Zuchmul.

She found the tool in the drawer under the housing and gave it to him, but before she could slide the drawer shut again, several of the tools bounced out, then the drawer came off its tracks and slid toward the hatch leading to the bunks. Just then Elias rolled out of his bunk, one hand on his head, where she'd removed the bandage.

As Zuchmul struggled to insert the tool accurately, he twisted to catch a glimpse of Elias. His expression was unreadable, but she knew he could smell Elias' blood.

"What's wrong?" bellowed Elias, gripping the hatch cowling and peering over his shoulder at Idom, then turning to look at Zuchmul again.

"Stand still!" ordered Kyllikki. To her surprise, Elias did. She sat down and thrust one leg over Zuchmul's folded knees to make a table and told him, "Lean your elbows on my leg. It'll steady your hand."

"Good. Hold it!" he grunted, drawing a bead on his target and thrusting the Radikov into the mechanism.

The Radikov lit up bright orange, spat, shrieked, and went dark and silent. Instantly, the jiggling stopped, and all they heard was the smooth whine of the gravitic drive. She repossessed her leg and they climbed to their feet, panting and grinning, Kyllikki between Elias and Zuchmul. The luren faced the controls, while, over his shoulder, Kyllikki noted the readouts claimed nominal function. She turned to Elias.

Without warning, the gravity gave one more lurch, throwing Elias into the chamber. As he staggered toward them, one of his feet came down into the loose tool drawer.

Dancing frantically, he grabbed at the overhead maze of equipment and caught a strut, regaining balance for a second. Then there was a loud snap, and one end of the strut broke loose. It slid out of Elias' grasp. The free end slashed down in an arc, aimed directly at Kyllikki's head. Elias staggered forward, arms flailing.

"Duck!" screamed Kyllikki, grabbing Zuchmul's shoulder as she went down. But the luren twisted to look for the hazard. The sharp end of the beam just missed Kyllikki's head, then slashed through the soft flesh of Zuchmul's throat.

Elias landed with a cry of pain.

A gout of bright-red blood fountained onto Elias and splashed onto the floor. The swinging beam reached the end of its arc just short of the gravitic panel and swung back over Zuchmul.

"Idom!" yelled Kyllikki, scrabbling around to examine Zuchmul while keeping her head under the beam's arc.

The pulsing fountain of blood subsided with a shocking finality before she could touch the wound.

"I killed him," muttered Elias, glassy-eyed. "I didn't mean to—Kyllikki—"

She thrust her hand behind Zuchmul's head and felt his neck, watching as the head moved normally. She felt no grinding of broken vertebrae. The beam had hit him sideways, slicing through the front of his throat and the main arteries at the sides, but not touching his spine.

Idom saw what had happened, and snapped, "Elias, help me!" He grabbed the flying beam to drag it to a halt.

Elias rose up and wrapped his arms around the beam, and their combined mass finally stopped the swing.

"I think he's all right, Idom," said Kyllikki.

Elias, arms wrapped around one end of the captured beam, cried, "All right?! He's dead!"

Idom knelt beside Zuchmul and turned the body on its side, inspecting the spine and the wound. "Missed by a fraction.

You're right. He should be all right." He looked up at Elias. "It's a good thing he's luren."

"Luren?"

"It's hard to believe, just reading about them I know, but I've seen them recover from worse."

Kyllikki watched Elias' expression. *He's never heard of luren.* Granted, there might be a few people in the Metaji who'd never heard of the only human race that routinely died and revived, but they weren't likely to be riding around in courier ships.

"Help me get him into a bunk," said Kyllikki. "That's not much of a wound. We've got to get him into stasis right away." She didn't dare think of the risks of stasis itself, never mind if the stasis machinery malfunctioned. He might never wake up, but she knew he'd prefer that to what would happen if he revived out here, without the help of his own people. And so would they.

chapter **three**

••••••••••••••••••••••••••••••••••••

The two men wrestled the luren's body into one of the bunks while Kyllikki read the manual on how to activate the bunk's stasis facility. As pod medic, she had been drilled in this routine, and knew that even for luren it could be fatal. Even the newest designs weren't reliable.

Very carefully, following the step-by-step diagrams, she primed the bunk and set the control probes in the body. She found three cautions specifically for luren suspected of being dormant, not dead. Idom hung over her and double-checked each move before returning to the pilot's station.

Only after the translucent cover had been pulled down, isolating the bunk, did she dare to think of the body in it as her friend, Zuchmul. Then she blinked back tears and clenched her hands together. They were cold and shaking.

A strong, warm arm came around her waist. She was too tense even to be startled.

"I guess he was a friend of yours."

She looked up into the face that had haunted her for days. His distinctive mental tone permeated her body.

She wanted to turn into his arms, lay her head on his

shoulder, and cry. Instead, not trusting her barriers, she tried to pull away. He held on to her, a move she hadn't expected. She was wearing a Com Officer's uniform. Who would treat a telepath like that?

"Elias, no." She freed herself.

He stepped back. "I only wanted to help."

A conviction came from nowhere. He didn't recognize the Com Officer's uniform. She presented her sleeve, stretching the device out for him. "I'm a telepathic communicator, with commercial-level skills, but sometimes when I'm upset . . . well, I wouldn't want to invade your privacy accidentally." It was hard to say after giving hundreds of earnest reassurances that she didn't read minds uninvited.

He stepped back and came up against the opposite bunk. "I'm sorry. I guess I'm upset, too."

He's a passenger, and I'm supposed to be crew! "Elias, we're going to make it to Barkyr just fine. We're not in any danger. So all you have to do is lie down on that bunk again, and let the healer do its job on your head. Meanwhile, I'll see about getting a meal together."

By the time she got the food on the table, cross-checking everything against the healer's readouts on Elias to make sure she didn't poison him, she had cheered up considerably. At least they could eat without guilt. Zuchmul wasn't starving anymore.

Maybe he'd planned to ride back in stasis anyway!

When she'd released Elias, he, too, had looked considerably less white-lipped and dazed. But he was as taciturn as ever during the meal. Idom related how it happened that his rescuers had arrived in a life pod. Elias listened with interest, but in the end, all he said was "I guess I didn't thank you enough. When I first saw you, well—I took it for granted that someone would come."

It hadn't seemed that way to Kyllikki, but she wasn't trusting her perceptions of Elias. The key to the working realm still floated like a seared afterimage in the back of her mind, and if her barriers slipped, the strange echo effect to Idom's words re-

44

turned and the shadowy impression of Zimor haunted her. As she poured a cup of steaming shaid, which she'd sweetened heavily, she asked, "Elias, I'm curious as to why you were traveling by courier, if you can say."

"It was by Imperial order."

Idom commented, "That sounds awfully melodramatic."

"Not really. Some people can afford to have what they want when they want it. It's my business to be what such people want." He raked Idom with a glance, then focused on Kyllikki. "I'm an entertainer."

Elias didn't seem to have any awe for Idom's colorful and distinctive uniform, even now that it had been cleaned and renewed. The astrogator had shed the dark-purple silk cape, but the white cassock and black robe underneath still showed not only the Guide Guild's insignia with *Prosperity*'s blazons, but also the sigils of academic rank normally covered by the cloak. However, Idom didn't need heraldic splendor to intimidate. He projected an air of understanding what was happening because of what he knew that others didn't.

"Etha Ckam told me you were," offered Kyllikki.

"When did you talk to Etha?" shot back Elias.

"We'd been exchanging traffic when she died."

"Oh." He looked stricken.

Ckam would have been wearing stripes identical to Kyllikki's, but Elias hadn't recognized them. Was he only now realizing Etha might have read his mind? "She said you were to entertain at a court function. What do you do?"

"Music. I sing, play instruments, dance a little."

"That doesn't sound very—exotic," said Kyllikki.

"My instruments are unique, I compose my own music, and I use a phonic scale that's . . . different. All my material is original. I'm told it appears exotic."

"What have you recorded? Do you use your own name? I don't think you ever told us your last name."

"Kleef. Elias—Kleef," he offered with an odd hesitation between the names. "No, I haven't recorded anything yet. If I do, I won't get any more rides on courier ships or yachts. The powerful don't want popular; they want exclusive, high culture, and rare."

What a position for a spy! Playing all the richest parties, the most exclusive clubs, court functions. If Zimor were to plant a spy, that's how she'd do it.

"Apparently, there's also danger in such a life these days," observed Idom. "Perhaps you should record."

"That's a thought. But now all my instruments, my notebooks—everything was lost with *Otroub.* And since I won't be getting paid because I won't be showing up, I'm broke."

"In that case," said Idom, "you'll be stuck on Barkyr, possibly as long as we will." He looked at Kyllikki.

It was a speculative look she recognized. Idom knew as well as she did that the healer's probe had given Elias' genetic makeup as human except for four or five small quirks.

Dressed now in the pod's brown coverall, Elias looked gorgeous. He had pale-blond hair streaked with white, a coppery complexion that almost matched the coverall, sizzling blue eyes, sculpted lips, and a gauntness that emphasized his muscular shoulders; taut, trim buttocks; and long legs with bulging dancer's calves. He couldn't be much older than Kyllikki. Idom, who considered most of her problems due to her recent, sudden celibacy, was matchmaking again.

Elias had not missed Idom's suggestive undertone, but he answered the older man's words. "Then maybe I'll have a chance to thank you both properly."

He'd never touch a telepath, she thought, *especially if he's a spy, and if he's Zimor's Bonded Dreamer, he's probably figured out who I am, might even be planning to capture or kill me for her. Capture, most likely. Shog.*

But nothing he said or did for the rest of that night supported that theory, and by the time Idom woke her for her watch, she'd discarded it again.

"The drive is humming along smoothly," he reported as he turned over the pilot's chair, "but the air scrubbers and temperature regulators have been erratic. Watch them."

She settled in place and eyed the indicators. "Don't mention it to Elias," she said. "It's probably nothing."

46

"It's possible they've been doing that all along."

"I'll read up on it just in case. Get some sleep."

But over the next day, the strange fluctuations increased. They alternately sweated or shivered, and occasionally panted as carbon dioxide collected.

Then Kyllikki regained contact with Lee. The flight of pods from *Prosperity* had nearly reached Barkyr, and every available craft was busy collecting the passengers. Every one of the pods had experienced an assortment of malfunctions ranging from serious to amusing, so nobody wanted to trust those pods to make a safe touchdown on an inhabited planet.

Lee told her, //There's no way they can spare a ship to come out and get you. How bad is your situation? Will you need to go into stasis?//

//I doubt it. We can make it, but we could use a little technical assistance.// And she explained their problem.

Under directions from one of *Prosperity*'s mechanics, Kyllikki and Idom stabilized the temperature, but couldn't do anything about the scrubbers.

Two more days went by, and they began using breathing masks when the carbon dioxide was high. Then they noticed a foul taste to the recycled water. They still had four days to go before they could expect pickup.

Idom and Kyllikki worked on the water recyclers all the next day, but had to reassemble them without much hope.

Over dinner, Idom said, "Even Zuchmul couldn't do more."

"I wish I could be more help," offered Elias, who had, after much careful instruction, taken over the galley chores for them, "but I have no mechanical aptitude."

"We noticed," said Kyllikki, reaching for the hot shaid.

"Kyllikki! Elias, she didn't mean that."

She was framing a weary apology when her shaky barriers were penetrated by a piercing whistle. She jumped, sloshing hot shaid all over her hand. The two men leapt to her rescue, blotting up the mess, searching for ice to treat the burn, and demanding, "What happened?"

Shog! //Lee! Pods aren't telepathically insulated like passenger liners! What's the matter with you?//

//Sorry. I've been trying to get your attention. Barkyr is under attack. A fleet of Teleod ships is coming from the opposite side of Barkyr, the side away from Station Prime, but the first attack destroyed Barkyr Defense. So the Paitsmun are already offering surrender. They've pulled back all their orbital craft, leaving half our pods stranded. Barkyr doesn't want to seem threatening to the Teleod fleet. If you have an option, change course. Don't come here.//

She relayed to Idom and Elias.

Idom shoved away from the table, towering over Kyllikki. "Tell him we don't have an option. We're coming in. We'll try a landing if we have to. I'm going to see what our screens are showing."

As she relayed that to Lee, her mind dwelled on what would happen if some zealous Teleod officer recognized her. Within days, she'd be back in Zimor's stronghold.

She shuddered. //I'll let you know if Idom comes up with something. Right now I've got to go—//

//No, listen!// returned Lee. //I know this is a sore point with you, Kyllikki, but you're the only one here who'd know. Is there any chance these ships have a communicator who can hear us like you heard that attack coordinator?//

He knows how I did that. She tried to think. //Lee, there's a chance they *might*, but it's a very, very small chance. My Metaji trainers told me I'm the only one trained in the Teleod who's ever tried the Metaji's com training and survived. I've never heard of any Metaji-trained telepath attempting the key images—you have to start that much younger than Metaji training. So I don't see how they could have someone who can work both systems.// She took a deep breath. //But since I can, they just might have someone.//

//I was right! That's how you did it!// The flash of avidity and horror that came with his words was very unprofessional. Then the disturbing whirl of mixed emotions was gone as quickly as it had come.

She admitted, //I can do it now, but not before that battle. I had to try *something* to stop those ships.//

//Hey, I'm not criticizing. Our escort did destroy the jump-cannon, so Defense got all the other ships before the Station blew. I'm just glad you're on our side.// But his contact voice was meticulously formal, not friendly.

Adopting her most professional voice, she urged, //Lee, think! *I* defected. Some Metaji telepath might have defected to the Teleod, without attempting to learn Teleod methods. So they could have someone who can hear us. Have you done a Search toward the fleet?//

//I've been afraid to. What if they spot me?//

She knew what his problem was. With Wiprin dead, he was in charge, but he wasn't ready for the responsibility. //Even if they have a Metaji telepath, they'd never send him to capture an obscure colony like Barkyr! And without such a telepath, the only way your Search might be spotted is if you get careless and emote. Basic emotion bleeds through, so any Teleod telepath working the realms might notice that.//

//So I've heard, but you never know what to believe.//

He was right to fear. She'd once seen a Metaji telepath yanked into the working realm. It had taken the poor woman a year to die. //Lee, a Teleod telepath would perceive your emotions as a distinctive but sourceless glow. They'd know they were being Searched, but not from where. We have to plan, and we can't unless we're sure communications are secure.//

//You're right. Their standard procedure is to kill all Metaji telepaths. But you ought to do the Search. At least you know what you're doing.//

There was nothing for it. She had to admit it. //Lee, I can't. Remember when you found me in the Window, and I couldn't control my barriers? I'm still getting headaches. I don't trust myself, at least not at such a distance. You're closer, and you're steadier.//

Reluctantly, he agreed and she left him to it, wrapping her silver brick wall around herself and finding to her dismay she'd also wrapped both arms around her middle and dropped her chin to her chest. Her hand throbbed cold.

Elias was standing behind her, muttering reassurances as if he really cared for her. When she looked up, he said, "Let me see your hand, Kyllikki. Is it blistered? A minute ago, you seemed to be going into shock."

She was faintly surprised to see her hand wrapped in a white cloth filled with ice. She unwound it. "No, it's not blistered," she said with some amazement as she got to her feet. "Come on, we have to talk to Idom."

Watching Idom work the scanners, she filled them both in on what Lee had told her.

Idom sighed. "And there's no avoiding it. We are about to become prisoners of war."

He flashed a display on one of the screens and turned it so they could see. Pointing, he said, "Those, those, and these over here represent Teleod ships. There's Barkyr. You can't see our pods on this scale, but they're here. In less than a day, the fleet will be in spectral range of the planet, at which point the surrender will become official. With no other habitat in the system, we've no place else to go."

"Do you suppose the Station got a message capsule out before it blew up?" asked Elias with real anguish.

If he were a spy, he wouldn't be upset about being captured. "I wasn't monitoring the Station at the time," admitted Kyllikki, "but later on, I'll ask Lee."

Idom muttered abstractedly, "His Search won't find anything. If the fleet had one of our telepaths, they'd be in direct touch already and the surrender would be history."

Elias offered, "*Otroub's* Guide claimed that Barkyr's importance in the war is its location. Doesn't that mean the capture won't go unchallenged?"

Idom watched the display, where the larger dots were separating into flocks of smaller ones. "For technical reasons, Barkyr's location is more convenient to the Teleod than to us. Still, as soon as the Imperial forces discover it's been taken, there'll be a counterattack. The Teleod knows it, so they'll be looking for valuable civilian hostages." He glanced up at Kyllikki. "The crew knows who you are. Can the Teleod telepaths get it out of them?"

"It won't take mind invasion. I'm sure there are crew members who believe I'm the spy who set this whole battle up. Someone is bound to mention it."

"Spy? What do you mean, spy?" demanded Elias.

"I'm a Teleod defector," said Kyllikki.

"And a loyal Imperialist now," added Idom.

"If they catch you working for the enemy . . . Kyllikki, they'll kill you . . . or worse." It was just what Lee had assumed, only Elias glowed with fear. Real fear.

She blinked it away and repaired her barriers, reassured that Elias couldn't possibly be Teleod. Whatever it was about him that eroded her barriers, it hadn't anything to do with Zimor or Dreambonding or spying.

She fixed her attention on Idom, who watched the display, counting the dots with the avid intensity he normally reserved for astrogation. "All they'd dare do with me is ship me home." *Probably.* "And, Idom, if they find out just who *you* are, they'll likely ship you home with me."

"They can't make me work for them."

"They might," she cautioned.

Out of the corner of her eye, she thought she saw Elias shudder. He covered it by turning to her and asking, "Is anyone going to tell me who I've been rescued by?"

"There's no point in keeping it from him," said Idom, fingering his beard thoughtfully. "Most of the crew knows anyway. Someone's bound to talk."

"Idom's one of a handful in the Metaji Empire who understands the theory of Pool construction and operation, of how one Guide or a pair of Operators can 'fold' a whole ship through a Pool that's built into the ship's framework and make it pop out where they want it to."

"And Kyllikki," said Idom, "used to be one of the Teleod's best Pool Operators."

Elias' eyes widened. "Yes. They use telepaths in the Pools! That's what this war is all about. Is that why you defected?"

"No. That's something I don't talk about." Zimor had used Kyllikki's talent as an Eight Families telepath and Bonder to make her into a powerful Pool Operator, but it had been the using she'd objected to, not the Operating. When she'd arrived in the Metaji, where Imperial policy called for the execution of all known Teleod Operators, her only chance for an exemption had been to volunteer for a "dangerous medical experiment"— retraining as a Metaji communicator. Part of the price she'd gladly paid to gain certification was the oath never to enter a Pool again, and having survived the mental probes and conditioning, she'd been given her freedom, as the law demanded. But very few below the rank of Duke other than Guild members knew the whole story. "I don't appreciate Idom bringing it up."

"Considering what he may face with us and because of us on Barkyr, he has a right to know," insisted Idom, examining Elias. "Of her own free will, Kyllikki has forsaken the Pools because, despite her retraining as a Metaji telepath, any transit she made would probably be just as damaging to the substrata of space-time as ordinary Teleod Operation."

"Lots of people seem convinced that's what's causing ships to disappear," said Elias.

"It's true," said Idom with all the authority of his Guild. "Every passage of a Teleod ship leaves a gouge behind it that can throw the next Metaji ship off course. Routes have become so damaged that now Teleod ships can't get through, and they're using stronger methods that leave deeper gouges. They think that solves the problem. They think they can keep on devising ways to punch across the scarred tracks. The only reason no one in the Metaji is afraid that the firmament will collapse is that our calculations show that civilization will crumble long before the damage is serious."

"You mean," he said cautiously, "no more interstellar travel?"

"Isn't that what I said?"

Elias' expression froze, but Kyllikki was certain she detected a frisson of real, personal fear beneath it, and a curious sense of bereavement. "I've seen the calculations," she said, "and I'm convinced the Teleod Operators are causing the problem. It can be stopped. It's political, not scientific. It can be done and it must be done."

"You see," added Idom, "Kyllikki will never add another scar to the crazing that's already there. She's doing all she can, at terrible personal cost, to help the Metaji abolish the Teleod Pool Operators before it's too late. For that, we owe her all the protection we can devise."

"Idom!" protested Kyllikki.

"It's nothing but the truth and you know it."

It wasn't anything of the sort. She was no Metaji patriot. She was just a refugee from Zimor's power. Unable to face her cousin down, she had run. "It doesn't matter why I'm here. If they catch me—"

"Sovereigns Be!" swore Elias. "Com Officers handle sensitive military traffic! If they can get into your—"

"They can. Not just me, but Lee and all the Paitsmun as well. The technique invariably kills the subject. That's why we need to agree on fictitious identities."

Elias shook his head. "It won't work—not for long."

"True, but they won't have many telepaths assigned to interrogating prisoners. I can get Lee to pass the word to protect us. It might gain us some time before someone slips or sells us out, enough time for what we know to go stale."

"Maybe," agreed Idom with a disturbing light in his eye.

She suppressed a shiver of foreboding, telling herself that Idom wasn't really foretelling the future. No science could do that, not even the one that could just count things and foretell where a ship would pop out of its Pool.

After that, they destroyed their uniforms and adopted the brown coverall the pod supplied. Idom insisted Kyllikki pick the new names, and she complied readily. She would be Kyllikki Abtrel, a trainee in *Prosperity*'s infirmary. Idom would be simply Idom Shigets, a very common name, and he could be listed as an in-system helmsman.

"You don't need a new name," she told Elias. "But I'll get Captain Brev to list you as a passenger, and you can continue to be a musician who's lost his equipment. The worst they might do is ask you to sing. But if they discover you were a passenger on *Otroub*, they'll take your mind apart to verify the reason."

Lee reported that his Search had found no trace of a working telepath in the direction of the approaching fleet. Kyllikki explained their plan, and he thought as little of it as they did. But he relayed their new biographies to the Captain, adding one for himself, and the Captain adjusted his log to support their claims. The Paitsmun were also cooperating, as their strategy called for their telepaths to disappear without a trace into the general population. Hours before the official surrender of Barkyr, the Guides' Guild office was closed, the personnel dispersed.

When the official surrender came, Kyllikki, Idom, and Elias gathered around the pilot's station, tuning and retuning the equipment to catch every crackling nuance of the invader's signal. Coherent spectrum conditions this close to the star were not good, and their receivers were old and far from adequate. They were able to hear Barkyr, but the fleet's transmissions were barely intelligible even after filtering.

At first, things went badly for Barkyr. The Attaché aboard the flagship of the fleet who was authorized to speak for the Teleod refused to accept the surrender from the Paitsmun who claimed to be Baron of Barkyr.

The Baron spent a good while attempting to establish credentials, but the Attaché was having none of it, and the Baron could not understand why. But Kyllikki did.

Schooling herself to remain strictly in audio-analogue, she gave a mental handclap aimed at the Paitsmun communicator she'd dealt with before the battle. //This is *Prosperity* Com Third. Tell your Baron that the Attaché will only deal with a human. She can't grasp the idea that a nonhuman might have ranking authority, and she may in fact have instructions to deal directly only with humans.//

The nonverbal consternation that came back from her opposite number on the planet's surface was eloquent.

//Kyllikki?// It was Lee. //Is that you?//

//It is, Lee. Did you hear what I told them?//

//I heard. Barkyr Control, this is *Prosperity* Com Second. My Com Third is absolutely correct. You must relay her information to your Baron for a decision.//

//Acknowledged, *Prosperity*. The situation is going to be much worse than we ever imagined. Thank you.//

Shortly after that, they heard the Baron break off and ask the fleet to stand by. There was a long silence.

The air in the pod had cycled through unbreathable and eye-searing back to tolerable by the time they heard a new voice, and they were now close enough to pick up some fuzzy visuals from Barkyr. "This is Sir Timend of Vrai, speaking for the Barony of Barkyr." The human insisted on direct contact with the Attaché and then spelled out the terms of surrender the Baron had offered.

This time, there was no temporizing. The Attaché issued counterterms, Timend counterproposed, and they settled with Timend gaining a few concessions Kyllikki hadn't expected, including the Baron's demand to have *Prosperity*'s refugees picked up immediately and brought down for medical treatment.

Not long after that, the fleet dropped a swarm of smaller ships, tenders, Captain's launches, and scouts, that shot on ahead of the fleet, querying the pods about their problems with a severe military efficiency. Then they assigned a pickup schedule. It would be another two days until Pod Fifteen could be met.

What surprised Kyllikki through all this was the way Idom sat and counted the Teleod fleet over and over as it came closer. The more ships he could distinguish on the poor resolution screen, the happier he seemed.

Kyllikki didn't argue. The random happenings of the universe, the relationships of numbers and probabilities were Idom's field, not hers. He had once tried to explain how he could trace probability waves by observing the manifestation of numbers. It only seemed like foretelling the future, he'd said, while actually it was just understanding the present, but she didn't see what difference it made if the approaching fleet consisted of two hundred or two hundred seventy-three ships. It was the people on the ships that mattered.

"I agree completely," Idom said when she put it to him. "I'd love to know how many people there are on those ships."

"And I'd like to know *who* they are," she countered.

That got his full attention. "Anyone high-ranking enough to recognize you won't be dealing with passenger-ship refugees. We'll keep a low profile and see what happens."

"They may not recognize me personally, but few Teleod citizens are unable to recognize the Eight Families!"

"Humans are humans the galaxy over," replied Idom serenely. "Speak, move, and dress like a working woman of the Metaji, and who could take you for an aristocrat of the Teleod? Even if you look somewhat like them?"

"The Teleod doesn't have aristocrats. The Metaji is an Empire, the Teleod elects its leaders."

"Politics! We both know what side you're on."

"I'm sorry. I guess the waiting is getting to me." It was only a question of time, and she'd be back on a Teleod ship, under Teleod law. "I'm going to check on Zuchmul."

She left Idom to his ship counting, and went aft to the bunks. Elias was lying in his bunk, curtain open. With one hand he tapped out a slow rhythm on the bulkhead while he whistled softly between his teeth. So far, he'd never offered to sing for them, but there was always music inside him, and sometimes it soaked through her barriers.

As she approached the stasis unit, he propped himself on his elbows. "Does it really need checking that often?"

"Probably not. There's not much we could do if it fails, and nothing we can do to prevent it from failing. But somehow it makes me feel better."

"I know what you mean. I feel guilty about what happened to him. If I'd stayed in the bunk, he'd be alive."

"There's no point to looking at it that way." She turned to examine him, wondering again about where he was from. His accent certainly wasn't Teleod, and his cultural assumptions didn't seem to form a pattern either. But then she didn't know much about the Metaji cultures. "If it would make you feel any better, talk to Idom about it. He could probably count the tools in that drawer that got loose, and the number of links in Zuchmul's radiation suit, and explain why the accident was inevitable." She gave a shrug and smiled.

He laughed. It was tense and a little rusty. None of them had laughed at all in days. But it was a real laugh.

She joined in with a chuckle. "All right, so I tease Idom. But what he really does do seems just that absurd to me. After all, numerical harmonics and probability resonances—accidents—aren't my field. Astrogation, Guild style, is the creation and control of accidents; telepathy occurs on a level where the concept 'number' is not defined. Elias, Zuchmul wouldn't hold you responsible, but Idom could tell you why you're not."

She bent over the stasis indicators. She leaned on the bubble that enclosed her luren friend, wondering if there was any hope for his revival. What would the occupation force do with a luren in stasis? She had to hold her breath against the tears. There was no time now for pain. Their lives were still in danger.

She didn't hear Elias move, but his hands came onto her shoulders and he pulled her back against him—the only way he knew how to offer comfort. And for the first time since she had threatened him with mental invasion for his trouble, there was no tension in him, just warmth. She firmed up her barriers and tried not to resist, remembering how the Paitsmun crewman had criticized her for her unconscious mannerisms. They could give her away both as a telepath and as Eight Families. If she was going to be Kyllikki Abtrel, Metaji paramedic, she had to practice.

"That's better," said Elias, and his voice was a caress. "It won't be too bad. If they catch you, they'll just ship you home. Surely, that's not so terrible a fate."

She whirled in his arms. "I'd be better off dead!"

"You can't really mean that?"

"I can and I do. Doesn't this war mean anything to you?"

"It does. Oh, it does. But," he said, glancing at Zuchmul's

shadowy form, "you have friends here, you must have had friends at home. They'd be glad to see you. They'd help you. It must have been terrible—to leave all that."

She studied his expression, wanting to thin her barriers and read the emotions that always whirled about him in glowing spirals. But it hardly took a telepath to feel the wistful yearning of an exile who lacked hope, nor the solid trust he had in her Metaji Communicator's principles.

She put one hand on the stasis case. "I had friends, yes, and a lot of them might side with me now—*if* there was any political advantage in it. But Zuchmul wouldn't care what anybody else thought or did. He'd defend me anytime, anywhere, against anything. And I'd do the same for him. Elias, that couldn't happen in the Teleod. Zuchmul is *luren*. Do you understand what that means?"

"But luren are human."

"*Here*, yes. *There*, no, not quite human enough."

"I see."

"Do you? This war isn't about enfranchising nonhumans or about protecting the firmament from permanent damage. It's about power, and the abuse of power. In the Teleod, the reins of power are in the hands of the Eight Families, and right now that's mostly just one person, my cousin Zimor, Lady of Laila. *The* Lady of Laila."

"I thought you said the Teleod elects its rulers."

"It does, but only members of the Families are eligible to be elected, and only wealth buys the right to vote. The Families control the great fortunes, which rest on the ebb and flow of trade. And all of their power rests on their control of the Pools, on control of ship movements. Destroy the Pool Operators, put the Pools into the hands of the proven impartiality of the Guides' Guild, and even the Families' telepathy couldn't keep them in power. Anyone, even a Paitsmun, could amass great wealth, or even political power. And the nonhumans outnumber humans."

His face had turned to stone. "I'd never heard it put quite like that before."

She didn't think she'd said anything that any Metaji news commentator might not have said.

"But if the hold of the Families on the Teleod is based on trade, why do they oppose protecting the shipping lanes from being destroyed?"

"The Families don't—not really," said Kyllikki. "Zimor does because she doesn't believe there's any real threat from the traditional method of Operation. She's convinced the Guild's crying doom just to break her power. It's hard to explain to someone used to thinking in Imperial terms. Here, the people who hold power don't get it because they want it—they get it because they're best suited to the job. And they have it for life, so they're not always looking over their shoulder wondering who's going to take it away from them. I mean, a Count or a Duke has to be really bad before the Emperor would remove them from office. And their incompetence has to be proved before the Imperial courts. There are laws here that prevent the kind of thing Zimor has been doing."

"What has she been doing?"

She missed the guarded tone of that question. "Oh, anything she pleases! She's insane, Elias, paranoid, and totally oblivious to the pain she causes as she pursues her own goals. There isn't anything that can stop her—except maybe the massed power of the Metaji Empire."

"So that's why you're here? Because you want to stop your—cousin."

"Elias, don't judge me too harshly. It's very hard for anyone raised in the Metaji to understand the use of military power as a political tool. That's why it took so long for this war to get started, but there is no other way to stop Zimor. However many lives it costs, it's fewer lives than will be lost if she's not stopped. I couldn't do anything against her. I just—ran. Ran away to hide."

"You really believe that."

"It's true. I'm not proud of it."

"Anything that your courage can't stand against has to be pretty formidable."

Shog! He really means that! "I've never had to use any courage here. It's a much better place to live."

"Are you sure? I mean, how much of it have you seen?"

"Well, I haven't met the Emperor, but I've dealt with some Counts, various Guild officers, and an assortment of ordinary people, a lot of whom were much less human than Zuchmul. There was even one Duke who wasn't human who treated me with respect when nobody else would. You won't value what you've got here unless Zimor wins this war. And then it will be too late."

"So after the war, presuming we win, will you go home?"

"I—I don't think so."

"Why?"

"Because home won't be there anymore, and I'm not the same person I was when it was home. Does that make sense?"

He cocked his head to one side and studied her. Then, gravely, judiciously, he nodded. "Strangely enough, I think it does. At least, I hope it will. It's certainly something to think about."

It didn't seem that difficult an idea to her, but she shrugged. "Where do you come from?"

He pulled her over to his bunk and they sat while he recited his life's story, liberally embroidered with tales of musical achievements, triumphs in contests, and great performances. Even though the grand moments he described were emotionally real to him, the rest seemed to be recited by rote from some biography or publicity release. It made her uncomfortable, and she had to keep reinforcing her barriers.

Before she found the right questions to ask, Idom called them to eat, and then she did a stint on watch in the pilot's seat. When she went to take her turn sleeping, Idom and Elias were still up, playing Thizan with an improvised board and pieces. Idom was winning and Kyllikki couldn't understand why. He wasn't that good at the luren game.

Wrapping herself in her most impenetrable barriers, she fell into a deep, undisturbed sleep, and woke thinking about the enigma of Elias. She had slept straight through without waking, and she never did that when Elias was sleeping at the same time she was. No matter how much care she took with her barriers before she lay down, she would wake every few minutes to find they were full of holes and her mind was dwelling on what she should have done and said during past confrontations with Zimor.

But this time, the shield of silver bricks that guarded her mind was still in place, reflecting away every wisp of thought. If Lee had been whistling as loudly as he could, it would not have wakened her.

"Kyllikki?"

She started, then saw Idom standing over her. "Yes?"

"At last. You've been sleeping as if you hadn't slept in days."

She swung her legs over the side and sat up, tugging her coverall into place. "How long did I sleep?"

"Two shifts. Elias went to sleep a while ago."

She peered into the adjacent bunk. Elias was curled on his side, his oxygen mask obscuring his features, one beautiful hand curved as if cradling an instrument to him. She peeled off her oxygen mask, which she always wore when sleeping now, and stretched. The air stank.

The air was so bad, and the water so slimy, that none of them had any appetite. Idom went to sleep, leaving Kyllikki on watch, waiting for the air to cycle back to breathable. She waited and waited, and for the first time began to doubt that the cycle would ever reverse. She counted the units of oxygen remaining for the masks, wondered how long the vacuum suits' supply might stretch to, counted the hours until they might expect pickup, and worried.

She was facing the fact that they weren't going to make it, that they'd have to risk stasis, when she was startled out of her reverie by the voice-com. "Pod Fifteen, this is Fleet Captain Iyadee's yacht, *Fine Time*, Pilot First, Drimar, commanding. Stand by for orbital correction data."

She grabbed for the transmission controls, fumbled, then produced a horrid squeal before she got it right. "*Fine Time*,

this is Pod Fifteen, uh, Kyllikki Abtrel, Medical Trainee. We—"
She broke off, reminding herself she was not a professional
communicator. It had been just luck that she had fumbled the
controls. Now she had to play it out. "Uh—we have an emergency, I think." She described the amount of oxygen left, and
read off the composition of the air. She slipped in the data on
their dormant luren in stasis as casually as she could, realizing it
would be foremost on a medic's mind. Omitting it now would
cause trouble later.

When Drimar wanted to talk about the orbital correction,
she called Idom, who likewise took care to stumble.

Kyllikki was sweating by the time they had forced the discussion to take three times as long as it should have taken, but
they won a higher place on the priority list.

chapter **four**

●●●●●●●●●●●●●●●●●●●●●●●●●●●●●●●●●●●●

Kyllikki dropped heavily onto one of the bare cots and stared at the worn and blotched floor between her feet. The high-ceilinged Paitsmun barracks had been hastily converted for human prisoners of war by filling the open floor with rows of bare cots, leaving just enough room for a slender person to stand between them. Kyllikki had chosen a cot on the wide aisle that ran the length of the space, which was drafty, filled with sharp echoes and human voices aching with defeat. She kept her barriers opaque in both directions, aching herself.

As *Prosperity*'s passengers and crew filed in behind her, a Teleod guard stood up on a cot and used a palm held amplifier to direct them, men to the right of the aisle and women to the left. Elias and Idom took cots across the aisle from her. The guard droned on in a Metaji dialect with a distinct Teleod accent, assuring them that a privacy curtain would soon be rigged down the center of the huge room, which seemed more like a space-yacht hangar than the luxurious accommodation it was to the Paitsmun. "Meals will commence at sundown, then you will be issued blankets. Tomorrow, you will be more thoroughly examined by our medical department."

They had already been through triage at the landing field where the small craft had deposited *Prosperity*'s refugees. Medical wagons, staffed by Barkyr's own hastily cooperative citizens, had taken away the most desperately ill passengers, but on order of the Teleod guards, had left Zuchmul's stasis unit sitting in the cruel sun.

Kyllikki had not let go of the unit even once after she, Elias, and Idom had detached it from the pod's bulkhead and wrestled it into the yacht that had collected them. She had clung to it while the yacht filled with survivors from other pods, and she had ridden down to the planet secured only by a makeshift safety belt attached to the massive unit. Once aground, several who had counted Zuchmul as friend carried the unit gently out onto the field. She had stayed with it until soldiers came for her. Even then, she had clung to the case with hysterical strength, repeating over and over how Zuchmul had to be revived by his own people, and they had to know, first, what had happened to him.

She had transcribed every detail in the unit's log, every bit she knew of Zuchmul's medical history and family affiliations, but she knew that wouldn't be enough. She had to go with Zuchmul, wherever they were taking him. Finally they peeled her away and forced her into an overcrowded truck that floated away across the pavement, Zuchmul's case receding into a tiny blot before she lost sight of it, abandoned out in the sun. *What if the protective fields aren't enough for a luren? What if they can't protect him against the direct sunlight?*

Somehow, in the middle of that long ride, she had found herself being held in Idom's arms. "Kyllikki, that was wonderful! Inspired. They'd never suspect you now."

Elias pushed up behind her, growling, "That was no act, old man. Here, let me."

He had turned Kyllikki into his arms, stroking her hair and making soothing noises until the truck halted with a jerk and they filed through security gates. The nonhumans had been segregated and herded by armed guards toward one of the looming buildings that dotted the flat, high-fenced compound. Then the humans had been escorted by the man with the amplifier, who never stopped talking reassuringly to them. No attempt had been made to reassure the nonhumans. Kyllikki knew why. Their opinions and feelings were unimportant.

Now, she sat on her bare bunk and heard the instructions and bland apologies, all very polite but firm, assuring them they'd be provided with bedding after they were fed.

Would the nonhumans? If so, she was sure there would be no attempt made to determine what sort of bedding would be adequate for each species.

Her musings were interrupted by another male voice. "Abtrel! Officer Abtrel, step forward."

A man with a palm amplifier paced past Kyllikki's cot, casting his announcement over the women expectantly, then moved on, the sound fading with distance and the incessant rush of hundreds of voices echoing off the cavernous ceiling. "Abtrel. Officer Abtrel, step forward."

"Kyllikki!" It was a penetrating whisper, and she started in surprise. Elias was squatting in the central aisle, pretending to be inspecting one leg of his cot, which was a bit shorter than the others, while over his shoulder he hissed, "Kyllikki! That's you! Kyllikki Abtrel! You'd better answer or they'll think you're hiding for a reason."

She gaped at him, then scrambled to her feet and pursued the guard who was calling her. "Sir! Sir! I'm Abtrel, Medical Trainee, *Prosperity*." The man turned to her, and before he could challenge why she hadn't answered sooner, she added, "I'm not an officer, sir."

He sighed and checked a display unit at his belt. "Come with me, Abtrel."

He scooped up her arm, trapping her elbow in such a way that she couldn't pull free, and marched in a long, measured stride toward the door. All eyes turned to her as they passed, but she had to pay attention to her barriers. The man who held her was a minimally sensitive telepath.

It was actually warmer outside than in, but the thin coverall was still not enough. It flapped in the breeze, and she felt naked. She concentrated on discerning the layout of the camp, concluding that it was a physical-training camp for Paitsmun entering the Imperial Service. The wide open areas between the buildings were laced with the typical Paitsmun running tracks, and in one field she saw hurdles, obstacles, and strange rope constructions scaled for Paitsmun.

To one end of the compound was a low, squat building with no windows and a bright-orange roof. That had to be the armory. At the far end, away from the armory, was the infirmary, and near it, an area painted in bright-green stripes marking a landing field. There was a small space yacht parked there now. She recognized the make and model: a fast, expensive machine favored by the Eight Families. As she watched, guards ran from the ship as the distinctive gravitic whine split the air, and the yacht took off.

They passed work crews raising towers to hold security sensors, and she read the signs: DANGER, SCRAMBLER EMANATIONS, KEEP OUT, all in Teleod scripts. It occurred to her that she didn't have to hide her knowledge of Teleod languages. Before the war, there had been free trade between Teleod and Metaji, so only her accent and intonation would betray her.

At the infirmary door, the guard turned her over to a group of armed women—large, tough women with the look of high-gravity training about them. As they pushed her through the big, transparent doors into a typical emergency receiving room, a thrill of fear gripped her. Their elaborate plan had failed. Drugged interrogations would be done by trained medical personnel. Considering what she knew of Teleod practices, she was suddenly willing to reveal her identity. *Maybe they only want a med tech to work for them?*

The emergency receiving corridor was lined with rolling cots waiting for patients. The air was colder here, designed to relieve physiological stress for injured Paitsmun. A few twisting, winding turns under the high ceilings and she was lost. They came at last to an office that had been carved out of the Paitsmun's idea of a treatment room by installing temporary buff-colored walls to define several reasonably sized areas.

But inside the office, instead of a desk, couches, lamps, and files, there was one metal chair rigged with sensor probes as well as a large display screen. Beside the chair was the familiar shape of a pod's stasis unit, activated.

Kyllikki tore loose from the guards and threw herself at the case, peering inside. She got one confirming glimpse of Zuchmul's face before the guards picked her up and put her in the interrogation chair. But they didn't activate the sensory probes, didn't strap her in.

"Stay there or we'll have to take measures," one of the guards warned her, her tone incongruously friendly.

Two of the women took up stations by the door, and the rest left. A silence descended in which she could hear the faint *tick-sh-sh-clack* of the stasis unit. She'd never noticed that sound in space, the other onboard systems making enough white noise to drown it out.

She knew the silent waiting was a war on her nerves, all very carefully metered. It worked. By the time the interrogators finally arrived, two women and a man trooping into the little room as if marching on parade, Kyllikki could not face the idea of giving up her life, her sanity, or Metaji military data to Teleod drugs, nor could she contemplate another meeting with Zimor.

One of the women spread a kit out on a high ledge and prepared an instrument as she said, "I am Dr. Itslin. You have nothing to fear, Officer Abtrel, for I will see that no harm comes to you. Hold out your arm."

She turned and, with swift continuous movement, grabbed Kyllikki's hand, shoved the blue sleeve up, and plunged a sharp instrument into Kyllikki's flesh. Swabbing off the dot of blood, she folded Kyllikki's arm up, saying, "I just took a small cellular sample for identification and immunization purposes. Purely routine."

Kyllikki's throat closed over a squeal of protest. If they processed her geneprint through Barkyr's Metaji register, they'd learn her real name. How many Lailas were there in the Metaji? How many would they think there were? Maybe they'd only check *Prosperity*'s data from Captain Brev's log tapes. Then her geneprint would read "Abtrel."

While Dr. Itslin worked, the man cleared his throat, consulting a noteboard. "I understand you're a friend of this luren." He nodded distastefully at the unit.

"Not really," she answered, thinking fast. "He's a colleague, a tech from *Prosperity*. I never met him before I got this job. But when the ship blew up, he saved my life, then saved the lives of all of us in the pod several times over." She lowered her eyes, keeping scrupulously to the truth as she painted a false picture. "I feel responsible for his 'death.' It was an accident, but I feel guilty. At least I've got to see he gets properly awakened."

"That's what you're here to discuss. Now, tell me, what exactly would happen if we shut down this unit and allowed him to waken?"

She gave the textbook answer. "He'd very likely die, permanently."

"But he would crave blood first, and be so crazed by his need that he'd kill for it."

She gaped at him.

"I see you know that little luren secret. What do you know of how his people prevent that from happening?"

"Just what anyone knows—that they don't tell how."

"It's known that luren revere the one who wakens them as a parent, and serve that parent's welfare above all others. But what exactly does a parent do to earn that?"

"Why are you asking me?" She pushed back in the chair, wishing she could put some distance between herself and them.

The woman who hadn't spoken yet leaned close to Kyllikki. "Because you know! And you're going to tell us."

The man restrained her with a hand. "Gently. Kyllikki is an intelligent woman. She's just upholding her own honor as a human in trying to protect his rights."

The woman pulled free of the man's grasp. "We'll use the probe, soften her up, and then call in one of the telepaths to pick her emotions apart."

The man turned the woman around and instructed patiently. "Only if we have to, but I doubt it will be necessary." He came to lean over Kyllikki. "Now, if I turn her and the telepath loose on you, there won't be much left when they're finished. But if you cooperate with me, you won't even have to go back to the barracks tonight. I've reserved a private room for you in the officers' hall, with its own heater, a nice bed, and usable plumbing. Now, keeping all that in mind, what exactly is done to parent a luren and earn his obedience?"

Suddenly, she understood. They wanted to waken and control Zuchmul, force him to use Influence to control the prisoners—or extract information. They wanted Zuchmul as a weapon. *His worst fear come true.* "I don't understand why you'd think I'd know such a thing."

The man knelt beside her chair. "There were many witnesses to your arrival. One was a telepath, of course. Living in the Metaji, you wouldn't know what that means. Our telepaths have skills your people would never imagine, and no law prevents them from using those skills. We know the truth about you, about how you feel about Zuchmul and his revival. The home planet of the luren is in the Teleod. We know a lot about them. We're going to learn a lot more."

The distinctive whine of the yacht landing shook the walls of the building, obliterating voices while she wondered why she hadn't spotted the snooping telepath, and what exactly had leaked through her barriers. A lesser telepath might have gotten only what she'd intended, a non-telepath's natural reflex barriers bursting from desperation.

As the noise abated, the man sadly shook his head. "If you really don't know how to parent a luren, we must experiment blindly. It'll go harder for him, I'm sure." He paused, and Kyllikki tried not to look too wild-eyed. "On the chance that you do know, we'll have to do a full exploratory interrogation."

The doctor began preparing an injector. Kyllikki's mouth went dry, and she could hardly breathe.

"Regardless of the results," added the man, "we will waken him. If you want it to go easier on him, you'll tell us what you know of the process now. After an exploratory, you won't be able to help him through his ordeal. If you tell us voluntarily, we'll let you see him through."

Slowly, Kyllikki moved her head in denial.

The other woman grabbed Kyllikki's arm to expose it for the doctor's injector. As the doctor approached, she leaned close to Kyllikki's ear and said, "He was drinking your blood, wasn't he?"

Kyllikki's mouth dropped open in shock. *At least they have no idea of the truth.* But because of the mistake, the occupation commander probably thought he had a rogue luren captive, a luren other luren would be hunting down to kill, a luren he could use with impunity.

The door opened and closed. A man wearing a commander's uniform with the six red triangles of a Master Coordinator on the shoulders stood facing Kyllikki. Mentally, she tensed. The man was short, somewhat overweight, with bushy eyebrows shading sunken eyes. She didn't recognize him, but he had the rank to entitle him to a yacht like the one outside.

He raked over the hardened surface of Kyllikki's barriers with casual precision, then dismissed her as what she appeared to be, a terrified paramedic. He gestured to her interrogators. "Come with me. All of you." He jerked the door open and stalked out, the three close behind him, leaving only the two women guards flanking the door.

Kyllikki let out a tremulous sigh that was almost a sob. The man had to be the ranking telepath with the occupation, and he had perceived nothing out of the ordinary.

Three more deep breaths, and courage returned. If she was the only Eight Families telepath on Barkyr, she had an advantage she had to use before it was too late. Mentally, she followed the group, using the Metaji Search technique and keeping the indelible key image obscured behind her barriers. She had no trouble following the man who'd questioned her; his worried mental jabbering was distinctive.

She laid her head back against the apparatus behind her and closed her eyes, eavesdropping shamelessly, suffering only a small twinge of conscience for her Metaji oath. After all, they were under Teleod law now.

"Commander Aarl, do you realize what you just interrupted? I almost had her—"

"You had nothing but a woman paralyzed with fear. But that's not important now. I have new orders direct from Zimor, The Lady of Laila."

"A diving capsule?" asked the doctor.

The telepath sighed in exasperation. "How else would I get direct orders? But this one was bumped and rerouted twice before it arrived. Results were expected long ago."

Kyllikki knew Zimor used her Pools to send message capsules all over, controlling the progress of the war. Their wakes were reputed to be much more destructive than those of ships, but Zimor neither believed that nor cared.

"Then your interruption was justified. What can we do?"

"This is classified, not to leave this room. I'll know if any of you break security."

"Agreed," they chorused routinely.

"One of our prisoners, someone whom I believe must have come in on one of *Prosperity*'s pods, is actually working directly for Zimor. She wants him extracted from the herd without blowing his cover. Then he's to be sent to the Dessiwan Internment Facility for potentially useful prisoners. I have his rebriefing tapes and documents."

The interrogator sat down at a desk and began pulling up data on a screen. "We don't have the detainees geneprinted and tagged yet, but I have the list of names they've provided. What name is the spy using?"

"The cover name is Elias Kleef. Something of a high-profile name in Imperial circles, I'm told."

He is Zimor's! And with that, she knew beyond all doubt that he was a Dreamer, Bonded to her cousin, Zimor's Dreamspy. There was no other way that Zimor could have known to launch that message capsule days ago. In fact, it must have been sent while he was in *Otroub*'s pod, expecting rescue from Barkyr—and ignorant of the intended takeover of the planet as well as Kyllikki's identity. *But as soon as Elias knew, Zimor knew. It's the nature of the Bond.*

The implications tumbled over each other in Kyllikki's mind, but her attention was called back to the pacing commander. "He's a triple-five operative, uniquely valuable though not irreplaceable, but he works, as I said, directly for Zimor herself. There was no facial view with the data, and no geneprint, no way to pick him out."

The doctor said, "We found Abtrel by just sending someone in to page her. Why can't we do that with this Kleef? He wouldn't have any reason not to answer the page."

The commander paced. "My orders are to get him out without anyone noticing. Where is he now?"

The man at the desk read from the datascan: "He came in on *Prosperity*'s Pod Fifteen, and was judged healthy. He should be in Building Five-eighteen-A. I have an idea."

"Well?" prompted the Master Coordinator.

"Make them answer roll leaving their buildings for the meal, and you and I will be watching Building Five-eighteen-A for Kleef; then in the dining hall, I'll take Kleef out of the serving line with some medical excuse, and you can have him in space before they finish eating."

"He'd still be missed," observed Aarl.

The doctor said, "We'd planned to resort them into different barracks tomorrow, increase stress before questioning, but we could do that tonight after the meal. That way, everyone will have lost track of friends and family, and one missing person won't be conspicuous."

They reached swift agreement on the plan, and since they had so little time, the interrogator sent orders for Kyllikki to be taken to a cell, a converted walk-in storage closet with one tiny vent and a camper's latrine package.

She let herself lose touch with the interrogator. She had to think. But one thing Kyllikki knew now. She had to escape. She had to steal that yacht and escape. She'd need Idom. Somehow the two of them had to capture Elias and get him to the Emperor. Elias was the only proof worth offering of the fact that

Zimor was raiding the interdicted Dreamer's planet, breaking the accord between Teleod and Metaji that had survived more conflicts than she could name.

If the Metaji Empire was really losing the war, this could turn the tide, this could be the weapon the Metaji needed—but only the Emperor could wield it. He'd have to find a way to convince the Eight Families to turn on Zimor. With Elias himself as proof, that wouldn't be impossible.

But she couldn't leave Zuchmul behind. She either had to destroy his brain so he'd be permanently dead, or take the stasis case with them.

chapter five

●●●●●●●●●●●●●●●●●●●●●●●●●●●●●●●●●●●●●●

Sitting on the blanket they'd given her, Kyllikki hugged her knees to her chin and abstractedly chewed her lower lip, staring alternately at the empty shelves of the windowless storage closet and at the door. It was a Paitsmun storage closet, but the Teleod soldiers didn't realize that Paitsmun claustrophobia forced them to make sure nobody could ever be locked into a small space. The soldiers had rigged a hasp and lock across the latch side of the door, but the door swung on mechanical hinges with pins, hinges set on the in-side. And there were only two unsuspecting armed guards out-side. She could walk out any time she chose, thanks to Zuchmul's teaching her all about clever primitive devices.

Just days ago, the thought of what would happen after she walked out of the cell would have kept her there. But now it seemed that something deep inside of her had decided that her life, like other lives, was expendable. Indeed, it was better to die than to sit quietly and let Zimor and her allies do as they pleased.

With that decision had come an overwhelming sensation of pure freedom, like the aroma of fresh spring air triggering an atavistic joy.

Even so, what she was contemplating was horrifying. In order to escape this prison, to accomplish her goals, she would have to place herself above the law, to become little better than Zimor in that regard. She couldn't live with that, but there was very little chance she would have to.

Strangely, at that grim realization, the tension sloughed off like a molted skin, all the fear evaporated, and for the first time since she'd decided to flee Zimor, Kyllikki felt like herself again.

Keenly aware that if she was going to move, she must move swiftly and decisively now, she nevertheless took time to lower her head to her knees, close her eyes, and check on the other telepaths who might notice and raise an alarm.

Securing herself firmly within the Metaji conventions but keeping her Teleod barrier key image of silvered brick, she Searched for and found Lee. He was sleeping, totally oblivious in his exhaustion. Far away at the edge of the compound, she noticed a group of Barkyr's traffic-control Com Officers, volunteers who had turned themselves in as the entire staff of Barkyr Control. They were heavily drugged and fully expecting execution. If any of them, or rather the undrugged ones hiding among the untalented, learned how she intended to escape, they would do their best to kill her. But with her brick wall adjusted carefully, she was confident none of them would notice her, at least for a while.

Slowly raising the key of the working realm from its perpetual dim glow to a brighter shine, she kept half her attention on the Metaji protocols while scanning the mental landscape defined only by mutual agreement of the Teleod's working telepaths. Several of them were going about their duties. Then she saw Aarl being summoned for some new emergency, his attention drawn away from finding Elias.

She didn't consider the Master Coordinator, or any of the others with the fleet, as an immediate threat to her plan. Aarl had to be the highest-ranking telepath here, or Zimor wouldn't be sending him direct orders. The six red triangles he wore denoted skills one step below the least of the Families' telepaths, a step he'd never be able to take because he lacked the genes. Kyllikki, though, was ranked just below the Families' top rank.

That counted for nothing when facing Zimor, but here it should be enough. If she took care.

As soon as she felt secure, she committed her first act as an outlaw of the Metaji, as an oath breaker. //Idom?//

Contact was instantaneous. He was still in the barracks, watching Elias standing at some distance talking with a group of men. She narrowed her attention so there would be no leakage, and sent, //Idom. It's Kyllikki. I need to talk to you.//

Idom's highly trained attention snapped to that inner voice, and then he raked his eyes across the women's cots.

//I'm in another building. You once gave me permission to address you this way. May I now? Please, Idom.//

//Kyllikki?// His mental voice was faint, diffuse, and blurred, but with intense effort she was able to distinguish his welcome from the background noise of his thoughts. He was not sending her that thought, though. He was no telepath. She was invading him to pluck it from his mind.

Either I'm going to go through with this, or I'm not. This is no time to get squeamish. //Yes, it's me, Idom. I've got to escape. Will you come with me? It'll probably get us killed rather than freed, but I've got to try.//

//Count on me. Do you have a plan?//

Her perception of the barracks dimmed, and she realized he'd closed his eyes to concentrate. //Yes, but it will require breaking every law that either of us holds dear. I can't do it without you to astrogate the yacht we're going to steal. It's a Teleod yacht with a Teleod Pool, but you should be able to use it. Alone, I could do nothing.//

The implication that if she could have Operated the Pool alone, she would have, told him where she stood. She expected a vicious refusal.

Instead, he countered, //I have a price.//

//First, I have to tell you my price. I will not leave without Elias and Zuchmul.//

There was a sigh of relief. //That was my price, Kyllikki. I will not abandon them.//

//You don't understand. Including them in this will cost

lives, our friends' as well as our enemies'. Worse yet, including Elias virtually guarantees our deaths.// She took a deep breath, clasped her hands and forced herself to confess. //Idom, he's Zimor's Bonded, a Dreamspy—captured from the planet of Dreamers and tape-indoctrinated.//

Idom's astonishment paralyzed his mind. She let him soak up the shock, and at last he asked the question she dreaded. //How do you know? How long have you known?//

//The timing,// she said and explained about the message capsule. //And any moment now, there'll be another capsule with orders about me, a capsule sent just after Elias first saw me, or first recognized me.//

//You don't know that he's Zimor's.//

//Yes, I do. The odor of Zimor floats around him like a cloak. I should have known right from the first, Idom, but I've never encountered a Dreamer, let alone a Bonded Dreamer, before, and they say it takes a lot of practice to learn to recognize them. He really doesn't seem any different from anyone else. I should have gone into his mind when I first suspected, but . . . I don't know why I didn't.//

//Do it now. Make sure.//

//I don't dare. Zimor will learn too much. I can't believe what she's done—what she's become since I left. If we have any chance at all, we have to keep her out of it.//

//Chance to do what?//

She recounted everything she'd learned and explained the details of her plan. //You see? We can't do anything. An accusation like this has to be handled at the Imperial level. If he can convince the Families that Zimor is raiding for Dreamers, they'll turn on her and the war will be over.//

//That's simplistic . . .//

//Maybe, but I know the Families. It'll work.//

In the formless white noise of his thoughts, numbers formed and sorted themselves, and then suddenly she couldn't follow the warped distortion as it folded in on itself.

She pulled back, telling herself that he wasn't insane, just thinking professionally. After a moment, she called, //Idom! If we're going to do this, it has to be now.//

His faint mental voice emerged from the noise again, posing her own major objection to the plan. //If you trigger a riot, lots of innocent lives will be lost. Those aren't riot-control weapons the soldiers are carrying.//

//If I dwell on that, I won't do it. Then Zimor will have you, me, Zuchmul, *and* Elias. I ran from her so my friends wouldn't get hurt, but now the war has turned more vicious than ever, and my new friends are threatened. Should I let her do what she wants, or should I try to stop her?//

He considered only a moment. //Let's try it.//

//All right. Wait.//

Trying not to think, she selected an undefended Teleod mind and insinuated herself into it, looking out through strange eyes. In the building converted into a human dining hall, an army of men and women had just finished setting up hot and cold serving tables and were filling the drink dispensers. A lot of the equipment was makeshift. Teleod planners had not realized what use of a Paitsmun facility to house humans would entail, but they were sparing no effort for the human detainees' comfort. Still, as soon as they smelled the unfamiliar Teleod spices in the food, it wouldn't be hard to engender suspicion in already highly stressed minds. But the key would be the nonhumans.

The captive nonhumans were housed in two barracks buildings at the far end of the compound, nearer the armory, not segregated by species. Already, the guards were lining them up to march them to their dining hall.

She shifted focus to another Teleod guard in the dining hall. The nonhumans would be provided the same Metaji-manufacture survival rations supplied on the pods, with only water to drink. They would all be required to eat together, a cruel hardship for some of them. Already, armed guards were in place all around the edge of the hall, and others were stationed at the door.

It would have to be the water; no Metaji citizen would suspect the coded food packets to be poisoned. But there were species here that would go into paranoia if watched while eating or drinking. *The Ye're'y, then. There are several families of them.*

She Searched for the interrogator and found him watching Aarl approach across the flat pavement outside the human barracks. A guard Captain was instructing the squad that would supervise the roll call as the humans were marched out. At a word from the Captain, they took up their amplifiers and went toward the barracks door.

Kyllikki sought Idom. He was in low-voiced conversation with Elias. ". . . course we can make it. And the reward for what we've learned will surely be enough to replace your instruments. The fame might even mean a command performance for the Emperor. Think of the connections you could make."

Elias studied his toes, which protruded from the ends of the sandals he wore. "Idom, what about Zuchmul? I won't go unless we take him along."

"That's what I told Kyllikki, but she was already planning on it."

He studied Idom for another moment as the guards worked their way down the rows of cots, using amplifiers to instruct them on how to answer the roll call. "All right. What's the plan? What do I do? When do we go?"

//Idom, don't tell him. The telepath may get it from him. Zimor certainly will.//

Idom started at her instruction, then answered Elias, stroking his white beard in that abstracted way he had. "Probably tomorrow. I'll give you a signal you can't miss."

//I hope that's good enough,// Kyllikki told Idom. //I know why you had to get his permission to risk his life, but, Idom, scruples are going to get us killed. He's the enemy. He's cooperating with Zimor voluntarily.//

//Then why did he insist on taking Zuchmul?//

//To make sure we'd be caught.//

While he thought that over, the guards took stations by the door, unslinging their weapons. They were keyed rifles, weapons that could be fired only by their owners, an expensive but necessary precaution in a prison. The Guard Captain climbed up on a cot, Aarl taking up a position in front of him. Then, consulting a noteboard, the Captain called names in a barbarous Teleod accent.

Peripherally, she noticed she was visualizing in depth and detail while operating within the Metaji audio-analogue. It was much clearer than when she'd gotten that single flash of Elias' appearance from Etha Ckam's mind. That, she now knew, had been an accident caused by Elias being a Dreamer. So much of what had happened to her could be attributed to the proximity of a Dreamer, she wondered how she could have refused to recognize it. Yet, as she'd told Idom, she had never experienced it before. Nobody had in centuries.

//No,// concluded Idom at last. //If Elias is a Dreamer Bonded to Zimor, it's not really his free-will choice whether to cooperate with her. His sanity depends on her now.//

//Exactly. And she knows it.// Knowing Zimor, Kyllikki realized that she had given her Dreamer *replaceable* status in order to keep people from realizing that her sanity depended on Elias, now, too.

As the roll was being called, people shuffled out into the aisle and obediently lined up, filing out of the building in an orderly stream, the Captain's voice working its way closer and closer to Elias' name. Kyllikki told Idom, //There's no time now. Just remember, everything he observes, she will know about the next time he dreams. Once he knows we've captured him, she'll know it. And that may be the end of us.//

A soldier trotted up to Aarl and delivered a message in low, confidential tones. Kyllikki was still loath to try to tap the telepath's perceptions, but Idom saw Aarl frown and snap at the man, who trotted away briskly, back stiff and head tucked in, as if expecting a blow to land as soon as he relayed the commander's instruction.

"Elias Kleef!" the Captain announced.

Shock rippled through Idom. Kyllikki braced against it as Idom urged, "Go. Don't attract attention."

Kyllikki felt Aarl's swift, professional scan of Elias' mind and was astonished when it became clear that, even after that close appraisal, he still didn't realize the man was a Dreamer. Suddenly, she didn't feel so guilty for missing it herself. Still, a Bonder should have spotted it.

Casually, not hurrying to catch up with Elias, the Coordinator detached himself from his post and moved with the crowd. Kyllikki told Idom, //Aarl doesn't suspect anything. I'll get the riot started with the nonhumans. Wait for the sound of the guards' weapons, then collect Elias and head for the infirmary. Aarl has the yacht's pass keys on him, and he will come running after Elias.//

//I'll move when the firing starts.//

"Idom Shigets!"

Idom started his slow march down the aisle, head down, feet shuffling like everyone else. //Kyllikki, the way they're treating everyone, there's bound to be a riot sooner or later. We're only triggering it a little sooner.//

//Thank you, Idom. I'm leaving you now.//

His caring about her conscience touched her deeply, which distracted her. As she disengaged, she found herself back in the supply closet, shivering. Her head ached, and she was sweating. It had been years since she'd done any of the basic exercises, and she knew now that there was a chance her physical strength would fail before she finished.

She braced her back against the wall and straightened her legs, forcing them to move despite the cramping, because in a few moments, she'd have to be up and running. Then, trying to ignore the throbbing ache centering in her head, she closed her eyes and searched for the contact she'd used before in the non-humans' dining hall, eyes that belonged to one of the guards posted along the side of the room. The nonhumans were filing past a table where men and women stood handing out food packets from coded crates.

Beyond them, another table supplied each of them with a cup—regardless of their oral physiology—and every fifteenth one was also handed a pitcher of water to carry.

From the way they moved and glanced at one another, she knew the nonhumans were convinced the treatment was not the result of ignorance but was a campaign of deliberate brutality designed to break their spirits. It took Kyllikki very little effort to magnify the simmering resentment by whispering a thought here or there. Then she went to work on the Ye're'y family in the middle of the line. She had no problem directing her informant's gaze toward the family. He was already fascinated as well as repelled.

There were the usual five adult Ye're'y, and they had three adolescents with them, one who had a wing in a badly wrapped support bandage. The Ye're'y were descended from unflighted avians, but needed their wings for balance. The child was stumbling, whimpering when the injured wing moved of its own accord. The Ye're'y walked on two legs, upright like a human, with two arms ending in complex hands, some of the digits with long, sharp claws.

In these prisoners, the claws had been cut recently, leaving bleeding stumps, which they protected as they moved. Kyllikki's informant stared openly, inspecting each of them and settling on the children, wondering idly if the amputated claws hurt, though he conceded there was no way they could have allowed prisoners to keep such natural weapons.

The guards refused to relax the single-line rule to allow one of the parents to help the injured child. The child's sharp features betrayed its misery.

One of the adult Ye're'y looked to be in shock, glassy-eyed, moving without real awareness. The others kept darting glances at the soldiers, who made a show of scrutinizing each creature who passed, telegraphing their prurient interest in private matters. Regardless of how long they'd associated with human cultures, there was no way the Ye're'y could keep their glands from reacting to those raking glances.

Kyllikki didn't even have a common Metaji education. She had no notion of Ye're'y sexual practices, but she was sure that three of these adults were bristling under what they perceived either as a sexual assault on their vulnerable genders, the other two adults, or as child molestation.

They seemed to be fighting off the impression, trying to

control their instincts, but abused as they had been, they were too worn out to suppress the reaction.

As she waited for the Ye're'y family she'd chosen to reach the water table, Kyllikki sought other nonhuman minds, directed their eyes at the guards, and floated whispers through their minds, ideas in tune with their emotions. Or, when she dared, she evoked an appropriate key and insinuated a ripe emotion into the nonhuman minds.

She tried to pick individuals who looked like fighters, strong or aggressive types. She was hampered by her own ignorance, for in many cases she couldn't identify gender or had no idea if the species had an aggressive gender. So she looked for clues to combat training, or at how the person reacted to a challenging glance from her informer.

By the time the Ye're'y family reached the water table, the room simmered with an ominous muttering. Carefully, she traced the key she'd chosen to work through for this task.

As one of the Ye're'y accepted the water pitcher, she gave him a sharp, definitive impression of danger.

He almost dropped the pitcher, then sniffed cautiously. She had to do nothing more. He threw the pitcher to the floor with a loud crash, stepped back, and into the ensuing silence yelled, "They've poisoned the water!"

Screams were followed by bloodcurdling battle yells, unleashing fury. As the prisoners attacked their guards, Kyllikki learned she'd chosen to use the one person whose proclamation would be believed by this group, one of the foremost chemists in the Metaji.

The building's windows, situated high up by the rafters, were broken by weapons fire, and soon after that the doors burst open to admit reinforcements. As soon as she was sure it would go on for a while, she left to find Idom in the human dining hall and, through him, located a mind belonging to the Guard Captain. Even though Aarl was nearby, waiting for Elias to be culled from the line, she had to take the chance. She grabbed control of the Captain, and had him say loudly to a nearby guard, "The animals must have discovered the poison in the water!"

He'd never remember saying that, but there was a good chance Aarl would figure out what his amnesia meant. It didn't matter. Either she'd be gone or dead.

It took a while for the riot to take hold among the humans. Word had to spread that "animals" to the Teleod soldiers meant nonhumans. Once the humans grasped that their friends and colleagues had been poisoned, which implied that they were probably next, there was no stopping the violence.

By that time, Idom had collared Elias, and the two men were nearly to the door. Aarl, struggling through the rioting mob, was after them.

Kyllikki disrupted the balance of a guard wrestling with a large weapon, so that when he fell, an opening cleared between Idom and the door. He went for it, dragging Elias.

Kyllikki pulled back to her bare closet and tried to get her body to move, but toppled and sprawled, prone, one arm flung toward the door. The pain was incredible.

Her head was the worst of all. Ghostly outlines and whirling, flashing scenes of violence superimposed themselves over the storage closet, which was close one second and distant the next; solid, then transparent, then solid again, until she thought she'd go into helpless spasms of retching.

But as she forced her cramped legs to move, the pain cut across the swirling realities leaking in from the minds she'd invaded and now could not shut out. She could almost hear her childhood instructor laughing. "And just what did you expect when you haven't communed in years? You may be Laila, but you're still just mortal flesh."

She humped up to get her knees under her chest. Her arms felt like dead tissue. Her chin stayed on the floor.

The instructor's voice continued, "And you're not even the best of Laila, arrogant child. You'll lie there until you die." The memory of receding footsteps, abandonment in a moment of need, stung as nothing else could have. She had been a spoiled child, self-indulgent, conditioned to expect an effortless life. She had hated that instructor.

But she had been right. Kyllikki had never put her whole self into her training, not daring to challenge Zimor's position in the ratings or preeminence in the Family. Now that she had dared, if she failed to get to her feet, all those killed in the riot would have died in vain.

She didn't quite know how it happened, but she was suddenly on her feet, lurching across the small room and slamming painfully into the door. That was the easy part.

She had no strength left for finesse. Like a clumsy child, she used one finger to trace the key image she needed, winding the line into its complex but compellingly beautiful knot. Teeth gritted, tongue pressed to the roof of her mouth against the painful rebellion of her whole nervous system, she flung the pattern at the two guards outside the door.

They slumped against the wall and slid down into a profound sleep. Their weapons clattered to the floor. It was a race against time now, and she could barely move.

She worked at the hinges. The spikes were not well oiled. Using the door handle, she lifted the door's weight, stretched to the limit of her reach, and twisted the top spike. Her fingers were slick with sweat. She wasn't going to make it. She had to get out by the time Idom and Elias arrived. And she couldn't.

Panting in half-audible sobs and grunts, she tried again, and yet again. Everything depended on her being set to take Aarl, and get the yacht's Pool key for Idom.

And then her fingers found a purchase, the spike moved, one link higher, then two. At last, the top spike was out. The bottom proved even harder. She shoved the top spike partway in to hold the alignment, then wriggled the bottom out.

She had to kick a shelf to pieces and ram the sharp edge into the crack of the door to pry it open. The door had opened just a crack and jammed, caught now on the makeshift hasp and lock. She needed a longer lever.

Ignoring a trickle of blood on her leg, and the shaking of her arms, she began kicking another one apart, trying to figure how to get a long piece.

There was so much pain, from abused nerves and from real physical pain, that more didn't matter. She was bleeding from several more cuts by the time she got her lever. Then she heard running feet. *Too late!*

She plunged toward the door and had the lever seated for one more bone-cracking try when the dulcet baritone penetrated her consciousness.

"Down this way, Idom! I told you I could find her."

Elias!

Feet shuffled to a halt outside, and through her crack she could see two blue-clad forms. "Sovereigns Be!" swore Elias over the guards' bodies. "What happened—"

"Kyllikki!" interrupted Idom. "Are you all right?"

"Dumb question," said Elias. "Kyllikki, stand clear, I'm going to ram the door."

She leaned against the wall next it, too dazed to react as Elias backed off and rammed his shoulder into the door. He did it again, and the unhinged side of the door opened.

She staggered out, and Idom's and Elias' hands grabbed her arms. To her shame, she wasn't able to shake them off and stand alone. They half-dragged her down the hallway until she finally dug in. "No! Zuchmul is that way." She plunged down a hall leading to her interrogation room.

Elias hung back at the door, but Idom charged in with her, examined the unit, and began shoving it on the roller base toward the door. "Elias, help me turn this thing!"

But Elias didn't move. His eyes were glazed.

Kyllikki knew why. Aarl.

"Stay here!" she commanded Idom, and scrambled over the top of the stasis unit to slide down into the hall, following Elias' gaze to where Aarl stood.

Shoving her hair back from her forehead and turning her face to display her Family's most typical profile, she adopted language and manner to fit and asked, "Commander Aarl, are you really going to defy Laila? Is that what you came to the Empire for? Treason?"

He did not drop to one knee and bow his head, but he did adopt a respectful stance, though his barriers remained hard. "Lady, I have been instructed by Zimor The Lady of Laila to conduct you to her. I may not take orders from you."

"When were these orders issued?"

"I received a Diving Capsule only moments ago. You have no choice but to obey the head of your Family."

Aside to Idom, she sent, //Stand still. Don't move!// And then she advanced on Aarl with one hand extended. "Very well, Commander. Your keys, and I'll be on my way." She put all the Family suggestivity behind it.

He reached into a hip pocket, but his hand never emerged. He backed away, eyes wide, defensive barriers tightening. "Lady of Laila, do not do this to me. I have my orders. Do not force me to commit treason. I must escort you. My Pool Operators are waiting onboard."

He wasn't exactly cringing, but it was awfully close. Acutely aware of her own exhaustion, she fumbled into his mind, hoping she wasn't so clumsy she'd derange his mind by accident. Then she had what she needed. The Pool Operators aboard his yacht already had the Pool chamber open. The pilot's board would be open, too.

She dropped her hand to her side. "As you will. Release my cousin's man, and we'll be on our way."

She half-turned to gesture to Elias, feeding the Coordinator a fantasy scenario in which she had staged her defection in order to penetrate the Empire and bring home these valuable prisoners. It was feeble, but it was all she had.

Suddenly, one of her informants, whose thoughts were still sloshing over her own perceptions, died. She lost her balance and went to all fours, her barriers dissolving into a swirling chaos. She couldn't even tell which one had died.

Aarl, who had realized the extent of her weakness, seized the opportunity to invade a Family mind—legally. He had his orders: dead or alive, with or without Family dignity, she was to be delivered to Zimor.

Flinching from the onslaught, she curled and rolled away, barely aware of her own scream as she was wrenched into a realm unfamiliar to her, a soldier's combat realm. The atmosphere was a dense, gray fog. The ground was scored with concentric circles, like a target. A key image occupied the center of the target—the gateway out of the realm.

But as she began to crawl toward it, a sheet of flame rose before her. Intellectually, she knew it was Aarl's projection, hardly anything she should have to worry about, but it was inside her mental barriers. It was *real*.

She had read about combat realms. The two challenging telepaths entered together, and the first one to reach the exit was the winner. When combat was serious, the one left behind was trapped there until he died.

She summoned a cloudburst. It hissed into the fire, but as it started to smoke and die, suddenly the rain turned yellow, and drops hitting the fire burst into roaring flame. She conjured a dirt mover to smother the fire, and wriggled closer to the exit. She might just make it.

Abruptly, the realm shimmered and wavered away. She died thinking, *I thought we'd do better than this.*

Some indeterminate period of time later, she felt strong arms lift her, a hard, cold surface under her chest, and movement. A meaningless rumble mixed with a more distant roar pierced by whiss-snaps. Rifle fire. Screams. Wheels on flooring.

She sat up convulsively and fell sideways off the stasis unit, ending on hands and knees facing back the way they'd just come. Aarl was sprawled in the corridor, head bent at an impossible angle.

Familiar strong arms came around her, swinging her up against a muscular, familiar chest. "Elias, put me down."

"I don't dare. Kyllikki, we don't have the yacht keys. He had nothing of the sort on him."

"His Pool Operators are aboard. They've got the keys."

Idom was pushing the stasis unit alone, now that Elias was carrying her. "I should have realized that," said Idom. "Now, how are we going to get them off the ship?"

"I expect we'll have to try to kill them," said Elias. "Kyllikki's all out of tricks for the day."

"You couldn't help killing Aarl. That was an accident," said Idom. "But if they're to be executed, it's a matter for the law."

Obviously, thought Kyllikki, when Aarl dragged her into

the combat realm, he had been forced to relinquish control of Elias. He had assumed, after all, that Elias was under cover, and thus Teleod at heart. But Elias had attacked, not considering what might have happened to Kyllikki because of it. *He's from the Dreamers' home planet. He has such odd gaps in his knowledge, his reactions can't be predicted.*

"Elias! Put me down! I can bluff it out. Maybe they haven't heard the orders, except that the yacht's to leave."

They rounded the corner into the hall leading to the emergency entry, outside of which the yacht was parked. Its shadow darkened the transparent wall at the entry. "Elias!"

He stopped and looked at her, weighing her suggestion, not defying a Laila order. *He's not Teleod.*

The paralyzing numbness of Kyllikki's mind and body had begun to wear off. Besides the prickles of returning nerve function, there was also a burning sensation, a residue from the phantom fire. The wounds in her legs stung. Every muscle trembled from strain, and she knew Elias could feel that shaking. With returning awareness, she could feel the warmth of his body soaking into hers as the vibrant—unmistakable—quality of his mind caressed hers. She didn't know how she'd failed to know the Dreamer. Even the Bond to Zimor, her shadowy presence woven through his perpetual soul-music, was obvious.

"Elias, I can pilot that model yacht, *and* they know I'm a Pool Operator. I can claim you're my trainee partner and I'm taking you and Idom home. But you can't carry me out that door. I have to walk. Or it will never work."

There was something in his eyes: admiration, respect, fear, a mixture? She couldn't read it. Her barriers were a shambles, her mind a sieve, wavering scenarios danced through the interstices of thoughts, and it was all she could do to hang on to the present reality.

Idom said, "I think she's right, and we're out of time. Put her down, Elias. See how far she gets."

But he held her in his arms as if she were a precious, fragile object. He was halfway into shock himself, and she wondered if it was because he'd killed a man who was acting on

Zimor's orders. But suddenly, Kyllikki no longer thought of him as Zimor's willing pawn.

"Elias," she insisted, "they won't be suspicious at how disheveled we are. We're coming out of a riot, aren't we? If we can talk the Operators off the ship, we won't have to kill them. And if I walk in there and issue the orders, they'll leave. Now put me down."

He lowered her feet to the floor, but kept one supporting arm around her waist. She clutched at his coverall, stiffened her knees, and forced a smile onto her lips. "See? I can make it. Let's go."

It was only a few more steps to the doors. But when Elias' arm left her to open the doors and help maneuver the stasis unit out, she stumbled. The yacht's entry ramp was down, and she felt the quiver of gravitics. In the planet's gravity well, the Pool was not activated.

Walking as normally as she could, she went ahead as the two men shoved the unit up the ramp. The lock tube led her into the main lounge, done in Laila yellow and black with all the deep, hushed luxury she hadn't known she'd missed. The Master Compartment was to her left, at the rear, with six smaller staterooms along that corridor. To her right, beyond a lock set in the forward bulkhead of the lounge, would be the crew's quarters, pilot's station, and the Pool itself.

She opened the first stateroom she came to. It was vacant, and there was enough floor space for the stasis unit.

Seeing the male Pool Operator picking his way back from the pilot's compartment into the large common room that was the central feature of the yacht, she grasped the back of a lounge chair for support and turned to call out the lock, "Be careful with that unit! Zimor wants it undamaged! Put it in the first room on the right."

Idom and Elias juggled the case around the tight turn, while the Operator watched, mouth agape. His youth was painfully obvious, his awe stemming from inexperience. Kyllikki adopted Zimor's most famous intonation and phrase as she displayed her profile toward the Operator. "Today, gentlemen, not next year."

Elias blanched, then bent to the job with muscles bulging and panic in his stance. But then, after all, stagecraft was his avowed profession.

She slowly turned her attention on the Operator as if wondering why he was still there. He backed up and went down on one knee, head bowed. "Lady of Laila, we are ready for takeoff as soon as Commander Aarl arrives, at his orders."

She let her eyebrows convey mild interest. "You haven't heard? A Diving Capsule arrives with direct orders from The Laila of Laila, and it's just ignored?"

He looked bewildered and guilty. She couldn't have sorted his real reaction from the cacophony sifting through her pounding head if her life depended on it. She gave an exasperated sigh and instructed, "I am Kyllikki—surely you've heard that name among Operators."

He gulped, eyes wide.

"This," she said, waving one negligent hand, "is my protégé. The other is my relief pilot. Commander Aarl is waiting. Take your mate and your pilot and go. Now."

The boy's head went all the way to his polished boots when he bowed. He scrambled away to collect the crew. The female Operator was the ranking officer on the yacht, but she didn't stop to question when she passed Kyllikki. She only paused to bow and murmur, "Lady of Laila, pleasant journey."

A clamor of boots on the ramp, and the three crew members were gone, hustling off in a near panic.

Kyllikki hit the closure levers. She didn't wait for the SE-CURE light, but made her way across the lounge, through the lock that divided the crew's domain from that of passengers. Past the crew's galley, she found the stair down to the Pool room, and sure enough, the security hatch was ajar. Crew's quarters were nestled along the sharply curved hall to her left and right. The doors were ajar, no one in sight. She called, "Idom! This way! The Pool's here!"

The Guide hurried across the lounge to join her, and surveyed the pilot's station through another open door. "No wonder you couldn't pilot the pod without the manual!"

"The Pool's down there," she repeated, gesturing. He

turned away and she went into the pilot's compartment. Things were so cramped up here that she could brace her hands on the bulkheads to keep from falling down.

Elias started to follow Idom down the ladder, but Idom closed the hatch in his face. Kyllikki eased into the pilot's chair. "Come here, Elias." The board showed takeoff clearance on standby. All she had to do was flick a switch and preempt a takeoff slot with priority clearance.

Elias settled into the chair at her right, inspecting the board, which was more complex than the pod's had been. All the displays and boards were lighted, holding on standby. He looked over at her anxiously.

She wiped her forehead with the back of her hand, absently noting the smearing of blood. She opened the circuit to Idom. "The course is set for a return to Teleod space. I don't dare change that until we're clear of Barkyr Control. They've got us locked into their computer and if we deviate, it will set off alarms."

From the board at her left elbow, Idom's voice said, "Use their programmed course. Don't worry about my course. Just get me away from the local gravity well."

Kyllikki glanced at Elias, knowing full well why Idom didn't give any details on the absurd feat he was planning. He'd told her he could make Veramai in eight dives, and now he was saying it didn't matter which way they went. But he couldn't explain where Elias could hear, or Zimor would know within hours and have another Diving Capsule filled with orders chasing them across the galaxy.

She released the countdown and the "Secure for Movement" alarms went off as Barkyr ground control gave them their clearance slot. "Secure!" she said. "We're on our way."

She turned on the outside alarms, warning everyone away, but screens showed that all the activity was now centered around the nonhuman barracks, with hardly an armed soldier anywhere on this end of the compound. They wouldn't have let her lift off without challenge otherwise.

The ship began to lift. It was nearly half the size of the

infirmary building and filled the touchdown pad, but the previous pilot had automated the tricky takeoff.

Under Kyllikki's guidance, the preset equipment answered each security challenge. They broke out of atmosphere and made for the Teleod at half the yacht's top speed.

They're not going to fire on us. I don't believe it. We got away!

The display monitor receded into a fuzzy, dim-wavering caricature of a pilot's board and she couldn't remember why she was facing a readout screen.

"Kyllikki?"

The last thing she remembered was wondrously strong arms and a hard, warm, friendly chest she wanted to sink into forever.

chapter six

••••••••••••••••••••••••••••••••••••••

Through a bleary haze, Kyllikki saw the rippling expanses of golden satin that surrounded her, glimpsed the white-and-scarlet coat of arms on gold and black, and knew she was in Zimor's private apartment, in Zimor's own bed.

Her body had been washed, her legs bandaged, and she was wearing one of Zimor's gowns. But she hurt everywhere.

She must have been caught by Zimor again, and dragged back to Laila for punishment. The memory of the last time Zimor had punished her was still an open wound, oozing confused impressions.

She recalled running, holding up her long formal skirts with one hand, breath coming in near sobs as she skipped down another endless flight of white steps. She paid no attention to the wooden-faced servants who stood on the landings. They would not help her. There was no help for her anywhere.

Knowing she had to reach the dining hall before Zimor did, she threw herself around the next corner and sprinted down the wide hall lined with images of each Laila of Laila for a dozen centuries. The plush golden carpet grabbed at her sandals. But she had to make it. If she could get there in time, Zimor would never discover what she'd found out.

Exhausted, she rounded the gargantuan pillar and faced the arch leading to the banquet hall, daring to hope.

But Zimor was there before her.

She was seated in the ornate, high-backed golden chair at the head of the table, with Kyllikki's place set in the center of the right side of the table, before a chair only slightly less imposing than Zimor's. But there were no other places set, and no live servants hovering about.

"You're late," observed Zimor.

Something was wrong. The room was never empty like this, not for supper. And Kyllikki was never given to preside over the right side of the table. As she settled decorously into her place, she said, "It won't happen again."

"I'm sure it won't," agreed Zimor.

No. This isn't right. That's not the way it happened.

Tossing herself to the other side of the bed, Kyllikki struggled to penetrate the confusion. She fixed her gaze on the folds of gold satin enclosing the bed, and fought the blinding headache to summon the key image that allowed her to build her barrier wall, one silver brick at a time. She made the bricks into perfect mirrors, blocking out everything so she wouldn't be confused by anyone else's stray thoughts.

She had found her cousin at the table studying some records while the servants prepared her a drink and a snack.

"Come in, Kyllikki. We must have a long talk." She indicated the seat on her right.

Kyllikki had taken the designated seat, finding the platter of delicacies before her arranged to form a pattern, a vaguely familiar one—a key image? She studied it, unsurprised when the servants failed to provide her with a drink. *Zimor knows. I know she knows.*

Rolling over again, Kyllikki squinted at the overlying images, the gold satin room, the platter on the dining table, and something else behind that. What had Zimor known? She did a key banishment. The design on the platter broke up.

Her eyes hurt, and somewhere deep behind her ears, her brain ached. A ghostly key image glowed darkly as she struggled to resolve the images into memory.

She had presided over the empty right side of the table, facing a platter of her favorite delicacies, and Zimor had said, "So you see, you've no choice. You must do your Family duty, and it must be soon. There's no time for all the formalities of a public marriage. I need you in the war effort. You're my best Pool Operator. It shouldn't be so difficult for an Operator to become pregnant."

Kyllikki shuddered. "You don't understand. We never complete the act—not with each other. It would destroy our ability to function together."

"It is you who do not understand. My order has already gone out. Your partner will be ready for you the next time you fling message capsules for me. My physician will see to it the exercise is effective."

She bit the pillow to stifle a cry. That was the horrible secret, and that was why she had run from Zimor.

But I got away. Her mind finally reassembled recent events. She had been retrained in the Metaji. *Prosperity.* Then *Otroub* and Elias. Prison on Barkyr. The escape.

Then a great blackness. How had she been caught and dragged back to Inarash and the Laila Compound?

Determined to penetrate the mystery before Zimor came for her, she added Metaji barriers to her silver bricks by summoning a background of white noise, an ocean beach, and setting a compelling limerick running in her foreconscious on an endless loop, then adding the babble of a loud party. In an odd way, the noise created a luxurious mental silence.

Now that she'd been caught again, she'd better figure out what had really been done to her before Zimor arrived.

Fragmented images floated into her mind—faces, veiled excitement, a secret meeting.

Yes, she had used key images to eavesdrop on a secret meeting of Zimor's most loyal followers. She had learned—something—something very important, not just to herself but to her friends who were organizing against Zimor. Now they'd have a chance to supplant Zimor and stop the war plans.

And Zimor had—had done what? The punishment had

been excruciating, Kyllikki knew. It had been the last thing that had happened to her before she ran. It had made her run. But what had it been?

There had been that insane dinner at the empty table. No. No, that was wrong. She had sat at Zimor's right hand, and there had been that tray with food arranged as a key image, one she didn't recognize. She had stared at it—and?

Zimor did something to my mind! To my memory!

An overwhelming, paralyzing horror crept over her, followed by wave after wave of defeat and hopelessness. In the midst of it all, Zimor's serene face floated, very pleased. Kyllikki's mind and body were Zimor's to use at her whim, and there was nothing she could do to change that.

She bit the pillow to stifle her screams of terror. Everything she remembered about the Metaji had been implanted by Zimor as a lesson. She hadn't gotten away.

The door opened softly, menacingly.

Kyllikki rolled away from it and screamed. Defeated, broken, she screamed her terror aloud, cementing her barriers in place, not with determination but with hysteria and panic. *Not my mind. Not my mind! Oh, please, no, not my mind!*

Someone circled the bed, and she twisted to the other side, sitting up and clutching the pillow to her face.

The draperies flew aside, and without warning, she found herself in a strange man's arms. *No! Not a child. I won't!*

She found a fold of flesh and bit down hard, then propelled herself off the bed. But he didn't let go. He yelled, and suddenly they were on the floor, twists of cloth binding them together. With his immense strength, he flipped them over so that he was on top, then got a grip on both her wrists, his legs trapping her legs, and held her still.

"Kyllikki! What's the matter with you?"

Familiar silky baritone. Familiar bright-blond hair. Clean, sharp features. Searing blue eyes. Fabulous shoulders. *Not even Zimor could make it so real.*

She stopped struggling, holding her breath, and the man— *Elias?*—disentangled the sheet, not a hint that he was going to rape her except the slight tumescence no humanoid female could mistake in a male. Even that subsided as he eased his weight off her, his concern eroding her barriers.

The door opened again, and a stocky elderly white-bearded man came in, calling, "Elias! What's—"

"Idom!" said Kyllikki, and reality turned inside out and lurched, twisting into something totally different than it had been. She was almost sick with the realization. "Idom! We're on *Shylant*, not Inarash! We got away?"

"Away clean," he agreed, "and orbiting an obscure star, waiting for you to come to."

She looked back at Elias. *Dreamspy*. That was real. He was Zimor's Bonded Dreamer. That was why she felt Zimor's presence so strongly.

The pain Kyllikki felt throbbing through head and spine she knew now was the result of what she'd done to start the riot, and that too had contributed to undoing Zimor's work.

It came to her in a rush with the crispness of true memory. Dreamers: the descendants of those illegally taken from their home planet centuries ago, secretly left to breed in an isolated preserve, rediscovered and used by Zimor to reward her Bonder followers.

Eavesdropping telepathically on one of Zimor's secret meetings, Kyllikki had learned of the scheme, and Zimor had obliterated Kyllikki's memory of it to protect her war plans from Kyllikki and the growing opposition among Kyllikki's friends. Then Zimor had planted that bizarre memory of forcing Kyllikki into a pregnancy.

Zimor had planned to spirit Kyllikki away while letting it be known she'd died of complications. Meanwhile, Zimor would have had her mind stripped to discover the identities of her friends, Zimor's opponents. By escaping and publicly defecting, Kyllikki had thwarted Zimor's plan and protected her friends. But Zimor was still in power.

But at least now Kyllikki remembered it all the way it had really happened. She wasn't sure which was worse, being threatened with a pregnancy, or with mindrape. Either was a sufficient reason to run.

But Zimor was still with her, staring out of Elias' eyes. With a gasp, she buried her face in another fold of cloth. *Bonders are, after all, known for instability. No, I'm not going insane!* Zimor was not inside Elias. Zimor only received Elias' dreams.

But the *power* throbbing from those eyes . . .

Kyllikki had heard that a Bonder was only half awake, half alive, without a Dreamer. The Dreambond brought the Dreamer to sanity and the Bonder to the full possession of the range of telepathic awareness. Looking into Elias' eyes and seeing Zimor, she could almost believe it.

With a shudder, Kyllikki shrank into herself, her mind throbbing and bruised. "Don't touch me. Please. Don't."

The two men retreated. Idom asked, "Kyllikki, what's wrong? Tell us what to do for you. We need you. I managed to make orbit here, but I can't read any of these manuals."

She remembered his plan. *Veramai in eight dives.*

And then she remembered Elias. "Idom!" She locked gazes with him, stricken. *Now Zimor will know we're headed for the Crown World, for the Emperor!*

Idom said, "I mentioned our destination after you fainted, but not why we chose it."

She scrubbed her face. "How long has it been since I passed out?" Her voice sounded strangely rational.

"Almost two days," said Elias.

She glanced at Elias, then locked gazes with Idom, not knowing what to say. Her suspicion that Elias was no longer Zimor's willing spy changed everything—except that whatever was said before him was as good as said to Zimor.

Idom said, "We can't move until we find out how to alter the automatic identification. And we need you to pilot. So we've been waiting."

And sleeping. Zimor knew they were headed for Veramai. In despair, she said, "The identification's no problem. This is one of Zimor's own yachts. But I'm going to eat first, and then we have to talk."

Idom said, "We seem to be provisioned for twenty-two people for months. We can stay here as long as you want. You should go back to sleep."

"No. We have to make decisions." With that she plunged into the bathroom, found some analgesic, got cleaned up and dressed in some of Zimor's less opulent clothes, slacks and tunic of pink shellsilk. *We need a new plan. And there must be no mistakes.* Zimor had raided the preserve of the Dreamers, and she had captured new stock—or at least Elias—from the Dreamers' planet. She was playing a bigger and more dangerous game than Kyllikki had thought.

Headache fading, she found the men in the lounge, a truly strange meal on the table before them.

She settled herself gently in the third armchair and regarded the repast, undecided if it was breakfast or supper.

Idom apologized. "We couldn't figure out the menus, so I picked some things from the protein scale at random."

"Oh." She helped herself to breakfast items, unable to tolerate the odor of the spiced delicacies. "I'll cook next time." She met Elias' eyes as she sipped a well-brewed cup of yarage, realizing that she had come to a decision. "Ah! Perfect. Don't you like yarage, Elias?"

"Is that what that is?"

Even shoring up her barriers to keep them from melting away in his presence, she could feel him straining at the lie. "Elias, you know what it is," she accused steadily, as she spooned warm sauce over a bowl of roasted blimny seeds and began to eat. "Laila practically runs on the stuff, though you won't find much of it elsewhere." She drained her cup, needing the fortification of the stimulant.

He started to protest, but she cut him off. "You spent at least a year there being tape-trained for this mission. You belong to Zimor."

His shoulders sagged and he lowered his eyes.

Idom opened his mouth but she chopped him off with a gesture. "So, tell us where you stand."

She chewed, aware of the delight her taste buds found in the familiar food, and also aware of a nebulous plan forming in the back of her mind.

Elias looked to Idom hopefully, but Idom said, "Kyllikki got the truth from Commander Aarl, who had orders for you."

He slumped deeper. "So if you know everything, how could you believe anything I said now?"

"Kyllikki would know if you were lying. I don't recommend it." Idom managed to sound truly threatening.

She mended her barriers and studied Elias. "Whatever we decide to do next, your life will be at risk. Whose side are you on, Elias?"

He straightened. "Yours. I was wrong to volunteer for Zimor's intelligence corps. I haven't sent her a report since you picked me up. Take my mind apart; you'll find that's true."

"Sent her a report?" echoed Kyllikki, silencing Idom with a gesture. "How do you send your reports?"

The agony in his gaze spoke to Kyllikki. The spy who turns can be trusted by neither side, and a spy who can't be trusted has to be eliminated. Barriers solid, she watched him give up his life.

"It's some kind of a telepathic trick, I'd expect you'd know it. I visualize a special pattern while I'm falling asleep, and go over what I want to send back to Zimor. She picks it up. She rescued me from these slavers who kidnapped me, and then discovered I have this rare talent and offered me a job. I thought—I really believed in the Teleod, really believed they had the best system.

"But then little things started to add up. I was thinking of defecting when the *Otroub* was hit. I don't think that was an accident. Somehow—I don't know how—Zimor knew and ordered me killed."

"You don't know how?" asked Idom, glancing at Kyllikki.

She risked letting her barriers fade, focusing on Elias for a moment. The crashing headache nearly blinded her, but she was convinced. "He doesn't know. Elias, Zimor didn't rescue you from slavers, she had you kidnapped. From your home planet. Where everyone has your talent."

Idom dropped his utensil with a clatter, staring at her.

Elias stared at her, fear throbbing in the air around him. *"Had me kidnapped!"*

"The images in your mind of the slavers—they were Zimor's men." She'd known it all along, but there was proof.

"Kyllikki, I swear I'm on the side of the Metaji in this. Don't send me back, please, don't. I'll do anything for you— anything. I'd rather die than be sent back there."

"Elias, does the term 'Dreamer' mean anything to you?"

"Dreamer." Scintillating blue eyes wide, he shook his head. "Should it?"

She repeated the term in the forms it took in various Teleod languages.

Again he shook his head. She tried Bonder, Dreambonder, Control, and then Dreamspy, all to no avail. Though peeps through her barriers produced more nauseating headache than real information, she could see he wasn't lying.

"Elias, she lied to you to get you to do what she wanted you to do."

"I figured that out. I was surprised by your idea of what this war was about. I'd thought—I'd heard people talking, of course, but they were Metaji leaders. Naturally, they'd spout their own propaganda loudly. But when I heard you say it, I began to doubt. And while we were imprisoned, I learned a lot. Zimor's way of using the Pools destroys—something. And she's no freely chosen leader."

"There's more," said Kyllikki. "And worse. Your home planet is the only planet in the galaxy where people Dream. Dreaming is the special state during sleep when your brain reprises the day's events, what's been learned, what's been discovered or experienced. Alone on your home planet, you Dreamed in disconnected snatches, sometimes distorted with emotion or mixed with memory, sometimes pure imagination. But ever since you met Zimor, it's been different.

"Since then you've slept soundly and well, wakening without stress. You've been more powerful, healthier and emotionally more stable, more creative in your art. You'd do anything not to go back to living a fragmented, fruitless, and emotionally tormented existence. That's why you took Zimor's job rather than her offer of a trip home, isn't it?"

"Kyllikki, I know you can read my mind—"

"I didn't get that from your mind. I got it from a textbook on Dreamers, and what I know of Zimor's style. And I'll also guess you don't know why life's been so good here."

"Are you going to tell me?"

She poured herself another cup of yarage. "Your telepathic link with Zimor is the source."

"Zimor is the source?"

Idom said, "The Eight Families are reputed to be the descendants of those who engineered the life on your home planet—designed it to complement their own psyches. The Eight Families have, in addition to their telepathic abilities, a gene that shows up in some of their children—like Kyllikki and Zimor—the ability to form a special Bond with a Dreamer."

"I'll tell him, Idom." She sipped from her cup and studied Elias, whose eyes registered growing shock. "Elias, when you sleep, you Dream, and you project to Zimor every event and thought of your day's experience, in coherent, sequential order—a complete report from a field spy. You don't need to visualize any image, and you don't get to choose what she learns. She learns everything you know."

He swore in some language Kyllikki couldn't identify. But the gist was plain. He felt violated. "Then Zimor knows we're going to—Kyllikki, we can't go to Veramai! Zimor practically controls the ports. We'd never make it off the spaceport grounds. And I'll be her number-one target."

"I think *Otroub* was a military accident. She sent a diving capsule to Barkyr to reassign you to Dessiwan, a camp that's so sensitive she wouldn't send you there if she doubted your loyalty. From the way the orders were phrased, she expected you to cooperate. But now that's changed."

"By now she must know what I think of her!"

"I'm sure of it. But what *do* you think of her?" She watched through her shields. It hurt like squinting into bright sunlight after hours of total darkness.

"Kyllikki, I swear if I'd suspected that I couldn't withhold anything from her, I'd never have taken this job."

Kyllikki believed him. Currents of revulsion shook his mental fabric when he thought of Zimor, but it was the Bond he was rejecting, not Zimor personally.

"Elias," said Idom, "you had no choice. If you hadn't believed her lies, she'd still never have told you the truth for fear some Metaji telepath would get it out of you."

"Idom's right," said Kyllikki.

"What am I going to do? I can't sleep! With what you've told me—Kyllikki, I swear I won't go to sleep again, I won't let her get another thing from me! Put me in stasis. You can do that, can't you?"

"*Shylant* is equipped, of course, but I don't think that's necessary. We've also got a complete pharmacy, and a drugged sleep, while unsatisfying, would be much safer than stasis."

Idom paused reaching for the yarage pitcher. "You have no idea how drugs might effect a Dreamer."

"They are genetically related to us," answered Kyllikki. "It's said that drugs affect them similarly. What I have in mind is a potion we use when—when the deprivation of being un-Bonded becomes too disturbing. It should stop a Dreamer from Dreaming." Should she tell them why she suddenly trusted that rumor? She'd heard it from some of Zimor's favorites, people she now knew as Dreambonded. "Elias, would you be willing to take such a drug?"

He barely gave it a thought. "Of course, but only if you're sure it'll be sufficient. I'd rather take the bigger risk and be sure she never gets another thing from me."

"Kyllikki, you can't be sure," objected Idom. "There can't be any real pharmacological data on—"

All right. "Yes, there can," she contradicted, and told them what Zimor had done to her mind and why she'd been screaming her head off like a foolish child. She recited the whole excruciatingly embarrassing incident with her eyes on her cooling yarage, finishing with, "I still haven't got it all sorted out. But now I think my failure to accept Elias' obvious identity as a Dreamer stems from how she suppressed my memory of having encountered her—illegal slaves."

Idom said, "Elias, what's been done to you is a capital offense in the Metaji as well as the Teleod, but what we've done in the last few days isn't exactly legal, either."

He brushed that aside. "If it's illegal to keep Earth humans on some kind of preserve, as if we're animals, why hasn't someone put a stop to it?"

Kyllikki said, "I tried, but I failed, then I ran away. I'm not proud of that, but I wouldn't be alive now if I hadn't. I've broken oaths and laws on both sides of the border, and I'll break more if I have to. Once what I've learned becomes public knowledge, once we produce you before the Emperor, this war will stop. The Emperor will know how to spread the truth through the Teleod. Most of the Eight Families will break with Zimor. She may take all of Laila down with her, and me, too, but the war will be stopped."

"It might not be so easy," said Idom. "The Families might not believe the allegations of a declared enemy. But we must start by presenting Elias to the Emperor."

"You make it sound so simple. The man rules thousands of planets and is embroiled in a war. Do you really believe three ordinary people can just walk in and claim his time?"

"There are options," said Idom grimly.

"I can think of a few possibilities myself, but we can't simply go straight to Veramai, if what you told us is true. If Zimor has operatives covering all the ports—"

"Oh, she does! I've been through several of those ports at odd times throughout the last year, and exchanged reports and recognition signals. She intends to take Veramai."

"You know," mused Idom, "that many spies on Veramai would account for how easily she took Barkyr." He arranged the tableware into a pattern. "This is Barkyr—and here is the Intarabi Front, and here, the Greening Line. With Barkyr, Zimor is now able to drive a wedge along here, using Barkyr as a supply base. These diving lines are still negotiable with some reliability, so she could attack here, here, and here, consolidate, then push for Veramai itself. Two years, maximum, and the war is ended—her favor."

"I didn't know you were a strategist," said Kyllikki.

"I'm not, or I'd have seen this right away just from the accessible routes out of Barkyr. But when you said she has Veramai's ports covered—it all made sense."

"I can't believe the Imperial forces don't know all this," said Kyllikki, her head throbbing. The medication was wearing off. "But that's another problem. We have to plan how to get through the port and onto Veramai first."

"I just don't see any way it can possibly be done," said Elias. "Doesn't the Emperor ever leave Veramai?"

"Certainly not during a war. It's the best-defended planet in the Metaji," commented Idom. "But, Kyllikki, he's right. I don't see how it can be done if there are that many people who'd recognize him—and us, for that matter."

"Simple," said Kyllikki. "We become something totally different. I have the codes for *Shylant*'s Incognito circuits, so we can change the identification into anything we want it to be. There are thousands of yachts just like this imported under that trade agreement of seven or eight years ago. We become a charter craft operating under the War Emergency Act. We stop at a couple of planets to pick up some passengers, maybe a relief Guide and a couple of stewards, then go right into Veramai's busiest port." She paused to judge the impact of that harebrained scheme.

"Incognito circuits?" asked Idom.

"Sure. This is Zimor's own yacht, if the most modest one in her fleet. It's fully equipped, and since it was deliberately sent into the war zone, I'll bet it's got a full set of Metaji identifications already inscribed."

Elias shook his head in negation. "Do you have any idea how much that would cost? Port fees, hiring a crew . . . Kyllikki, you've never had to deal with the realities of handling money. It just won't work."

"The financial resources we'll need are aboard." If there was no Metaji currency in the safe, there would surely be jewels to go with the dresses in Zimor's closet. "But Idom, can you find a port where we can set down empty and not attract attention, yet come away with crew and passengers?"

"Probably. But we'd need new biographies for ourselves. At Veramai, our real names or credentials would trigger all the computer records, and Zimor's people would notice. We'd need ship's uniforms, and we'd have to change all the Teleod signs and programs. I'm not sure if that can be done."

"It may take a few days," conceded Kyllikki, "but this model was designed to be sold in the Empire. The alternate labeling has to be in the display programs somewhere, and all the mechanical specs will satisfy Imperial Port requirements. This isn't going to be easy, and it certainly won't be without danger—" She broke off, studying Elias. "It's your life, Elias, not to mention your sanity. To verify your link to Zimor, the Imperial physicians will have to do some nasty things to you. You'll be a prisoner of sorts."

"I'm not in any position to avoid risks, and one thing I'm sure of; I'm going to get Zimor for what she's done to me no matter what it costs. One thing I'm fairly certain of; neither of you is on Zimor's side in this war. One more thing I'm willing to take a chance on; you know more about what's going on than I do, and I'm now fairly sure I'd have been on your side from the beginning if I'd really understood how the Metaji governed itself. I've always had an aversion to anything calling itself an empire."

Kyllikki couldn't fathom what forms of government had to do with the real issues, but she said, "No, you can't just go along with what we decide. You have to understand and choose to take the risk with us. That's why I took the risk of telling you all this. You must understand and choose."

"I understand all right. We're none of us likely to live through this. I accept that."

"That's not the risk," she countered, rubbing her brow with shaking fingers. "Remember how you felt about being sent back to your own planet?"

His face paled.

She drilled her gaze into him. "Remember I said your sense of well-being comes from the Bond with Zimor? Under this drug, you won't Dream, and if you don't, you will gradually lose your grip on reality. It won't be like it was for you before Zimor took you. It will be much worse. I don't know how long you can take it, but it won't be very long. I don't know if the effects would then be reversible."

"As I understand it, it may be just as bad for Zimor."

"Not quite, but she won't be pleased. It's you I'm worried about, though."

"If I go crazy, put me in stasis."

"And if you die from stasis, there goes our evidence. Also, I don't recall ever seeing anything on whether a Dreamer Dreams while in stasis—for all I know, they do!"

"A minute ago, you were all for disguising ourselves and making a mad dash across the Empire, talking as if it would be easy. Now all you want to do is talk me out of trying."

"No. I want you to understand that for you, the risk is not just to life but to sanity."

He didn't hesitate. "The faster we do this, the less the risk. Let's get started."

She studied him one more time, enduring the throbbing ache in her skull, then slammed her barriers up. She stood up, clutching the chair back until her knuckles turned white. "I'll check out the Incognito programming and see what we have to work with. Idom, sketch out a course to someplace there's a Guild Station so we can get you an assistant. Elias, clean up the table, check on Zuchmul, and then begin stowing Zimor's belongings. I'll move up to crew's quarters, and we'll make the big room our most expensive accommodation."

She went to work with a will, but after an hour of tedious adjustments and stupid blunders, she had to take another dose of the analgesic. That kept her going long enough to change the yacht's name to *Winning Number*, a good Metaji name that came with a fictitious Imperial history.

She broke into the fixed file and added the sale of *Winning Number* to the three of them in equal shares, with its conversion into a passenger charter which they'd only recently registered out of Barkyr. At least, nobody could get records from Barkyr to check on that, and with the changes she'd made, even if Zimor's operatives knew *Shylant*'s pre-packaged aliases, they wouldn't spot her.

They chose new names, which she inserted. Idom decided to risk taking the name of a Guide he knew to be missing on a recent trip, Sharom Idim. He had the man's vital statistics, close enough to his own that he could pass if no one knew either of them. He had to have credentials, though, if he was to try to hire an assistant, and *Winning Number* needed a Guide with a good reputation to attract passengers.

Satisfied with her artistry at last, she forged the appropriate seals and closed the files, setting the new specifications into the identification beacon. When her eyes would hardly focus, she checked on Zuchmul, then sought out Elias in Zimor's bedroom. The emblems had been removed from the bulkheads, and the marks covered by artistic use of the draperies from the bed enclosure. All the storage compartments were empty, Zimor's possessions crated for storage or just heaped in the center of the room.

"Where did you get the containers?" she asked, plucking at a heap of clothing.

"The hold. I evicted packages of chemicals so I could use the crates, and put the loose packages in an empty locker. I'll get all this stowed away tomorrow."

She nodded, selecting a gown and a robe, another pair of pants, and a tunic. "Where's the stuff from the bathroom?"

"Bathroom? Oh."

She went into the bathing compartment, all glittering blackstone and gold, with a large tub. Zimor's well-stocked pharmacy supplied the analgesic she needed and the potion she had promised Elias. "Here, dissolve a dose of this in shaid or wallor juice, and by the time you shower and change for bed, you'll be ready to sleep."

He took the cylinder in the palm of one hand and stared at it curiously. Determined not to make another mistake with him, she asked, "Do you know how to use the dispenser?"

"It produces a foam, right?"

It was a safety dispenser designed to prevent overdose, the sort of thing children learn to use almost before they can talk. She sighed. "Wait a moment and I'll show you."

She made a sling of the robe and selected some items from

the cabinet. "You can crate all the rest of this, but put it where we can get at it in an emergency. Come on."

She led the way to the galley where she filled a glass with chilled wallor juice and put it on the counter before him. "Hold out your hand, flat," she ordered. Then she positioned the container, looped the sensor around his thumb. "Hold it over the glass and press until it stops foaming."

He did it and, upper lip curling slightly, he watched the green foam sink into the purple juice, and effervesce.

"It doesn't taste as bad as it looks," she reassured him. "Now this container won't dispense for you again for a day." She checked the gauge and added, "It's still almost full, so it should last you until we get to Veramai."

He was eyeing the glass dubiously. "And I won't dream?"

"No," she replied, trying to sound positive.

He brushed a strand of that pale-blond hair off his forehead and straightened his shoulders. Then he lifted the glass and drained it in one smooth motion.

Putting the glass down, he agreed, "Not so bad."

"I'll see you for breakfast," she said and gathered her things off the counter. "Good night, Elias."

Without turning, he replied, "Good night, Kyllikki."

She tore herself away, refusing to think how it might have been had things started differently for them. *He loathes the concept of the Dreambond, not just Zimor. He'd never accept me in her place. Besides, it's illegal.*

Clutching her pack of things to her chest, she tore through the lounge, hurled herself into the room she'd chosen in the crew's quarters, and flung her things into drawers.

She went to bed, but rest would not come. Rolling from side to side, she blamed her restlessness on the constant pain. It felt as if every nerve in her body had swollen too large for its sheathing tissue. When she could find a comfortable position and almost relax, memories of Zimor would flash into her mind, and she'd twist away from them, the physical movement starting the pain again.

Perhaps she should have joined Elias in using the potion.

She had saved out another container of it. It was no farther than her own lavatory cabinet.

But she heard Idom next door, settling down to sleep, and she didn't want to disturb him with noise. She didn't want him to know she wasn't sleeping. If they trusted her judgment, trusted her plan, this time tomorrow they could be on their way. Idom had spent the whole day working in the Pool room, preparing a route for them. Just a few more details and they'd be ready to go. She could hold together that long, and the pain would subside eventually.

She yanked the cover over her head. But as she forced herself to lie still, she became more and more tense, Zimor's presence almost tangible in the room. *Shog!* she swore. It was her barriers, Elias' proximity, a Dreamer's proximity, naturally eroding away at her already shattered control. She hadn't been able to hold barriers really steady since *Prosperity* was attacked, and before that she'd been struggling with a monumental case of contact deprivation. It was small wonder she was lusting after the Dreamer, and getting nothing but Zimor's shadow between her and his mind.

She was about to give up and drug herself into oblivion when she heard a moan that turned to a muffled cry.

She was on her feet before she could think, and when the cry turned to Elias' voice raised in a scream, she tore out of her room at a dead run.

chapter **seven**

••••••••••••••••••••••••••••••••••••

Elias was sitting up in bed, back braced against a corner. Feet kicking and arms protecting his face, he cowered yet fought bravely, if ineffectually.

The room filled with shadow pictures: Zimor, coldly elegant in flowing white gown, descending an all-too-familiar staircase; Immertoid and Kagin slavers, using multicolored firecable restraints on human victims; Zimor, leaning over her state dining table, asking for help to stop Imperial aggression into Teleod space; Kyllikki twisted in gold satin sheets, screaming; a deserted sandy beach, long-legged seabirds, blue sky framing a single Kagin space yacht, which loomed larger by the second; Kyllikki in Zimor's clothes, sipping steaming yarage, looking very much like Zimor; Kyllikki bending over *Shylant*'s controls reading data into the Incognito program, and behind Kyllikki, as she programmed, Zimor usurping Elias' place, watching through his eyes.

Without stopping to think, Kyllikki dived across the room, tackled Elias, and rolled with him onto the floor. "Wake up! Wake up, Elias, you're Dreaming!"

Her barriers in tattered shreds, Kyllikki felt as if she were wrestling Zimor, a slender woman, not a solidly muscled man. Zimor's face loomed in front of Elias' features, contorted, eyes screwed shut as she cried, "No! You're mine! You won't get away! You won't!"

"I will!" grated Elias. He seized Kyllikki's arms and shoved as if she were the enemy to be escaped from. "You filthy imitation of a woman!" But all his efforts could not rid him of Kyllikki's grip. It was as if he were strapped by invisible restraints, enslaved again in mind if not body. Eyes rolled halfway back into his head, Elias growled alien invective and snarled, "I won't tell you! I won't!"

Kyllikki dug her nails into his ear cartilage. "Elias, wake up!" She bounced the back of his head on the floor trying for a sharp enough pain to draw his attention outward.

Suddenly his eyes opened. For an instant, it seemed he knew her, and then a vagueness shrouded his gaze and Zimor was there, conscious now of Kyllikki. Then Elias struggled back to the surface, only to submerge again, crying out for help in a tone that reminded her of the helpless wails of despair she herself had emitted under Zimor's power.

Zimor renewed her attack, and all trace of Elias' personality faded. Black waves of a familiar disorientation billowed into Kyllikki's consciousness. She knew in her bones it was useless to struggle against Zimor's will.

Distantly, Kyllikki felt Elias' strength rolling her over, then rolling again and yet again until he had her pinned against the base of a wall. But most of her attention was on the key image that wove through the misty curtains surrounding her mind, a slow building of a swirling, knotted pattern traced out by a glowing ember, a point of light as intense as the substance of the hottest star. It was trapping her mind in a webwork, inexorably drawing her mind through the symbolic cloud of dark mist into a private realm.

No, not my *mind. Elias'.*

She struggled out of the trap far enough to see Elias' physical features overlaid with Zimor's wavering form. Zimor grated with Elias' voice, "You won't get him! He's mine!"

Kyllikki heaved her body around Elias'. Ending up on top, she ripped aside her barriers and reached for the link to Elias that she had so craved and feared, the Dreambond.

It was like trying to invade Zimor's mind, not a Dreamer's. There was a rubbery resistance, and Kyllikki slipped, missed her grip, and tumbled into the roiling black mist, her body becoming black mist. *She's pulled me into a realm she controls!* All around her, the key image was still being etched into the billowing black clouds, the key image that permeated Elias' mind, defined the Dreambond.

She could see the entire pattern, partly etched in fire, partly glowing dimly like the key she couldn't banish. Kyllikki suddenly knew that if she let Zimor complete the evocation, she'd be trapped in Elias' mind, trapped and extinguished.

She reached out her ghostly hands made of black mist and seized the fiery point of light. Pain such as she'd never known shot through her. Suddenly, Elias was there, slapping at her hands in a feeble attempt to dislodge her grip.

She tightened her hold on the bit of light, counting it a major triumph that she had stopped its juggernaut advance. Elias seized one of her wrists, heaved with all his strength, but here in this realm, his physical strength counted for nothing. Still, her concentration wavered, and the point of light escaped her, resuming its journey, but more slowly.

Clearly, Elias' own, independent will opposed her, for the emotional truth of Elias' existence lay in the Dreambond, in serving Zimor. He had capitulated. *No! You won't!*

Her misty hands closed on Elias' equally misty throat, and she squeezed with all her might.

A voice pierced through her being, a dearly familiar voice. "Kyllikki! What are you doing!"

It was Idom. Hands grabbed her, warm, fatherly hands. Her body was solid, physical flesh, not black mist, and her real hands were on the warm, pliant flesh of Elias' throat. "You're strangling him, Kyllikki!" He pulled her away from the writhing form beneath her.

As soon as her hands lost contact with Elias, the writhing

black cloud disappeared from her consciousness. The room no longer held phantoms; Elias' face was his own. She knelt on the floor, gasping, wrapping herself in silver bricks solid enough to reflect everything away from her mind. "Sovereigns Be! I never—I can't—I didn't—"

"I know, I know," said Idom, bending to examine Elias. "It's all right. He's alive."

She crawled over to them. The entire battle with Zimor must have occurred during the few seconds it took Idom to arrive, assess the situation, and act. Yet she gulped air as if she hadn't breathed in hours. She peered over Idom's shoulder and saw Elias wasn't thrashing anymore. Icy fear gripped her guts. "Elias Kleef, don't you dare die!" *I can't be the murderer of a Dreamer!* And yet, that's what she'd been willing to do. If she couldn't have Elias, she wouldn't let Zimor have him, no matter what he wanted. It had nothing to do with the war or ideals. It was personal.

But it hadn't been Elias' conscious will aligned against her. It had been the reflex of a Dreamer threatened with a severance of the Bond. Her response had also been reflexive. And as always, when it came to Zimor, Kyllikki had lost.

Steeling herself with all her remaining courage, she thinned her barriers. Only on the very edge of her raw and abraded senses could she detect the hint of Zimor that signified the Bond. Elias' Dreaming state had at last been fully disrupted, and as she solidified her barriers and looked at his face again, she saw his eyes coming into focus.

Idom asked, "Are you sure you didn't overdose him?"

"Underdose, if anything. He was Dreaming!"

"You're sure?" Idom turned to her.

"Well, what would you call it?"

"Did Zimor get any of what he Dreamed?"

"She got it all, but I don't know what 'it' was. It was so mixed up." She told him what she'd seen when she first entered. "I'm sure she saw me programming the Incognito circuit. Elias had come in just as I was finishing. I thought I'd shut down before he glimpsed the screen, but I wasn't fast enough. When he Dreamed, Zimor got it all."

"Dreamed," muttered Elias.

They snapped around and found him gazing at them blearily. Kyllikki said, "Yes, you were Dreaming."

He shook his head. "That was no Dream. That was a *nightmare*."

"A what?" she asked.

"Sorry. I guess if nobody in this galaxy dreams but us, then you wouldn't have a word for *nightmare*. It's like imagining a horror, and it's somehow worse because it's imaginary, not real." He wiped his face with one hand. "It was as if I was a slave again, and Zimor, instead of rescuing me, was torturing me—and then you came and fought her for possession of me, but I was sure you only wanted to torture me, then kill me. Crazy. *Nightmares* are crazy."

Idom protested, "Kyllikki, you said a Bonded Dreamer dreams coherently. Has the drug broken his Bond?"

"I wish it was that easy," she answered. She tucked her legs under her, aware for the first time that her gown was torn up the side all the way to her armpit. Miserably, she confessed, "Elias, it may have felt like what you call *nightmare*, but it was real. It actually happened."

"You mean—you wanted to kill me?"

"No! I fought Zimor—I just reacted when she attacked me. I fought her—for possession of you!"

Idom repeated, "Zimor attacked you? From halfway across the galaxy!"

"I've never heard of anything like it, either, but theoretically there's no distance limit on the Bond. Elias was Dreaming, which opened the contact to Zimor, and if it's any consolation," she said to Elias, "it was no fun for Zimor, either. She'll be dreading the next time you Dream." She mused, "She might be wondering how much of that was real." *If she's doubting her sanity, it could be an advantage.* On the other hand, Zimor wasn't the type to doubt her sanity.

Easing himself to his feet and sitting on Elias' bed, Idom said, "Kyllikki, tell us exactly what happened."

She detailed the entire experience. "But," she finished, "I've no way to know what she got before I arrived, unless you remember?"

"I'm sorry. None of that sounds familiar. I fell asleep, as you said I would, then there was a horrid *nightmare* of grasping, strangling, torture, and *that woman*." He sighed, resting his forearms on his bent knees, the back of his head against the wall. "I'm going to kill her."

"I know how you feel," said Kyllikki.

"From you, that sounds ominous."

"I didn't mean it that way. I'm trying to keep my barriers up and respect your privacy."

"Kyllikki, I was *joking*. You saved my life again, and I thank you. It's not your fault the drug didn't work."

He'll never take it again. Now what are we going to do?

Idom heaved himself to his feet. "I'm going to make a pot of shaid. Aren't you cold in that gown, Kyllikki?"

Elias levered himself up, using the wall for support. "I'll help. I'm afraid if I lie down, I'll fall asleep."

Kyllikki went for her robe, and took another dose of analgesic. The pain was worse than before she'd gone to bed. She picked up the spare cylinder of sleeping potion, checked on Zuchmul, and joined the men in the lounge, finding them arguing over the dangers of increasing the drug dosage versus putting Elias in stasis. Elias was for stasis.

She took a mug of the hot juice drink, sweetened it to kill the taste, and curled her hands over the steam.

". . . hear me, Kyllikki?" asked Idom impatiently.

"There's only one clear fact," said Kyllikki dully. "We can't include Elias in our decisions."

"In that case," said Elias, "stasis is the only answer."

"It's not worth the risk," she replied. "Stasis is useful only when you face certain death otherwise. Risking death for a purpose isn't the same as courting death. For our purpose, we need you as a live witness, an exhibit in a legal battle." *Shog! I'm such a hypocrite.* Their purpose had been far from her mind when she'd attacked him. Still, she'd been trained to detach the personal, to take the point of view needed to manage an inter-stellar civilization.

Glumly, Elias said, "An exhibit. Fine, I'll be your exhibit, but not if I have to go through that again!"

"You won't have to!"

"Oh? So what's the alternative if not stasis?"

They were almost shouting, and she couldn't help from retorting even more loudly, "I'm not going to tell you!"

He subsided, stunned. "No. You shouldn't."

Leaving his half-full cup, he got up and stalked toward the crew's quarters. She went after him, pulling the extra drug cylinder out of her pocket. Grabbing his elbow, she pressed it into his hand. "Here. This'll deliver another dose, and with the first only half worn off, it'll knock you out completely. Try it, Elias. What have you got to lose?"

"Like you said before, my sanity as well as my life." He did not close his hand on the cylinder.

She proffered the container again. "This *will* keep you from Dreaming. It just takes a larger dosage where an active Bond is involved. I should have realized that."

He regarded her for several long moments, then took the container. "Promise me something. Promise me that if—if it comes to insanity, to being trapped in *nightmare* for the rest of my life, you'll make sure I don't suffer long. Can you promise me that, Kyllikki?"

No! But if she were in his place, she might well ask the same. She moved her head in assent. "I'll see to it."

"Then I'll try this." He took the cylinder and turned away, his retreating back bowed. There was little of the Elias she'd come to admire in this man. She went after him again, stopping him opposite the crew's galley. "Elias, have you ever had a *nightmare* before?"

"I used to—all the time, until Zimor 'rescued' me."

She threw her arms around his chest and hugged him as hard as she could. "I'm sorry. I had no idea. This time you'll sleep without Dreaming, Elias, I promise."

His arms came around her, hesitant, strong as solid rock,

gentle as soft music. The music that always haunted his mind flowed into her. *Barriers!* She withdrew, pushing back. "Go back to bed, Elias. I have to talk to Idom."

He nodded and went. She closed the hatch to the crew's area behind him, and returned to the table. Idom leaned back in his chair, stroking his beard and rocking gently.

She settled beside him and refilled her mug. "I'm glad I can't imagine what it's like to have that happen to your mind when you sleep. I don't know how they survive it, but I've heard their planet is seething with life, and most of it Dreams un-Bonded. *Nightmare.* What a nasty-sounding word. Of course they'd have a word for pathological Dreaming."

"You're babbling."

"I know."

"You've got a plan."

"Some demented fool might call it that."

"You're going to have to tell me."

"We've got to break the Dreambond with Zimor before we try for Veramai and the Emperor. Stasis is too dangerous, and the double-dose strategy may not work. He'll be more and more uncomfortable, unrested, nervous, irritable, or depressed. He could become deluded enough to believe he has to discover what we're planning, and he could succeed. He'll be so in need of Dreaming that he could fall asleep anytime during the day, and she'd know our plan. So it's obvious: we can't go to Veramai until we've broken the Bond."

"I didn't know Dreambonds could be broken."

"With luck, Zimor won't either until it's too late."

"Tell me. Tell it all to me."

"I told you Zimor threw a key image at me, but I didn't tell you—do you know what a key image is?"

"Vaguely. Imaginary patterns a Teleod telepath uses."

"Well, I'd never seen that key before, but—don't ask how—it showed me how to fight Zimor for possession of Elias. I'd actually almost won—almost transferred the Bond to myself—when Elias disrupted my concentration. He pitted his whole will against me. He couldn't help it." She squeezed her eyes shut, firming all barriers, ignoring the dizzy, whirling pain that swept through her at irregular intervals. "I behaved disgracefully."

"So how do you plan to avoid doing that in the future?"

"Wish I knew." She sipped at the hot, sweet juice and told herself that she had to tell it all to him.

"But now you have a plan, a plan based on something you learned during your disgraceful attack on Zimor for possession of Elias? An attack which would never have happened had you not miscalculated the dose of the drug?"

"Yes. I know it's all my—"

"—responsibility," he finished doggedly. "Kyllikki, forgive yourself. As things stand right now, we're not so much worse off than we were yesterday. We're better off, in fact, because we've learned something that may help us defeat Zimor. Now will you tell me what we've learned?"

"I learned what I've known all along, that I can't win against Zimor. But I also learned that Zimor might not always win, if faced with a team effort."

He refilled his mug with steaming shaid. "What do you mean, team effort?" He raised his mug to take a sip.

"Luren Influence."

He slopped hot shaid over his hands and swore. When they'd mopped it up, he asked, "Did you say luren Influence?"

"I did."

"Kyllikki . . . that's not legal."

"Zuchmul would do it for me. I know he would. There isn't any legal way to do this. Dreambonding is illegal everywhere, so there's no legal way to break such a Bond."

"You can't parent a luren."

"Of course not. We've got to take Zuchmul to be properly revived. As soon as I can talk to him, I can figure out how to do this. Influence can make people believe the unreal, do things based on that belief, or feel emotions. I'm not sure how it works. Maybe Zuchmul doesn't know either, but he's good at using it."

"How would you know?"

"Monitoring luren is one of the Com Officers' jobs on-board a ship, remember? I watched him a lot. He's good. He's careful, and very ethical. We were on that pod with him for days without his Inhibitor, and he never overstepped the bounds. The Families are sensitive to luren Influence, re-member?"

"Hmmm. You plan to have Zuchmul distract Zimor while you wrench the Bond away from her? Get Zimor to strike at Zuchmul with her Family reflex? I don't think that's a good plan, and I doubt Zuchmul would go along."

"That's not what I had in mind, but I'm not sure what will or won't work. The mechanism governing Influence must have the same character as that governing the realms, as well as the one governing the Metaji system. The Bond is something else. But all four have to be governed by aspects of the same princi-ple. Geneticists agree there are relationships between the luren, the Dreamers, and the Families. They're not three separate things, but aspects of one thing. So with a bit of experimenta-tion, I think Zuchmul and I can pry Elias loose from Zimor."

"What if Zuchmul does not wake up at all?"

"Dormant luren survive stasis a lot more often than live humans do."

"Can't argue with that. But suppose he is revived and does agree to your scheme, and Elias is freed of the Bond, and you can somehow manage not to Bond with him. How do we then prove to the Emperor that he was Bonded to Zimor?"

That gave her pause. "I don't know how that's done in the Empire, but there must be a way. After all, you can't have a law and no way to enforce it. In the Teleod, there's the Verifier, Brain Printing, and telepathic examination, as well as older tests invented for just this purpose. Bonders who saw they were about to be caught often suicided, which does break the Bond. So there had to be objective methods of determining if the Dreamer had been Bonded, and if so, to whom. Breaking the Bond shouldn't make any difference."

"That's way outside of my field, and I wouldn't know who to consult about it."

"Can you get us to somewhere there's a big established luren community? Where another revival won't be conspicuous? With a library big enough for you to find out what procedures the Empire has for evaluating a Dreambond or its residue?"

"Would Insarios do?"

"How would I know? I've never heard of it."

"It's in the Four Stars Region, and has the largest luren citadel in the Fotel Duchy. Lots of traffic."

"Sounds ideal."

"What do we tell Elias?"

"That it's none of his business where we are or where we're going. I'll take the stasis unit to the citadel. Revival probably won't take more than a day or two. Zuchmul really wasn't hurt all that badly."

"You're determined to do it this way?"

"Do you have a better idea?"

"No," he answered grimly.

"Look, if you don't like what you learn at the library, at least then Zuchmul will be awake, and maybe the three of us can think of a better idea."

"Three of us; not counting Elias, of course," he mused. "Actually, breaking the Bond might be less dangerous than the original plan, which involved so many people, so many strangers, any of whom might have been on Zimor's payroll. This is a three-step plan that risks only the four of—" He looked up at her suddenly, eyes boring into her. "How many containers of that soporific do you have aboard?"

"Just two. Or there might be more in the hold. Zimor uses a lot—well, she used to before she Bonded Elias."

"Where in the hold?"

"Look it up on the inventory screen."

He lunged to his feet and went into the galley. With her help, he paged through the inventory, then exclaimed, "Kyllikki! There are *three* cases of that stuff aboard! Three! We can do it! This's a much better plan. It'll work. I knew it all along. You're the key to this mess."

If she hadn't known better, she'd have said he was crazy.

But Idom's prediction was right, as usual. From then on, everything went smoothly. Elias slept without Dream or *nightmare*, they made Insarios in three neat dives, and by the time they arrived, Kyllikki's physical condition had improved markedly. She'd been able to sleep for the first time in a long, long time, and the persistent headache had subsided.

Approaching Insarios, she handled the Communicator's job smoothly, introducing herself as Kaitha Ray, Com First of *Rising Tide*, an independent charter out of Wayward Cluster.

The registration was Idom's suggestion, one almost as hard to check from Insarios as a Barkyr registration would have been. The Wayward Cluster was an ill-defined mass of artificial habitats that occupied the center of a star desert, its main industry provided by ships crossing that desert. Their story of having just bought the ship made more sense with that kind of a registration.

She had the documentation ready for transmission, sure that all was in order. But when Insarios Control told them to wait in orbit, she sweated. She was tempted to switch to Coherent Spectrum for the next contact, but restrained herself, thinking that might have seemed suspicious.

She waited a long time, then thought that such patience might seem suspicious and was on the verge of demanding a landing berth, when she decided *that* might seem suspicious.

Idom came up the stairs from the Pool room, wiping his hands on a towel. "What's taking so long?"

"I wish I knew."

He sat down next to her and scanned nearby space for sign of defense installations. She explained the displays. "An artificial solar-orbit habitat here. Three heavy projectors on that airless moon of the fourth planet."

Insarios was the third planet from its sun, but the sun was small and pallid, with a skewed visible spectrum.

He studied the emplacements. "Isn't there something along this line, out farther in solar orbit?"

"Not according to their public information. Why?"

"Best departure line."

"Oh." She played with their monitors, examining space in that direction, finding nothing. "Idom, why would Defense be along a departure line? We came in along the best approach line, and passed their fortified moon and the solar-orbit Defense Station. They all sounded our transponder and questioned me thoroughly. We had two ships pacing us for half the distance. Now Ground Control is shredding our documentation. Why defend the *departure* line?"

"No reason. But if we're in a hurry, that's how we're going to leave." He pointed out his target dive point.

They spent some time planning various retreat vectors, Idom charting routes to Veramai. At least it occupied the time. Four times, while they waited, Elias called from his quarters. "What's taking so long?"

The third time, Idom retorted, "Just practice with that voder in case you have to use it."

"You're sure it's a good idea for me to play nonhuman?"

"I told you," replied Kyllikki, "we have to change our profile in the records or any cursory check could identify us for Zimor's agents. But they'd never expect this."

"We're not even sure she has spies here," argued Elias.

"But we have to assume it. You can bet that she's looking for us with everything she's got."

They were kept waiting half a planetary rotation, and then, finally, were granted a berth. Immediately, a truck pulled up to take *Rising Tide*'s Captain, Kaitha Ray, to the Portmaster. She went armed with every sort of documentation she could think of, plus an array of negotiable instruments from Zimor's safe, more than enough to pay all fees.

Having never done this before, she sat in waiting rooms and stood in lines with the bored Captains of other newly arrived ships, some in expensive uniforms, some in soiled coveralls, some in nothing but their natural scales or feathers, and tried to blend in.

In every office, in every waiting room, in every line, at every console where she had to input data or establish solvency or prove her identity, at every point where she was questioned by a port official, there were armed Baronial guards stationed conspicuously.

She had a lot of time to inspect them or the likeness of Tshiv, Baron of Insarios, that adorned every official portal. The Baron was an Effein, a very humanoid species evolved on a heavy-gravity world that was one of the original twenty-two signatories to the Imperial Compact which had established the Metaji throne. Kyllikki was not an expert on Imperial heraldry, but she gathered from the elaborate crests the Baron wore that Tshiv was closely connected to the Effein Dukes, one of whom was the Duke of Fotel, ruler of the Four Stars Region.

At first it bothered her that she couldn't distinguish the Baron's gender. The knobby charcoal-gray tegument, oddly articulated hands, and slightly distorted bodily proportions were all that hinted at a lack of a genetic connection with the varied races of humanity until she remembered that Effein had no sexuality humans would recognize. They were, despite the haunting similarity of form, not at all human.

Their strength and agility had led a disproportionate number of them into the Crown's armed services, so she wasn't surprised that half the guards were Effein as well. They wore burgundy velvet dress uniforms and full headgear that displayed all their honors, orders, awards, and, for all she knew, lineage as well. No two helmets were alike, but all the Effein sported a stiff crest of sparkling-white bristles.

One strolling guard wore a helmet that was a work of art. It dripped with so many medals that the Effein jingled with every movement. Kyllikki decided this was the officer in charge and the Effein used the musical sound of the helmet to assert authority. But that only worked on other Effein.

Undismayed, the officer inspected each guard, spoke a few quiet words, swept the roomful of ships' Captains with narrowed eyes, then marched off, leaving the guards sharply alert, hands close to the very real weapons they carried.

Twice, Kyllikki watched this performance before she realized that, after the Effein left, the guards focused on her. The third time, she decided that the officer entered every area just after she did. That time, she caught the Effein watching her. The elaborate helmet obscured the gray-skinned features, but it had to be the same Effein. There couldn't be two helmets like that.

Still, she began easing the automatic barriers she'd lived behind since the battle with Zimor. She was, after all, the Com Officer as well as Captain, and most Metaji telepaths couldn't barrier the way she did. She relaxed enough to monitor the seepage from the Effein officer.

There were few telepaths in this area, and most of them were officials in the adjacent office questioning Captains. None of them were Communicator material. They wouldn't notice her amidst the waiting Captains' roar of anxiety.

She watched the Effein with her mind, keeping her eyes on Baron Tshiv's portrait and taking care to adhere to her Metaji oath, doing only what would be expected of any telepath of her ostensible rating. She got a single, clear impression of the Effein's mental signature, enough to pick him out of a crowd of his fellows. She'd never encountered such a joyful zealousness before. Zealots were almost always grim folk. This one was an idealist, a satisfied idealist.

The Effein was inspecting his guards at the exit when she left. Without looking back, she walked briskly to *Rising Tide*, carrying all the stamps, seals, and bits of hardware that had to be attached to various parts of the ship's anatomy to thwart unauthorized lift-off. *Rising Tide* was legal.

She and Idom managed, half from vague memories, half from the sketchy instructions, to get it all attached well enough to satisfy the Inspectors who boarded several hours later. At least her Effein was not with them.

The Inspectors were more suspicious than they should have been with an unarmed yacht. But they accepted the story of a Thaener nocturnal asleep in Elias' room, exhausted from working the Pool as astrogator and now into his three-day sleep cycle. No one would consider disturbing a sleeping Thaener, and astrogator apprentices had garnered a prestige they'd never had before the war.

After a cursory inspection of the hold, cracking open a few cases to find clothing, food, and medication, the three Inspectors left, but not without thoughtful backward glances. That made Kyllikki nervous. Most of the items in the hold were of Teleod manufacture, and though luren still imported such goods, loyal citizens wouldn't have them.

"Idom, what would it take to get those seals off the Pool and the gravitic drive?"

"Not much. They're a formality, more to prevent accidents than to force compliance."

"What if we took them off now?"

He shook his head in negation. "We might be inspected again. I don't think they were satisfied with the story that we'd inherited the cargo with the ship."

She told him about the Effein guard. "But I got all the clearances anyone else got."

He pondered that, pacing and tugging on his beard. Then he turned, Guild robes swirling about him, and said, "The best way to allay suspicion is to go about our business."

She agreed and patched into the local communications lines to the luren citadel. Despite the busy period at the luren infirmary, she got Zuchmul an immediate spot by claiming that the antique unit might break down at any time.

According to their new cover story, *Rising Tide* had been hired to have a luren revived and transport him to Hayelma, where there was another small but thriving luren community. They'd be paid only if they delivered him there, paid enough to refit their ship and go into business.

The hole in the story, which they hoped would not come to light until long after they'd departed, was Zuchmul's true identity as crew of *Prosperity*. There was no way to hide his full family designation, as it was necessary before the luren would revive him and provide him with a new parentage and family affiliation. These affiliations, Kyllikki understood, were cumulative, and there were rules that had to be strictly followed in choosing who might properly revive him this time.

Kyllikki had been entrusted with her friend's full identity, and though it had taken her some hours of hard work, she was sure she had remembered it all properly.

She knew it would go no farther than luren private records, and those records probably did not contain his last-known employment. Luren had odd ideas about privacy, and rarely cross-indexed onto the major-data networks. It would take legal action or one of Zimor's spies to discover where Zuchmul had been revived, when, and by whom.

So Kyllikki hired a transport and driver, and escorted the stasis unit to the luren citadel.

It was a buff-colored, high-walled complex of windowless buildings connected by roofed and sealed walkways on ground level. The buildings were low and flat, but extended many stories underground.

Originally, she understood from the maps provided at the port, the luren citadel had been built far outside the boundary of Port Confluence, but over the years, industries, embassies, and residential areas had crept up to and surrounded the luren. Needing to control magnetic and particle emissions in their environment, they had fortified their buildings and burrowed underground. Now, no nonluren was ever allowed in beyond the reception area of the citadel, which was governed by luren law, not Imperial.

Within those walls, luren walked free of the protective garments they needed elsewhere, and they used Influence as their culture dictated.

It wasn't a place any sane human would want to wander into, but the security was tight. As Kyllikki's driver turned off a wide boulevard that led to the planet's Baronial residence, she saw they were in a narrow street ending in the two huge, formal gates of the luren citadel. They stood half open, but there were glittering lenses in the gates, tangle-field projectors atop the walls, heavy guns she couldn't name, and two armed guards outside the gate. They were luren in full solar-protection gear and wearing conspicuous Inhibitor collars. That wasn't nearly as intimidating as the sight of a rank of armed guards on the inside of the gate, none of whom were wearing Inhibitors.

Before they arrived at that gate, though, they had to pass through a Baronial checkpoint where guards in dark burgundy field uniforms surrounded mobile pieces that looked capable of destroying the luren citadel. As her car pulled up between bars that trapped it fore and aft, Kyllikki saw a small three-wheeled scooter stop at the other side of the guard post. On it was her zealous Effein officer.

She was left standing outside her vehicle as the Effein inspected the guards, speaking to each privately. Then, it took them twice as long as it should have to clear her through the checkpoint. They wanted to uncover the stasis unit, which had been shrouded in protective material for daytime transport, and shine a light into the case to record the luren's appearance.

"You can't do that!" shouted Kyllikki. "You've no idea what kind of harm the sun or your light might do, never mind the magnetic flux around here!" She gestured to the mobile gun emplacements with their standby lights in full evidence.

"They'll fix him up inside," said one Effein guard.

"Are you a physician?" she challenged. "Do you know luren? By what authority can you torture an innocent citizen of the Empire?"

Shouting and gesticulating, Kyllikki snatched the corner of the shroud from the guard's fingers. Only then did it occur to her that she was opposing a legitimate officer of a very loyal Baron of the Empire.

chapter **eight**

●●●●●●●●●●●●●●●●●●●●●●●●●●●●●●●●●●

Off to Kyllikki's right, one of the luren guards posted outside the citadel gate started toward the checkpoint. The Baron's man saw her coming and backed away from the stasis unit. Before the guard had come halfway, the barricade in front of Kyllikki's transport lifted and the Baron's man nervously waved them through.

As Kyllikki's driver stopped at the gate, the luren woman in guard uniform moved alongside, handing Kyllikki a noteboard displaying a form. Signs posted on the guard shack and over the gates bore the luren's concentric circle crest and the legend: WARNING—YOU ARE ENTERING LUREN TERRITORY AND SURRENDERING ALL RIGHTS TO PROTECTION FROM INFLUENCE.

Kyllikki knew that by custom luren didn't use Influence in the public areas and she was ready to sign the standard waiver without a qualm, but her driver balked.

"This is as far as I go. That'll be fifteen, as we agreed." The woman got out to unload her cargo compartment.

Kyllikki climbed out, holding the noteboard. "I've got a stasis unit with a dormant luren here. What do I do?" She signed her assumed name and returned the noteboard.

The guard glanced at Kyllikki's signature. "Do you have an appointment, Ray?"

"Yes," answered Kyllikki.

She inspected the unit as the driver wrestled it out of the cargo bed and set the wheels on the ground. The shroud, left unsecured by the Baron's man, slipped aside. The guard lunged forward to yank it back into place, but hesitated, peering at the unit before she refastened the shroud. "I've never seen one like that before. You sure it's working?"

"Yes."

The luren squatted to inspect the wheeled framework from Barkyr. The fittings had never quite matched. "It's not secure." Rising, she called to a luren in the guard shack. "G'rel, here's another one for you, and it's a problem."

The man came out, wincing as the sunlight hit him. He, too, shook his head in wonder as he squatted to inspect the unit's underpinnings, and then the archaic unit itself. "That's the third or fourth today. I'll get a float." He started to go back inside, but Kyllikki's driver stopped him.

With a nervous glance at the Baron's men, she said, "I can't wait here. Move this so I can turn around."

G'rel and the woman guard exchanged glances, then closed on the stasis unit and lifted it, carriage and all, putting it down inside the gates, giving the transport ample room.

Kyllikki drifted through the gates to wait beside the luren guards who weren't wearing Inhibitors.

Her feet were hurting by the time four luren turned up with an antigravity unit, muttered and swore as they rigged a way to affix it to the stasis unit, plastered a coded label on the unit, handed Kyllikki a stub with the same code, then led her through one of the many doors opening off the courtyard. The sign over it read: MEDICAL EMERGENCY RECEIVING.

Without pause, the four escorts marched across the waiting area, past the counters and offices, then eased the unit through a gate over which flashed signs saying: NO ADMITTANCE, HAZARDOUS ACTIVITIES, and INFLUENCE FREELY IN USE. As they passed that point, they removed their Inhibitors with a practiced flourish that bespoke profound relief.

After Zuchmul disappeared into the citadel, Kyllikki suddenly became aware that she was obstructing traffic. Ahead of her were desks, counters, data consoles, and a bewildering array of signs, few of which seemed to pertain to her problem. Behind her, defined by a square of red carpet and rows of seats, was a waiting area filled with people.

There were lines at most of the desks, but the people in the waiting area all possessed some sort of color-coded noteboard. Few of them were human. None were luren.

She was reading the signs hanging from the ceiling, flashing over the desks, or sprouting up from the floor on movable stands when a Ye're'y came out of the waiting area, wings folded tightly. "You brought in a luren in stasis?"

"Yes, I did," Kyllikki said with relief. "Do you know the procedure?"

"This is your first time here?"

"Yes."

"Ah. Well. The luren. A friend of yours?"

Kyllikki almost said yes, but then remembered her cover story. "No. I'm Captain of *Rising Tide*. We do charter work, and we were hired to bring this luren here."

Kyllikki was on the verge of thinning her barriers to assess the Ye're'y's stare when the stranger proffered a data card. "I work for D'sillin Escort Service. We serve the luren community of the Four Stars Region, and we're the best Dormant Escort Service insurance money can buy. If you're planning to compete with us, I suggest you'd do better to join us instead. We can use good ships, especially now, with so many chartered out to fight the Teleod."

Kyllikki said, "An interesting proposition. I'll think about it." The name "D'sillin" sounded ominously familiar.

The Ye're'y inspected Kyllikki again. "Think carefully, Captain of *Rising Tide*. If you seek profit, we will hear from you very soon."

"My next port of call is Hayelma. After that, I may look you up if I come back to the Four Stars."

"Speak to us before Hayelma, Captain. We dislike seeing helpless luren maltreated, here or in the Teleod."

"In the Teleod," she said, "few ships would take this commission. It's one thing to deliver a stasis unit to a hospital, it's another to take a revived luren passenger."

"Is that what you were commissioned to do?"

"What's your interest in the matter?"

The Ye're'y shifted, wings flexing. "There's a profit in preying on luren, but in the Four Stars, we've found a better profit in protecting them when they're vulnerable. You may not be from the Fotel Duchy, and may intend to leave, but you are here now. By special appointment of the Duke, with the support of Baron Tshiv, D'sillin protects the luren of the Four Stars, *and all luren visitors.*"

Protects? thought Kyllikki. *Or polices?* "I'm beginning to understand."

"Good. Then we'll be hearing from you or we'll speak with your luren about the other choices of transportation."

Kyllikki opened herself to the Ye're'y's emanations but found no menace, just a tranquil security that was itself a kind of threat. "In that case, you'll hear from me. Now where do I go to sign my client in for treatment?"

The Ye're'y indicated a long line. "Follow the blue arrows with the numbers in blue circles. You do see blue, don't you? That female Hayelmin in grickle-skin boots is standing under the blue number one."

"I see it. Thank you."

Again the Ye're'y weighed Kyllikki's appearance as if accustomed to judging humans. Kyllikki was wearing an outfit of Zimor's, serviceable black slacks and bright-striped tunic, not overtly Teleod, but not well-fitting either. It looked expensive, which lent her an air of authority. The Ye're'y said, "We'll be expecting you. Ask for D'sillin."

"I'll do that." Kyllikki went to join the line. When she looked back, the Ye're'y had vanished.

By the time she reached the desk, her feet were really hurting, even though the gravity was barely above norm on this world. As she obtained a noteboard with the proper forms and instructions and retired to the waiting area to fill them out, she resolved to get herself some proper shoes.

The line was not long for Step Two, which required her to insert her noteboard in a slot and enter what information she had on Zuchmul's history. The terminal presented her with a pager and sent her back to the waiting area.

She was getting hungry as well as anxious when the pager finally directed her to desk number four, where a luren man was reviewing the data she had given, while on an adjacent display he had a picture of Zuchmul's capsule. It took her an hour to satisfy the luren about the operational specs of the stasis unit, a model on which they had no data at all.

In the end, he said, "This may take two to five days. I understand your instructions require you to wait."

"That's correct. His passage is paid to Hayelma."

"Well, I can see why you couldn't have taken him there directly. I assure you we have the experience with archaic equipment that they don't. You'll be notified. Thank you."

Five days! Suddenly, Kyllikki doubted Idom's prediction that the plan was going to work. As she left the citadel, looking for public transportation, her palms were cold and sweaty, and she was so tense she jumped at every loud noise.

She had figured on two or three days' grace on Insarios before they could be traced, but not five. And now there was the added complication of the D'sillin Service, protectors of luren by appointment of the local Duke, a relative of the Baron of Insarios.

It made sense that a nonhuman Duchy would harbor luren, a human race hardly counted as human but which contributed greatly both to the sciences and to trade. But if luren were so privileged here, why had that Baronial guardsman tried to lift the shroud protecting Zuchmul? In fact, why were there Baron's men guarding the citadel at all? And why had that Effein officer turned up as Kyllikki arrived with Zuchmul?

Then she remembered where she'd heard the name D'sillin before. From Lee. D'sillin had owned *Otroub* and had been trying to recall it, probably to transport orl, just when the

Teleod claimed that the Duke of Fotel had kidnapped the heir to Sa'ar. Kyllikki had concluded the Sa'ar had been lost in the ordinary way, but what if Fotel was really dealing with the Teleod's luren? No, more likely Zimor's lies were creating distrust between the Effein aristocracy and local luren, and maybe, for all Kyllikki knew, between the Duke and the throne.

Whatever Zimor was up to this time, Kyllikki could only hope it had nothing to do with her. But one thing was clear: they had to get out of the Four Stars as quickly as possible.

When she reached the port shopping district, she called the ship and left a message for Elias that she was on her way to order the ship's uniforms and other supplies. As a sleeping Thaener, Elias would not answer, but one code phrase said that Zuchmul was safe in the citadel.

Idom was at the Guild House dealing with formalities, and that was another time bomb under them. He had decided to use his own name despite the risk that it would alert Zimor's spies. Under his own identity, he had the right to sign on a Thaener apprentice without bringing him into the Guild House or explaining to anyone, but his very presence would surely be noted and the story taken off-world by the next departing Guides. And Zimor's spies would hear of it.

Two days, maybe three. That was as long as they dared sit here, yet they needed Zuchmul. They had to wait even if it took five days. *Besides, I can't abandon him to face whatever's going on here all alone.*

Still, everything went smoothly that first day in Port Confluence, and when Kyllikki told Idom of her experience at the citadel, ending, "We can't leave without Zuchmul, but we can't wait five days," Idom nodded thoughtfully.

They were alone in the crew's galley, and Idom was trying to process Metaji-packaged provisions through Teleod equipment to produce something edible. He turned from the second charred mess he'd made and said, "You'll have to visit this D'sillin and allay suspicion. Sign up with them if you have to. After that . . ." He shrugged.

"I can do that, but it won't be enough. I keep telling you, we don't have five days!"

He lined up three new meal packets on the counter, then tapped each one in turn. "At the hospital, you said there were five blue-circled numbers, but you were directed from one to two to four, and never hit three or five, correct?"

"Yes, but—"

"And," he interrupted, "when you ordered the uniforms, it cost you three hundred local credits, exactly?"

"Yes, but—"

"And," he insisted, "when you ran into trouble with the port officials, it took three officers to get it straight?"

"Yes, but—"

"At the third office you spotted the Effein 'zealot'?"

"Yes, but—"

"You're leading us up onto a probability crest. I don't know how far it's going to carry us. Zuchmul's rejoining us may change everything, but in three days, Zuchmul will be here. Go call Elias for supper." He turned back to his chore and on the third try produced three perfect meals.

Over breakfast, she had to ask, "Idom, some things have come in threes, true, but not everything. Counting Zuchmul, there are four of us. Only one Ye're'y approached me, one Baronial guardsman took an interest in me, there was one broken voder in the hold, and it only took one try to get the uniforms. But it took five tries to fix the voder. How do you know it won't take five days for Zuchmul to return? How do you know what to count?

Elias shifted his gaze to Idom, and Idom calmly poured himself more shaid before answering. "Here's a proposition for you. You teach me how to construct, use, and recognize key images, and I'll teach you how to recognize, use, and extrapolate probability structures, how to distinguish ridges, threads, sinks, singularities, points, crests, peaks, runs, punctures, and whorls from background noise. Deal?"

"I see," she replied, deflated. "It takes a lifetime of study and training, not to mention talent."

"And even I make mistakes," admitted Idom somberly. "In the world of theory, everything is clean-cut and sharp edged. In the real world, all the structures penetrate and affect one another. But this I know: Zuchmul will return on the third day, most likely in the third trisect of the day, but after that—I can't begin to guess."

"What do you mean?" asked Elias. "When Zuchmul joins us, we'll be four—"

"Exactly. There's a lot of energy bound up in this trinary cresting, and when it breaks it can go to literally anything. There's no controlling the breaking of a crest; it's pure chaos at that point, but I do have considerable experience with pure chaos—the majority of my life's work has been in that field—so I'm not dismayed by the prospect of counting a dive into a purity unstructure."

Rapt, Kyllikki listened with more than her ears. Though he hadn't revealed any Guild secrets, the texture of his emotional glow had become deeper, richer, more intense, and oddly cleaner. Here was a man cramped and deprived by the war, forced into a kind of professional exile as hopeless as her own and hungering for his true place as much as she did for someone to commune with since she couldn't have a Bond.

Idom took a long pull on his shaid, studied them, and realized he'd lost them. "Well. Now, I must find the Port Confluence Library and complete my task."

They all rose, then Idom paused in the act of turning away. With an impish grin dancing on his lips, he added, "It took three tries at the Guild House to get a library pass."

They all laughed and Kyllikki said, "All right, I believe you. I have only two errands in mind, but I'll see if I can concoct a third on the way."

She'd meant it facetiously, and the matter faded from her mind as she headed for the Panspecies Catering office at the edge of the field. Oddly enough, as early as it was, she was third in line at the counter.

Before she'd taken Zuchmul to the citadel, she'd decided to stock three stasis tanks of fresh orl blood for him, not two.

Tanked blood was the best they could do since the yacht couldn't accommodate live orl.

As she filled out the forms and tendered payment, she considered Idom's errand at the library. He hadn't mentioned in front of Elias that he had to consult the legal section. But even that shouldn't trigger any alarms that Zimor's people might have set into the system. Working Guides were always into the library systems counting things, trying to figure new safe routes between the planets of the Metaji. But then, why had it taken him three tries to get a pass?

The whole situation made her nervous, so she decided to walk to the D'sillin Service office, hoping the exercise would steady her. Checking the map, she set out briskly along the most direct route through the business district.

Most of the stores were still closed, but food shops were opening, delectable and distressing aromas wafting into the breeze to entice customers inside.

At one corner she paused, captivated by a display of musical instruments from all over the galaxy. She went up to the huge screen filling the entire wall beside the door and watched as the display cycled through its set sales pitch. These were instruments sold by the previous owners for emergency credit. Some were master level, concert-quality instruments. And a few of those were even affordable.

Elias! His emotions marched to a cadence, his thoughts were orchestrated in chords and movements, and if he couldn't have his own, at least he deserved something of this quality.

She pulled the touchpad out from under the display screen and keyed up all the stringed instruments the store had. There was one high-quality harp—the very simplest of all instruments, each string set to sound one note, but with adjustable tensions to allow tuning to any scale. She entered her order for the instrument, noting that she would return to pick it up at local noon when the store opened.

Then she set off again, her step considerably lighter.

The Escort Service office occupied the underground level of a large building about halfway between the field and the luren citadel. The reception-area lighting was dim, but the fact that she could see at all meant it was nearly painful for luren. The signs were duplicated in luren script, and it appeared that at least half the employees were luren, the rest a scattering of every species and race in the Metaji. The luren wore Inhibitors but no protective mesh.

"I am here to see D'sillin," Kyllikki told the luren at a desk situated behind a counter. The woman rose and leaned on the counter. "Do you have an appointment?"

"No," Kyllikki answered, tendering the data card she'd been given and telling her story. "I can return another time."

"I doubt that will be necessary," said the luren woman. "Will you step through here, please?" She indicated a gap in the counter arched over with a security scanner. If there was a light barrier to indicate the scanner was working, it was set at some wavelength only luren eyes could detect.

Kyllikki walked through the scanner's field, then followed the receptionist through a tunnel closed at both ends by heavy doors, then into a well-appointed sitting room from which three doors led deeper into the complex. "Please wait here a moment," said the receptionist and went through one of the doors. The label on it was in luren script only.

Kyllikki had just selected a seat designed for a human when the receptionist returned. "D'sillin will see you now."

"Thank you," replied Kyllikki and went through the door into near total darkness. For visitors' convenience, dots of light outlined the bases of the furniture and walls, just barely illuminating the floor enough to allow one to walk with confidence, but leaving the upper reaches of the room in shadow. Kyllikki crossed the room, her footsteps muffled in the dense floor covering. She paused before the desk, conscious that the luren behind it was examining her with interest. *D'sillin is luren. Why am I surprised?*

"Captain Kaitha Ray?" asked the feminine voice.

"Yes," answered Kyllikki with a squeak in her voice.

"I'm wearing an Inhibitor. I have the light turned down because my eyes have been strained recently. Do you mind?"

"Uh, no."

"Please be seated."

"Thank you." Her legs began trembling as she sat, and her mouth was dry. It was almost as if she'd been inundated with some sort of fear-inducing drug—or Influence. But it couldn't be Influence. She'd have reacted to that violently.

"Tell me, Ray," said D'sillin quietly, "when were you given the commission to transport Zuchmul to Hayelma?"

Zuchmul! She hadn't given the Ye're'y Zuchmul's name. "Is that any concern of yours?"

"It wouldn't be if you hadn't come into the Duchy. If I am to allow you to work for us, I must know why you have no orl accommodations aboard your ship, and why you ordered stasis tanks sent to your ship, not orl."

"Our contract specified the stasis tanks. Since we do not intend to take another luren-transport contract, we've no need for such an expensive item. And it's only six to ten dives from here to Hayelma. I have two Guides aboard. Three tanks is a five-hundred-percent safety margin."

"Two Guides, one of whom is a renowned Master who prefers the law library over routing research. Why would a small, independent charter that can't even afford to carry orl list such a Master as Guide?"

"You certainly have your sources of information." *How did she find out about the library!*

"Captain, I am luren. We are neutral in this war. The Four Stars is one of the few places luren are welcome, and I intend to keep it so. No luren, even a transient, will have reason to accuse the Baron or the Duke of failing to guard their best interests. No one else will have cause to see the Baron or the Duke as favoring us. Baron Tshiv is loyal to the throne, as is the Duke. As neutrals, our presence on Insarios is no threat to the Empire. Do you understand me?"

"The Baron must never regret harboring this community."

"Good. My company protects the *neutrality* of the luren of the Four Stars. Your ship is Teleod, and your Guide is—inappropriate. Your client is unable to speak for himself, but you are making no effort to provide for him properly. Are you Teleod or Metaji? Is he your prisoner or your passenger? If you are Metaji carrying a paying passenger, then why do you resist joining our service? We would provide you with orl facilities, and the stock to fill them, plus passengers and Guides proficient in Four Stars routing. You could leave here with a full load, not just one passenger."

Kyllikki scrapped Idom's idea of pretending to join the Escort Service, then disappearing. Trying to sound patient, she said, "We are a Metaji ship carrying a passenger, and we are just passing through the Four Stars. I take what ship I can get, what Guides I can get, and I try to make a living despite the war. An *independent* living. That's all."

Kyllikki felt D'sillin's luren senses focused on her, though without Influence. "So you won't join our firm?"

"I tried to make that clear to your representative."

"Very well, then you should have no objections to our picking up your contract and transporting your client, just so it won't appear to anyone that the Four Stars allowed a luren to be transported through here unwillingly."

The Duke was accused of kidnapping a Sa'ar, and now they're all nervous. She used her cover story. "We get paid when we deliver our client to Hayelma. We've invested—"

"I can have your stasis tank and blood fees refunded, and you may lift today, saving port fees. There's no reason a luren should suffer inconvenience to travel the Four Stars. You've brought him halfway and have been paid half your fee. You've no reason to object."

"I've given my word, backed by my personal honor. That can't be bought."

"Really? Independent charters don't make much profit. Suppose I offered you double the fee you received to bring Zuchmul here, along with my personal guarantee that we'll transport him to Hayelma on whatever schedule he chooses."

"You could afford to do that only if you told him we'd abandoned him, so he'd have to pay you. We're just starting in the charter business. What would that do to our reputation? I have a contract. I'm going to fill it."

Both the woman's hands slapped onto the desk. "What if Zuchmul doesn't want you to fill it? What if he'd prefer to travel with us?"

Kyllikki's heart stuttered. Zuchmul didn't know about the invasion of Barkyr, about Elias being a Dreamspy, or even that the person who signed him into the infirmary was his friend, Kyllikki, not Kaitha Ray, a hired charter captain. At least she'd put Kyllikki down as the person who had hired Kaitha, but had listed the venue of the contract as Wayward Cluster. Zuchmul would be bewildered and confused, with no reason to return to *Rising Tide*, a ship he'd never heard of.

Trying to seem perfectly collected, she rose. "Given a *totally* free choice, which would include an interview with me, I'm sure my client would prefer the arrangements already made for him. I bid you success in your ventures, D'sillin, and warn you to stay out of mine."

With that, she made her way back out of the office and hardly paused when her eyes squeezed shut in pain as the light hit them. She stalked past the reception area and out onto the walkway, squinting. She wasn't proud of the way she'd handled the interview. Somehow, she felt, a Laila ought to have been able to do better than that.

On the way back to the ship, she bought the harp and a case, tuning tools, and three spare sets of strings. It was worth, she was sure, ten times what she paid.

She sauntered back to the field as if she hadn't a worry in her head, glad that her feet didn't hurt in her new shoes. The harp was a burden, but she took time to see if she was being followed. She wasn't a total amateur at that game. She'd often given her bodyguards a hard time when she'd wanted privacy. She did spot an Effein she had seen outside the D'sillin offices. He was still there after three turns.

She led the Effein back to the ship and swung jauntily up the ramp. In the lounge, she spread open the harp case on the main table and called Elias up from the hold where he was repacking things to make them seem like old, prewar imports.

He came up the ladder into the crew's area, then out into the lounge, wiping his hands on a towel. He halted when he saw the harp. "What's—"

The expression on his face was worth the effort of lugging the instrument all the way back to the ship.

His bright-blue eyes glittered, and his cheeks flushed. A reverent smile blossomed, and his hands twitched. But he restrained himself at the last minute, and the hands clasped together. If she'd needed any more proof that he really was a professional musician, the manner of that restraint—the intense need to touch, followed by the ingrained habit of respect for another's instrument—would have convinced her.

"Kyllikki, it's beautiful. May I—"

"It's yours. A present."

"What?"

"I don't even know what sort of instrument you've lost, but I do know that nothing can replace it. When I saw this—I wanted you to have it."

Reverently, he lifted the harp. It fit into the crook of his elbow and against his shoulder like an amputated limb suddenly replaced. When he sounded the strings, she was glad she'd had the proprietor tune it so Elias could hear the resonance at its best in that first moment of acquaintance.

As the sound filled the lounge, Elias was transformed before her eyes. The harsh, tense planes and creases of Dream deprivation that had settled over his features like an ugly mask suddenly vanished. It was like watching a Teleod telepath engage and commune after a long austere discipline.

She found herself sharing his pleasure as he listened with his whole body to the pure sounds.

When the intensity had mounted to where she knew she couldn't stand it another moment, he silenced the strings and breathed, "Kyllikki, this must have cost a fortune! Three fortunes! I can't accept—"

She told him what she'd paid.

His face froze, then went blank, and when he looked again at the harp, it was with vibrant regret. "It must be stolen. You'll have to take it back. Kyllikki, this is a concert-grade instrument—probably handmade—"

"No probably about it. Turn it over. Look at the imprint. The proprietor didn't know what he had. Maybe I cheated him, but he didn't cheat me." She described the store where she'd found it. "It's not stolen. You can keep it."

She thought he was going to cry, so she turned to the main galley and said, "I'm going to have something to eat, then go out again." She knew she had to get a message through to Zuchmul, preferably before D'sillin talked to him. But she wasn't luren. She couldn't go where D'sillin could. She was dependent on the luren to tell her when he revived.

She couldn't discuss any of this with Elias. She had to wait until that evening to tell Idom all about D'sillin. After a fruitless day spent alternately pacing the citadel's waiting area and standing in line to ask questions every time the desk clerks changed, she was too depressed to inject any hope into her narrative.

But even so, Idom reiterated his prediction that Zuchmul would return in three days. If they could string things out that long, they could get away.

Elias was in his room with the harp while they sat in the lounge with the hatch closed. Idom reported, "At the library I worked through a sequence of references leading into the Dreambond material, to make it look natural. As you predicted, the Imperial Court has retained Verifier and Brainprint equipment. I don't know where they'll find trained technicians to run them, but the law accepts the results of both tests, when the results agree, as proof of the Bonding. But, for the Brainprint test to identify Zimor as Bonded to Elias, we need Zimor's Brainprint."

"No problem," answered Kyllikki without thinking. "It's a matter of public record for identifying Family."

"In the Teleod, maybe."

"You think there are no Imperial spies in the Teleod?"

"Good point. But it'll take longer while they send for the data, and it'll be harder to get them to take the risk."

"Don't forget I am—or was—a Lady of Laila, and the Imperial records show I'm a Bonder. Don't you think my accusation might carry enough weight?"

"Hmmm. If we can get to the right people, yes. And I think we *can* get to the right people."

The second day they took delivery on their stasis tanks and the uniforms, and other supplies. And Kyllikki haunted the waiting room in the citadel, asking after Zuchmul at ever shortening intervals, until the clerks became nearly uncivil.

But every so often, she noticed one luren woman watching her. The luren's work kept her moving through the waiting area. As a result, she often paused just beyond the warning signs to adjust her Inhibitor, and then moved behind the counters to speak to the clerks. Occasionally, Kyllikki saw the woman talking to the luren gate guards going on or off shift, coming in for treatment for exposure to the sun. Several times, Kyllikki recognized the woman who had been on guard duty when she brought Zuchmul in.

It didn't take telepathy to know they were talking about her. But even when she made herself as receptive as she dared, she detected no malice or even disapproval.

Often during her vigil, Kyllikki saw D'sillin workers bring in stasis units containing dormant luren. The escorts never sat in the waiting area. Apparently, D'sillin had a special clerk just for D'sillin clients. That night, she told Idom, "That Ye're'v was waiting for me. We're not going to make it through tomorrow. If they've been checking records—"

He asked her a series of questions focusing on the numbers she'd observed. She had most of the answers, for she'd had nothing to do all afternoon but count. He went to the pilot's station to run calculations, then paced the lounge. "You shouldn't go to the citadel tomorrow."

"But why?"

"More an inspired guess than a calculation. But think about it. What can you really expect to gain? You've left all the messages for Zuchmul it's possible to leave. They have their laws. If D'sillin can isolate him from us, she will, and your presence won't stop her. Then Zuchmul will decide and act for

himself. As I understand, he won't have to go through that waiting area to get out of the citadel."

"True, but—"

"So you stay here and we leave when Zuchmul arrives."

"At the moment, he has no reason to prefer going with us
over staying here or letting D'sillin take him to Hayelma. *He*
doesn't want to go to Hayelma! If he tells them so—"

"We're approaching the breakup of the crest. My advice is
that we should all stay aboard tomorrow." He fell into a morose
silence and refused to be drawn out any further on the subject.
After a while, he retreated to the Pool room, where he spent the
evening feeding the data into the astrogation library that he had
gleaned from Insarios' public files.

Kyllikki refused to go down to the Pool, especially in this
particular ship, and had told him so often enough. He was hiding behind the heavy insulation that prevented her from picking
up a whisper of emotions or thought.

Elias was once again shut up in his cabin, tuning and experimenting with the harp, but she couldn't have discussed the
problem with him, either. She paced and nibbled spiced nuts
until she'd eaten too much, then drank iced wallor until she
thought she'd float.

In the end, she decided that her desire to be at the citadel
was purely self-indulgent, a childishness she couldn't afford if
she intended to face Zimor and win. It came to her then that a
lot of her actions had been prompted by the same desire to
avoid emotional pain. Even her refusal to enter a Pool room
was based more on avoidance of painful memories than on a
desire to defend her oath.

If she couldn't withstand the temptation of entering a Pool
room—even when the Pool was locked down with a port seal—
how could she wrench Elias away from Zimor and *not* Bond
with him?

She found herself at the top of the stair leading down to the
Pool room, staring at the closed hatch. It was closed, not dog-
ged, and no privacy lights were on. She marched down the
steps, let her hand fall on the familiar levers, give the familiar

amount of pressure, and feel the hatch move aside with the familiar oiled smoothness.

She stepped through, giving the familiar half-turn to the right, and deliberately let her eye fall on the Pool which she had entered with uncounted numbers of partners.

It was an ankle-high raised disk of purest black, circled by a deeply incised collar with the directional markings clearly legible, markings that Idom would ignore when he used the Pool with Metaji methods. Locked down, the Pool's surface appeared to be a shining black mirror, dark and flawless, bottomless, beautiful . . . seductive.

She noted the port's sealing cable bisecting the blackness, short-circuiting the internal mechanism. It would be the work of moments to remove the seal, but while it was in place, she could even walk on the surface beside a male focus, even reach into the Pool with her mind, and still not activate it, not sink into it, not become one with it and her partner, not take the ship through it with her into—somewhere else. The desire, though, was still in her, the needs coming over her unbidden as she knew they would.

She could see herself venturing into that Pool, and beside her—beside her, Elias, bright-blue eyes sizzling, shoulders square and proud, and the smile of knowing anticipation welling up from within him as he reached—

"Kyllikki?"

She shook herself, forced her eyes closed, and wrapped her arms about her middle and faced him squarely, trying to shut the awareness of the Pool out of her mind. "I came to tell you that you're right, and I'll stay aboard tomorrow."

"Good." But as she plunged up the stairs, she thought she heard him breathe, "Probably."

chapter **nine**

....

"I'd say it's time to ask for departure clearance," said Idom.

They were all in the lounge sharing the wait. They had worked steadily toward this moment, practicing, stowing supplies, studying the yacht's systems, and rehearsing alternate plans. And in each scenario, they had assumed Zuchmul would have returned by now, or at least sent word.

Outside, a slashing storm drove hail against the yacht. But the weather hadn't slowed traffic; vehicles rated for such a busy port could deal with worse.

Elias objected. "Idom, we can't leave without Zuchmul." He compared Kyllikki's grim expression to Idom's. "Can we?"

Idom said, "If he doesn't come soon, he probably won't."

"The citadel told us maybe five days," said Kyllikki for the third time in an hour. "The Baron's officers know it. I refused D'sillin's bribes to desert Zuchmul. When we ask for clearance before hearing he's coming, what'll they think?"

Elias ran his fingers through his hair, making it stand up in white-blond spikes. The pale hair only emphasized the haggard, bruised look his face had acquired since the drug had blocked off his dreaming. But somehow his harp music had substituted for the dreaming, and his hands were steadier. "How should I know what they'll think? But I owe Zuchmul!"

They had finally told him about reviving Zuchmul because there'd be no way to hide that. But they hadn't told him why they'd risked it, and Kyllikki hoped that, if Zimor found out, she'd discount it as more of Kyllikki's folly. "And you're paying. You don't have to understand it all yet."

"Just promise me you'll explain it sometime. Idom said the local Baron is loyal, his Duke is loyal, and security is tight here. So why not just tell our story to the Baron?"

Kyllikki glared at Idom.

He shrugged. "How many loyal Barons and Dukes are there in the Empire? Zimor couldn't deduce anything from that."

She relented. "Elias, you know her intelligence network. Do you really think that if we go from Baron to Count to Duke, we'd reach the Emperor before she found us?"

"Doesn't sound too likely," he agreed. "But if we do it in a very public way—make news headlines—"

"I'm Laila by birth, you're Zimor's Bonded and have spied on the Metaji voluntarily, while Idom is a famous scholar expected to be more interested in science than politics. We've all been prisoners of the Teleod, and our escape sounds implausible even to me. The public would be screaming for our executions. How could we prove our loyalty to a Baron or a Count who doesn't even know us?"

"Well, but how can we prove our loyalty to the Emperor? How can we even get an audience?"

The only way she could think of to prove their allegation against Zimor was to get access to the Brainprint equipment and the Teleod Family records, which were available in the Metaji only at the Imperial level.

"Sometimes," said Idom, "I really wonder about you, Elias. It seems as if your early schooling pounded all the imagination out of you."

His eyebrows rose, but before he could rally to his own

defense, Kyllikki said, "Don't blame him, Idom. Dreamers would have to school their children very strictly because the incidence of stress-insanity, especially in dense population areas, is very high."

"Have you been to Earth?" demanded Elias urgently. "Do you know where it is?"

"Is that what you call your planet? No. I just know that a society of un-Bonded Dreamers is basically an insane society with high crime and violence and large numbers of mentally dysfunctional individuals." She squirmed out of her chair. The thought of Elias un-Bonded, teetering on the edge of that legendary state of insanity, was too much for her. She rose. "I'm going to wait in the air lock. The pilot's and owner's clearances are logged in, all the bills are paid, and we're on internal power. Ask for a departure slot anytime you're ready. But just remember—Zuchmul may still be unconscious for all we know."

She stalked across the lounge and down the access to the outer lock. They had left both hatches ajar, guarded only by the routine alarm system, which had been set off twice by the hail. Each time they'd come running, thinking it was Zuchmul.

Now she settled on the lip of the outer hatch, knees drawn up to her chin, heels braced against the cowling where ship's gravity and planet gravity met in a peculiar barrier that tickled the bottoms of her feet through her boots. When she hadn't been sifting through the war news, listening with horror to the consequences of the loss of Barkyr, she'd spent the day here, and now the light was waning and she was back.

She stared into the rain, watching it sluice down the ramp and form crusts of ice. Ground vehicles, sealed against the weather, scuttled to and fro among the ships, but there were few pedestrians other than Paitsmun, who leapt into puddles, splashing as they called greetings to one another.

She dissolved her barriers and Searched for Zuchmul's busy mind.

The sky darkened to an ominous orange hue. The nearest ships became smudges behind curtains of rain, their occupants telepathically shielded by the bulkheads. The Com Officers of departing or arriving ships were active in Window Rooms or, as with the yacht, Pilot's Bubbles. Kyllikki exchanged polite hails, oddly gratified that she was easily taken for a weak telepath. That supported her identity as a charter Captain of more use to the war as an independent than as a conscript.

Her new uniform was dampened by the rain and she was beginning to shiver when, in the far distance, she detected a faint but familiar whiff. Zuchmul. Confused. Doubtful. Changed. He was wearing an Inhibitor, but the difference was more than that. She'd read that revived luren displayed altered telepathic characteristics but wouldn't explain why.

Still, as she tracked the emanations, she was convinced this was Zuchmul, a very scared Zuchmul. She didn't dare do anything to betray her real abilities. There were too many good Com Officers around, and both the port and the Baron's own security guards had their telepaths.

She stood and palmed the intercom switch. But then she noticed that Zuchmul was no longer approaching.

"What is it, Kyllikki? Zuchmul?" came Idom's voice.

"I'm not sure. Could be just wishful thinking . . ."

Then she noted that among the sealed port service vehicles, cargo handlers, and personnel transports was a disproportionate number of Baronial guard vehicles. Each of those sported a burgundy stripe along the side and a roof fixture she'd thought was an ornament. Now she saw, as one of the vehicles cruised between *Rising Tide* and its nearest neighbor, that the roof housing peeled back to reveal a weapon. And in that particular vehicle, she detected the crisp joy of "Zealous," the suspicious Effcin guard captain.

The car glided out of sight around a cargo lander.

Zuchmul moved again, the veil of nascent Influence around him throbbing within the confining Inhibitor field.

//There! That's the luren! East of berth 433, behind that yellow tanker.//

The strange telepath's silent cry echoed in Kyllikki's mind for several seconds before she realized it was a Baronial guard tracking Zuchmul and alerting other telepaths in other Baronial vehicles scattered far across the field. Suddenly, they were all converging on the luren.

"It's him. Break the seals and get ready to lift!"

They'd never practiced an emergency lift-off without Kyllikki at the pilot's station. Still, she didn't dare move from the lock. She could see Zuchmul flitting from parked vehicle to docked ship to cargo pile as he tacked across the field toward them. He was a wraith, a gray shadow against gray, rain-slicked pavement, but to her perceptions he was limned in a glow of constrained Influence, throbbing with fear. A burgundy-striped car slewed around an occupied berth and rocketed across an open stretch of pavement directly toward Zuchmul's hiding place, its gun turret peeling back.

She had to take the chance. Using her every skill to keep it private, Kyllikki whispered directly into Zuchmul's mind, //Zuchmul, this is Kyllikki. Dive to your left!//

He hesitated, then heard the approaching vehicle. Without raising his head above the containers shielding him, he scrambled to his left, but not quite fast enough.

The vehicle's gun was a tight-beamer shooting a narrow cylinder of coherent energy. It was set on puncture, not slice, so it drilled a neat hole through the cargo containers and pierced his ankle.

His pain lashed through Kyllikki as if it were her own, and she realized her barriers had dissolved, the ever-present key image pulsing behind her consciousness. //Zuchmul, they are going to your right. Keep circling left. I'm coming.//

She was out and down the ramp before she could think. Around the yacht, out of sight from the hatch, was an empty berth encircled by loaded cargo handlers, awaiting an arrival. Their crews were huddled in a toolshed, all now watching the action in the distance, not their vehicles.

Kyllikki tumbled into the operator's place on an open truck attached to a train of three trailers, one with a cargo crane on its rear deck. It was vibrating, powered up and ready. Frantically, she searched the controls, then stabbed at glowing touchpads. The hitch released the trailers and the truck lunged forward with more power and speed than she had dared hope. She almost drove it onto the landing pad before she found a way to brace herself against the rack designed for a Paitsmun and steer at the same time.

She sideswiped another truck with a howling screech, and then careened toward Zuchmul, barely able to spare time to tell him, //I'm behind you in the little truck. Get on as I circle.// He glanced toward her, but kept moving, dragging his injured leg and keeping low amid stacks of containers.

Sudden wind slammed into the truck, throwing her off course just as one Baronial car spun its turret and fired at her. The shot blasted a hole in the ground where she would have been if not for the wind, and her heart slammed into her throat. At that same instant, the world went dark gray and filled with the hiss-crack of a hard-driven wall of hail.

The car that had shot at her lurched and skidded out of control, crashing into two others that were converging on Zuchmul. *Three. It's still working!* She slewed around to approach Zuchmul, who was wedged between two containers. Her knuckles were white on control knobs built for a Paitsmun, and her whole right side stung where hail had lashed her. Peripherally, she was aware of the Baron's telepaths yelling at each other in total disarray, and one mysterious concept came up repeatedly. Ripper. She couldn't imagine how two unarmed people could be terrorizing armed guards, unless they thought she was armed with a ripper. Whatever that was.

Pavement erupted on her left, spraying hot chunks onto her pants. Over her shoulder, she saw the car carrying "Zealous" closing on her, the gun turret tracking her. A loudspeaker said in an Effein voice, "By authority of Baron Tshiv, you are ordered to surrender to answer charges of treason." The warning was repeated in mechanical tones in three languages. "We are authorized to use lethal force."

Kyllikki leaned out and shouted to Zuchmul, "Get on!"

In a shuffling run, Zuchmul matched with the truck and leapt, catching the open framework, and dragging himself aboard. As his mass landed off-center, the truck, not built for high-speed turns, almost toppled over. Kyllikki struggled with it, her erratic course causing several shots to miss. As she turned back into the teeth of the wind, the shield in front of her quickly iced over, opaque.

One stark-white luren hand shrouded in fine mesh slid behind her as the other hand wrapped around one control knob. "Let go!" Zuchmul shouted in her ear. His voice was drowned out by the searing whine of a shot hitting the truck's crane.

She relinquished the knobs to him and found how to heat the forward shield. Zuchmul got the truck under control, continuing to zigzag across the icy field, as he yelled over the roaring din of hail and the pursuit cars closing in, "Give me one good reason not to surrender!"

"If you do, the Teleod will win the war and Zimor will revive the Triumvirate using dominated luren!" As she said it, she realized it was very probably true. Why else had they wanted total control of Zuchmul?

Their bodies were pressed together, putting her inside the field of his Inhibitor. She winced as his luren senses raked through her. Then he glanced at the semicircle of vehicles converging on them from the rear. Since the crash, none of the Baron's drivers dared top speed.

Zuchmul asked grimly, "Which ship?"

"That one. The yacht just beyond the empty berth."

He looked it over as the truck built up speed, two wings of ice water rising on either side of them. "It's Teleod!"

"Stolen!"

He skewered her with goggled eyes.

"Idom's astrogating!"

He nodded and stuck his head out around the icing shield, trying for more speed. To their right, another truck dragging a long train of trailers began to move toward them on a collision course. She could barely make it out as a shadow in the dim, dirty light, and she couldn't hear it over the increasing roar of the storm.

She twisted to watch the pursuers, who couldn't yet see the truck-train. "Faster, Zuchmul! It's going to hit us!"

Long teeth bared, he straightened their course, racing the truck-train. At that moment, the car just behind them hit a hole dug by the guns, bounced, and toppled. Kyllikki slammed her barriers into place, cringing as several telepaths screamed in shock as crash restraints immobilized them. Three cars plowed into the downed car and the others peeled off to avoid the pile. Several regained control and resumed pursuit, "Zealous" among them.

Then Zuchmul passed the truck-train, which moved behind them, then halted, cutting off her view. Only then did she identify the driver. Elias.

With the sound of cars crashing into the truck-train, and the ambient shock immobilizing all the telepaths in the area, Elias dived from his truck, hit the pavement in a roll, and came up running toward them.

Zuchmul glanced at him and hunched down to nurse more speed from their straining engine. Kyllikki clamped her hand over his, and shouted, "Slow down!" Then she squirmed free of the driver's rack and wormed her way around the crane. She saw Elias, arms flailing, try for a mounting grip, but his hand slipped on the ice-coated rear deck.

Kyllikki hooked one knee over a strut, then reached out beyond the rear hitch. As Zuchmul slowed, Elias' hand closed on her wrist, securing his purchase on the cuff of her uniform. He dived forward and almost made it. Desperate, Kyllikki reached over his back, grabbed his waistband, and heaved with all her strength.

Elias' feet left the ground and he teetered over the rear end of the truck as it bounced, swerved, sped up, then slewed to a halt, throwing Elias's head against icy metal.

They were at *Rising Tide*. As Zuchmul scrambled out of the cabin, she pushed the dazed Elias off the rear bed and jumped after him. Swaying, he grabbed her hand. "Come on!"

Zuchmul paused at the bottom of the ramp watching them, then, seeing they were moving, he scrambled up the icy ramp to the lock and, as their feet gained the ramp, the luren hit the ramp retractor. Using both hands on the slick railings, they reached the top just as the ramp came level.

"Secure it!" she said, running for the pilot's station.

Idom had completed the departure sequence, and as she threw herself into the pilot's chair, Kyllikki heard the Effein traffic controller screaming, "—accused of treason. Move and you'll be blasted from the sky!"

She twisted to look at Idom, who worked the Com Officer's displays as he muttered, "I can't find anything they could get us with. I've set the departure line so I can dive soonest. You have ninety seconds to hit my window."

She thumbed on the internal speakers and said to the traffic controller, "*Rising Tide* lifting. Clear my sky, I'm going. *Now!*" She rammed the controls home.

Another voice cut across the traffic controller: "All ships! All ships! Rippers sighted, bearing six-three-three. Clear the field!" Emergency sirens blared from the speakers and her monitor showed three black triangular shapes against the dim yellow sky. Now she knew what "rippers" were: funnel clouds with winds intense enough to knock a ship out of the sky. One was headed for the traffic-control building.

But it was too late to stay safely ground-anchored. The gravitics had lifted the yacht just as Kyllikki's board registered the lock sealed. Instruments now showed distance and time to the dive point Idom had selected.

Then the nearest ripper hit the traffic-control building, stripping away every external communications device. All the ties with traffic control went dark and silent. "I hope no one was outside!" said Idom.

She shook her head. "But what about us?" They climbed slowly above the port, compensators screaming as the wind buffeted them.

"There are three funnels," he said. "Forget the air law. Lift hard. Give it everything we've got."

Teeth clenched, she shoved aside all the safety locks and hit the emergency boosters. All Zimor's equipment was upgraded to military standards. This low in atmosphere, they would leave a trail of destruction behind to rival the storm.

Wasting power, the yacht screamed into the sky, only a slight tremor betraying how close to the limits they'd stressed the gravity compensators. In seconds, they were through the clouds, and moments later above atmosphere.

Kyllikki armed the intercom and told her passengers, "Secure for dive." She turned to Idom.

"On my way." He plunged down the stair to the Pool room. His voice came over the intercom. "Thirty seconds."

She spotted a couple of small fighters driving toward them, carrying enough fire power to reduce their yacht to atoms. However, the fighters could intercept only if the yacht tried to clear the system before diving. Idom had calculated a dive spot that was technically inside the system, one that was open only when all the other planets were grouped on the other side of the system's sun, as they now were.

Kyllikki knew too much of Pool functions to watch the dive point approach with equanimity. She held her breath, eyes wide as her displays died and the lights blinked.

She felt the Pool open and swallow Idom, the Pool room, the whole ship. As a passenger, she shouldn't have felt it, but it was there, compelling her to summon the key image she'd always used in the Pools. She barely subdued it.

When the lights and the display flickered and blinked back on, she felt a glow of undischarged arousal, something that should not have been there, had not manifested in a dive since she'd abandoned the Pools.

She hugged herself, shivering, and read her displays. They were in a huge, lazy orbit around a planetless red giant star. Idom's voice rattled through the ship. "Dive completed. All equipment secured. Location confirmed."

"Confirmed," she answered and blanked her displays so Elias wouldn't see, and possibly give Zimor their location. The chair squelched as she rose, and water puddled on the floor under her. She wrung her hair out, and joined Idom as he came up the stairs. Together they went into the lounge.

Elias and Zuchmul were limply draped over their chairs, staring at each other. There was blood on Zuchmul's right boot, but he grinned through his mesh mask at Idom and Kyllikki, then winced when he tried to rise.

"I'll get the medkit," said Kyllikki, pushing him down.

Elias slid out of his chair and knelt to ease the boot off. "Is it bad?" There wasn't much blood.

Zuchmul peeled off his goggles. "No, no, don't bother. It'll be all right."

But then Elias had the boot off and Kyllikki could see the angry red holes in each side of the ankle between the tendon and the bone. Elias said, "You were lucky. But it must hurt like crazy. Why isn't it bleeding more?"

As Kyllikki opened the first-aid kit, Zuchmul took the boot out of Elias' hand and inspected his own wound. "It's a neat hole. It doesn't even need a dressing."

Kyllikki had stocked a variety of luren supplies. "This time I've got the right analgesic for you. Hold still!"

She sprayed the vile-smelling stuff on the wound and held the foot when Zuchmul winced. It formed a transparent film and also disinfected the wound. "I'd say stay off that foot for a couple of hours until it finishes healing."

Zuchmul agreed, then his eye came to Elias, who still knelt, watching the nearly visible healing. "You're right, it does hurt—uh, I'm sorry. You just saved my life, but I don't know your name."

Amnesia! It was common after prolonged dormancy, she knew. But Zuchmul had recognized and trusted her.

"I'm Elias Kleef. Don't you remember? You saved my life and I caused your accident. Now we're even."

"You're the man we rescued?" He blinked, squinting against the ambient lighting through his protective inserts. "Yes, I do recognize you but not your name, and I don't recall the accident." He looked up at Idom, then down at Kyllikki. "The last thing I remember is bringing him aboard our pod. When I found out how much time had passed and that I'd wakened on Insarios, I thought surely you were both dead. Then when I saw your name on the commitment forms, handing me over to a charter originating in the Wayward Cluster, I figured something truly bizarre must have happened. And now—"

"Uh, Zuchmul—" interrupted Idom, glancing at Elias.

Simultaneously, Kyllikki said, "I think I should tell you the whole story in private, Zuchmul."

Elias rose and pulled her up by her elbow. "You should get into some dry clothes first. We all should."

Idom put one arm out to help Zuchmul up. "Kyllikki has some uniforms for you, and stasis tanks to feed you. It'll only take a few minutes to change, and meanwhile I'll tell you about the capture of Barkyr."

"Capture—!" He pulled away from Idom.

Idom slid his shoulder under the luren's arm. "Don't put any weight on that ankle yet!" He began the story while they went toward the passenger cabin they'd given the luren.

Kyllikki had to pull away from Elias. The warmth of his body, even through two layers of sopping-wet clothing, was reaching her in a way she knew she mustn't allow. And the caress of his mind was too pleasant. "Thank you, Elias. I'll only be a few minutes."

She slipped into her cabin. Once the door was shut, she sagged against it, pierced by an incredible longing that left her in throbbing confusion. It wasn't like the purely physical attraction she'd felt at first sight of him. Now she knew who he was. She'd fought Zimor for him. She'd heard his harp, if only faintly through the bulkheads. And she'd seen him risking his life for hers today. *I won't fall in love with a Dreamer!* Life was hard enough. She didn't need stupid complications that could only end in pain and misery.

She flung herself into the shower, scalding the scrapes and bruises, and sprayed herself with a healant. Examining her reflection, she saw one side of her face was red, pocked where hail and gravel had hit her. Her throat was raw from yelling, and her whole body felt pulverized.

In a fresh uniform, she returned to the lounge to find Zuchmul perched on the back of a chair swinging his injured foot and sipping from a lidded container. He wore a ship's uniform over his fine-mesh protective suit. The Inhibitor was visible through his open collar. He seemed more at ease than she could ever remember, but there was a residue of tension over-laid by a burning curiosity.

Elias was already there, and Zuchmul was saying to him, "Idom told me about the accident, and I don't think we're even. You risked your life for me. I owe you, if you want to keep score. But I'd rather just be friends."

Idom came out of the galley juggling three hot-meal trays. "Now, no more talk of our problems. Come and eat." To Kyllikki, he said, "I explained to Zuchmul that Elias has agreed to let us do the planning."

Elias brought a pitcher of hot shaid and Zuchmul joined them at the table, the first time she'd ever seen him do that. Of course, one couldn't very well bring an orl into the dining sa-loon of a passenger liner, but she had to ask, "Zuchmul, I've been told that using orl blood from stasis tanks is a real hard-ship, but you don't seem upset about it."

He cradled the covered mug between both hands and stud-ied it somberly. "It's an improvement over the pod."

"I guess they were right," she said.

"Whoever they were, they probably hadn't spent many years in space. *Prosperity* was the first berth I'd ever had on a ship large enough to carry orl."

Kyllikki dipped a crisp cake into a bowl of sauce and twirled it thoughtfully. "Are you avoiding the question?"

"Yes." Zuchmul grinned at her, and suddenly he was the old Zuchmul again. "If what you said at the port is true, then that makes any hardship worthwhile."

The two other men glared at her, avid with curiosity, but she ignored them. "So it is a hardship. I wish I could have done better for you."

He took another drink. "Actually, as stasis tanks go, these are top quality. Where did you get the money?"

It was Kyllikki's turn to grin. "Zimor provided it, along with the yacht. She goes for top quality."

Zuchmul cast an appreciative glance at the furnishings and nodded. "You stole it from her?"

"Not exactly," replied Kyllikki.

Idom said, "I only got as far as our imprisonment on Bar-kyi. Since all of that is old news by now, you may as well tell him about the escape."

So Kyllikki, with a few comments from Elias and Idom, recounted their departure from Teleod-occupied Barkyr. At first mention of Elias' being a Dreamer bound to Zimor, Zuchmul's eyes went round with shocked comprehension and his lips silently formed the word *Triumvirate*. "Sovereigns Be, Kyllikki, you meant it literally."

"It was supposition. But it could be true." Elias was puzzled, which was just as well. No use giving Zimor ideas. But Idom understood. "Wait, Zuchmul. There's more." She took Zuchmul into Zimor's cabin to finish the tale.

When she finally fell silent, he stared at her blankly for several minutes before he whispered, "I knew it had to be something truly bizarre." He leaned his elbows on the small table between them and propped his forehead in his hands.

She had sealed her barriers, concentrating on including each salient detail that had gone into her decision to try to break Elias free of Zimor. "You can see why we had to take so many risks to get you back. What I don't understand is why you came back with all the Baron's men chasing you."

"I didn't exactly understand it at the time, either, but now I can. I first became suspicious when D'sillin herself came to talk me—me, an insignificant space mechanic—into abandoning a charter hired to take me to Hayelma. She promised to give me passage to Hayelma free, if I'd send Kaitha Ray a polite note of dismissal. Kyllikki, did you have any idea how much I'd pay to avoid going to Hayelma?"

Astonished, she laughed at his aggrieved tone. "No! Idom picked it just to divert suspicion. We never intended to go there. But why would you—"

He cut her off. "Personal reasons. It's not important. But suddenly everybody wanted me to go there. D'sillin assumed I knew why and kept grilling me about it. The only person who really knew was the one who'd paid my fare through to Hayelma. So I called for the commitment forms. I *really* got suspicious when they questioned me about that. But then I saw your name, and I knew the only way I'd unravel this mystery was to get to *Rising Tide*. By this time, I had decided I didn't like the way power was working in that citadel." He broke off, assessing her expression.

"I wasn't too happy with the way they did business either. I told you about their waiting room, and—"

"That's not what I meant. It's the way they were using Influence—there's an atmosphere . . . Well, I doubt it would make much sense to you, but it made me suspicious. Then a woman came to see me, one who works in the outside waiting room. She told me about Kaitha Ray, a charter Captain who had gained an instant reputation in the citadel for standing up to the Baron's men who wanted to expose a stasis unit to the sun. She not only stood up to them, but made them back down without the help of the luren guard, who always had to intervene in such instances.

"The woman described how you returned to the waiting room to pester everyone for news of me, and she described you. People are very individualistic to luren senses, you know. There was only one person Kaitha Ray could be. I had to find out why you were using an alias. The more polite resistance D'sillin and her people put up, the more determined I became." Pensively, he added, "I'm not sorry."

"Does that mean you'll help me free Elias?"

"No."

chapter ten

•••••••••••••••••••••••••••••••••••••••

Kyllikki's heart fell. The exhaustion held at bay only by willpower now swamped her. "Well, I'm not sorry we got you back. You're still my closest friend in the Metaji."

He drew a breath to reply, then thought better of it and commented, "That's not the impression I got at dinner."

Shocked, she just stared at him.

"It doesn't take telepathy to see how you and Elias—"

"I *pity* Elias. I thought you'd want to help him, too."

"I didn't say I wouldn't."

"But you said—"

"I meant that solving the mystery of Kaitha Ray and the Wayward Cluster yacht *Rising Tide* was worth an indictment for treason to the Metaji, to which, as a neutral, I've never owed allegiance. I love delicious irony as much as any luren. Elias is another problem. I'm not convinced I *could* help, I'm not convinced that helping the Metaji win would be proper for a neutral, and—do you have any idea what kind of a violation of Metaji and luren law using Influence like—"

"You'd have Elias' consent."

"Would I? You haven't told him any of this, have you?"

"No, but I told you how he feels about what Zimor's done to him. And you saw today he's no coward."

"Hmm."

It was the most noncommittal noise Kyllikki had ever heard. "Assume he asked you to. Would you do it?"

He rubbed his hands together, the mesh gloves making a scratchy sound. "Also assuming I *can* do it, whatever exactly 'it' is, my answer is maybe. It needs thinking about."

"I guess it would. There are, as you once pointed out to me, good reasons for the laws governing luren, reasons I don't know. Would it do you any harm to Influence a human?"

"I doubt it. But is he really human?"

It was a serious question. She launched into her theory of the genetic relationships among luren, Dreamer, and Bonder, and how their talents should combine to dissolve a Bond. The theory had incubated deep in her mind for days, and as it spilled out, she marveled at the insights. Zuchmul listened as she addressed each of his objections in turn, then he halted her with a gesture. "I haven't understood half of what you just said, and I'm too tired now. I'm a mechanic, not a theorist. Maybe after I've had some sleep—"

Guilt seized her. "And you just walked out of the hospital! They hadn't discharged you yet, had they?"

"No. I had to break out of there."

"Break out—!"

"They didn't want me rejoining you." He toyed with the empty covered container that had held his meal. "Now I can see why. They don't know about Elias, of course, but they're convinced you're Teleod spies who've kidnapped me to use me. That must be what they told the Baron, to get him to bring out the guard. It's the strangest feeling to find you *did* take me in for revival because you wanted to use my abilities."

The old Zuchmul would not have said such a thing unless he meant it as an accusation.

For the first time since she'd begun her recital of events, Kyllikki softened her barriers and examined Zuchmul. The dif-

ference in him was astonishing. He was somehow older, more
mature, solid in the manner of someone drawing on decades of
accumulated knowledge. He wasn't accusing her, he was merely
bemused. She said, "I hope you know I'd have brought you to
your people eventually, regardless."

He raised his gaze from the container and met her eyes.
There was a great welling of emotion in him, so intense it was
unreadable. "Yes, I know."

"Is that why you didn't surrender to the Baron's forces on
the field? It's not the act of a neutral to defy Baronial authority.
You do want to see the Teleod lose, don't you?"

"I don't want to see them win."

"That's not a neutral stand."

"Yes, it is. I'd prefer to see a stalemate and an end to the
fighting. That's the best outcome for luren trade."

"Idom says with Barkyr in Teleod hands, they can cut the
Empire in two, take Veramai, then gobble up the pieces."

Before he could answer, she saw her opening. "Zuchmul,
listen! Our plan has the best chance of creating your stalemate!
The only way to preserve both civilizations is to oust Zimor
from power. The rest of the Families can be convinced to abandon the use of Pool Operators, and then the Empire would have
no further reason to press the war. The best way to turn the
Eight Families against Zimor is to expose what she's done with
Elias, and for all I know we might find I was right about her
ambition to subjugate a luren and create a new Triumvirate. It's
so in character!"

He crossed his injured leg over his knee and rubbed ab
sently at the wound. "So you say we can't expose her unless we
can reach the Emperor, and we can't reach the Emperor unless
I help you sever her Bond with Elias. But you said he hasn't
been Dreaming because of this drug. Why can't we just go to
Veramai with Elias using the drug?"

"I told you what happened when it failed. It's going to fail
again, soon. Did you take a good look at that man?"

"He looks sick, worse than when we rescued him."

She nodded. "He's fighting, and that's why the drug has

worked this long. You can't die of suffocation by holding your breath, and a Dreamer, especially a Bonded Dreamer, can't not-Dream. It's already threatening his sanity. What he did at the port—Zuchmul, I think he's courting death."

"A telepath's assessment?"

"No! He's got to have his privacy, especially from me. He knows that. He won't even talk to me about it." She wrapped her arms around herself and shivered. "But he doesn't have to. I can feel it. That's what you sense between us, not affection: the Bonder/Dreamer attraction."

"Wouldn't that get worse without the Bond to Zimor?"

"Yes. But even now, I feel Zimor everywhere. Waiting. Can we take *her* into the center of the Empire and still claim to be loyal subjects?"

He sighed, stared at his ankle. Kyllikki was sure he would promise to help, but the silence stretched on. Eventually she said, "If you won't help break the Bond, we'll devise another scheme. Elias has volunteered to go into stasis. I'm not sure that would stop his Dreaming, but we can try. Or maybe we could feed him false information about our plans, send Zimor off in the wrong direction, then try to get through her spies on Veramai. Or perhaps we could ditch this ship and take passage on a commercial carrier."

Zuchmul thought about all that, eyes closing heavily. "Neither Teleod nor Metaji condones the use of Influence on nonluren. It's a capital crime. This is *not* a simple problem." He continued to knead his ankle as he added, "Blood Law requires me to protect the interests of my new parent." He shot her a quick glance, then focused on his ankle. "She's highly placed in a trading family, and luren traders have won the trust of the galaxy because we *do not* ever use Influence in our dealings with nonluren."

"I see. Settle the war and you've provided a good trading climate for your new family, but if you do it by illegal use of Influence, you've disgraced them, and maybe forfeited your life." She sighed and got to her feet. "But I'm not so sure nonluren would condemn you for it. All luren might be honored for your courage."

He put his injured foot down and eased his weight onto it. "Blood Law looks at things a little differently." He limped to the door with her. "I must think about it."

"Your attitude toward law seems to have changed."

"Of course. I've changed. Everything's changed."

His voice shook. With her hand on the door, she turned to reassure him, but suddenly he was very near, limpid dark eyes in a stark-white face of elegant features. He had been reaching around her for the door release, so she turned right into his embrace. He didn't move.

The warm stirring she had ignored returned with a vengeance, paralyzing her. Every bit of her skin became exquisitely sensitive, her uniform harsh against her. *He's hungry!* She recalled his words. *"There is a rage to the hunger that comes then."* He'd referred to spontaneous revival, but now D'sillin's scorn of tanked blood made sense. Even after a normal revival, the hunger would be intensified.

With his free hand Zuchmul touched the side of his mesh mask and it fell away, baring his face to her. He drew closer, and she couldn't retreat. She'd rarely been so aroused, even when prepared to descend into a Pool. *That* sort of arousal she knew how to manage; *this* was different. It lacked the repellent quality his starvation had induced.

Slowly, Zuchmul reached for the torque around his neck, the Inhibitor. He paused as his fingers touched the catch, watching her intently. She couldn't breathe.

With a gesture that had become familiar to her in the citadel, he released the catch and peeled off the Inhibitor. Then, one hand braced against the door, the other holding the Inhibitor behind him, he leaned over and kissed her.

His lips adored hers, worshipped gently, and withdrew.

Every cell in her body glowed with pulsing abundance.

Their eyes met, his Influence a caress, gentle, controlled, not threatening to trigger her Family's reflex.

Abruptly, he turned away, flipping the torque about his neck and latching it with a snap. Another deft motion and the veil guarded his face again. "I'm sorry. I shouldn't have done that."

She hit the door release and fled into the lounge.

She came to a halt in the middle of the floor, facing toward the crew's quarters, wishing he'd follow, dreading it.

A rich baritone asked, "Kyllikki?"

She yelped, spun, and found Elias rising from one of the deep chairs, his harp on the floor beside him.

He stopped barely arm's length from her. "What's the matter?" He cut off, eyes narrowing. "Did he hurt you?"

"No!" She gulped air and lowered her voice, pasting her barriers together hastily. "No, of course not. I'm—I'm tired. I'm going to sleep." She tried to walk away from him with dignity, but when she reached the hatch leading to crew's quarters, she glanced back. Elias was watching her. Behind him, on the other side of the lounge, Zuchmul had paused with one hand on the door to his cabin, the one they'd stored the stasis unit in, waiting to see what she'd do.

Without breaking stride, she plunged into her room, ashamed that she'd run like a virgin. Somehow she had two men jealous over her, men who were both forbidden to her for very good reasons. And all she wanted was for one to save the sanity of the other. If Zimor ever found out, she'd laugh herself sick.

After hours of fitful sleep, Kyllikki went out and found all three men huddled over breakfast at the lounge table, heads together, all talking at once. They fell silent as she fetched herself a plate out of the warmer and joined them. Zuchmul put his covered container down and said, "Kyllikki, if you can convince me this has any chance of working, I'll try to help you and Elias."

"But—" Her protest died in bewilderment.

"It's got to be today," said Idom.

"But why?"

She looked at Idom. He looked at Elias, whose head was moving from side to side in what she now recognized as the signal for no. "I didn't sleep at all last night," he said. "I can't go on much longer—I told Idom—I guess it was an ultimatum."

"Elias admitted he's been hallucinating off and on for more than a day now," said Idom. "Veramai's six dives from here, and we can expect to spend a couple of days in the approach pattern. He can't go another eight or ten days, Kyllikki. So I told him what you're planning."

Her mouth opened but she aborted the protest.

Elias said, "When Zuchmul came in, I told him I wanted him to do it." He shoved the food on his plate around, then looked up at her. "No, actually, I begged him to do it."

His face was blotched, maybe from the ice storm, or maybe from tears. Kyllikki splashed yarage into her cup, and studied Zuchmul. "Why did you change your mind?"

He glanced at Elias, then focused on Kyllikki. "Last night—well, life is very precious at a new awakening. I didn't realize my only reason to say no was that it would mean forfeiting life—permanently—by committing a capital offense. That's a stupid reason. I wasn't thinking clearly. I owe Kyllikki my life. She and I owe Elias our lives from yesterday. Whether I do this or not, we're all likely to be killed trying to put this case before the Emperor, and she's right. This could end the war, with everyone winning—even luren. How can I refuse to risk my life to save millions? How can I refuse to *give* my life to save millions? So."

Elias shook his head. "No! I can't let you—"

They were all talking at once again, and it took a long time to convince Elias that someday they would win Zuchmul's case in court and get him cleared of any crime. Though Zuchmul never accepted the possibility, Elias did and once again asked Zuchmul to use his power to prevent him from clinging to the Bond with Zimor.

When Zuchmul had again agreed, Idom added, "Today."

Kyllikki said, "All right. Today, then."

They sat over the remains of breakfast as Kyllikki explained what she wanted to do, and why she expected it would work. Idom listened raptly, sometimes asking a pointed question or offering bits of theory. They experimented gingerly to discover if Zuchmul could use his power and still avoid Kyllikki's reflex.

She didn't know the vocabulary of Influence, so it took some time for her to describe what he was safe doing. As they mapped the edges of her reflex, Zuchmul learned quickly, and adhered to those limits with a sure precision that inspired her confidence.

Then they experimented on Elias, with Kyllikki in telepathic touch while Zuchmul found ways to dispel the hallucinations that floated through the Dreamer's perceptions.

Before long, they got into another wrangle about the theory behind what they were doing, Kyllikki again insisting that Influence, telepathy, and Bond were all aspects of one thing. Something in the way she phrased it made Idom slap both hands on the table and look at her in astonishment.

"What did I say?" she asked.

He waved that away, stared into space intently, then demanded, "Before Teleod Operators descend into the Pool, they induce sexual arousal, don't they?"

Her cheeks flared hot, but she kept her voice clinical. "Yes, of course. But then it continues to build."

"And they use a visual image of the destination to set the target path, not a numerical harmony, right? They don't *hear* numerical harmonies?"

"That's right. Targeting is all visual."

"Why haven't I seen it before? Kyllikki, your theory is right as far as it goes, but it doesn't go far enough. The two kinds of telepathy, Influence, and the Bond are really four aspects of the same thing, but *what* thing? The Pool is an artifact designed to make use of that thing." He looked from Zuchmul to Elias with a triumphal smirk. "And here you two are squared off against each other, subconsciously driven by that very thing." His eyebrows rose. "Or maybe not so subconsciously. And I never saw it."

"What?" asked Kyllikki.

"Sex," announced Idom.

"Idom!" complained Kyllikki.

"That doesn't make sense," said Zuchmul. "The Teleod uses sexuality in the Pools, but the Metaji doesn't. Since they work even better without the sexual element, obviously the Pool mechanism has nothing to do with sexuality."

"Wrong!" said Idom and shifted his scrutiny to Elias. He folded his arms across his chest. "Can you tell me that music doesn't interface with sexuality? And if the basis of music isn't number, then what is the base?"

Elias glanced from one to the other of them and shook his head in such pathetic bewilderment that Kyllikki had to say, "Of course mathematics is the basis of music, and nothing's more sexual than music. Most known species have a centralized nervous system that's basically numerical. Numbers are the subjective/objective interface. Every child learns that in school."

"Do Pool Operators ever use drums?" asked Idom.

"Well, it's a recent practice, but yes—"

"And now your theory has five elements: key images, audio-analogue, Influence, the Bond, and the Pool." He shoved his chair back and made a straight line across the lounge for the corridor leading to the crew's quarters.

They stared after him.

Kyllikki said, "I doubt if we'll see him for a while. So, while he's busy, why don't we get this over with?"

She led the way aft to Zimor's room, stripped now of all heraldic paraphernalia. With a flick of the wrist, Kyllikki turned the lights down and told Elias, "Kick your shoes off and get in the bed." She stripped the top cover off and flung it around her like a cloak, stationing herself cross-legged on one corner of the bed. "Zuchmul, can you drag up a chair and work from over there?"

He grabbed a chair that had been at the table and, with one toe, he released it from its floor mount, then swung it over beside the bed one-handed. "Position isn't important."

She felt the throb of gathering Influence, raw and unshielded by his Inhibitor. He had more power now than she had ever felt before, but more control, also. "Ease off with that," she told him.

He closed his eyes and the bone-penetrating power waned, but it was gathering, leashed tightly.

Gingerly, Elias slid into the bed and drew up the other cover. "As tired as I am, I don't think I can just go to sleep. Even the drug didn't put me to sleep last night."

"Zuchmul will take care of that. Just get comfortable."

"Zuchmul," said Elias, "don't let the nightmares start."

"If they're anything like those hallucinations, that won't be hard."

"I'm not sure it's exactly the same," said Kyllikki. "A Dreamer has a four-part cycle. This will take a while. Will you get cold?"

"No. I'm fine. Will Zimor know he's sleeping?"

"When he starts Dreaming."

"How will you know?"

"I'll know."

"I feel like a specimen," sighed Elias. He squirmed.

"I'm sorry," said Kyllikki. "This is awkward for all of us. But would you prefer the floor of one of the crew's cabins? Or the middle of the lounge?"

There was more than enough room on the enormous bed for all of them without any intimacy. But they had decided to use it before Idom mentioned sexuality, and now all three adults were as discomfited as adolescents.

"Let's just get this over with!" said Elias, rolling onto his side so he faced Zuchmul and away from her. "Zuchmul, see if you can put me to sleep."

They hadn't dared practice this part. She firmed up her barriers, drew the cover around herself like a tent, and focused on key-image drills, summoning total concentration.

"He's asleep," whispered Zuchmul. "Can you talk?"

She blinked and came partway out of it. Zuchmul was a deep shadow against shadows, but his power throbbed around him like a ruddy glow. She felt a tremor of defensive reflex, as he wavered. "What is it?"

"You didn't tell me he had false memories. They weren't planted by luren, though. I don't know if I can work around them without dislodging them."

Planted by luren! "I didn't know luren could—"

In a level, expressionless whisper, he said, "I don't think any luren *could* do anything this sophisticated. Detailed information has been implanted. What will happen if I disturb them and he suddenly remembers he never learned these things? Will his sanity survive it?"

Thanks to Zimor's meddling, Kyllikki knew just how unsettling such a penetration could be. Maybe it was something like a *nightmare*. "We have to risk it."

"All right, I'll take your word for it."

"Now I have to get ready to do this. Remember, I want to get at that Bond before he starts to Dream, before Zimor becomes involved. When I signal, feed him a fantasy that's so engrossing he won't notice what I'm doing."

"I'm ready."

She snugged her back against one of the posts that had held the golden canopy, then melted away all barriers and picked up her drill where she'd left off, surprised how easy the discipline was. As she concentrated, she became less aware of her aching body, of the rhythmic throb of luren power, and more attuned to the sleeping Dreamer.

It was unlike anything she'd ever observed in states-of-consciousness training in either Teleod or Metaji. Without effort, she became utterly absorbed in that rhythmic process, the stepped coordination between the brain's song and the heartbeat and respiration, utterly alien but complementary to her own.

Everything in her yearned to fall into that symphony, to become part of it, to soak in the pure sensation of pastel harmonies. *No!* She had to shake her head, scrub her face with both hands, then forcibly break her respiration pattern.

"Something wrong?" breathed Zuchmul.

"No. Did you know he has music inside him even when he sleeps?" *And some of it's in color.*

"Is that what that is? Should I do anything yet?"

"No. Wait." She adjusted her barriers to keep only a tenuous contact with Elias, then traced the key image of the working realm and entered the vast and formless landscape of the mind. It was a dangerous maneuver. If she had dragged Elias' consciousness with her, it could have been the end of him. But her old skills had returned, maybe even enhanced. The gray substance of the realm was hers now to work into any shape she desired even while she was conscious of Elias sleeping just an arm's length from her physical body.

She made the orientation key image under her feet, her working floor, provided pillars to define her space, and an arched roof, symbol of her barriers protecting her. Only then did she summon the memory of Zimor's Bonding image and direct herself to approach that Bond.

She formed a lane defined by a broad ribbon of green light flanked by rows of her distinctive pillars. As she walked the lane, she became aware of a waxing rhythm and melody. Approached from this direction instead of through Elias' mind, the Bonding image was a large rectangular frame braced along both diagonals. The intricate knot pattern was formed by a black filament, the pattern repeated in each of the four triangles of the rectangle. All four repetitions seemed to be formed of one continuous filament. And therein lay its only vulnerability.

Cut that filament anywhere, and the entire knot could then be unraveled, if one but knew the correct sequence.

She had divined that sequence when she'd seen it in his mind. What she saw now agreed with that memory. Only, from this perspective, she saw the frame as embedded in the wall of dark mist, forming a window into Elias' mind, a window screened by the knotted filament.

Behind the screen, the bright blobs of color danced in Elias' peacefully sleeping mind. He wasn't Dreaming yet.

Over her head, from the center of the frame where the diagonals crossed, a thick black cable, pulsing and writhing like a living thing, soared off into the mists behind her, connecting the image to Zimor. That cable divided into the filament which formed the knot pattern within the frame and came out on the other side, she knew, wound into another cable extending from the frame down into Elias' mind—growing roots into his consciousness.

Seen from this perspective, it was easy to discern just how

to break that Bond, but she knew that it wouldn't be easy. The instant she touched cable or filament anywhere, Zimor would be summoned, and so would Elias.

During the *nightmare*, she had almost been drawn against the image from the other side, yanked against it by Zimor, who must have expected the knotted filament to cut Kyllikki's mind into a million pieces as she was forced through the pattern like thrixal root through a sieve.

She had to prevent that from happening this time, and she had to devise a way of snapping that filament. She was under no illusions about how tough it would be, especially once Zimor's consciousness began tracing it, wakening the dark substance with the energy of life. She'd seen how searingly brilliant Zimor's point-consciousness was even at this distance from her Bonded.

Behind the window into Elias' mind, the colored blobs began to coalesce into shapes that hinted at form and meaning— the kind of images she'd seen Elias Dream before. But now there was an agitation, due, no doubt, to his long deprivation. That could bring on premature Dreaming and perhaps, for all she knew, *nightmare*. So she set to work at a feverish pace.

First, she erected two flanking columns of her own pillars along a path beneath Zimor's cable, made them tall but strong, so that when Zimor followed the cable here, she would have to pass between Kyllikki's markers, essentially traversing Kyllikki's territory within the working realm.

At irregular intervals, she erected her own key-image traps, huge webworks across the path. Only the cable of the Bond itself passed through those traps. If Zimor was careless or hasty, she'd be at least annoyed by the traps.

Next, Kyllikki erected traps that only she could pass through all along the path that led from Elias' window back to her own floor and roof, protecting her line of retreat.

Then inspiration struck. She made the very last trap something no one trained in the Teleod would expect: pure, paralyzing *sound*. Sound could disorganize the central nervous system. For good measure, she went back to Zimor's approach line and added two traps consisting of the dull, almost inaudible throb that induces fear. She backed away from it as she armed it, wondering if it was such a good idea. Zimor often said fear was a tonic to her.

Noting how the whirling blobs of color behind the screen of the Bonding key now seemed to be people, she bent to her task of creating tools and weapons.

When she'd created everything she might need, and had hidden it all in mist or beneath the floor, or inside her pillars, she took one last look at the people forming behind the window and raced back to her floor, to the spot where she'd appeared. Orienting swiftly, she surfaced in her body and whispered to Zuchmul, "Now!"

Then, without waiting to feel the Influence gather and focus on Elias, she returned to the realm and raced back to the Bonding image. Already, Zimor's side of the cable was vibrating, and Elias' brilliant colors had become Idom and Kyllikki in the lounge, voices edged with fatigue and anxiety, saying exactly what they said when they'd decided that Elias would not be part of the planning.

He was recapitulating events since the last time he'd Dreamed for Zimor.

Trying to ignore that and trust Zuchmul, Kyllikki bent to heave a huge two-headed clamp into place along a stretch of filament in the frame. As soon as the second head latched on, she heard Zimor scream. *Trap one?*

Without looking behind her, Kyllikki bent to seat the rear end of the clamp in the socket in the floor, and then to winch the clamp's heads apart to stretch the filament out of shape, distorting that segment of the key image.

Until the clamp was freed, Zimor could not get at Elias, and if Zuchmul succeeded, Elias wouldn't get at either Zimor or Kyllikki. She took the rotary saw she'd made, energized it with her personal force, and braced it into the holder over the filament. Why hadn't Zimor made any other sound?

Grimly, she rammed the whirling saw blade against the filament, holding in her mind the key image for severance and visualizing the thread parting with a resounding snap.

A cold hand grabbed her shoulder and spun Kyllikki away. She smashed into one of her own pillars. Dazed, but still holding the visualization, she saw Zimor scrabbling at the clamp. She had never been good with machinery.

Gathering her feet under her, Kyllikki noted Zimor's disheveled appearance. Never, in any training exercise, had Kyllikki succeeded in marring Zimor's symbolic appearance.

But the cable overhead was now glowing brightly in the wake of a searing point of light, the locus of Zimor's consciousness. It had almost reached the center of the frame. To either side of the cable, where the point of light had passed, Kyllikki's pillars were wavering and indistinct. She was now in Zimor's mind as much as Zimor was in hers.

She gathered up one of the weapons she had prepared, a large sheet of damp darkness, and crept up behind Zimor, who was struggling to stop the whirling saw. Hurling the sheet over Zimor, sticky side down, she retreated.

Unfortunately, Kyllikki was too hasty and the sheet only clung to Zimor's back and shoulders. Still, she straightened, offended as she fought free of the noxious thing, and searched for Kyllikki, who was hiding behind one of her pillars. With the spinning saw still attacking the filament and the moving point of light now tracing its way around the Bonding image, Zimor unaccountably paused to refurbish her appearance.

In a flash, the ragged drapery of her gown was mended, the blistering sores on her skin and face disappeared, and her hair resumed its impeccable coiffure. She glided toward Kyllikki's hiding place with a stately stride. She had discovered that the only way to stop the saw from severing her Bond was to break Kyllikki's concentration.

Briefly, Kyllikki closed her eyes and reinforced the severance key and the vision of the parting filament. It was easier this time, as if the saw had made some progress. Then she glanced at the Bonding image and saw only a dim mist on the other side. Elias' consciousness had been drawn far away. Had Zimor noticed yet?

Kyllikki reached inside the pillar and grabbed the pump she'd hidden there, then began circling away from Zimor, back toward the Bonding image, so Zimor would have to turn toward it, eventually noticing its darkness. If she hadn't felt it already, that sight would shake her.

She didn't have to best Zimor, but only harass, divert, and delay her long enough for the saw to work.

Warily, Kyllikki circled as Zimor closed in on her. The pump in Kyllikki's grip gave her pause, though, and Kyllikki almost made it back to the saw before Zimor sprang.

She hit Kyllikki at waist level, and they both went down, the pump flying out of Kyllikki's grasp. They rolled, Zimor dragging them away from the saw.

Kyllikki relaxed, closing her eyes and concentrating on the severance key and the visualization, feeling it get easier with Zimor's attention diverted. With the barest corner of her mind, Kyllikki tangled one hand in Zimor's gown, and when Zimor rolled over onto her again, Kyllikki used the motion and the merest whisper of a thought to rip the fabric—which was nothing more nor less than Zimor's own mind. It was the most real damage she'd ever done to Zimor.

She screamed and recoiled. Kyllikki scrambled free and dived for her pump while, with a tiny free corner of her mind, she ignited the incendiary film she'd laid over the ground. Zimor was no longer standing on the patch when it burst into flame. She was advancing directly at Kyllikki, a snarl on her face and a coil of bright-gold fire looped between her hands like a throwing rope.

The rope, Kyllikki knew, was charged with Zimor's own mental energy, a part of her self, and if she could complete even one turn of it around Kyllikki, Kyllikki would be paralyzed, bound in thrall to her cousin. Her mind would cease to function independently; the weapons, the tools, the realm-defining pillars, and even her floor and roof would disappear. There would be no way for Zimor to guide Kyllikki back to her body, even if she wanted to do so.

Against lethal force, Kyllikki's little pump seemed so inadequate, but it was all she had.

Desperately, she backed toward the frame of the Bond image and aimed the pump, showering Zimor with a black sticky oil reeking of flammable hydrocarbons. It was Kyllikki's oldest and most effective trick against Zimor's strength. Each time she filled the pump with something more filthy or disgusting, and it always broke Zimor's concentration. This time, it didn't. Zimor calmly extinguished the burning rope and advanced. But Kyllikki lunged for the saw and rammed her whole weight down on it, her entire mind centered on forcing it through the filament before the glowing point that was tracing the knot pattern around the frame reached this segment and grabbed her mind as it had before.

The filament gave a little, and she checked the progress of the moving point that had nearly killed her last time. It was white-hot against the dimness of the realm beyond the Bond screen, but it wasn't moving.

Kyllikki whipped her head around to where Zimor stood, fully expecting her to be closing in again with some new lethal weapon. But the woman was staring slack-jawed at the Bonding image, or rather through it to the formless charcoal mist beyond. *He's not dead. The Bond image would disappear if he were dead.* Kyllikki brought everything she had in her to focus on the filament under her saw, and bore down hard.

The filament parted with an audible twang.

Zimor's scream blended with Elias' agony.

Kyllikki fell forward, nearly cutting herself before she could dissolve the whirling saw and the twin-headed clamp.

As she rolled on the ground, Zimor crumpled, and the Bond knot began to unravel, the ends whipping around and around the frame, disappearing like burning fuses.

Kyllikki humped to her knees, then staggered to her feet, knowing that she had until those ends met to retreat. But she paused beside Zimor, who was kneeling, curled over her pain and sobbing, suffering something Kyllikki had never known, the severance of a Bond.

She couldn't find any pity for her cousin. She took off for her protected pathway as fast as she could move. Within moments she was back on her own floor. Only after she opened her physical eyes did she start to shake. But then she found herself wrapped in Elias' arms.

chapter eleven

●●●●●●●●●●●●●●●●●●●●●●●●●●●●●●●●●●●●

Luren Influence beat at her from behind. In front, even through layers of cloth, she felt Elias' intense arousal.

Battered, stripped of all resistance, she couldn't help her response. And now there was no tinge of Zimor's presence, just the rich music that was Elias, a free Elias unaware of the amputation of the Bond. Something in her that had never really been touched before woke and demanded, needed, this man. *If only he weren't a Dreamer!*

But he was, and she was un-Bonded, open to him on all levels. Inwardly, she saw the brightly colored shapes she'd glimpsed through the Bonding image now gathered in full force, orchestrated to a symphony. When Kyllikki had cut the Bond, Elias had been held in Zuchmul's Influence in a reality more attractive to Elias than the Bond.

His head was thrown back, eyes closed, bliss wiping years from his age, as he breathed in a heavy, unmistakable rhythm. But he was unaware of her. His eyes flicked back and forth, visible proof of Dreaming. His gathering Dream invaded her, building on the foundation of the fantasy Zuchmul must have chosen.

She was with Elias in a pavilion walled by transparent draperies that billowed in a zephyr breeze. Beyond the draperies, rocky terraces fell away to a brilliant blue sea dotted with boats. Perfume laced the air. Their couch was cool satin. And there was nothing but the two of them. //"Ah, Kyllikki!"// he groaned. //"At last! Now! Now . . ."//

It's going to happen, and he'll wake to find—

She stiffened her arms against his chest, finding herself bound by twists of the blanket she'd wrapped around herself. She called, "Zuchmul! Stop it! Zuchmul, no!"

But he didn't hear her.

Jerking her head around, she saw Zuchmul in his chair, feet propped on the bed, head lolling back, mouth open, hands clutching the arms of the chair until the tendons stood out, as if in dread of impending ecstasy. His lips shaped her name over and over. *He's lost control of it!*

She stopped struggling and marshaled her last remaining strength. Directly into both men's minds, she projected the stinging pain of a slap. //No! Wake up!//

Zuchmul came out of it first, his feet crashing to the floor as he gasped, *"That's* a Dream?"

Elias croaked out a strange word, but his eyes focused on her before he doubled up and began screaming.

"The Bond!" she yelled at Zuchmul. "I broke it. Get me out of these blankets!" Zuchmul fumbled her free and spilled her out on the floor. Clutching the side of the bed, she dragged herself back to Elias. She couldn't breathe for the hot vise of pain clamped on her guts. *No, it's his pain.*

She got control and, crawling onto the bed, she peeled one of his eyes back and found only white.

"Kyllikki, you shouldn't—"

"He's dying! You don't know what I did to him."

He pulled her back against his chest. "He'd rather die than Bond again. Let me see to this as we planned."

He's right. Sovereigns Be, but he's right.

Influence gathered, beating through her and Elias with a searing heat. Dimly, she felt the nervous tremor of reflex building. Zuchmul was exhausted, too, his precision gone.

She scrambled to the end of the bed and flung herself out of the room. With the door shut behind her, she was able to reassert control, but she clutched at the bulkhead. Too pulverized to reassemble her barriers, she gulped in the sweet air, utterly free of Zimor's taint. *Zimor's gone!*

"You succeeded," said a weary voice echoing in her mind. *Not that again!* She knew she hadn't spoken aloud. "Don't touch me, Idom." It came out as a tremulous whisper, not a command, but he stepped back warily.

Knees shaking, Kyllikki propelled herself toward the crew's quarters. "Elias may be dying. I don't think you should go in there, though."

He followed her across the lounge, which had taken on the proportions of a landing field. When she faltered, he made abortive gestures at her but she waved him off. Without being asked, he closed the hatch to the lounge behind her. When she had sealed herself into her cabin, she collapsed on the bunk, surrendering to Elias' pain, Zuchmul's fumbling aid, and Idom's roiling anxiety. At least they swamped out her own soiled feeling. *Without a qualm, I left her there to die! I'm no better than she is.*

They were alone in space with not another mind within her range, so when Zuchmul finally prevailed over Elias' pain and alleviated Idom's anxiety, the ship's insulation was able to provide Kyllikki with enough peace so she could restore her own barriers and lapse into an exhausted sleep.

She woke to the awareness that, despite her callousness, her cousin had probably survived. Kyllikki had won much too easily. Zimor would be enraged now, much harder to vanquish.

Barriers tight, Kyllikki emerged to find Idom puttering in the galley while Zuchmul was picking up litter and straightening the furniture. It looked as if they'd kept a long vigil. Zuchmul stopped as she approached, his Influence drawn up tight about him and subdued. "Are you all right, Kyllikki?"

"No permanent damage, anyway."

Idom came out carrying a pitcher of yarage and some mugs. He gave her a once-over, then set the things on the table and said, "I fixed you a hot meal."

"Thank you. I'm ravenous."

"Good. Zuchmul, I've got Elias' tray about ready—unless you want me to take it to him."

"No, I will." He avoided her and went to the galley.

"How is he?" called Kyllikki, as she poured yarage. Elias' presence was a droning hum lacking the melodies that had persisted even when he couldn't Dream. *But he's alive, and Zimor will be trying to get him back.*

Zuchmul emerged with the tray. "I stopped managing the pain about halfway through the night, but he kept sleeping. This morning he's recovering. He's tough."

Kyllikki agreed. "Tell him I'm sorry it hurt so much."

Zuchmul glanced back. "I'll tell him." He left.

Idom was standing in the galley watching her. She sipped her yarage. "How soon can we start for Veramai?"

"Are you going to pretend nothing happened? Can't you see how embarrassed Zuchmul is about that fantasy he built?"

They've been talking all night. She buried her nose in the steam from her mug. "I'm embarrassed too, but that's not usually lethal. Underestimating Zimor can be lethal. How soon can we dive?"

He continued to examine her.

He's upset, too. From behind her barriers, she guessed why. "Idom, I didn't mean to bespeak your mind directly in the hall last night. I apologize."

"You've my permission for that anytime. I trust you. But Zuchmul is worried you won't be able to trust him again. We'll never make it on Veramai if we don't trust each other."

"You're right." The yarage suddenly tasted vile. "I'll talk to them, but first we have to start for Veramai. There will be plenty of time between dives." A Guide usually made one dive per waking period. One Guide, six dives, six days.

He turned into the galley and his voice came to her. "I'm ready as soon as I have a pilot who's not fainting from hunger." He emerged with a tray of steaming mismatched food.

Zuchmul returned with his covered mug freshly filled and assumed his now accustomed place at the table. "I think he's all right. He said he'd be out soon, but I told him to take another long nap first." He raised his eyes to Kyllikki. "Was I right? We're going to dive now?"

"We have to. We may already be too late."

Idom asked, "What could Zimor do? She probably figures we're going to Veramai, but she can't guess which port."

"I don't know what she can do," replied Kyllikki glumly, "but we won't like it." She told them how Zimor had used a lethal weapon. "She's decided to kill me. The only way to win now is to move faster than she imagines we can."

"I think I can make Veramai in five dives."

"You said six! Minimum."

"Six staid and predictable dives, or five theoretical, thus dangerous, dives. Is it worth saving a day travel time?"

"How much risk?" asked Zuchmul.

"Who can say? But I'd like to test the theory you and Kyllikki gave me yesterday. If true, it'll revolutionize our concept of Triumvirate technology, including the Pools."

"And if it's not true?" prompted Zuchmul.

"We'll get lost."

"That doesn't scare you?"

"It's never happened to me. Every time I've missed a target, I've been able to get back. But there's always a first time. Would you rather six-dive?"

Kyllikki met Zuchmul's eyes and found agreement. "No! Five it is, if Elias agrees to the risk."

Elias did agree, and the first dive went smoothly. Then they argued about how to approach the Emperor.

Elias said he was known to four of the Imperial Heirs, all of them human males. At the time he'd performed for them, he had not known that they were only four of a hundred Heirs from whom the next Emperor would be chosen, and that almost all the races, species, and sexes were represented among that hundred. Elias had thought he was dealing with the sons of the Emperor. Still, any of those four might do.

Zuchmul objected, "Zimor knows you know those men. She'll have them watched. Besides, there's a war on. Most of the Heirs are out risking their lives for the Empire and vying for support in their bids for the Throne. We need to go for someone who's likely to be on Veramai now."

Kyllikki suggested one of the women who had sponsored her for retraining as a Metaji telepath. "She held the rank of Duke for twenty years. But she's too old to be out on the battle front, and handles the policing of the Communicators. She has the Emperor's ear, socially and professionally."

"She'd know your oath is compromised," objected Idom.

Idom was mentor to the head of the Guild, who was the Emperor's closest adviser in the war, and Zuchmul had a relative who was the luren Ambassador to the Throne.

Idom knew something of the security at the different ports of Veramai, and Elias knew quite a bit about the depth to which Zimor's spies had penetrated port operations. Every morning over breakfast, they argued, then Idom took them through their dive, and Kyllikki handled the traffic with passing ships, giving a different identity after each dive while asking for the war news. They decided on the identification they'd use for landing at Veramai, not seriously expecting it to divert Zimor, but hoping to avoid attention.

Just for that reason they chose to go into the busiest port, the one at Vindara, the Emperor's official residence. The entire planet, plus several moons, held the offices of government, but Vindara itself was the central hub where the major decisions were made and announced.

Vindara Port had, of course, the largest number of Zimor's spies, but she knew that Elias knew that and she might, therefore, expect them to avoid it. Vindara had the tightest security, but security was vigorous everywhere on the planet. It was the most expensive of the ports, but they had an expensive-looking yacht and perfectly valid credit instruments. All they needed was an hour to get clear of the ship, and then they'd trade identities again and disappear into the hallowed precincts of the Guide's Guild College.

The strongest argument was that the Guild headquarters, the luren Embassy, and another of Kyllikki's connections, a former Imperial Heir, resided in Vindara advising the Crown. So if one plan failed, they had alternatives.

As they argued through all of this, redressed the yacht to pass customs, chewed over the war news, learned their new names, pored over maps of Vindara, and planned where to meet if they got separated, Zuchmul strove to get Kyllikki alone.

She did her best to elude him. She didn't need any more complications. She and Elias had mutually agreed to forget what had almost happened between them. Neither wanted to start anything they dared not finish for fear of arousing their mutual need to Bond. But the stress remained, drawing her nerves taut, leaving her no strength for Zuchmul.

Each time she heard Elias' voice, she remembered his mental voice uttering her name, fraught with intimacy. She wasn't just a woman to him, nor just a Bonder. If that were all she was, he'd avoid her. Instead, he, like Zuchmul, took every chance to sit near her, to work beside her in the galley or the pilot's station, to bring her snacks, and even to offer to rub the knots out of her back after a dive.

Often, she'd catch Elias in mid-gesture and remember how he'd first approached the harp she'd given him, and the burst of pure joy that had lifted her then. As the shock of the dis-Bonding receded, his inner music returned, and, despite her barriers, it spilled over into her mind like a silken balm to her nerves. Though the frustration of being near a Dreamer made her want to flee him, his music drew her inexorably.

Over and over again, she recalled the moment on Insarios when she'd seen Elias on the truck-train behind them, blocking the pursuit. She pictured his mad dash across the icy pavement, and felt his weight as she had hauled him onto their truck.

One day, after their evening meal, she asked, "Elias, where did you learn to tumble like that?"

"Hmm? Like what?"

She described how he'd jumped from the moving truck.

"As a kid, I wanted to be a stunt man." He smiled shyly. "Most kids want to grow up to do dangerous things."

"A stunt man?"

"On primitive worlds," he explained, "a writer uses his computer to write words, not actual scenes, then live people have to do the things the writer has written down, pretending it's all real. Then other people watch the recordings just the way you would, except it's only audio and visual."

She gaped at him. It was inexcusably rude, but suddenly the incredible adjustment he'd made became real to her, evoking a stunned admiration for the man that threatened to burst out of her and splash into all the minds around her.

Peripherally, she glimpsed Zuchmul watching her with a desperate expression. Instantly, he turned his face away, and only then did Elias' voice come through to her. ". . .all illusion. Mostly it isn't dangerous, but when I was a kid I thought it would be—well, heroic work. So I learned a lot of the skills, only to find out later that I'd rather sing."

Idom said, "You've never sung for us. I'm tired of the sound library of this ship. Would you sing?"

Kyllikki realized with an abrupt shock that she'd never turned on the sound in her cabin. She hadn't missed music because adding anything to Elias' music would have created noise. *And I thought my barriers were so good!*

Shrugging, Elias went to get the instrument.

Zuchmul stirred in his chair, and Idom looked at him questioningly. "Will harp music bother you? It's not a powered instrument, so there wouldn't be any magnetic flux."

Zuchmul squirmed again. He had his Influence drawn up close around him, a pale flickering corona with hardly any power to it, his equivalent of being barriered. It worked, too, for it made it very hard for Kyllikki to discern his emotional state. If she hadn't caught that strange desperate expression a moment ago, she wouldn't have known he was lying when he said, "Oh, no, it won't bother me."

Elias returned before she could think what to say, and Zuchmul donned a mask of polite endurance. As Elias tuned the harp, she decided that the flash of desperation she'd seen was akin to the silent tension Zuchmul radiated before a dive, which wasn't at all like him, especially not when Idom was the

Guide. But after the dive, he'd behave normally for a while, then fall into a contained agony.

He'd been fanatically careful with his Influence since they'd freed Elias, but he hadn't taken to wearing the Inhibitor again. He'd asked lightly if anyone minded his not wearing "that thing," and explained that it was the one thing about life as a spaceship crewman that he loathed.

No one had had any objections, and for a while he'd carried it on his belt loop, but then it had remained in his cabin. And no one missed it.

Now, she thought she understood. He regarded the use of Influence on Elias as such a major breach of the covenant that allowed luren into space that he had already sacrificed his life. Ultimately, there would be no way to hide what he had done. He regarded himself as awaiting execution. There was no more reason to suffer restriction to earn privilege. His life was over. No wonder he was brooding and desperate. Ashamed for avoiding him, she decided she'd find the strength to take him aside and let him talk it all out.

Elias struck a chord, finally satisfied, and said, "I haven't mastered this thing yet, but is there something particular you'd like to hear?"

"Something original," said Idom, "that you composed."

"How about this?" His fingers created a ripple of sound and his voice seemed to grow out of that background.

Setting a rhythm and moving lightly from chord to chord, he sang the story of their escape from Barkyr, broke into another key with a wilder tempo, and sang the destruction of Port Confluence by rippers. He made it seem like a hilarious comedy of errors, with Zuchmul the real hero of the day. When he lapsed into silence, Kyllikki locked gazes with Elias and her laughter filled the room, harmonizing with his as both voices rose. She was laughing at the weird sensation of hearing with her ears what she had been living with in her mind all this time. She was glad she'd gotten him the harp.

The sound of his laughter twining through hers was a bone-deep joy; she didn't want it to stop, but eventually it had to. Then she noticed Zuchmul was withdrawn, suffering.

Elias didn't notice, but Kyllikki didn't need telepathy to sense that the luren's endurance was breaking. He had chosen a seat next to Kyllikki, with Elias across from him, so she had to turn her head to look from one to the other. But she knew that when she looked at Elias, Zuchmul's attention focused exclusively on her.

Oblivious, Elias created a ripple of luxuriously rich, slow, rhythmic sound. He sang in some Dreamer language, but the meaning came through her barriers carried on pure emotion. And when he was done, she knew his aching need and wanted to go to him and be what he needed.

She flung herself to her feet. "Excuse me. That was lovely, but I'm very tired. Good night." She almost ran for the crew's quarters.

The harp complained as Elias set it aside and started after her. "I'm sorry, Kyllikki, I shouldn't—"

"No," said Zuchmul, his voice husky. "Let her go."

Idom said, "Thank you, Elias, but I think we've all had enough for tonight. We dive first thing in the morning."

As she closed her door behind her, she heard Idom's tread coming. She leaned on the inside of the door. She'd done a lot of that lately. Then she flung herself on the bed, clutching a lump of bedclothes to her middle. There were tears that needed shedding, but they wouldn't come. She wasn't even sure why they were there, but they wouldn't come.

In her adolescence, she'd been trained in the most severe school, and behavior such as this simply was not to be tolerated. She had the strength; she would just have to use it. She got up, stripped, and lay down on the floor to do the set of exercises she'd adopted to stretch and strengthen the muscles that had taken such a beating on Insarios and might take worse on Veramai.

She'd coordinated the exercises with the set of key-image disciplines she had recently begun practicing again. They gave her strength to live with the perpetual glow of the working-realm key that kept visuals bleeding into her mind.

She worked up a good sweat, pushing five and ten repetitions beyond her current tolerances, and it helped.

When she'd finished, she told herself she felt better, showered and groomed meticulously, dressed for bed, and lay down to sleep. But there was no sleep in her. She nearly tore her pajamas by twisting in the same direction. *What I need is to take Elias down into the Pool!*

Only the Pool offered relief so profound that nothing could stir up this need for days and days.

Shocked fully awake, she realized she was in a state she had learned how to induce quickly before a dive. She had years of experience with the state. The most powerful sleeping potion wouldn't help. Only one thing, other than the Pool, would, and it wasn't available.

Idom? No. He'd never expressed that sort of interest, and besides, he needed his sleep. He had to dive tomorrow. Fleetingly, she wondered if Guides experienced the same relief after a dive that Operators did. But if they didn't use sexual energy to power the dive, then why should they?

She stilled her prurient thoughts, mended her barriers, and grabbed a robe. Perhaps a hot drink would help. She slipped into the crew's galley, shut the door and turned on the lights to search the menu. She didn't want alcohol, but there were other sorts of tension-relieving beverages. The crew's choice, however, was much more limited than what Zimor had kept for herself. Kyllikki turned the light off and made for the passengers' galley.

The moment she stepped into the lounge, she knew it had been a mistake. A pale-pink mist of Influence filled the whole room. Zuchmul rose from his chair.

The lights were dimmed and filtered down to a ruddy orange, the closest the ship's lighting could get to that preferred by luren. Her hand had already automatically begun to raise the lights. Seeing her gesture, Zuchmul clamped his hand over his eyes, his field of Influence contracting about him. "Please don't!"

She snatched her hand back. "I won't! I'm sorry."

He took a step toward her, then stopped, gazing raptly.

She'd never been feasted on like that before.

She wanted to dash back to her cabin, to hide from the intensity, but her gaze was held by his eyes. He wasn't wearing his protective inserts. It was the first time she'd seen his eyes naked. They were human, with pale-purple irises. The pupils were contracted to pinholes in what was to him bright light. She could have truly blinded him had she finished her gesture. And she remembered her resolve to talk to him. Her mother had taught her that the debts of friendship always came due at the worst possible time, but still had to be paid without complaint. She advanced a step. "You shouldn't have risked sitting in here like that."

He nodded. "But it was worth it. You're—beautiful!"

"You've never really seen me before! You've never seen any of this before, have you?"

He agreed. "Because of the lights. The filters have to shift the spectrum and nothing looks—right."

He thinks he's going to die and he's avid for life. Her problems shrank to insignificance. She went to a chair near where he'd been sitting. She noticed he wasn't wearing his protective mesh suit either, so the place he'd been sitting must have been chosen for its magnetic character. Would the presence of her body alter that? The whole lounge must be an endurance trial for a luren, especially an unprotected luren.

"Zuchmul, why are you sitting out here at all?"

He perched on the foot rest of the chair opposite her. "I couldn't sleep. And you?"

"The same. But probably not for the same reason."

He was examining her now at close range, his veil of Influence a diffuse cloud about him. "What we're doing, what we face the day after tomorrow, what we've already done—is enough to keep anyone awake. Except Idom. He's exhausted after every dive, and he's too old to be working like this."

"Is that why you're so—scared—before a dive?"

"Scared? Kyllikki, I've been in space for—" He buried his face in his hands. "Oh, what's the use!"

She firmed up her barriers and said, "Don't insult me.

Your mind is your own. If you want to lie to me, go right ahead. I'll figure it out the way anyone else would."

He laughed. It was a strained, tense laugh. "Kyllikki, I'm not dive-shy. I'm scared it will take too long to get to Veramai, too long until—until I can access orl."

"Oh . . ." *Korachi!* she swore to herself. *It's not dying that's getting to him—it's dying by starvation.* "Idom's good. He won't get us lost. Day after tomorrow—"

"If we don't get lost, we'll be at Veramai and waiting in the landing pattern. There won't be orl available until after we convince the Emperor. Maybe fifteen days."

"You could go directly to the citadel from the landing field." As soon as she said it, she regretted it.

He bowed his head. "That would be worse. My only chance is for Imperial sanction. It's just—"

He stopped, eyes wide, lips compressed over words he would not speak. Knowing she'd almost gotten it out of him, she moved over to sit beside him, holding her breath when he flinched away from her. "Just what?" she prompted in a lower voice. "If you're not going to leave us on the landing field, if you're going to go with us to the Emperor, then I think I have a right to know what's bothering you."

He was silent, gathered into himself.

"We may be in a lot of danger," she continued. "We may have to depend on each other. Right now you're shaking inside so badly that I wouldn't trust you to keep your nerve. It makes me want to wrap you in my arms and comfort you." *Why did I say that?*

But it was too late. The words were out and Zuchmul was already halfway across the lounge, heading for his cabin. Without thinking, she lunged after him and arrived just in time to slip through the door behind him.

He whirled, gasping as if she'd stabbed him in the gut. His hands came up to push her back into the passageway, but he stopped himself, clenched his fists, and forced them back to his sides. "It's all right. I know you didn't mean it."

"But I did mean it," she contradicted.

He frowned and retreated a step, shaking his head, almost as if she hadn't spoken intelligibly.

"No matter how tightly barriered I might be, I could never miss the tension that's almost breaking you in half. But you've got to *tell* me the cause. I'm not going to invade your privacy." It was a shot in the dark, but the only time people in the Metaji acted so skittishly was when they suspected she was peeking.

Bewildered, he said, "But you just did."

"I did not! If you can't trust me—"

"What's trust got to do with it? You're standing inside my threshold."

"What?" She was inside his cabin. She looked around the dimness, not seeing anything particularly private. The walls, floor, and ceiling were shrouded in protective mesh she'd gotten from the citadel, but there were no private possessions. The bed was a smaller version of the one in Zimor's room, but still had its canopy, a crisp white material against which she could make out the magnetic-field-generating apparatus she bought so Zuchmul could sleep peacefully aboard ship.

Very carefully, he enunciated, "You just invaded my privacy, but I know you didn't mean to hurt me, so don't worry about it. Just don't do it again."

"I'll promise, just as soon as you tell me what I did."

"You came into my room uninvited."

She backed up to the doorway. "I'm sorry. I thought we were friends. I wanted—" She had to swallow tears. She made it into the hall, and finished, "I wanted to help you."

She turned and fled back to the lounge, almost furious enough to turn the lights up out of sheer spite. It would make him slam his door shut instead of standing there watching her. But she couldn't bring herself to inflict more pain on him. By the time she reached the middle of the lounge, she was running.

Her foot hit something hard and she went down on her face, stifling her outcry. *Stupid! Dumb! Some Laila!*

She sat up, kneading her foot, and the tears burst out of

nowhere. She tried to stop, but that just made it worse. By the time he reached her, she was crying uncontrollably.

"Are you hurt?" He knelt and examined her ankle. Then his hands flittered all over her looking for injury.

She wrapped her arms around his neck, buried her face in his shoulder, and stopped resisting the tears.

chapter **twelve**

....

"Oh, Kyllikki, we *are* friends. Always and ever, Kyllikki, and you're welcome in my home. More than welcome." He gathered her against his body and carried her back to his cabin, cushioned by a private fog of Influence.

His power carried only his genuine feelings, without the least attempt to alter her perceptions. His need to make amends gave her a sense of security, and, perversely, that fueled her catharsis. She wrapped her arms around his neck and clung to him, trying to muffle her sobs.

This was the first time she'd felt his body without the protective mesh between them. He was all bones, but, even thin as sticks, his arms were stronger than Elias'.

He lowered her to the bunk effortlessly, cradling her head against him. Then he eased down beside her, his lips found her temple, and she was unaware of the convulsive sobs melting away. Her whole attention centered on those lips as they told her he'd meant it when he'd said she was beautiful. By the standards of his people, she must be ugly indeed, dark-skinned and grossly over-fleshed. To her, his chalky skin and stick figure build were not attractive. But his lips said she was beautiful. And for the first time in a very long time she believed it.

He kissed away the tears, then reached her mouth, and she knew what had been bothering him. She should have known when he kissed her that first time.

This had been smoldering in Zuchmul for a long time, suppressed by the constraints of law and custom. Now Elias' presence had inflamed it, and she herself had breached Zuchmul's defenses by inducing him to use Influence on Elias.

He shifted against her, and she could feel the throbbing strain of his excitement as the kiss altered. The sharp demand she knew as his hunger became a gentle giving as he interested himself in her response, following the trail of her desire with his luren senses without imposing any image or feeling on her.

He didn't have to. She wanted it. *But I don't dare.*

One of his hands hesitantly invaded the bodice of her pajamas. She wasn't sure if her soft flesh was repellent to him or if he was asking permission.

Gently, she worked her hands up to his face, finished kissing him, then breathed in his ear, "Zuchmul, we can't."

He collected himself. "It takes months for fertility to return after revival. But my need is very great, and my love is greater still. Your need fills this ship. There's nowhere to get away from it. I know it's Elias you want, but you don't really hate me that much, do you?"

"Do you know what orgasm does to a telepath's barriers?"

"Do you know what orgasm does to a luren's Influence?"

"I don't think either of us ought to find out." With care, she could prevent herself from taking a non-telepath out onto the planes, but she'd never had to before.

He edged away, leaving her room to move. "If you really want to leave, I won't stop you. But this time, turn the lights to your visual spectrum before crossing the lounge."

"Could you stop me?"

"Yes."

"How?"

"Influence."

"I'd react. I might kill you."

"You'd react, but not with the reflex. Observe."

His power contracted into that pink shell she knew she wasn't seeing with her eyes. The pit of her stomach clenched up tightly, the need to cry returned, and she clutched at him, bereft in the absence of his Influence, her reflex quiescent. There was a cold chill as if he'd taken his arms from around her.

"See? The Eight Families' reflex seems to be triggered only by the *imposition* of image or emotion. I wouldn't dare employ that function near you, which is why I had to use Elias' own most powerful fantasy to capture his attention."

As he spoke, the pink shell expanded to include her, and all her muscles thawed. "It seemed to me," she murmured, trying to distract him, "that Elias was holding *your* attention!"

"Even with such a subject, it shouldn't have become that kind of a . . . mutual . . . thing. I'd no idea how compelling a Dream could be. Must be akin to Influence."

"We ought to talk to Idom about that." She had a horrifying thought. "If there's something undocumented about a Dreamer's response to Influence, what about a Bonder's response? This might be dangerous for us."

"That's true. I've never even heard of anyone doing this with a human, let alone a Bonder. But I'm not doing to you what I did with Elias. I wouldn't dare. I'm just embracing you. As I would a luren woman."

Relieved a bit, she touched his cheek. "I like it."

He plucked her hand away and held it hard. "Don't tease me. Say yes or no, Kyllikki."

"There's still something you haven't explained. I keep asking and you keep avoiding. The stasis tanks aren't sufficient. Somehow you're starving because I ignored D'sillin about the orl, and if this will help, then—"

"No! You owe me no debts. All I offer is the release we both want, that we both need before facing Veramai." He brought her hand up and kissed the palm.

His interest, his attention was focused on that one little

spot, and it did wonderful things to her. With an effort, she whispered, "You're avoiding again."

He put the hand down between them, edging just a bit closer. "We've always considered that humans prefer not to think about how we feed. It's the most unhuman thing about us. Perversely, I suppose we want to be accepted as human."

"And I'm Teleod. Does it show that much?"

"No! No, it's not you. It's me. It embarrasses me."

"Are you going to tell me, or do I have to go read computer files for six or seven hours and hope to stumble on the right fact?"

He sighed. "There's more to feeding than just blood. That's why the emphasis on freshness. The stasis tanks are very good at maintaining that freshness—that *life* in the blood—but not perfect. There's no substitute for orl, especially after a long dormancy in those older stasis units. I know you'd have provided for me if you could have. But I'd rather be here than on my way to Hayelma in one of D'sillin's ships! I made the choice, not you. Does that settle it?"

"No. Sometimes, I *feel* your hunger. It's all tangled up with arousal, but it's not pleasant."

He shrank back, gathering in his power. "I'm sorry. I should never have—"

"But you have. And I want you to." She felt his confusion. "*Sometimes* it's pleasant, and I don't know what the difference is."

He thought about that. "I think I do. It's intensity. To be savagely honest, twice now—on the pod, and after I returned—I've taken that touch of *life* I've needed, taken it without your consent. No wonder you fear me. I let you see no hint of my shame." She tried to object, but he laid a finger across her lips. "And the intensity is greater now. The longer the dormancy in stasis, the longer the ensuing sterility, and the more intense the need to resume sexual activity. I haven't yet. I left the facility before I could. But, Kyllikki, it can be only by your consent."

"I'm not convinced it would be right for either of us."

"There can't be anything—permanent—between us. But

tonight, you have a need, and so do I. Right now, Metaji and Teleod law aside, it would be harmless, and it doesn't make sense for us to go to our separate beds and toss and turn and ache when our lives and the future of the galaxy could depend on our being rested when we arrive at Veramai. If you don't want me, go to Elias. His need is at least as great as mine, and fills this ship like a drumbeat."

"But you said that long stasis sharpens sexual needs."

"Yes, until fertility returns." He stroked her cheek. "Don't be concerned for me. I've been properly revived, and acquired a splendid new family. You don't owe me anything. I shouldn't have asked. I know you prefer Elias."

"But that's just as impossible as it is between you and me." *And there are moments when I'm not so terribly sure I wouldn't prefer you.*

"He doesn't look at you the same way he regarded Zimor."

"You don't understand. The Dreambond is addictive. His craving will get worse and he'll convince himself he wants me when what he wants is the Bond, but if I let it happen, he'd hate me."

"I think you misjudge him." Zuchmul laughed. He planted a kiss on her forehead and breathed, "What sane male of any species would believe this conversation! I've got you in my bed, nearly undressed, completely aroused, and I'm trying to talk you into going to someone else!"

"As if you—" —*really love me?*

"As if I what?"

"The law against luren/human sex makes no exception for sterility or contraception because people who do get this intimate often do—crazy things—for each other. If I were some stranger you'd never see again, offering a cheap thrill, it'd be different. But as it is, can you just—start this, then forget it ever happened? Because, Zuchmul, the most we could have is the few days until we reach Veramai. I think it might do us both some good, maybe give us the edge we'll need on Veramai, but only if we can let go of it before it's really gotten started. Can you do that?"

She felt him move as he realized she was making an offer. She shored up her barriers, determined not to watch him make this decision.

After a very long time, he ventured, "You could let go very easily because it's really Elias you want."

"You mean, I'd be using you as if you were some stranger offering a cheap thrill?" She edged back from him, searching for the side of the bunk. "I want to keep your friendship, Zuchmul. It means a lot to me."

His hands clamped on her arms. "You misunderstand." He turned her to him and smoothed back her hair. She knew he was devouring every detail of her appearance, here where the colors and shadows were right and he could see clearly. "Because of your feeling for Elias, you will not be hurt—and I—well, it would be worse for me to have nothing to let go of, no memory to cherish."

"That's not usually the way of it for humans."

"True. Humans wrote the law without consulting luren."

"You know, if we do this, it'll become known while we're trying to prove what Zimor did to Elias."

He was silent, but she understood. He had given his life to stopping Zimor and wanted a warm memory to take to his grave. But he wouldn't beg. He dropped his hands and lay back on the pillow. "But I will be with you, and be your friend—always."

And all her resistance collapsed.

He was slow and careful, agonizingly slow, more fascinated with her responses than his own needs. She set herself to remain wholly within his level of reality and not to reach into him, and she felt him taking similar care with his power. Gradually, she found herself trusting, relaxing into the ultimate moment when her barriers disintegrated on every level and their gifts twined in a triumphal shout.

It was a strange effect. The luren outlook was—not human. And yet it was. For that one brief moment, she seemed to possess Influence and she knew it wasn't telepathy. It accessed the mind in a different way and dealt with knowledge from a different idea of reality.

When it was over, she felt as if she'd been stripped of a whole sense, deafened somehow. She would gladly have given her birthright to possess Influence.

Gasping, Zuchmul pressed his cheek to her shoulder, physical shudders racking him as if he suffered fever chills.

She could feel sweat standing on his forehead as he clung to her, his breathing becoming more labored. With her barriers so much diaphanous tissue, she was filled with his thoughts, but they were incoherent with some kind of shock. And she'd been so careful not to invoke the realms or bring his mind into any sort of real communion.

She could only hold on, rocking him and making soothing noises. "What have I done? I didn't mean to hurt you. It's all over now. See, we're separate again. It's all right now. You can trust me. Your mind is your own."

At last, he pushed away and stroked her face again. "Ah, no, Kyllikki, you can lose your barriers with me anytime you like. You're so sweet. And a first time—a first time is like no other time." He trailed his lips down her arm to her hand, murmuring in the luren language. In moments, they were both ready to try it again.

He began on her shoulder, which became instantly convinced of its beauty.

"Do me a favor," she suggested.

"Hmmm?"

"Don't treat me like a fragile virgin this time."

He didn't.

After the third time, when she got a chance to return the favors, she fell asleep.

She woke wondering what might have happened if he'd been forced to wait another four or five days, until they reached Veramai, to resume sexual activity. She wouldn't have trusted his judgment even to fix a food processor! If nothing else, that should be an argument in their favor, and she knew the legal defenders who could make the most of it.

But she didn't have a chance to discuss that with Zuchmul. He was already in the shower, and it was late. Idom couldn't dive without her at the pilot's station.

Robe clutched around her, she stuck her head in the bathroom door and told Zuchmul she was leaving.

Elias was in the lounge, putting breakfast on the table while Idom puttered around in the galley.

They both saw her closing Zuchmul's door.

Elias stared, face frozen, mind radiating pain.

Kyllikki repaired her barriers. "Good morning," she said as she padded barefoot through the lounge. She knew they'd found the lounge lighting set for Zuchmul's eyes and wondered what they'd made of that.

As casually as if she'd come from her own quarters, Idom said, "We'll reach the dive point in an hour and a half."

She didn't stop as she passed Elias. "Keep the yarage hot. I'll be right back."

When she'd showered and dressed, she found Zuchmul just sitting down with his own covered mug, warily watching Elias.

She took her place and reached for the yarage pitcher.

Zuchmul said, "Elias, you probably noticed Kyllikki coming out of my cabin this morning."

"I did."

Zuchmul held a perfectly serene expression. "She and I had a terrible misunderstanding last night, and I wanted to make sure that no one else risked being sworn at by a seasoned space mechanic."

Idom grinned. "What did she do?"

"Quite innocently, she stepped across the threshold of my cabin. I wanted to be sure neither of you ever does that without my specific invitation. If you enter that cabin, even when I'm not on board, I'll be able to point to each foot- or handprint. It could make the room useless to me."

Idom said, "I'd assumed it was just a cultural preference."

"No. It was all I could do to keep from leveling Influence at Kyllikki—and you know how long I would have survived had I done that. Afterward, we talked for hours."

Elias asked, "Is that all you did?"

"Elias!" warned Idom.

Zuchmul gestured Idom to silence. "Elias, she's yours and has been since the moment she laid eyes on you. Nothing I can do or say will ever change that, and I wouldn't want to if I could. Does that answer your question?"

"Not exactly, but it will do."

Kyllikki said, "Zuchmul is entitled to his opinion."

Idom said, "Kyllikki, pass the yarage pitcher."

She did and said, "Idom, after the dive, Zuchmul and I have to talk to you."

"I was planning on two dives today, if the first one goes right." Having captured their attention, he continued, "I'll need Kyllikki to monitor the traffic around our first emergence point. If we come out where I expect to, I may be able to count into the next dive almost immediately and hit the approach pattern to Veramai. After that, I can rest and Kyllikki can work."

Zuchmul met Kyllikki's eyes. That was one day less they'd have together, but one day less until Zuchmul would have his orl.

She took a fresh fruit from the pile in the middle of the table, then peeled the cover off her breakfast tray. For the first time in days, the food smelled inviting.

Even Elias' frustration didn't dampen her appetite. He wasn't as depressed as he had been, and there was a brightness to his inner music, an optimism.

Later, as she was settling into the pilot's station, running the shields away from the hull to open the Com Window, she noticed that not only was all trace of Zimor's shadow gone, but the working-realm key that had lurked in the back of her mind since Barkyr had faded overnight. It was as if her whole being was suddenly able to take a deep breath, free of pain or constriction. She felt strong, able to meet the next challenge. And somehow, everyone on the ship, even Elias, had felt the same release of energy.

That was something else to talk to Idom about. Later.

She went through the pilot's dive routine, something she'd learned from the Teleod ship manual's description of Metaji practice. It was particularly easy since Idom had taken them far

203

off the traveled routes, where, he said, there was less chance of running afoul of Teleod damage. All she had to cope with was the tuning of the gravitics to the local mass distribution, and that was automated.

But when the flickering twist of the first dive was over, they emerged among scattered traffic and she became busy exchanging greetings with other Communicators.

The biggest topic was the closing of one of the approach gates to Veramai. Speculation was rife that a fleet was being gathered, some kind of a massive counterattack in response to the taking of Barkyr. Some of those coming from the farthest reaches of the Empire were reporting a sudden thinning of the Imperial forces on all fronts. Estimates of the size of the fleet being assembled escalated with each new ship to report in.

She relayed it all to Idom, ending, "Conservatively they've committed between two and three thousand ships. What do you think they plan to do?"

"Attack Inarash. Laila's not the only Family that headquarters on the planet. That would be as good as the Teleod taking Veramai. The Empire will annex the Teleod."

"And it will become a guerrilla war, a grudge war that will never end. We've got to hurry!"

"Takes time to launch a fleet, Kyllikki. If that's what they're planning to do, we'll make it." Then his tone changed. "Good. I've got it. From this direction, they'll have to put us down at Vindara Port. But we have to dive now." He dictated a new course, then instructed, "When we emerge, pay attention to the gossip. I need a size estimate on that fleet if it's not just a ploy to divert Teleod attention." Idom warned everyone to secure for dive, and then they were running into their new dive point.

This time they emerged at the far edge of the Veramai traffic pattern, and Kyllikki had to use both hands to order course adjustments while she exchanged greetings with half a dozen other Com Officers.

Thanks to Idom's meticulous drills, the new identity flowed easily into her mind. By sheer luck or Idom's mystic skill, all the Com Officers she dealt with were strangers, so there was no challenge to her fictitious identity. The yacht's beacon was chattering as it answered other ships' queries, and her screens rapidly filled with identifications of other ships as the yacht collected answers from their beacons.

Right on schedule, she raised the regional traffic control, Veramai Outstation Six, an artificial planet anchored in interstellar space and supporting not only traffic control and mail services but also some of the most sophisticated defense installations anywhere.

And the gossip was thicker here, speculation rampant. Kyllikki took notes.

Like dozens of other craft entering the approach pattern, the yacht was required to spend hours in maneuvers, while instruments analyzed them. Zuchmul waited it out in his insulated cabin, which showed as a dark blob on the security scanners. That required a port inspector to board, but they had long since readied the yacht to pass as what they claimed she was. The inspector, a harried Ye're'y, very politely asked Zuchmul to vacate the room, provided him with a radiation shield, trained instruments through Zuchmul's door without crossing his threshold, apologized for the inconvenience to a neutral, explained that no luren ship with proper identification would be so challenged, and left.

Heaving a sigh, Kyllikki said, "Never happens like that in the Teleod, neutrality or no."

"In the Teleod," said Elias, "it would be a telepath doing the inspecting, and we'd never get away with this." Kyllikki recalled how upset he'd been when he'd discovered that Teleod law required all telepaths to inspect minds at random rather than protecting privacy as in the Metaji.

"There are very few telepaths," she offered, "and they can only spot-check. Some spies always do get through."

Zuchmul was completely silent.

In the end, the yacht was secured in its slot, tied in to the regional automation controls, and Idom announced to everyone, "Secure and stand down."

As Kyllikki set the pilot alarms and closed her Window, she said over the intercom, "I'm amazed we've gotten this far. Are the numbers with us again, Idom?"

"Not much of a pattern yet, but six seems to be doing us some good. I'm not too thrilled about that, though. I need more data."

"I may have it," she replied. "See you in the lounge."

It had been nearly twelve hours since anyone had eaten, and she was grateful to find Zuchmul in Zimor's galley preparing hot food while Elias set things on the table. She called to Zuchmul brightly, "I didn't know luren could cook!"

In the same vein, he replied, "Someone has to feed the children! Hot soup in three minutes. Go wash."

She headed for the crew's galley, the nearest unused sink, and Elias followed her, blocking the door as she splashed water onto her face. "What happened between you and Zuchmul that Idom has to know about?"

Scrubbing the towel over her eyes, she scraped together the remains of her strength and remembered her comment that morning. "Oh, that too. Maybe it's related. I meant to tell you to sit in on it with us. It could have to do with Dreaming, but theory is Idom's department." She offered him the towel. "Want to wash?"

He took it but didn't move out of the door. "Kyllikki!" It was half-groan, half-plea. "Don't you care at all?" His music had become strident, and she shored up her barriers.

"I care enough that I couldn't stand it if you came to hate me the way you hated Zimor."

"It's not the same—"

"Of course it's the same. Bonders and Dreamers are attracted to each other—they are *always* willing. You don't want to get close to me. I'm *not* any better than Zimor!" She hadn't intended to say that.

"That's not true."

"I behave just like her." Her bitterness astonished her, and at his automatic denial she couldn't stop herself from retorting, "I left her to *die* in the working realm! My own cousin, and I didn't feel a hint of remorse at the time."

That stopped him. Then he asked, "What did you feel?"

"Nothing."

"She might be dead."

"No. I realized later she didn't need my help. But at the time—when I thought she did—I didn't care."

He moved into the tiny space, close enough that she could feel his body heat. "What do you feel now?"

It had never occurred to her to ask herself that, but the answer was very clear. Self-loathing. The tears of relief flooded hotly, and suddenly he had his arms around her. It was worse than with Zuchmul. She'd thought nothing could exceed the pure physical greed the luren aroused in her, but this did. It touched a core place that had never been touched before.

She slid around him and fled into the lounge to find Idom surveying the table. "You look tired," she offered, trying to sound normal.

"Physically, yes. And I'm starved."

"Zuchmul's made soup."

"What!" He started for the galley, but just then Zuchmul emerged carrying a tray. On it were three covered bowls. The bowls didn't seem melted, and the covers weren't shriveled. Even a luren could cook once the machine knew how to read the instruction codes.

There was a sparkling cold aperitif waiting in everyone's glass, and a decanter of light-green wine on the table. Zuchmul smiled. "I thought we should celebrate while we have the chance." He set the food trays on the table, then brought his own covered mug and sat with them.

They toasted Idom for his triumphal feat, and feasted convivially, limiting the conversation to trivialities. Remarkably, all the flavors in the meal Zuchmul had concocted fit together perfectly, and when he brought out a frozen confection to top it off, they all groaned, "No more!"

But even that went down smoothly. "Zuchmul," said Idom, "you should have been a chef on *Prosperity*, not a mechanic."

He laughed. "But I *like* fixing machines!" Then he told them of a luren friend who worked for an interspecies catering service and who had taught him several surefire combinations. "So you see, I'm no artist. It's just that we had all the ingredients from one of his lists on board!"

But as they all laughed, Kyllikki caught Idom counting the items on the table and brooding. Then he raised his eyes to Zuchmul. "But you only consume one thing."

Zuchmul swirled his empty mug. "I'm not too sure that's the case—from a Guide's point of view, anyway."

"If it weren't," said Idom, half-facetiously, "that could introduce a serious counting error sometime."

"I don't see how," said Elias. "If one thing has two or three components, it's still one thing."

Kyllikki said, "That's right! You counted containers of that sleeping potion, then cases of it. The drug has to have ten or more components, and the containers even more, and—"

"But considering that numbers don't have an inherent sequence—" said Idom.

"What!" challenged Elias, suddenly alert.

Idom elaborated, "That six isn't five plus one. That six is six and nothing more nor less. Universal Discontinuity Principle."

Elias made a questioning noise, frowning.

Idom added, "That all things are aspects of one thing, but that the one thing has components separated by no-thing."

Elias' eyes took on that same wary look he'd had when they'd discussed the mathematical basis of sexuality, as if he doubted their sanity.

"So," said Idom, focusing on Zuchmul, "is there another component to the luren's diet, other than blood?"

"Everyone's always taken it for granted that there isn't, but suddenly I'm not so sure."

He glanced at Kyllikki, then Elias, and finally donned an air of resignation and said to Idom, "I've always considered that *yanforz*—oh, I don't suppose it translates except as 'life,'—is a component of blood. But I've had three experiences lately that seem to belie that. Kyllikki insists I have to tell you about one of them, so I suppose I have to tell you about all three."

There was no obvious sign of the embarrassment that always made Zuchmul avoid this topic, but Kyllikki finally understood why Zuchmul had created this meal for them. He had wanted them all relaxed, himself included.

"The first incident was when I succumbed to the urge to kiss Kyllikki. What I needed was there for me. But she turned me away. It was almost worse than nothing. It took the edge off the hunger for a few hours, but then—there was the memory of it."

Elias squirmed.

Zuchmul leaned toward the other man and offered, "If this discomforts you, you don't have to stay, but I must tell Idom."

Elias was almost expressionless as he answered, "Just tell me one thing: Did you sleep with her?"

"Yes," said Zuchmul. "After we had intercourse. Three times. I don't think Idom needs any graphic details. He is well experienced in such matters."

Idom betrayed no reaction except disappointment and a little, distant, fear. "I could have wished for six, but that would be asking a bit much."

That comment earned him Elias' best stare.

Zuchmul added, "What I said this morning about Kyllikki—it still holds."

"She doesn't think so."

Zuchmul shrugged, the gesture of the interstellar traveler loath to pass judgment. Then he launched into an explanation of why he shouldn't have left the citadel so soon, describing in clinical detail what a newly wakened luren needs and why.

"So," Zuchmul finished, "the next day, when we tackled the breaking of the Bond, I was not as objective as I might have been." He recited every detail of Elias' fantasy, how it had become a Dream and how he had been trapped in it until Kyllikki shocked him out of it. "Kyllikki thinks it's important that a Dreamer dominated an Influence projection. At least I think that's what happened." He turned to Elias. "I did describe your own vision, didn't I?"

Elias' skin was so red it seemed purple, but he nodded, a single taut jerk of his head, then added in a strangled voice,

"But I had no idea you—anybody—I thought it was just a dream. My own, I mean. Private—"

Overcome with Elias' embarrassment, Kyllikki thickened her barriers, then captured Elias' hand and dragged his attention onto her. "Do you see how you feel? Your dreams are private—not to be shared. Not even with me. It's all right, Elias, I only caught the end of it, and I thought the setting was lovely. And you were—magnificent."

He swallowed hard. "Thank you."

She let go of his fingers and asked Idom, "So is it possible? Influence and Dreaming are akin?"

"Maybe," he said. "Zuchmul, you said there were three events, and that was the second."

"Oh, the third was last night. I found out why Kyllikki had rejected me. I had taken *yanforz* from her without consent. This time, she consented—and more. The law against mating Dreamer and Bonder may have stemmed from some bit of Triumvirate lore that was lost along with their Pool science. Outside of the context of intercourse, my need was a threat to her. Within that context, I fed from her and she was not depleted. To the contrary; she is well—as she has not been since before Barkyr. I am well for the first time since I wakened. It doesn't make any sense. It wasn't as it might have been with an orl. Yet both hunger and need abated without the taking of blood. I conclude *yanforz* is not a component of blood, but a second thing luren feed upon."

He fed from me. As horrible as it sounded, she was willing to do it again. *What if it's as addictive as Bonding?* Aloud she said, "All of us seem to have been affected—by something. A weight has lifted. Idom, how could what Zuchmul and I did affect you two?"

Idom looked from Kyllikki to Zuchmul, comparing them, then said, "If a Dreamer can make a luren Dream, and a luren can feed from a Bonder without taking blood, then my theories are definitely incomplete. This needs thinking about. But emotion is the carrier wave of both telepathy and Influence, and neither Elias nor I are immune to emotional atmosphere. It could be as simple as that."

When it was clear Idom wasn't going to say anything more on the subject, Kyllikki got up and began to clear the table, and Idom helped. In the privacy of the galley, he muttered, "If I were you, I'd be thinking about the law. You may win the war for us only to find you've lost your own battle."

"I don't see any way out of this situation except to do the right thing, not the legal thing, and hope to change the law."

"Hmmm. May as well try to move a planet as to change this particular set of laws. They're the foundation of interstellar civilization."

"I know." She had rarely experienced such misery. The whole after-dinner conversation had been a torment for Elias, and she hadn't dared give him sympathy for fear he'd think it an invitation. And as bad as it had been for Elias, it had been a worse trial for Zuchmul.

Idom put his arm around her shoulders and squeezed. "I'm your friend, too, Kyllikki. Do what you must, but do it boldly and with confidence because you know you're right."

Then he was gone, and she was left to cram the rest of the trash into the recycler. When she came out, Elias and Idom were gone, and Zuchmul was waiting for her.

Somehow, when she was alone with him, the idea of his feeding from her in some mysterious way wasn't as repellent. Before long, she was convinced it was harmless. They spent that night together, and two more. Only four nights, interrupted several times by the piloting or Com alarms as the traffic became thicker, but they were four nights Kyllikki would treasure forever.

Just a few hours before they were scheduled to enter atmosphere, Zuchmul took her to the door of her own cabin and kissed her one last time. Then he said, "It's time to let go. But I will be your friend—always."

It was a lot harder than she'd anticipated, but she returned his steady gaze. "Always, Zuchmul. No matter how bad it gets, I will be your friend."

The next time she saw him, they had touched down at Vindara Port, and the four of them were gathered in the lounge to await the Port Inspection team. She was drenched in sweat from the long, arduous, tedious job of landing, and he was now fully dressed in protective mesh, ultraviolet blocking ointments, and the Inhibitor. He had a pair of sun goggles looped through his uniform belt.

Pacing, Idom asked, "Do you have any idea what could be taking so long?"

"No . . . but . . . they put us down next to a huge cleared area. Let me go see." She went forward to the pilot's station and put the outside scanner image on the lounge screens, telling them by intercom, "Look, there's still nobody on that part of the field. There are blue vans and trucks everywhere—and isn't that an Imperial car?"

The elaborate conveyance, tall enough to stand up in, with walls that could be rendered fully transparent, was never sent out for anyone of rank less than a Duke.

Idom said, "Somebody important is arriving. They may just leave us in here until they clear the field."

Zuchmul said, "See if you can tie into some local-events coverage, find out what's going on."

Elias told them the most likely channel to be covering an arrival. "I think that's their equipment over there—see the red logo?"

It took some doing with the Teleod equipment, but she locked in the frequency and Elias turned out to be correct.

They got a good view of the rows of seats set up under a canopy where dignitaries were waiting wearing bored expressions and all their formal Imperial orders. A wide strip of the landing field had been scoured and polished to a high gloss to let those arriving walk from the landing berth past the official greeters to the Imperial car without getting their shoes soiled.

Kyllikki found a broadcast in an intelligible language. ". . . so it won't be long now until the Duke of Fotel arrives on Veramai. With Barkyr lost and the Teleod forces driving toward the Four Stars and other primary Effein holdings, the Duke's arrival may just mark a turning point in the war. We have it from reliable sources that Fotel plans to discuss surrender with the Emperor."

chapter **thirteen**

●●●●●●●●●●●●●●●●●●●●●●●●●●●●●●●●●●●●●

"I don't believe it!" exclaimed Zuchmul.

"It's what Effein would do," said Idom. "With Barkyr taken, Fotel's got the main route to Veramai, and now the Imperial ships are being withdrawn. I can see him threatening surrender. Effein don't fight without a physical advantage."

Zuchmul replied, "No, I'd have heard on Insarios if any such thing were brewing. Everyone there was worried about anti-luren sentiment, not Effein defection. Baron Tshiv rewarded any hint of Teleod leanings with severe penalties and interpreted anything that wasn't pro-Mctaji as Teleod leanings, challenging our neutrality. No, I say Fotel and all his Effein are not just loyal, they're committed to the Empire's stance in this war. This is something else."

From the pilot's station, Kyllikki heard the announcer talking. "Listen!" she said, adjusting the lounge speakers.

". . . death threats against the Duke. So security is tight and the Duke's arrival time is unavailable. While we wait, here's a report from Zuting in the Capital."

The scene switched to a Paitsmun who arrived with a leap

and bounced up and down while recapping the situation. "The Ambassador from Eff to the Imperial Court denies all rumors about the Duke of Fotel's trip to Veramai. The Ambassador says the conference pertains to the succession in time of war, and that no Effein-controlled territory will be ceded to the invaders. Here is the Ambassador."

An Effein's nobby gray skin filled the screen, a face seen above an array of heraldic decorations. The Ambassador said, "*Rumors* are a method of information exchange relied on by non-Effein races. There are no Teleod sympathizers hiding among the luren of the Four Stars, and my government does not favor the advice of luren over that of others. No luren has advised us to surrender. They guard their neutrality."

The coverage went on as Kyllikki returned to the lounge.

"Kyllikki," said Elias, "listen!" He was bent over Idom, gripping the back of the Guide's chair and watching the announcer. "He said security is on to an assassination plot against Fotel, and nobody denied *that* rumor. Zimor has more agents here than anywhere in the Empire, and *by chance* we've been directed to a berth next to the Duke's. Is this Zimor's work? She's had almost five days."

Idom nodded. "They're well-constructed rumors. Security doesn't know which way to look. Everyone has a motive to assassinate the Duke: Imperialists for his threat of surrender, Teleod patriots for his denial of surrender, and luren for his infractions on neutrality while looking for hidden Teleod sympathizers. No matter what he does or says, he's a prime target for every zealot around. Zimor might not even have to send an assassin. Very neat."

Kyllikki shook her head. "But why would Zimor want to get rid of the Duke of Fotel? His successors are also loyal, right down to the Baron of Insarios."

"That's easy," said Zuchmul. "The Four Stars have always been considerate to luren. But Tshiv has changed. He's pathologically suspicious of the citadels."

"No, there are too many in the succession before him. Unless that's the succession he's come to discuss, not the Imperial Succession." No, it just wasn't Zimor. "She must have some new advisers."

"Zimor's not above using rumors as weapons," said Elias.

"This isn't her *style* of using rumors."

"That's not important," said Idom. "What we need to know is whether Zimor arranged for us to be set down *here*."

Just then the seldom-heard voice of the yacht announced: "Attention. Port Security approaching the main lock. Attention. Port Security seeking admittance. Onboard security overridden. All ship's functions under external control. Main air lock opening now. Boarding party entering. Attention, Port Security on board."

Kyllikki, in her role as Captain, hurried to the passage leading to the air lock and shut off the warning. They had been under external control and heavy artillery surveillance since they entered atmosphere, but that was as routine as this boarding. She fought her leaping heart back to normal and waited.

The first man to enter the lounge was huge. He carried a bunch of Port Seals looped onto an official ring hung at his waist. In one hand he had a snooperscope to inspect for contraband, in the other an official Port recorder. Except for the scowl on his face, he was what Kyllikki had expected.

Behind him, shoulder to shoulder, came a pair of heavyset armed men in guard uniforms. They drew their weapons, fanned out, balanced on their toes, eyes darting about.

Behind them, there were more people. That wasn't normal.

Kyllikki asked the Port Inspector, "How many Inspectors does it take to clear a merchant into Vindara?"

The Inspector dumped his equipment on the dining table, drew his side arm, and went forward to the crew's area.

Three more uniformed men entered: a luren flanked by two more very large, strong humans. The humans had the luren's arms in a come-along hold, and one of them held a noose of nerve-wire around the luren's neck, his thumb on the control. The other held a projector that could blast a luren's nervous system right through protective mesh. He aimed it at Zuchmul.

Through his mask, Kyllikki saw a wildness in the captive's eyes. She didn't need Zuchmul's shocked recoil to know he was a Feral luren. His hunger pierced her like a hot knife, a vicious hunger she had never sensed in a luren before. Yet, still, there was some sanity left in him, for he did not challenge the nerve-wire that could inflict pain or death.

Zuchmul said something in the luren language, and the captive replied, his gaze centering on Kyllikki.

"Shut them up," commanded a woman's voice.

The last person to arrive was a tall, slender woman, also in Port uniform, but with enough decorations and Imperial Orders on it that it was barely recognizable. Kyllikki deduced she was some minor noble, or pretending to be.

The prisoner surged forward against his bonds, teeth bared at the woman. She gestured and the luren's guards jolted him with pain from the nerve-wire. He sucked breath through clenched teeth and slumped, unconscious.

"Shog!" swore the guard. "I told you we shouldn't have brought him. Nothing's gone right yet."

The woman looked around, glanced down the hall to the passengers' rooms, then grinned at the distraught guard. "Wrong. Revive him. Our luck's just turned." She called out to the one who'd gone into the crew's area. "Bitsin! This is *Shylant*! I'm sure of it now. Get the real records, not their faked ones." She turned to the two others. "Duksh, check out the passengers' cabins. Minthar, the hold. Make sure there's no one else aboard."

Bitsin came back from the crew's area with an official record case in his hand. "This is it, Treglar. They were the ones who trashed Port Confluence."

The woman took the red-striped case and strolled toward Kyllikki. There was something in her walk—the way she *possessed* the deck she walked on, never even checking over her shoulder to see that Bitsin was covering her, totally disregarding Zuchmul—that alerted Kyllikki.

She softened her barriers and listened with everything she had as the woman said, "So you're Kyllikki, Lady of Laila." The tall woman looked down on Kyllikki, raked her with a hauntingly familiar gesture of the eyes, and added, "Make no mistake. We can handle you—oath-breaker."

//No!// Kyllikki's mental outburst bounced off the woman's barriers. To Kyllikki's perceptions, she was sheathed in a wall made of shards of mirror glass with beveled edges fitted this way and that, reflecting back a crazy quilt of images. Kyllikki studied her visually.

The woman was Eight Families. Surgically altered, maybe. Probably Azmei or Beditzial from her manner.

As recognition flashed through Kyllikki with stunning force, she slammed up her barriers, putting all her strength into isolating her mind. She barely felt the woman's assault when it came. The woman studied Kyllikki pensively, then, from a pocket of her uniform, she drew forth a palm-sized chunk of shiny green material. With the snap of a wrist, she shook it out into a sheet of thin film shaped into a hooded cape.

Kyllikki recognized the Teleod device and felt herself blanch. Buried within the film, monomolecular threads formed a circuitry pattern which, when energized by a telepath's nervous system, interfered with the telepath's perceptions in the realms. If she went out, she'd never find her way back.

The woman grinned as she settled the film around Kyllikki's shoulders and fastened it with the hood drawn close around Kyllikki's face. "Yes, of course, you'd understand. But let me just warn you. Try anything and I'll have your friends flayed alive in front of you."

Beditzial. Definitely Beditzial, Kyllikki concluded, knowing the woman meant what she said. *But not a Bonder.*

As Duksh and Minthar came back, reporting the rest of the ship empty, the woman glanced at the lounge screen.

Kyllikki noticed Elias edging toward Zuchmul and tried to catch their attention. Three guards were covering them with drawn guns; this was not the time for hasty moves.

Idom was still seated before the display. He was an old

man, not regarded as a threat by the guards. He seemed to be concentrating on the display, but Kyllikki knew he was aware of everything around him. He said, "It appears you're here to kill the Duke. You must have had traffic control put us down here so you could use *Shylant* as a base. Very clever. You must be good at moving fast to grab opportunities." He added toward Elias and Zuchmul, "Faster than any of us."

The leader ignored Idom and studied the display as she spoke to her men. "We don't have long to wait."

"How long?" demanded the captive luren, eyes blazing.

His guards tightened their grip, but the leader went over to him, scrutinizing him. Kyllikki assumed she was reinforcing a mental hold she had on the luren. "N'hawatt, have I ever failed to deliver on a promise to you?"

He made a noise.

"When you've killed my target, I've protected you."

He agreed.

"There have been times when you didn't control your hunger for human blood, and I had to punish you."

Unblinking, he stared at the woman, and Kyllikki knew she was working inside his mind—what was left of it.

Her voice lowered to an intimate tone that betrayed to Kyllikki how she felt the luren's hunger. "Now I've one last promise. Kill the Effein Duke and not only will you have these three humans for yourself, but we'll take you home."

A flash of objection crossed the luren's face, a flicker of sanity quickly squelched by the woman's hold on him. "N'hawatt, we practically own this port—our retreat is all arranged. In a few days, you'll be back on Inarash, where we can cure you of this—problem. You'll have earned the cure. Then you'll be free to return to Lur. *Believe* me, N'hawatt. I can do what I say, and I will do it. *Know* that."

Kyllikki looked to Zuchmul and saw his revulsion growing as N'hawatt succumbed to the woman's lies. She caught his eye and shook her head in warning. His lips tightened.

Kyllikki watched the Beditzial as she turned away from the Feral, secure in her control over him. Zimor was using Dreamers and Beditzial was using captive luren. Where were the decent people of the Teleod? What was going on there?

The woman walked to the hatch into the crew's area, turned and waved the red-striped recording case as she ordered: "Watch them all carefully. I'm going to transmit this with our report on this yacht's Teleod identity, and how it was allowed to escape from Barkyr to take a luren courier to Insarios." She turned to her captive Feral, working her planted command images as she said, "With them convinced the luren are in the war on our side, the Emperor will surrender. N'hawatt will be credited with saving billions of lives."

Definitely Beditzial. The way the woman savored the effect her nonsense words had on N'hawatt was pure Beditzial, but Beditzial turned vicious. It made Kyllikki vaguely ill to realize the woman was a distant relative. But who?

When she left, silence was broken only by N'hawatt's labored breathing. Everyone watched the video coverage, which cut between shots of the Duke's yacht descending under Port control and interviews of those gathered to greet the Duke.

Elias and Zuchmul exchanged glances, sizing up the guards, shifting their weight. Idom stared tensely at the display. The woman had made a typical Beditzial mistake—overconfidence. She should never have allowed her prisoners to realize they had nothing to live for, nothing to lose.

There was no way they would ever be allowed near the Emperor now, no way they could even get a message through. And if N'hawatt survived killing the Duke, he'd be allowed to kill them, too. Even if he didn't survive, they were doomed.

N'hawatt's restless squirming caught Kyllikki's eye. The luren was suffering, fading in and out of contact with reality. What if she could reach him, lift the Beditzial's compulsion keys, or even just loosen them? What would the luren do? Especially, what would he do if he understood what was really going on?

But she couldn't reach him as long as the green cloak was around her. The flimsy thing would not have held Zimor, but Kyllikki had never been able to beat it in training.

Training! Metaji training. Just in the last few days, since she'd been sleeping so well, she had become able to banish the ghost of the working-realm key that had haunted her since Barkyr. It always came back, but it took longer each day. So she ought to be able to work in audio-analogue without triggering the cloak. For a while. Theoretically.

Meticulously, she erased the realm-key image, then thinned her barriers. The white-noise rush of the non-telepaths' internal dialogues washed over her. She suddenly realized that neither her barriers nor the cloak had completely blocked her awareness of Elias' music. She was so used to it, she hadn't noticed, but now it burst into her awareness, a strident fear and anguish.

She focused her attention on N'hawatt, sorting him out from the general babble. She found a somber muttering in the luren language and behind it the rapid, nonverbal thrum of emotion that gave meaning to the words. Without being aware of how it happened, she began seeing the images flittering through his broken mind, half-formed memories randomly juxtaposed in the sort of chaos common to drug addicts.

The content of his maunderings riveted her attention so strongly that she summoned an entry key, needing to get into his mind to guide his thoughts.

She felt the monomolecular circuitry respond and whipped herself back, slamming her barriers shut.

She looked around the lounge. Nobody had noticed her gasping. They were absorbed in the display. After a few heart-stopping moments, she relaxed.

She had summoned a key and had nearly walked into the luren's mind before the cloak had responded. She reconstructed exactly what she'd done, and thought about every experience she'd ever had with the green capes.

I'm stronger than I've ever been! The device that wasn't strong enough to hold Zimor wouldn't hold her, either. If she was careful. Not Beditzial-careful. Laila-careful.

Tentatively, she dissolved her barriers and resumed contemplating the Feral, simultaneously keeping her gaze wandering around the room so no one would suspect.

In her brief excursion, she had learned that he was from the Teleod, and had been a technical factor on Inarash, a luren trader who could get rare and unusual components. He had been supplying a project of Zimor's set up inside the Laila compound. The images connected to these memories were lucid, probably predating his captivity, but not by much.

And then there had been one that made no sense at all. She had thought it part of the insanity, but she had to be sure. This time, she worked her way into the luren's identity, slipped past the key images implanted by the Beditzial, not daring to try to dislodge them, and groped for the memories she wanted.

The luren had been in the Laila compound to try to talk Laila's technical buyer into taking a substitute for some device normally imported from the Metaji. He had passed a large empty building with rows of windows near the top.

Kyllikki recognized it as the hangar where Laila craft were maintained. The huge double doors had been open that painfully sunny afternoon, and a crowd had gathered by the doors, talking. Not being luren, they didn't mind the sun.

The luren had edged into the hangar. Had to know if something important was going on. He might have some item they'd need. After all, that was his business.

But inside the hangar, deep in what would be shadows to non-luren, a huge Pool was sunk into the hard bedrock that underlay the hangar. Curious, the luren edged around the door. Pools couldn't be used anywhere near planets or suns. They had to be carried to the appropriate spot, where the fabric of space-time had the right shape, and used there.

That much any schoolchild knew.

He crept to the edge of the railed pit that held the device and looked down. Even though it was a hugely outsized thing, the rim had been manufactured by Ansarios Beditzial's factory on Inarash, and the Pool field itself appeared to be from Standard Operators' shelf stock. The apron surrounding the pool and its attendant control monitors and devices was filled with components unfamiliar to the luren.

Kyllikki recognized it, though. It was a typical Operator's-training setup with research recorders. The research objective was frighteningly clear: to find out what would happen if a Pool were activated on a planet's surface.

As the memory developed, the luren became more agitated, fighting to break away from Kyllikki's direction. But she held him to it, using a lot more force than was kind.

Zimor appeared in the luren's memory, and abruptly, other telepaths took his mind in thrall—the beginning of his captivity. It was all confusion until Zimor ordered the luren secured with a tangle field and rolled into a corner while the business was completed.

All the luren's overwhelming emotions of that time swamped Kyllikki, triggering memories of her own helplessness before her cousin.

Controlling her rage, she watched as the meeting was addressed by a Dreamer. The luren factor had not recognized this woman as a Dreamer, but, after knowing Elias, Kyllikki did. The woman had infiltrated the Metaji Guide Guild's College at Vindara and had stolen their secret research on Triumvirate Pool theory, some of it Idom's own work. She was at this meeting to attest to the genuineness of the material and to report on her training as one of the Operators who would descend into that huge Pool. Her partner would be a young man of the Azmei Family, a powerful telepath.

Teleod scholars explained and vouched for their theory derived from the Metaji research. The new key image they had designed would prevent the Operators from *going* anywhere with a sizable chunk of the planet in tow.

Kyllikki knew that the Metaji was way ahead of the Teleod in theory, and she didn't believe the Teleod scholars understood a word of what they'd stolen.

But when she forced the luren's memory through to Zimor's actual plan, she understood why her own scholars would *say* they understood and take the chance.

Zimor was offering her followers what they wanted, and she had them convinced she could deliver.

"When this Pool has done its job," Zimor told them, "no Metaji ship will be able to traverse space. *You* will control trade and travel here as well as throughout the Metaji. Which means we will control the entire civilized galaxy."

As they reacted to this, Kyllikki found out who was unequivocally with Zimor and who was unsure. And by noticing who was missing from that meeting, she deduced who was against Zimor, and that, in fact, the majority of the Eight Families was against her.

Alliances had shifted since Kyllikki left. Power and wealth had shifted, too. She'd deduced some of that from the news filtering across even during the war, but now she saw how precarious Zimor's position had become. She had a few very wealthy supporters, people situated in key positions, people who would benefit directly from gaining a monopoly on galactic trade. They, in turn, had a hold over the majority of the Eight Families, a hold that was slipping as opposition mounted. Zimor's control at this moment was absolute, but it depended on her Pool's success. She had to ram it through before her opposition raised doubts about the theory, or about who should reap the benefits. *Or before they figured out that she had no intention of using the Pool and letting them share the power, that her real objective is to revive the Triumvirate with her at the apex?*

Kyllikki withdrew from the luren's mind, numbly wondering if insanity was infectious. She had no evidence for that final supposition except her dislike of her cousin.

She glanced about the lounge. The guards were still alert, though more than half their attention was on the display. Idom's head was turned as if he were watching N'hawatt, but his attention was on Kyllikki.

She smiled at him. //Idom, it's Kyllikki. I have to talk to you.//

//At last, child! We have to—//

//Listen to me.// She related what she'd learned, including her belief that the Pool project was a diversion. //Her Pool won't work, will it? Can what they stole have taught her how to subjugate a luren into a Triumvirate?//

//No! It's not relevant, but, Kyllikki, she can't—//

//She'll try it unless we stop her. All of this—all of it—the attack on Barkyr, the use of Elias as a spy, the plot against the luren, everything she's done to us—it's all a diversion, whether from the Pool, the Triumvirate, or something worse. Loud, noisy diversions are her style.//

//Kyllikki, if that Pool is used the way she plans to use it, no Pool will ever be useful for travel again.//

//Then we've got to stop her.//

//How?//

//I don't know, but I'm through trying to get others to deal with my problems. Zimor is my problem. Always has been. I should have taken her apart when we were kids. Now if I can't do it . . .// How could you run an interstellar civilization with sublight transport? There weren't many planets that were totally self-sufficient. Billions would die. But here she was half a galaxy away and helpless.

Behind Idom's head, she could see the Duke's yacht finally settling into its berth. Among the welcoming party heraldic banners were unfurled, sound projectors filled the air with the anthems required by protocol, and dignitaries shuffled into their proper places.

The Beditzial returned, motioned to N'hawatt's guards, and went toward the main air lock, calling over her shoulder, "Bitsin, get down here and cover us. I'm releasing him as soon as the Duke appears." Bitsin followed, which left only Duksh and Minthar in the lounge. *Beditzial overconfidence.*

Kyllikki caught Elias' eye. //Elias, it's Kyllikki. Don't look at me, just listen. When the Duke appears in his air lock, I'll drop Duksh, you and Zuchmul will tackle Minthar. Wait for my signal. All right?//

//Then what?//

//I don't know, but we've got to stop them. Let me talk to Zuchmul.//

But Zuchmul was absorbed in the display, which showed the gathering crowd beyond the secured area. A contingent of luren had appeared, a very conspicuous group that was pushing up to the security barricade. One of them was talking to a Port guard, gesticulating vigorously. The reporter's microphones picked up the sound of the voices but couldn't resolve the words against the crowd noise.

//Zuchmul, it's Kyllikki. We've—//

He darted a glance at her, then whipped his attention back to the screen, fairly screaming at her mentally, and she realized he'd been frantically trying to attract her attention. //That's D'sillin! Kyllikki, D'sillin's going to get the blame for this!//

//Figures. We've got to—//

//No, you don't understand! N'hawatt is related to D'sillin! Kyllikki, I've got to kill him. I owe it to him. *And* I owe it to D'sillin!//

//All right. But can you handle him?//

He glanced at the guards still in the room, then toward the passage to the air lock. //Keep them off my back, and I can take him out. He's—he's insane.//

//I know.// She relayed her plan, then added, //After that, you get on through the air lock and go after N'hawatt. Ignore everything else. Just go.//

He agreed, and she told Idom to get the guards' weapons any way he could. At the air lock, she would tackle the Beditzial, and Elias and Idom would be left to deal with Bitsin and the two who had guarded N'hawatt.

She barely had time to get them all to understand and agree when the Duke emerged from his air lock and paused to display himself to the crowd.

//Go!// Kyllikki gave the signal as she threw an image at Duksh, grabbed the energy net of his mind, and yanked. He dropped before she felt the green cape begin to respond. She threw the cape off and was struggling with the hood tie when Elias and Zuchmul hit Minthar.

The knotted tie loosened enough that she could peel the hood off her head, though it was still anchored around her neck. But suddenly she was free of its deadening feel. Then her senses reeled as Minthar died, his neck broken.

As she snatched Duksh's side arm, he groaned, but she knew he'd be out for hours. She ran for the air lock right behind

Zuchmul, who tore his Inhibitor from his neck and flung it aside. She pounded through the passage on his heels and shot Bitsin in the back as he was aiming square at Zuchmul.

Simultaneously, she shouted, "Grenmer Lady Beditzial!"

It was an inspired guess, but who could the woman be other than Ansarios Beditzial's eldest daughter?

The woman turned at the sound of her own name, mouth open, shock suffusing her countenance, her paralyzed thoughts locked behind protective barriers, overconfidence shattered.

In that split instant, Zuchmul leapt over the falling body of Bitsin, pushed the astonished woman into N'hawatt's two guards, and bounded down the ramp after N'hawatt.

Grenmer grabbed the weapon from the guard she'd knocked down, rolled over, and fired at Kyllikki. The cape hood around her neck smoked and shriveled.

Kyllikki threw herself prone, aimed the familiar weapon— a Teleod spitfire—and drilled a hole through Grenmer Lady Beditzial's forehead. It was almost like target practice.

Grenmer slumped, a dead weight against the two foundered guards, and Idom and Elias opened fire over Kyllikki's head, stitching a line of blood across the guards' bodies.

Determined not to retch, Kyllikki pulled her feet under her and propelled herself over the fresh corpses, Elias on her heels. *Killing shouldn't be that easy.* But Elias had been right. She'd defended herself, but without joy.

Fighting down all reaction, she squinted into the sunlight at the scene she'd been watching on the display, only from a confusingly different angle. There was a security barricade strung between *Shylant* and the Duke's ship, but N'hawatt had cleared a section of it by Influencing two of the guards to extinguish a pair of the projector poles that created the barrier field.

They stood beside their stations, eyes blank, faces slack, staring at nothing. Beyond them, N'hawatt was cutting a swath through the scattering of ground-service technicians and Port officials waiting to do their jobs. In his wake, Zuchmul ran faster than Kyllikki had ever seen him move.

The Duke started to parade down the polished strip on the landing field, the sun striking his reflection in the burnished area. It must be hellishly dazzling for the luren.

She knew she couldn't catch up, but she ran anyway. Twice Elias overtook her, then she pulled ahead just as N'hawatt breasted the last row of people between himself and the Duke.

The more distant guards were finally reacting to the disturbance, and someone grabbed Kyllikki, swinging her around to halt her.

Elias' fist connected with her captor's jaw, and she spun around again, just in time to see N'hawatt start to launch himself at the Duke.

Running, she sent, //N'hawatt, no!// She threw him a vivid picture of the dead bodies aboard *Shylant*.

He hesitated, the power going out of his legs as he began his leap.

Just as his feet left the ground, Zuchmul put all his power into Influence aimed at N'hawatt.

Still running, Kyllikki felt a wave of disorientation strike her, saw the Duke turn into a writhing *thing* with too many arms, something no doubt from luren mythology, and felt her reflex start to react against Zuchmul's Influence.

She tried to stop, a scream gathering in her throat as she resisted the reflex, then stumbled, arms flailing, legs weakening.

She went down on all fours. And suddenly, a horrid, gurgling scream rent the air, and it was over.

Head clearing, she struggled up, grabbing Elias' arm and starting forward again.

N'hawatt's brains were spattered on the ground and splashed on several shrieking bystanders. Two guards stood over the corpse. The Duke pulled himself up from a defensive crouch, pointed at Zuchmul and roared, "Kill the other assassin! He's not wearing an Inhibitor either!"

His men whirled to bring their weapons to bear, other more distant guards converging on the action. Some of them were telepaths coordinating the tightening of the security cordon. Doubling her speed, Kyllikki solidified her barriers, bracing herself against the inevitable. *So this is how it ends.*

At first Zuchmul didn't see her and Elias coming. He drew himself to his full height and faced his death, head high and proud, face calm, but then he caught sight of Kyllikki.

chapter fourteen

∙∙∙∙∙∙∙∙∙∙∙∙∙∙∙∙∙∙∙∙∙∙∙∙∙∙∙∙∙∙∙∙∙∙∙∙∙

Kyllikki never broke stride. Ignoring the shock waves of emotion pouring off Zuchmul, she swooped in, grabbed his arm, yelled at the Duke's guards, "He just saved the Duke's life, you idiots!" and thrust the luren at Elias. "Go!" She tossed her gun at the guards, and spat, "We're unarmed!"

They dodged the missile and six rifle shots hit it simultaneously. The Teleod spitfire exploded, gouging a crater they had to circle. Kyllikki ran, the guards firing as they came.

Kyllikki caught up with Elias and Zuchmul, retreating along the only open track, the way they had come. The guards N'hawatt had put out were still out. The ones converging from the sides avoided the bodies. There was no telling what someone might do under Influence. Most of the bystanders had retreated from the area. The few who were too confused or fascinated to move blocked the guards' field of fire.

A shot burned a hole in the cape, which still fluttered behind Kyllikki. Over her shoulder, she spotted the lead guard gaining fast, firing as he moved. He yelled to his squad, and they spread out to snare their quarries.

Kyllikki put on another burst of speed. She gained on the

longer-legged men, mostly because Elias was half-dragging the dazed luren. Elias gasped, "Where to?"

"Where's Idom?" she asked.

Zuchmul shook his head as if to say he had no idea.

"The ship!" she decided. //Try for the ship,// she told each of them mentally.

The landing field stretched in every direction, and Port vehicles and riot-control squads were already moving in on the action. There was a hot stitch in her side, and though she could see *Shylant's* ramp, she knew she couldn't make it.

And then a large white cargo van plastered with official logos careened into their path. *They've got us!*

But the van squared off in front of them, the vehicle slowing to their pace but not stopping as it presented its rear doors to them. She expected the doors to fly open revealing armed guards blasting away, or Imperial troopers who would jump down and surround them.

But when the doors flew aside, there was Idom, one hand clutching a rail, the other reaching toward them. "Hurry!"

Beside him was D'sillin and another luren. "Quickly, brother!" she yelled, reaching toward Zuchmul.

Zuchmul caught her hand and was inside, turning to grab Kyllikki as the other luren hauled her in and threw her into the depths of the van. It was filled with soft bundles—clothing or linens. She fell into the pile beside Zuchmul, sucking huge, wheezing breaths into her lungs.

Elias landed nearly on top of her and the doors slammed, locking them into pitch-darkness as acceleration pulled her toward the doors. Zuchmul and Elias each caught one of her arms, anchoring themselves somehow.

Several shots from heavier guns, probably mounted on pursuit vehicles, pierced the walls overhead. Every so often, the van swayed alarmingly. They were alternately flung back toward the front, then pitched toward the doors again. All Kyllikki could do was pant. She had no strength left to scream. She had almost caught her breath, her throat agonizingly dry, when the van skidded to a sudden halt.

The doors flew open again, admitting an eye-stabbing light, and D'sillin commanded, "Out! Move!"

Other luren dragged Kyllikki out the doors and propelled her toward another fully enclosed vehicle, painted with the luren concentric circles denoting diplomatic clearance. She collapsed onto a bench set along the side of the van and found herself in Zuchmul's arms, his mesh protection harsh against her. Elias slid into her other side, his uniform as clammy with sweat as her own.

The doors slid shut; other doors slammed, shaking the vehicle; then it rocketed away from the Port service van.

Before long, the pace slowed, and Kyllikki heard everyone, all the luren included, letting out shaky sighs.

Zuchmul told them, "We made it. We're safe."

His hug became barely intimate, then he withdrew. The darkness glowed the dim orange of bright luren lighting. As Kyllikki's eyes adjusted, she made out shapes and a hint of expression on the faces of D'sillin and the three strange luren. They had removed their Inhibitors. The van was technically luren territory.

D'sillin grabbed an overhead bar, and, swaying with the vehicle's motion, came to stand over Zuchmul. She studied Kyllikki grimly. "Where do you want us to let you off?"

Idom said, "The nearest Guild facility."

"No!" said Zuchmul. He got to his feet and peeled the mask from his face to look D'sillin in the eye. "Come over here; I have to talk to you."

She hesitated, then followed him to the end of the bench near the driver's cabin. Zuchmul backed her into the corner, invading what Kyllikki considered to be D'sillin's personal space. He spoke in the luren language. The air throbbed with Influence, a virtual jousting match performed under the elaborate protocols that made Influence part of the language.

Still, it didn't take a linguist to see that Zuchmul wanted something and D'sillin objected vehemently.

Zuchmul argued, lost, then moved closer, lowered his

voice, and his tone altered, perhaps to a more formal mode, a command or demand. His field of Influence was calm, solid.

D'sillin became very still. The other luren on the benches watched the confrontation intently. D'sillin glanced at them as if to say, *I have no choice.* Then she put her right hand on Zuchmul's right shoulder, and he put his left hand on her left shoulder.

Zuchmul slid back into place beside Kyllikki and gave her a reassuring squeeze as D'sillin returned.

Kyllikki noted how she placed herself a little farther from the non-luren. She studied Kyllikki once more, then scrutinized Elias and Idom, returning to Kyllikki as she said, "Zuchmul, you are truly serious about this?"

"Absolutely. Do you need it witnessed?"

"No. It is between us for the moment, but it won't stay that way. I don't think you know what you're asking."

"I do. She's Eight Families. But the others are more easily dealt with. There is a long and complicated story that must be recorded. It must be done in chamber. *First.* It is my right. It is the right of my Blood."

D'sillin's gaze flicked to him, then settled on Kyllikki. "Well, woman, are you——"

Zuchmul cut in. "I told you her name."

"Kyllikki, Lady of Laila," said D'sillin pensively.

"Just Kyllikki," corrected Kyllikki in a hoarse whisper.

"Kyllikki, then. Do you know what your—" She glanced at Zuchmul and amended, ". . . what Zuchmul has promised for you?"

"How could I?"

D'sillin shook her head in despair. "How well can you really control your reflexes, Lady?"

Suddenly, Kyllikki understood. She stared at Zuchmul in shock, but answered D'sillin. "Not too well, but I do try. I wouldn't want to hurt anyone who wasn't trying to hurt me." She paused, then added with the intonation only luren used, ". . . or those of my Blood," meaning not genetic relatives but those to whom a life-debt allegiance was owed.

Understanding what it meant for a member of the Families to utter a phrase not considered properly human, the luren shook her head again, glanced at Zuchmul, then admitted, "It is his right. The three of you, if you pledge on your lives to obey luren law, may come into the citadel to record your vision of events for the sake of Zuchmul and his Blood."

"She means," said Zuchmul, "if you break law and custom, your lives will be forfeit; but if not, you have diplomatic asylum, and all that's my due is also yours." He searched their faces. "My privileges aren't negligible, but my obligations are far-reaching, and they'll also be yours."

"Could I get a message to the Guild?" asked Idom.

"Covertly," replied D'sillin, "but not privately."

"Good enough. If Zuchmul needs me, I'll come."

Elias said, "Me, too."

Kyllikki agreed. "Keeping in mind that we don't know your laws or customs, and have no idea what our obligations would be, you have our pledge."

D'sillin said, "Zuchmul, they've no idea what you ask."

"That's so. But I know them. I trust them."

Her power rippled around her in a luren shrug. "You're responsible for them now."

Cryptically, he said, "You wanted Sa'ar, you've got it."

She stared at him again, then went to the driver's cabin to issue orders. As D'sillin's attention shifted away from her, Kyllikki felt as if a hot light had suddenly gone out, and the gravity diminished.

Zuchmul slumped. "You may wish you'd let them blow my head off."

She put her hand on his arm, alarmed. "Zuchmul—"

He put his hand on hers. "You will help me, won't you?"

His entire attention was on some fierce challenge he had yet to face, something more important to him than his own life or theirs. She could only respond, "We're friends—always. And that's what friends do—help."

He seemed to come back to himself as he withdrew his

hand and she released his arm. "You have no idea—Kyllikki, Elias, Idom—I'm afraid I've been very selfish . . ."

Elias said, "No. You've a right to ask anything of me."

Idom said, "And me; but Kyllikki learned some things from N'hawatt that change everything."

Kyllikki felt the loop of the green cape's fastening cut into her neck. Zuchmul started to help her work the knotted tie loose and free herself from the fabric as he said, to Idom, "Everything Kyllikki does or says changes everything. But if she can exonerate N'ha—" The moment he touched the green material, he made a revolted sound. "What is—*that?*"

She took it from him and explained why the Beditzial had wrapped her in it. "But as long as it doesn't surround me, it has even less effect. Still, I'd like to get rid of it."

"Here," said Idom. "Give it to me." He flexed the material. "What's it made of?"

"I don't know."

"Zuchmul, what did it feel like to you?"

"Slime. Worse."

"No end of surprises," mused Idom, as he folded the cape and stuffed it under his Guild robes.

As they neared the citadel, Zuchmul briefed them hastily on what they would face immediately, sidestepping questions about what would be expected later. "Contrary to popular rumor, you won't be wantonly attacked, but you must stay with me and do as I say."

The limousine did not go into a courtyard entry to the citadel, but rolled down a twisting ramp and discharged them in a huge parking garage filled with official vehicles.

Here, the lighting was for luren, though the five luren with them did not remove their outdoor eye inserts. She concluded that the lighting where they stood was bright by luren standards. The bright area, though, was surrounded by what seemed to be pitch-blackness, and was probably normal lighting.

There was a large counter set into a corner, separated from the traffic by a transparent shield in which signs in luren script flashed. In the office behind the counter, several clerks worked.

The counter sloped down toward the customer's side and presented a number of consoles for the use of those walking up to the counter. The displays were invisible to her, and what script she could see, illegible.

The counter looked exactly like the check-in desk at a busy hotel or travel-booking office.

D'sillin paused at the counter and tapped in some commands at one of the consoles, then she gathered her three luren around Zuchmul for a few words. She seemed to be offering things while Zuchmul declined, accepted, or negotiated. It was all done in bursts of Influence and luren language. A moment later, D'sillin made a few more entries at the console, then led her people off into the pitch-darkness, leaving Zuchmul and the non-luren alone.

Zuchmul herded them into the narrow channel between the transparent shield and the office window, and tucked them up against the end wall. "Wait here," he muttered, examining the console D'sillin had used. Then he turned back to them and repeated in a firmer tone, "Stay right there. Don't move. All right? Don't do anything."

They all agreed, and he worked over the displays.

Meanwhile, vehicles departed and arrived, and luren stepped up to the counter to do business in a quick, abstracted way until they noticed the three intruders.

The first time she was inspected by Influence, Kyllikki tensed, but it was nothing that would trigger her reflex. Zuchmul did not notice the other luren until the man spoke. Zuchmul rattled off an explanation that mentioned D'sillin's name, and the man gave them a dubious once-over, finished his business, and left.

The next was a woman, but this time Zuchmul countered her rising Influence before it focused on the intruders, recited a version of the explanation, and resumed his task. She completed her business, then lingered outside the shield, considering what to do about them. Eventually, she left.

Zuchmul continued working while variations on this occurred several more times, once with a clerk from inside the office. Some querents took it upon themselves to step close to Zuchmul and offer low-voiced advice.

At last, Zuchmul accepted some tokens that spilled out of a slot with a musical tinkle. "That takes care of that," he said, "now come over here." He took them to a machine at the far end of the counter, inserted a token, and told Kyllikki, "Put your hand in the slot."

At Kyllikki's hesitation, he sighed, replaced the token with another, and stuck his own hand into the dark slot. A rubbery membrane sealed around his wrist; the token popped up, then the seal released his hand. He held up the token. "A key. You can't do anything in the citadel without one, and it won't work unless it has a record of your handprint. It doesn't hurt. Much. I mean it won't hurt you."

"Oh," said Kyllikki, feeling foolish. The machine looked nothing like an identity programmer. But then she realized that the radiation it used had to be confined. She slipped her hand into the slot and felt the seal grip her wrist. A moment later the token popped up.

Zuchmul gave it to her. "It taps my personal credit."

It didn't look like a key, but then when you had to control magnetic fields, you built things differently. After the men had accepted theirs, Zuchmul led them into the dark, the way D'sillin had gone. It wasn't quite as black as Kyllikki had feared. Zuchmul lined them up against a wall and said, "Wait there."

Elias called, "Where did you go? We can't see!"

Zuchmul reappeared. "Neither can I. I have to take out these shields, so I can read the signs and see where we're going. I'm at the sink, right here. Now wait."

They waited tensely. Every time luren came by, they scrutinized the strangers and began to question them. Every time, Zuchmul provided his explanation. Kyllikki was intensely curious about what he was saying but kept her barriers up, determined not to react if anyone brushed her with a more pointed use of Influence.

Meanwhile, Kyllikki noticed a faint but pervasive odor she couldn't place. And despite the kaleidoscopic patterns of Influence among passers-by, and the noise of moving vehicles, there was an underlying sense of *silence*. The air was as fresh and clean as any springtime meadow, except for that intrusive odor. Even so far underground there was no sense of oppression or dampness. Despite D'sillin's warning, there was no sense of danger and no real hostility from anyone after they'd heard Zuchmul's explanation, though reactions ranged from simple astonishment to flat rejection.

When Zuchmul returned, he stood with them looking about as if for the first time, then announced, "There it is. This way." He struck off across the traffic lane, then shortened his stride. "The flooring is smooth. I won't walk you off a step without warning. Can you see well enough to follow me?"

"If you don't get more than a step or two ahead."

She felt his Influence expand to enclose them all, and his sense of confidence in the familiar, a subtle relaxation of vigilance, helped. He took Kyllikki's arm, and the two of them walked just in front of the two men. As they crossed the traffic lanes, Kyllikki peered this way and that, unable to see more than an arm's length. He brought them safely across the garage to a wall where he inserted his key. A door flew open to admit them to a foyer that was warm and carpeted but just as dark, despite the dim glow of what seemed to be decorative lamps among comfortable seats.

Chilled in her clammy clothes, Kyllikki began to shiver in that welcome warmth.

Zuchmul used his key again, and a moment later they were in a lift that plummeted nearly in free-fall. Elias gasped, "I thought we were underground!"

"We are. We're going down to the eighteenth level. I doubt any Imperial telepath could find Kyllikki down there."

"No, I wouldn't think so," she agreed. "How many underground levels are there here?"

Zuchmul studied the lift controls. "Twenty-three, with another eighty-three above ground. This citadel is a hundred times larger than Port Confluence on Insarios. I didn't know D'sillin kept offices here, but it makes sense she would."

"She obviously has a lot of prestige here," said Idom.

"Yes, you could say that," allowed Zuchmul as the lift stopped to admit three luren.

They were conversing as they entered, heedless of those already in the lift. As the doors closed, one of them nudged another, then all three gaped at Kyllikki, Idom, and Elias.

Zuchmul made his explanation in an offhand tone.

The luren looked at each other, surreptitiously scanned the three strangers, and fell silent until the lift stopped to let them off.

Zuchmul relaxed when the doors closed, then the lift moved to the right. At the next stop, he led them down a curving passage, broad, low-ceilinged, carpeted, and dark. Several times, Zuchmul said, "This way," and turned a corner.

It felt as if they'd completed a circle when he finally stopped at a door. "This is it." His key opened the door, and it was just as dark inside as out, dark and stuffy. The door closed as Zuchmul adjusted the invisible lighting, turned on a sound system and changed the bizarre music to the soothing sound of waves on a shore. He asked, "Is it cool enough in here for you? I turned down the thermostat. Your rooms are off this hall and have their own air controls." He took Kyllikki's hand on one side and Elias' on the other.

"Idom, put your hand on my shoulder. I've got the lights up as far as they'll go. I'll try to do something about that later. This is your room, Kyllikki," he said, leading them all inside. "It has its own facilities—the door is over there on that wall. The rest of us will share the facilities at the end of the hall. Later I'll arrange a change of clothing and some way to feed you all. We'll be left alone today, but by morning, you'll have to be prepared to face some very critical people."

Kyllikki said, "Just tell us what we can do for you."

With a weary sigh, he replied, "You must address a group of people who have authority over me and mine. It's—oh, I couldn't begin to translate it. Can you just consider it a kind of religious exercise, a sacred obligation?"

Religious? They'd never discussed religion, but she didn't know why she should be surprised. Every human race had an abundance of religions, though most humans ignored their culture's practices except in moments of ultimate stress. *He thinks he has to die—permanently.*

"All you have to do is tell everything that happened to you while I was dormant, everything we did afterward and why. This will be a—public—event. But we must include every intimate detail." His tension was thick around him, holding overtones of guilt and fear.

Oblivious, Idom said, "Good. It's time to tell this story to anyone who'll listen. When can I send that—"

"They won't be just listening," blurted Zuchmul. "Influence will be in full use. Kyllikki must be drugged."

"What! There's no drug that can prevent reflex—"

"Yes, there is."

"Sovereigns Be!" said Idom. "How does it work?"

"I don't know," said Zuchmul, "but it has been tested. It was done legally, on criminals duly denied extradition to the Teleod courts and sentenced to death under Blood Law. The survivors were properly executed, and the experiments were stopped when the drug was perfected. That was decades ago, but every citadel stocks it."

"I don't believe it." said Kyllikki.

"Would you more readily believe that luren would willingly remain helpless before the Families? Our reputation for protecting our privacy is well earned."

Elias drew away. "You brought us here to be killed—"

"No! You will leave in good health when you choose."

"You're not telling the whole truth," accused Kyllikki.

Contritely, he agreed. "None of you will retain clear memories when you leave. Our privacy will be maintained."

Feeling betrayed, Kyllikki started, "Zuchmul—"

"No, listen! There's more at stake than my personal honor. The reasons for what I've done will make great differences in hundreds of lives. When the Duke's guards were closing in on me—Kyllikki, I ran from them with you because I realized it would be selfish to die and leave everyone else to contend with my guilts."

"Especially because we can prove you're innocent," said Elias.

"No. Not me. My relatives. My survivors. You're here for them, not for me. And you will leave without me."

"Then we shouldn't do this now," mused Idom. At Zuchmul's despairing protest, he told Elias and Zuchmul about Zimor's plan to activate a ground-based Pool. "It's not going to do what she thinks it will, so Kyllikki has decided to stop Zimor, and I'm with her. But, as I count, we can't do it without you. So your family may have to wait."

After a long, somber silence, Zuchmul said, "Idom, it can't be stopped. The convocation will occur tomorrow morning. You will be called. If you refuse me . . ." He strangled back a sob. His Influence was drawn about him like a clenched fist, and all Kyllikki felt was the pervasive anguish that had been there since he'd turned from the Duke's guards. Living was worse than any death would have been.

She drew him into an embrace. "We'll be there."

"So we'll be there," said Idom grimly. "You said it would be a public proceeding. Then we just have to be sure the right authorities are also there or at least listening. If we can convince enough of them that what we know of Zimor's plan is true—then perhaps they'll help us."

"They'll be there," assured Zuchmul, "but helping you would mean abandoning the policy of neutrality, and I—"

"Then we need to reach those who can change the policy."

Zuchmul moved to the bed and dropped down beside Idom. "That's not impossible, but it would take D'sillin to—" He cut off, rose, and charged out of the room.

"What's the matter?" asked Elias.

"Communicator—can't you—no, I don't suppose so. I hadn't thought of that. I'll be right back. You can explore. It's safe here."

While he was gone, they groped around Kyllikki's room until they'd found drawers, cabinets, the facilities, and a desk with communications and data-display equipment that seemed to be disconnected.

Kyllikki poked at the controls. Zuchmul's voice burst from the speaker. "Kyllikki? Is that you?"

"Yes."

He told her how to turn on the visual display, but though he could now see her, she could see nothing but dim shadows that might or might not have been there.

"Well," he said, "I'll leave it activated anyway." He explained that each room had a console but that only the use of the key in the main console could open the billing accounts. The arrangement seemed reasonable to Kyllikki, considering what trouble children could get into, but Zuchmul replied that this area of the citadel housed no children. "I may be crazy enough to bring you here," he commented, "but I'm not naive enough to try to manage you around children."

The inaudible door signal interrupted him and, moments later, he brought an armful of clothing, two brass candle holders with ornate glass chimneys, and a box of fat candles.

"D'sillin's messenger said that someone bought the candles for party decorations, then discovered they produce an irritating light. Maybe they'll help. Here are some loose robes to change into for tonight, and there will be someone by later to take your measurements for something to wear tomorrow. I have to go out now, but when I come back I'll bring you something to eat."

"Where are you going?" she asked.

"Physician's exam. They have to make sure I'm healthy and sane enough to do this now. Oh, not again. Excuse me."

"What is it?" asked Kyllikki, hastening after him.

"Door. I hope the curious aren't descending."

She lost him at the entry to the large reception room, but sensed the direction when the door opened, admitting a puff of outside air. And again there was that distinctive odor. She worked her way closer as Zuchmul conversed with people outside, his long-restrained hunger erupting. They were just shadows against shadow, but then Zuchmul reached out and made two tapping gestures accompanied by rippling surges of Influence.

He was about to close the door when Kyllikki made it to his side. She could discern three figures outside and felt the heavy pall of Influence shrouding them. The odor was overwhelming. And Zuchmul was shaking.

As the three retreated, she softened her barriers in unabashed curiosity. *Animals!* Her eyes showed her the dim shadows of three human figures, but her other senses insisted it was a luren and two docile animals. "Orl!" she exclaimed. "That odor. It's all over the place. It's orl!" She realized how rude that sounded. "Oh, consider that unsaid!"

Zuchmul shut the door. "Without further thought. I hope the odor doesn't bother you too much. It's everywhere. I sent them away because I didn't think you'd be comfortable with them in the apartment. The cages are just down the other hall over there." He gestured to a point opposite the hall that led to the bedrooms.

"You mean someone came to deliver your dinner?"

"Routine courtesy for new arrivals."

"But how will you—I mean—I know how hungry you—"

"I can't dine until after the examination. They'll be kept just around the corner in the common cages. I have to go now. You'll be safe here as long as you don't open the door for anyone, and ignore the . . . well, you won't notice it anyway. I set up the console to take messages."

"Good. I never knew luren hearing differed so much!"

He paused half into the corridor. "It doesn't. The signals are distinctive magnetic pulses. *Controlled* ones."

"Oh." The door shut, leaving her in a dark, alien world.

Elias called, "Zuchmul, it was great of them to send us candles, but there's nothing to light them with."

"He's gone," she answered, crossing the room by feel.

Stumbling and groping, they searched the apartment for the means to make fire. Short of dismantling a wall and arcing two power cables, there was nothing. There wasn't even a kitchen. *Of course not. No children, no food.* They tried searching the orl cages and the area where the food for them was stored, but that was empty except for a stack of tightly sealed kegs which she assumed held orl food.

Kyllikki sat on her bed amid the pile of clothing and candles, sorting it by feel, while the two men searched her bathroom. She said, "I don't like the idea of taking a shower in the dark, using strange plumbing—" The box of candles opened, spilling the hard cylinders all over the bed. Groping after them, she found a flat cylinder, cold and metallic. "Hey! I think I've found it!"

It took another few minutes to get the thing to work, and when it finally did flare, she had hold of it upside down and nearly dropped the flaming gadget onto the bed. With both of the men shouting advice, she managed to light one of the candles. It made a very satisfying yellow glow that was almost too bright for them after hours in the dark.

They explored the apartment by that light, looking for something to use as holders for more candles, but there was nothing. Still, two candles made life suddenly bearable.

As she showered, finally getting warm, Kyllikki found herself singing the tune burbling through the back of Elias' mind. Even though she knew it was wholly irrational, the simple light of one primitive candle made it seem possible to convince the luren authorities to abandon their neutrality and defeat Zimor. The war was as good as over.

Still humming, Kyllikki was standing by the bed, toweling her hair and letting the air dry her body when in the hall, Idom cried, "That's it!" Her door flew open and Idom charged in. "Kyllikki, you've got to tell me about—" He backed up. "Hurry up. I need information."

Elias strode after him, calling, "Idom, what's going—"

He stopped by the door while Kyllikki was still staring at it openmouthed. He was carrying the other candle lamp. It outlined his features beautifully and made his hair a damp golden crown. The music in him flowed through her like a caress. The robe he wore was tight over the shoulders, displaying every sculpted line while it clung about his pectorals and hips, where luren were so much narrower.

She lowered the towel around her and finally, he broke his gaze off and charged down the hall.

She dressed and joined them, bringing her candle. Idom broke off questioning Elias about the experience of being Dreambonded, then turned to Kyllikki, and with an urgent, avid tone he quizzed her on the use of the monomolecular material in disrupting a telepath's perceptions in the realms.

"But there was no effect at all on your abilities with the audio-analogue?"

"No, and after I got used to it, I had no trouble with the keys, either."

"Then I think I know how it works to—"

The door opened and Zuchmul cried out, "Sovereigns Be!" and turned his back on them, juggling the load of trays.

"The candles!" said Kyllikki, and blew them out.

Zuchmul came into the room, letting the door close behind him. "D'sillin was right. Nobody would want to use those at a party!" He set the trays on the table. "The meal isn't anything like what I was able to do for you on the ship, but Lur exports massive quantities of these products, and not just to the citadels. *Somebody* must be eating it!" The faint odor of orl clung to his clothing. "I'll put my protectors in. You can relight the candles."

Kyllikki sighed, "Zuchmul, I think the lighter is on the bed in my room, or maybe in the bath."

"I'll get it."

When they'd taken the edge off their hunger, Idom, in one of his more distracted tones, asked, "Zuchmul, how could we ever convince all those luren we have to face tomorrow that they have to let you come with us because you have to enter that planet-based Pool with Elias and Kyllikki?"

Kyllikki choked.

chapter fifteen

● ●

Zuchmul was the first to get over the shock. "Idom, Elias and Kyllikki would *never*—and besides, luren are forbidden to descend into a Pool!"

"The law is there to prevent a Bonder from grabbing control of a luren and forming another Triumvirate."

"Kyllikki said that could be what Zimor wants! What we've done already skirts awfully close to—"

"No!" said Kyllikki. "I'd *never*—"

"I know," assured Zuchmul. "But that's not the only reason luren are forbidden into the Pools. Idom, Influence is one of the least-understood functions—"

"Of course," Idom replied. "That's what my theory—the one Zimor stole—was about. Kyllikki picked up on it when she figured out how to cut the Dreambond. Influence can't be understood alone, but only as part of Dream and Bond. As space, time, and thought are not the separate things they appear to be, so Bonder, Dreamer, and luren are not separate. The Bonder spans space, the Dreamer spans time, and the luren spans thought. Influence transforms emotion into vision, into motive, into action, into *existence*. It uses a veritable riptide of pure energy—and through the depths of a Pool, under certain conditions, it could reach to the ends of creation."

Idom wasn't given to exaggeration.

Elias' eyes took on the wild look Idom's explanations usually evoked, but this time he emanated a wariness more appropriate to dealing with a dangerous madman than a theoretical scientist. With exaggerated quiet, he said, "Zimor was going to send a Bonded pair into the Pool—and you said that would permanently destroy the usefulness of the Pools for astrogation. Now you—"

"No, no, Elias. Given what Kyllikki says about the monomolecular circuitry in that cape, and considering what happened between you and Zuchmul when Zuchmul helped break the Bond, it's absolutely clear that Zimor's experiment would result in a sort of "crazing" of the firmament—a network of real cracks, not just furrows, gouges, and scars. It may be even worse if her pair uses drums or music." Oblivious to Elias' condition, he commented to Kyllikki, "When you told me that, I finally understood why things have been getting worse so much faster."

Zuchmul said, "I see. It all has to do with music. Dissonance and silence are as much a part of music as harmony is. It's the patterns that count—patterns govern the transformation of energy. And matter is Influenced energy."

What?! Kyllikki squeezed her eyes shut. She hadn't slept since before the final approach to Vindara Port, more than a day ago. Small wonder nothing made sense.

But Idom seemed to think it did. "Influenced energy?" he mused. "Yes, I suppose it is, if my theory is true, which is, of course, where Elias' musical bent comes in."

Elias, struggling for composure, asked, "Do we have to understand your theory to understand the difference between what you want us to do and what Zimor intends?"

"No. Zimor wants to send down a Bonded couple without a luren anchor, and the result will be destruction. You and Kyllikki will go down and Bond *within* the Pool—using Zuchmul. He's the key, the fifth element, the harmonizing numerical that makes it a cleansing, not a severing. You see,

Kyllikki will define the parameter of space, Elias that of time, and then direct Zuchmul's power. Or it would be equally valid to look at it the other way around: that Zuchmul will use Influence to define the key image and Kyllikki and Elias will power it, thus reversing the damage."

Scooting forward, Idom arranged the remnants of their dinner into two circles, placing two things in one circle and four in the second. "That's a bit abstract. It's easier to see by counting into the numericals—"

Zuchmul interrupted, "Idom, you need someone skilled with Influence. I've spent most of my life wearing an Inhibitor and learning to avoid using Influence."

"No, look." He put two knives between the two items in the first circle, and another between one of the elements and the circle. "Zimor's experiment. Bonder, Dreamer, Pool—a three-element system. Bonder and Dreamer are linked, as are Bonder and Pool—an open three-element system with one double Bond, the Dreambond, the Dreamer needs it as much as the Bonder. And one single Bond, between Bonder and Pool.

"The Dreambond is a two, so you have three elements, plus one double Bond and a single, the one between Bonder and Pool—which makes three elements and three Bonds. But what Zimor's advisers can't see because they don't understand numericals is that they've reinforced the triune quality without actually shadowing a six." He met Elias' gaze and interpreted. "Like a chord with one missing note replaced by a note just a quarter tone off true." Elias winced as his imagination supplied the sound. Idom added, "The energy raised—and it would be considerable!—would simply go wild. There'd be no way to control it."

"How far would the destruction go?" asked Kyllikki.

"Probably at least galactic in scope. But even if it's only half the galaxy, it'd extend from Inarash to Earth and to Lur, taking a huge chunk out of the Metaji and the Teleod. Neither Operators nor Guides will be able to use the Pools in the crazed region. The damage would reduce the range of all telepaths, perhaps even to zero. Gravitic drives surely won't work normally."

"That's hard to believe," said Kyllikki.

"Maybe. But that's why it's so urgent that I get all of this to the Guild. If this theory is correct, then after the crazing is done, my scheme for reversing it won't work."

Zuchmul said, "I still don't see why me."

Idom looked down at his impromptu diagrams. "I thought I explained." He took a deep, patient breath, and named the three elements in his other circle. "You, Elias, Kyllikki." He started moving objects to represent the different Bonds between the elements, rattling off numbers as he went.

Kyllikki halted him. "Wait. Just tell us what Zuchmul is other than a great space mechanic."

Idom looked at her, startled. "Kyllikki, what is he to you that you would defy law, custom, and common sense to have sex with him? If you hadn't, you know, this whole plan wouldn't be possible." She made a bewildered sound, and he added, "So why do you keep saving his life?"

Her mouth opened, but nothing came out.

Idom answered her silent protest. "Oh, of course you don't know what you're doing. But that doesn't matter—"

With a sigh of relief, Zuchmul got to his feet. "The door," he explained. "Must be the clothier." But when he opened it, he said, "D'sillin!" He called over his shoulder, "Blow out those candles, please?"

Idom and Elias extinguished the lights.

D'sillin's step whispered into the room as she spoke to Zuchmul in flickers of Influence, then told them all, "I came prepared for the candles—if I may, Zuchmul?"

"Certainly, though it's not necessary to—"

"But it is. This way, we can all see—a little. Relight the candles for your guests. I'll be right back." She went down the hall to where the orl were usually kept.

Elias said, "I've no idea what's become of the starter."

Zuchmul hunted on the table. "Last I saw of it, it was supposed to be me in Idom's diagram. Yes—this is it." Fire flared, and Zuchmul quickly relit the two candles.

They heard water running as Zuchmul resumed his seat, saying, "I don't exactly follow your reasoning, Idom, but I trust you. If, after the Recounting, I'm allowed to accompany you to Inarash, I will. The only way that might happen is if D'sillin helps us. So now we've got to tell her everything. But I don't know how to convince her!"

Kyllikki said, "We've got to try."

Zuchmul warned, "She came to tell us something, not to listen to what we must reveal tomorrow. Let me handle this."

D'sillin returned and paused. "Those candles do produce a ghastly effect. I hope it won't make what I have to say seem more frightening than it is."

Zuchmul relinquished his chair to her as she approached. "You'll get used to it in a few minutes." He began to gather up the scattered food containers.

"Don't bother, Zuchmul. Sit down. This is important. It may, in fact—forgive me, but it may be more important than your Recounting, which might have to be postponed."

Zuchmul folded onto the bench seat beside Elias, the field of Influence around him throbbing with shock.

D'sillin folded her hands. "Yes, I know, but please believe we're not impious. This threatens all the Blood."

D'sillin shifted her attention to Kyllikki. "According to my physician's report on Zuchmul, I did you a grave injustice on Insarios. Ignorance isn't maliciousness, and despite the penalty, you didn't let him suffer once you discovered your error. Consider all my harsh words unsaid."

"Without further thought," replied Kyllikki, stunned that their private indiscretion had shown in the physician's report, and shocked that D'sillin approved.

D'sillin returned to Zuchmul. "I have reliable confirmation that the last message from N'hawatt was not the garbled meanderings of a Bloo—of a deranged mind."

Kyllikki demanded, "N'hawatt got word out to you after Zimor captured him?"

"What do you know of that?"

"What do you know of it?" she returned.

D'sillin looked to Zuchmul, who said, "Kyllikki, D'sillin

has the rank here. She asks; you answer. Anything else is worse than rude. She's on Veramai as an official of a group of allied families, which, because you had me awakened on Insarios, is now allied through me to another, older, group, creating a powerful majority voice. I'm a kind of linchpin in this alliance, which is why my Recounting is so important, and why anyone's listening to me at all, but even I don't have the status to question D'sillin. Just tell her how you learned what happened to N'hawatt."

From what Kyllikki had learned in school, lurèn never achieved political majorities, which was why they were so hard to deal with. "D'sillin, I didn't mean to be rude. I searched N'hawatt's memory and got the story of his capture."

D'sillin's silence became icy. Illicit sex was one thing, mental invasion quite another.

Zuchmul said, "Out of context, that sounds even worse than what I've done. But not only did she make it possible for me to delay N'hawatt, she also killed the Beditzial who had him—I think because of what she learned from him."

Reactions flowed through D'sillin, then she thawed. "The Blood owes you all much, not just for preventing the assassination, but for bearing the blame for the plot. I went to the landing field to present proof of the Teleod plot against Fotel and us. Later, when they'd seen that I'd presented it *before* the attack, they accepted that the luren community was not backing the Teleod assassins. Now, even the Duke blames only the few who were there, assuming that even a luren can be a traitor."

"He blames us," said Zuchmul. "Personally."

"Yes," replied D'sillin. "If N'hawatt's mental privacy was the price, then, Kyllikki, your transgression was not only legal by Blood Law, but obligatory."

"Blood Law does not apply to me."

D'sillin glanced at Zuchmul, and there was a swift exchange of Influence. She answered Kyllikki, "It does so long as you're within our jurisdiction under Zuchmul's protection, and so long as you observe our Law. Therefore, a false trail has led your pursuers offworld, and as long as you handle your telepathy under the same Law governing Influence, as you did with N'hawatt, we see no problem with your behavior that needs reporting to your superiors."

"But we can't stay here," said Idom.

"I'm here to arrange your departure in such a way that you will not be caught and killed."

"D'sillin," said Zuchmul, hands clutched in his lap, "I beg to be allowed my Recounting tomorrow in chamber. You can't deny me."

"I shall not deny. But you may be willing to delay after you've heard me out. The assassination plot was engineered by Zimor of Laila as a diversion. We must not be diverted." To Kyllikki, she explained, "When you arrived so fortuitously on Insarios, I suspected you were the leader of this plot. We knew only that a woman of the Families was holding N'hawatt captive. We thought N'hawatt had managed to die and you had taken Zuchmul in his place and had some hold over him. When you refused to be reasonable about his travel arrangements, I grew certain. When he fled the citadel, I felt I had to save him, even if it meant sending the Baron's men after him. I made an error."

"An understandable one," granted Kyllikki. She looked to Idom, who seemed to agree, and only then did she notice how very silent Elias had been. His inner music was muted, as if he was worrying a private problem, not listening.

D'sillin continued, "But now I've learned Zimor's real plan. She expects to win this war with one blow that will put all interstellar transport—and thus all trade—into her control. The wealth of Lur is based on trade. We can't allow her to win. She knows it, and so tried to set the Metaji to war against us. We can no longer remain neutral. The vote is now in progress, but because of the alliances through Zuchmul, I don't doubt the outcome. Before the sun rises, we'll be at war with the Teleod."

Zuchmul looked at Kyllikki, then asked Idom, "You're sure she didn't know what she was doing?"

"Kyllikki? No. She can't count," said Idom.

D'sillin looked from one to the other, then asked, "Did

you discover from N'hawatt that Zimor has built a giant Pool sunk into the crust of Inarash? That's the planet where the Laila Family is based." She glanced at Kyllikki. "Well, I suppose you know that."

"I do," said Kyllikki, "and yes, N'hawatt's memory of his capture was very clear. D'sillin, please excuse me if this is impertinent, but though I'm astonished at how much you've discovered, there's a lot you don't yet know. May we tell you what we know of this Pool now?"

D'sillin inspected them and assented.

So, taking turns, they told the entire story, with Idom's interpretations interspersed with each event. Beginning with the attack on *Prosperity* and their rescue of Elias, Zuchmul's dormancy, and their escape from Barkyr, they recounted the discovery that Elias was Zimor's Dreambonded spy, Elias' reaction to the truth, Kyllikki's first battle with Zimor for Elias, then their version of events on Insarios, Zuchmul's decision to aid Kyllikki in freeing Elias, and finally the odd feedback effect Zuchmul experienced from Elias, which magnified the effect of Elias' frustrations on Zuchmul's hunger and led to the breaking of yet another law.

At Idom's dry, scholarly description of Elias' fantasy about Kyllikki, D'sillin finally nodded, darting a glance at Zuchmul, a glance shrouded in Influence which he allowed to beat through him without resistance. "I see why you desire the Recounting now. It makes your actions seem—inevitable, even a defense of the Blood, anticipating the declaration of war by only a few days." She asked a short question in the luren language and Zuchmul replied in a monosyllable.

Kyllikki was holding her breath, waiting for the nearly palpable Influence to abate. But whatever was carried on that powerful wave, it wasn't triggering her native defense.

Seeing her distress, Idom said, "If Zuchmul hadn't had the courage to help Kyllikki break that Bond, we would not now be able to reverse the damage the Teleod Operators have done to the firmament."

D'sillin's attention riveted on him. "Reverse?"

"Reverse." Idom picked up the tale, filling in with deductions that had only come to him later.

D'sillin again interrogated Zuchmul in the luren language, focusing her Influence on him, but eliciting only monosyllabic replies. Noticing how Kyllikki was squirming, she gathered her Influence close to herself, and prompted, "So then you arrived here at Vindara Port, intending to reach the Emperor with the tale of Elias' identity?"

"Yes." Kyllikki told of the arrival of the "Inspectors," her identification of the Beditzial, and again tried to recall every detail she'd learned from N'hawatt.

Zuchmul interposed, "She didn't decide to help N'hawatt because of me. In the life pod, I'd explained what it could be like for a luren to be—well, she *understood*."

"I see," said D'sillin.

They each told their versions of the chase after N'hawatt. Idom recounted how Kyllikki's description of what the green cloak could do crystallized his theory. Then he explained his theory in a tightly organized way that made it more convincing. Kyllikki noticed when Elias began to listen, though still wrestling his personal devils.

The candles had burned down as Idom fell silent at last, and D'sillin said, "We wanted to ask you to leave for Inarash tonight to destroy that Pool before Zimor uses it—just you three, because Kyllikki would know how to get into the Laila compound, Idom knows Pools, and Zuchmul can get you through the border and across the Teleod on luren ships. But now you're telling us you can use that abomination to restore reliability to astrogation?"

"Only if Zuchmul, Kyllikki, and Elias agree to ignore even the more sensible portions of the law. And what I'm asking of Kyllikki is more than of anyone else because—forgive me," he said aside to Kyllikki—"she's got to go into that Pool using that drug Zuchmul mentioned, the one that would allow a luren to use heavy Influence on her. Without it, there's no chance for this to work. D'sillin, a supply of it could be sent with us, couldn't it?"

Nodding, she looked at Zuchmul, then asked Kyllikki, "You agreed to go to his Recounting suitably drugged?"

"I hadn't agreed yet, but I would have." She glanced at Idom's shadowed eyes, wondering why she hadn't understood when Idom had described his experiment to begin with.

As Elias had become more restive, Zuchmul had settled into a serene calm Kyllikki hadn't seen in him since before Barkyr. Now, without the driving tension that had been behind every previous request, the luren said, "The Recounting is my right. I'm not sure I can relinquish it. I'm not sure that if I do, I'll be able to do what Idom requires of me." He added to Idom, "I'm not unwilling, just unsure of my strength without the Recounting first."

D'sillin said, "We have your transport off Veramai arranged, and a line of contacts for you to use, some on my own ships, some on Sa'ar ships. Timing is crucial. My best information is that the Teleod forces are massing for an assault on Veramai. That could be another diversion, one calculated to bring the Imperial fleet here to defend us."

"Is that what those ships are here for?" asked Idom.

"Maybe. Other sources say the Emperor is planning to take Inarash at any cost."

Idom said, "If they take those ships that far as one fleet, they'll lose maybe fifty percent in transit."

D'sillin agreed. "However," she said, "it won't be long before one or both of those fleets moves. One source hints that Zimor plans to work her Pool when the Imperial fleet is in transit and wipe it out totally. We wanted the Pool destroyed before that happened. Whatever Zimor's schedule, she'll probably move faster when she finds her assassination has failed."

Kyllikki remembered now what she'd learned from N'hawatt that she hadn't mentioned, and she told them her deductions about the Teleod political situation. "So Zimor has other reasons for pushing her project through."

"Then it may already be too late, but if Idom is correct, if there's a chance not just to stop her but to reverse the damage, we have to try, no matter the cost."

Idom nodded assuringly. "On the way here from Insarios, I checked out part of my theory. By the time we get to Inarash, I should have the rest proved out."

"Forgive me, Guildmaster," said D'sillin, "but we'll have to subject your theory to peer review before you implement it. The final go-ahead will be given to you by citadel relay, and should arrive at Inarash when you do."

"That certainly sounds reasonable," agreed Idom.

They all knew that the luren maintained their own communications network, and that it often functioned faster than anything either Teleod or Metaji had.

Zuchmul said, "You'll never be able to remember what Idom's said, let alone explain it to another Guildmaster."

A trifle hesitantly, D'sillin produced a recorder from the folds of her clothing. It was luren manufacture, heavily shielded, which explained why Zuchmul hadn't sensed it operating. She handed it to him. "The substance of your Recounting is there, if devoid of formalities. It's enough for me that Kyllikki said she'd testify under Influence. Do you certify that everything said in this session is as it would have been said in Chamber?"

"Every word of this story as it has been recounted before you is true as it would have been said in Chamber." Holding the recorder in both hands as if it were a fragile jewel, he recited his entire name, followed by some luren formula. Then he handed her the recorder.

In a slurred accent, D'sillin recited her entire name. It took her a lot longer than it had taken Zuchmul, and she followed it with a similar formula. Then she handed the recorder back to him. "Run a copy for yourself."

The face he turned to her was nearly worshipful, but then he rose and went to the desk in the corner where he inserted the recorder and set up the copying.

Worried, Idom asked D'sillin, "So you'll have a copy of my theory. Who did you intend to get to review it?"

D'sillin rose. "I'm not familiar with the roster of

Guildmasters," she said, going to the desk and standing behind Zuchmul. "May I, Zuchmul?"

"Of course." He shifted aside to give her access to the command pads, but Kyllikki caught him staring at Idom.

D'sillin ran data onto the screen, and as Zuchmul handed her the recorder and took his copy, she asked Idom to spell his complete name, title, and identification code. "It appears there are only ten in this part of the Empire who can be counted as your peers, and none of them is on Veramai. The Imperial forces have conscripted them, as you were."

"Ten?" asked Idom, sitting forward. "Who?"

She read the names. He asked about someone else, and Zuchmul fingered the display. "Deceased."

Idom groaned. "She's the only other one I'd have expected to figure this out, given the data." He scrubbed at his face, the years suddenly heavy on him. "I think the recording will convince them by itself. I hope it's all on there. I was editing heavily for a nontechnical audience."

D'sillin came back and gave him the recorder. "You can add anything you like, though keep in mind I'm not sure who we can reach before you get to Inarash."

For Kyllikki, D'sillin's casual mention of their destination evoked an image of home in her mind and the reality of the plan crashed in on her. She'd sworn never to return to Inarash, and she'd meant it. She'd sworn never to enter a Pool again, and she'd meant that. Now she'd have to do both, and Bond a Dreamer, too. She'd killed the Beditzial without a qualm, and now had discarded her sworn word with the same cold determination. *Just like Zimor!*

Her eyes met Zuchmul's and she realized that she was faced now with the same dilemma she had thrown at him when she'd asked him to use Influence on Elias. And her answer was the same. The only reason she was reluctant was that she could see no way to survive and rebuild her life afterward. That was a stupid, selfish reason, given the stakes.

D'sillin said, "If there's any hope of your getting to Inarash in time, you must leave now." She turned to Zuchmul and folded his hand around the recording cylinder. "If you don't return for a more formal Recounting, I'll get this accepted. It is clear that it was not by your will that the Recounting was omitted. We owe you much, but more is required of you. Will you go now?"

"Yes. If the others agree."

Idom got to his feet. He held his empty hands out. "As soon as I change clothes, I'm packed."

"I've sent for suitable clothing," said D'sillin.

Kyllikki stood. "Then I suppose we're all ready."

Elias rose and moved to her side. He nodded silently, but the music inside him rose to a crescendo that was half joy, half terror. He was going back to face Zimor, too. And perhaps he'd realized at last that being Bonded to Kyllikki might not be any better than being Bonded to Zimor.

chapter **sixteen**

●●●●●●●●●●●●●●●●●●●●●●●●●●●●●●●●

They were taken out of the citadel in a
cage full of orl, Kyllikki drugged to the eyebrows so she would
not strike at the luren who were controlling the orl with Influence.

Half the controlling luren kept the orl stirred up emotionally, while the other half blanketed the cage with a thick
pall of calm. It was hoped that the Imperial searchers who were
telepaths would not perceive the fugitives through that cross-
hatching of emotions, images, and turbulence.

The turbulence itself wouldn't attract attention because the
outside of the cage was plastered with VICIOUS symbols to keep
all but luren Port Inspectors out. It worked, though Kyllikki felt
too sick to pay attention to the danger.

They stayed in the orl compartment until after the first
dive. By then, the drug was wearing off and Kyllikki became
more aware of their situation. She was placed on a stretcher and
floated to sick bay, which was as dark as the rest of the ship.
Gradually, the realization stole through her that yes, they had
made it. She was on her way—home.

They were given a compartment like the apartment in the

citadel, but much smaller. The luren were able to provide food without attracting attention because the ship carried Communicators and Guild Guides who had to be fed. Not being luren, they kept strictly to their own, segregated, insulated quarters and were unaware of the intruders.

Several hours later, Kyllikki's appetite returned. When Zuchmul was sure she had recovered fully from the drug, he went to find his own meal and Idom succumbed to exhaustion, disappearing into one of the tiny sleeping compartments. It was the first time she'd been alone with Elias since Idom had decreed they must form the Dreambond.

Their sitting room, lit by portable emergency lights, not candles, barely contained Elias in his mad pacing. She was ready to creep slowly to her room, sure she would sleep for a few days, when she realized that she couldn't relax with Elias so close and so anxious.

She folded herself back into her chair and watched the Dreamer. She still liked what she saw: a trim, powerful build, strange pale coloring that arrested the eye, and, even frantic with tension, he bore himself with a lithe grace.

She admired how he'd been dealing with the tormenting stresses building in him since the Bond had been broken. Few men could handle intense emotion without repressing totally. She fell to speculating on what a Dreambond would be like. People said it was like living two lives, but the Dreamer didn't bring the Bonder just knowledge or even another emotional point of view. Dreaming induced a deeply satisfying rest that would make her feel more awake and alive. All her senses would be enhanced. Her telepathic range and sensitivity would increase, which wasn't something she was looking forward to. She cut off the thought. Even if they survived the Pool, the law wouldn't permit them to exist in the Bonded state for long.

Abruptly, Elias spun on his heel and jabbed a finger at her. "You were right!" He vilified her name in some language and repeated, "You were completely right!"

"About what?"

"I want to do this only because I want the Dreambond

back! I keep remembering how I used to sleep so soundly and feel so good in the morning. *This* is normal for me, but I feel *sick*! I never wanted *you*, I just wanted the Bond; I wanted relief and I didn't care how I used you to get it! So I told myself I was in love with you until I believed it!"

She winced. "Don't yell. Idom needs his sleep." Then she was instantly ashamed at scolding him.

His lips stretched into a snarl and he turned his back on her, stalking about the room in a circle. He tried to shove an easy chair out of his way and discovered it was bolted down. He swore, threw himself into the chair, and curled down to cradle his face in his hands. Kyllikki could feel him holding his breath against a surge of emotions.

She went over to his chair and knelt so she could look up at his buried face. With great trepidation, she softened her barriers and stroked the backs of his fingers. "Elias, your yearning for the Bond isn't the only reason you're attracted to me. I feel the strident sexual tension—"

He jerked away from her touch as if scalded, then hissed, "Go to Zuchmul if you're bothered! You don't want me, and I don't want you!"

Hand poised in midair, she found her courage and whispered, "If there'd been a way to make love to you without being tempted into Bonding you to me, I'd have done it long ago. You're exactly the sort of man I always fantasized about having for my very own. I can't stand to see you suffering." She sighed, but it came out nearly a sob, which she barely managed to twist into a chuckle. "Before Barkyr, I used to think my life was complicated!"

He turned to look down at her, and deep inside, she felt something happening. It was like nothing else she'd ever felt before, and she wanted it. *Do Dreamers have barriers?* They weren't telepaths, but she'd observed how a luren could use Influence as a kind of barrier. Wouldn't the three genetic strains all have barriers specific to their talents?

If so, the Dreamer's barrier didn't shield the mind but something else. His mind, his own private mental realm, was as open to her as any human's was.

In the dim emergency lighting, his eyes seemed to reach down and kiss her soul, enfolding her innermost being, offering to make her safe and complete at last, fulfilling a need she'd never known was there.

"No!" Idom's voice sliced through the moment, and he charged into the room. "Not now! Not here!"

Kyllikki pulled back and, one hand massaging her scalp, she focused on Idom, patching up her barriers. He was wearing a loose sleeping robe, his beard and sparse white hair in spiky disarray. She got to her feet. Somewhere under the ringing shock, she was vaguely aware of the door opening to admit Zuchmul, but she ignored it.

"Don't worry, Idom. I've no intention of—"

Elias rose. "It has nothing to do with you, Kyllikki. I am not going to do this. Find yourself another Dreamer, someone who won't use you as selfishly as Zimor used me. Good night." He shouldered past Idom. Idom reached out and grabbed his elbow and whirled him around.

"There's no time to find and prepare another Dreamer! Weren't you listening to D'sillin?"

"So let's just destroy the Pool and stop Zimor the way the luren wanted to. We don't have to try to reverse—"

"Do you know how many ships have been lost in the last year?" challenged Idom.

Elias broke off, staring at him, and Idom quoted figures, region by region, then quoted the strength of the Guild five years ago and compared it to now. "If we defeat Zimor, bar the Operators from the Pools, and leave the damage alone to keep swallowing ships, the Guild will not be able to supply enough Guides for commerce to continue. Illegal shipping will use Operators because it's safer. Soon, legal shipping would be clamoring for Operators for critical cargoes and to protect important lives—then how would 'unimportant' people feel? In less than a year we'd be back on the same road to total disaster. No, we must use the Pool to repair the damage, *then* we must destroy it."

Rubbing the back of his neck, Elias said, "I can't believe the fate of the galaxy depends on me!"

"It doesn't," said Idom. "It depends on *us*. All of us. We have to find the harmonics that bind us. War is just energy gone into wild discharge. That same energy can be sequestered inside the system to bind its elements. The greater the energy, the greater the peace it produces when sequestered. We are a rough analogue of the Teleod/Metaji system. If we can find our harmonics, then peace will spread from us in a chain reaction." Noting the silence, he explained, "That's an extension of Shideow's Sixth Theorem."

As always when Idom talked theory, Elias began to look a little wild-eyed. Reassuringly, Idom gestured to the various lighting fixtures about the room. "Shideow. The principle behind common utilities."

Elias took on a very strange expression. Again Kyllikki wondered what his basic education had been like, if he'd had any at all. "Idom, it sounds like it ought to be easy, but I've no idea how to put it into practice."

"Oh, it won't be easy," answered Idom. "My first task is to devise the images Zuchmul must project within the Pool. Yours is to draw me a diagram of the Bonding image you'll be using for Elias. It has to emphasize three, six, and five."

Kyllikki folded her arms around herself. "I haven't given it any thought." She turned to Elias. "Elias has to consent first. I need to access his mind to construct the image, the part of his mind that's still raw and hurting."

He seemed close to panic. Kyllikki kept her barriers tight, not wanting to know what was behind that look.

Zuchmul moved from where he'd been by the door, saying, "Elias, I may be able to help you sort this out, if you'll let me use Influence on you again?"

"How could I stop you? It's a luren ship."

"Refuse permission. It *is* a luren ship." He went to the Dreamer. "Can you trust me? Let me help?"

"How could you do anything about—"

Zuchmul took his elbow and steered him toward the sleeping compartments, saying, "Your problem is that you can't tell how much of what you feel for Kyllikki is the attraction to a

Bonder, and how much is attraction to Kyllikki herself. Just let me block out the attraction-to-a-Bonder part of what you're feeling, so you can explore the tangled mess underneath and straighten it all out. You'll feel a lot better. And maybe you'll decide that saving galactic civilization doesn't require a moral crime, just a legal one. Or—maybe you won't. But at least it will be a genuine decision, one you can stake your life on."

The door shut, cutting off Zuchmul's voice.

Idom said, "Why didn't I think of that?"

"What?" asked Kyllikki, still staring after the men.

"Luren! They can do all sorts of things they're never allowed to do except among themselves. But we're under luren law—I should have thought of it!"

The next morning, Kyllikki emerged, expecting to struggle with the tiny warmer the luren had provided for their meals, and found Elias had already produced a pitcher of hot yarage and some of the gooey mess luren children were fed for breakfast. "Join me?" he asked amiably.

"Sure." She collected a mug and a bowl and began ladling condiments onto the tasteless stuff.

"Kyllikki," he said, putting a hand over hers as she reached for some spice. "I've been awfully crazy lately. I thought I got sane after you broke the Bond for me. But really I've just been getting crazier and crazier."

"It's not your fault. I've admired you because you haven't gotten even crazier. And even at your worst, you weren't trying to hurt me."

"Is it really true that you didn't dare sleep with me, even once? Would it have formed a Bond?"

"You mean you didn't believe me?"

"Did I have any reason to?"

Sovereigns Be! Non-telepaths! "Yes, it's true."

"Kyllikki, you feel it as badly as I do, don't you? But Zuchmul didn't block it out for you."

"It?"

"The—intense sexual attraction that isn't really love, but almost violence?"

"It isn't quite that bad for me. I've been trained not to let the need go sour like that. But I needed Zimor's sleeping potion sometimes. Sometimes, it doesn't help. As for Zuchmul, we agreed—it would only be until Veramai."

"He loves you."

"I know. But . . . my mind was always on you."

"That's what he said. He talked as if it was almost a business deal. But I could tell—you're special for him."

"But now he must be fertile again and I'm Eight Families."

"It must be hard to make love to someone whose reflexes can kill you for a natural expression of passion."

"You're not jealous then?"

"Not anymore. But underneath that compulsive need for you, Sovereigns Be, Kyllikki, I do love you."

"I know," she assured him. "That's why you'd rather let galactic civilization crumble than exploit me to assuage your compulsive need. And that's one of the reasons I love you. Underneath my compulsive need, that is." She'd meant it to sound flip, but suddenly she had to avert her gaze because she felt the barriers shimmering away into nothing again.

His hand tightened on hers. "It'll be all right. Surviving this won't be worse than dying while doing it."

Kyllikki wasn't too sure about that. If they survived, eventually the law would probably force them to separate or die trying. Still, that could take years, and if they succeeded, would society repay them with torment and death?

For Elias, anyway, breaking this Bond would be death. He could never survive another such trauma. She marveled that he didn't hate her for what she'd done to him. But he laid the blame for that damage on Zimor, not Kyllikki.

He let her probe his mind, and she sketched the Bonding key for Idom. Immediately, he suggested modifications. That night, she slept on his ideas, which didn't seem workable. Then they conferred again, and Kyllikki tried to rework the numbers of twists, corners, and loops to suit Idom while still reflecting the essence of the two of them.

As she worked with Idom's parameters, she began to get ideas. Could she design a Bond that would break without traumatizing Elias? Could she put that brittleness under his own control? And, while she was at it, could she give him control of what his sleeping mind transmitted to her?

School, naturally, had taught nothing of how a Dreambond was constructed. Still, almost everything else done with keys was based on the same principles, and she had seen Zimor's Bond. Zimor wasn't an original thinker; possibly both her Bond and her Pool were unmodified applications of some ancient Triumvirate text. Did they have a common principle?

She tried discussing it with Idom, but even though he almost seemed to make sense, his reasoning lacked a whole perceptual dimension. So she worked alone.

When Idom wasn't worrying about the competence of the Guides or fretting over the *feel* of a dive they'd just completed, he worked with Zuchmul on the visual images he wanted used, and Zuchmul practiced until Idom was satisfied.

They changed ships, again hidden among orl, Kyllikki drugged. This time, the drug didn't make her quite as ill, and so she was acutely aware of the *lacking* in her mind. But the luren were terribly polite and anxious to make her feel safe, and in the end she came out of it with no ill effects.

They spent the next leg of the trip strictly within their small cabin. Because of this ship's design, there was no choice but to house Zuchmul's orl in the cage at one end of the cabin. The sleeping compartments were nothing but bunks like those on the escape pod, so there was virtually no privacy. Zuchmul took to feeding only when Kyllikki and the men were asleep, and he was always nervous that his habitual use of Influence on the orl would trigger Kyllikki's reflex.

At the border along the Greening Line, they stayed at a citadel for two days while Zuchmul arranged their passage. This was one of the places where the Sa'ar clan dominated, and trade had once flowed freely across the border. It still did, though they made it appear that all the ships dealing with the citadel came from and returned to the Metaji. In fact, a good half of them were from deep in the Teleod.

When she mentioned her dismay, Zuchmul chuckled. "There are those who'll be unhappy when the war is over because they'll have to pay taxes again. But it will be worth it if we stop the loss of ships. Or so their accountants have told me." Then he added confidentially, "I'm glad all luren aren't like that!"

They had some bad moments when the Imperials sent their own luren hirelings in to search the citadel for fugitives matching their descriptions, but as Kyllikki learned, Blood Law prevailed for all luren at all times. As soon as they understood the Blood lines that protected the intruders, and the real reason the Imperials were searching for them, the luren searchers became instantly blind, deaf, and dumb.

Zuchmul explained, "The Imperials know we have higher loyalties than to the Emperor, which is why we can never become Imperial officers or hold a royal title. Those men were hired to search where Imperial law forbids non-luren intrusion, and if we had been real criminals, they would have turned us in. Blood Law would have required it."

"They will anyway," predicted Kyllikki, "as soon as some telepath interrogates them officially."

"But they'll remember searching and not finding us."

"Influence can do that?"

"Provided the wielder is sufficiently powerful. With D'sillin's backing, our journey is mandated and protected by the most powerful elders of the community."

A few hours later, they were again smuggled onto a ship, this one much larger and fully staffed by Pool Operators whose Port documents claimed they were Guild Guides. As on all luren ships, the non-luren were housed in a separate area near the Pool, and Kyllikki never saw them, never learned how they came to be running the border for the luren.

They took a roundabout way out of the system, five days to the first dive to avoid detection of their method of travel. Idom became more and more tense and withdrawn, waiting for that first dive. No matter how many times Kyllikki told him, "It doesn't feel any different to passengers than traveling with a Guide," he still paced and fretted.

Finally, Elias snapped, "You're being ridiculous, Idom! The chances of getting lost are greater with the Guides."

Before Idom could protest, Zuchmul added, "This ship would be traveling this route with or without us. Our presence isn't causing more damage to be done."

Idom sighed and sat down at the small desk they used as a dining table. The ship and their quarters were bigger, and though they had been provided little but cold rations, they could now dine without orl snuffling in the corner.

"I suppose it is irrational," Idom admitted. "But I can't count, sitting here in this room. I've no idea where we are. When I knew the Guild had staffed the ship, it didn't matter. I've deadheaded all around the Metaji while catching up on sleep. But I've no idea who's certified the competence of these people. After all, if they're smuggling, they can't be legally certified!"

Zuchmul said, "Don't bet on it. Do you really want me to trace down their experience and training?"

He made an exasperated sound. "No. They wouldn't be trusted with a Sa'ar cargo if they weren't good. I've just been cooped up in the dark too long."

"I can't let you wander around the ship."

"I know. I'm not asking. It's too dark to count, and if I carry a light, I might injure someone's sight. I told you, it's not rational." He got up and went to his room to pace in private. After the first dive passed successfully, he calmed down and buried himself in the plans Kyllikki was formulating for getting them into the Laila compound.

With the help of standard equipment rather than the luren-built displays that she couldn't read, Kyllikki had created a detailed graphic of the compound as she remembered it. The luren provided current maps, and Zuchmul, using an apparently blank screen, added the most recent modifications the luren knew about.

Laila security would be using top-rated telepaths and the most sophisticated hardware. With the war, it would be tighter than when Kyllikki had left. And, she cautioned Idom and Zuchmul, in the Teleod, telepaths were not restricted in the use of their abilities. The Metaji telepaths tracking them had only been allowed to "listen" for spontaneous mental output. They had not been allowed to probe minds, and had to account for the source of every fact they acquired.

A Metaji citizen could sue for damages in the case of mental invasion by a telepath, and often could win large sums or be acquitted of crimes discovered by invasion. The offending telepath lost everything, often including his life.

But in the Teleod, an Eight Families telepath answered only to the head of the Family. Others were trained and employed by a specific Family and answered to any member of that Family. Considering the network of alliances and power balances among the Families, in practice that meant all trained telepaths, Family or not, were under Zimor's control.

When she was sure everyone understood that, Kyllikki presented her plans for sneaking into Laila and for creating diversions and breaking in. As a last resort, she considered a simple ruse: either with herself as the repentant cousin returning with Zuchmul, the luren who had thwarted the assassination of Fotel, as her prisoner; or with herself as Elias' prisoner, the Dreamer pretending to be desperate to resume his Bond with Zimor at any price.

Despite his heroic efforts to conceal it, Elias' desperation was clear for any telepath to read. All he'd have to conceal was his personal loathing for Zimor. As she watched him studying the map of the Laila compound, Kyllikki again admired the man for hanging on to his sanity. He met her eyes, and her admiration threatened to turn to a searing rage at the fate that put genetics and politics between them.

Choking back her emotions, she said, "Those are the best ideas I could come up with."

"You mean," said Elias, studying the map of the Laila compound, "you grew up inside those walls and you don't know any secret underground passages, dank tunnels, or crawl ways carved into the stone walls?"

"What?" asked Kyllikki, bewildered.

"I used to read a lot of adventure fiction, and castles always had secret tunnels, a way for the King to escape in case of invasion. The heir apparent, returning to recapture his throne, *always* knows secret passages the usurper doesn't know because when he was a boy, he played in them!"

"Hmmm. I wish this were a story! If Zimor were a usurper, this would be a lot easier."

Idom said, "The emergency escape routes are off the roofs by various sorts of vehicles armored in various ways and protected by emplacements anchored to the ground. There's no way to use the escape routes to get in."

Kyllikki sat up straight. "But there *are* underground connections among the buildings, secured, of course, but . . ." And she was off propounding a plan requiring Zuchmul's use of Influence to get them by guards. "Would you do it, Zuchmul?"

"I wouldn't dare—not in a Family compound."

"I suppose you're right." When she found herself concocting ever wilder schemes, such as dumping a ton of the reflex-repressing drug into the water supply of the compound, she called a halt to the planning session.

They changed ships one last time, laying over at a Teleod citadel that seemed identical to the ones in the Metaji. Zuchmul had become adept at supplying the bizarre needs of his charges, and they were quite comfortable, both in the citadel and on the new ship.

Kyllikki, Elias, and Idom now interacted casually with luren who weren't wearing Inhibitors. They had learned that there were elaborate rules of custom and Blood Law governing the use of the power of Influence, rules that resembled to a large extent those governing the social use of telepathy. Since they did not have the power of Influence at their command, no responsible adult would impose Influence on them.

But they still could not wander freely within the citadels. Now that Kyllikki was within the Teleod again, some luren could be tempted to sell her whereabouts to Zimor. After all, Blood Law or no, luren were only human. So her identity was revealed only to Zuchmul's relatives who needed to know.

Likewise, Elias' identity was kept quiet. But even Idom had to remain in their quarters, for any stranger free in a citadel would set the gossip mills raging, and Influence was a way of life for luren. Curious luren could have accidents.

Often, entering a new ship or citadel, Zuchmul would bring up his Influence in an exchange of greetings with strange luren, then flinch away from Kyllikki, apologizing for his life-long habit. But at such moments, she was always still affected by the drug and not in danger of reacting.

When he went out alone, Zuchmul returned with luren gossip to augment the sterile and heavily screened reports on the Teleod news channels. Though the war looked somewhat different from the Teleod side, as if Metaji resistance were crumbling and Teleod victory imminent, Kyllikki didn't pay attention to battles and victories. She concentrated on news of the Families: who had died, who had had children, who now owned what, who had voted with whom, who'd been seen with whom.

Between the news, Zuchmul's local gossip, and clues she'd picked up from the unfortunate N'hawatt, she pieced together the view from Zimor's vantage. She was almost afraid of the surge of optimism that vision brought. Clearly, the balance of power was shifting, and Zimor must be desperate.

The movement was still amorphous. No one had come forward to risk leading a rebellion—at least not since Zimor had eliminated the last one to try.

Four days out of Inarash, Kyllikki discovered the existence of the ground-based Pool was still not general knowledge. Though all members of the Eight Families knew that something was brewing, very few knew what.

The ones who did not know were suspicious of the ones who did. One day, as Zuchmul returned from his meal, Kyllikki was pondering how to use that suspicion to their advantage. She was startled when he said, "Tomorrow morning, we'll arrive at Inarash, and we'll be staying at the largest citadel—the one nearest Laila. With luck, D'sillin's message should reach us there by—what's the matter?"

"Nothing," said Kyllikki. Somehow, she'd distanced the project into an academic exercise. Now it was real again.

She went through the evening meal, almost a ritual by now, grappling with that reality. During these quiet meals, she had developed the habit of softening her barriers. Gradually it had come to be expected that she would speak to her companions' minds, and listen to the thoughts they returned to her. This routine had developed slowly after they'd stopped using meals as an occasion to argue, and after she'd stopped sleeping with Zuchmul. They all knew she needed mental contact, so they offered it freely. It wasn't enough. She needed to commune with another telepath, and would have welcomed even a Metaji telepath under Metaji protocol. But this night, she was suddenly obsessed with memories of real, Teleod, communion.

Even so, the concession by her friends helped. But when she retired, she did her mental and physical exercises, and went to bed wondering how many more times she'd sleep without Dreams. Would the Bond obviate the need to commune?

She'd done her best to design her Bonding key for Elias' benefit. And having seen the melting gratitude on Elias' face when she'd explained her design, she couldn't replace any of those traits with something to help herself. But what telepath would touch her after the Bonding?

After a restless sleep, the drugged trip from the landing field to the citadel got to Kyllikki in a new way. The effect of the drug seemed to change every time she used it, and this time it left her wide awake and hyperaware of every wisp of Influence controlling the orl.

During the removal of the open-sided cage from the ship and its insertion into a closed truck, they had been jammed between the rear wall of the cage and the feeding trough, an area used to stock the feed machines. They were out of sight of anyone outside the cage, but cramped between metal walls with just enough room to stand or sit sideways. Kyllikki had elected to stay there rather than go out among the animals in the dark.

The truck lighting, of course, was for the orl-handlers. The sides of the truck were insulated, blocking the Influence fields of the handlers from any passing Family member who might react reflexively. But they also shielded telepathically, leaving Kyllikki in an isolated cocoon.

She was sitting hunched over her knees when one of the orl decided to join her. The jouncing ride upset her stomach, and the animal odor made her gag. She squirmed, and found herself hugged by a small furred primate that stank. "Uhg!" She pushed at the creature.

Zuchmul wormed in beside her and held out his hands to the orl, murmuring something as he impelled the orl to come to him. Kyllikki felt the wave of compulsion wash through her. "I hate orl!"

Zuchmul propelled the small primate away. Then he squirmed around to lay prone and propped his chin on his hands. "We'll be there soon."

Feeling like a petulant child, she put her face in her hands and began to cry. "I can't *stand* these creatures!"

"It's the drug, Kyllikki. It wipes out a brain function you've always counted on, which makes you feel helpless." He reached out a hand. "Come on, come into my mind. Let your barriers down, Kyllikki, and come to me."

Feeling like an utter idiot, she flung herself into his mind and his arms, trying not to sob disgracefully. If the drug affected her like this during the descent into the Pool, there would be no hope.

But the moment she was enfolded by the luren mind, she felt Zuchmul shrouding them both in his Influence, putting his power at her command. The urge to cry disappeared, and she knew he'd been right. Her perceptions of the world around her altered, and she felt safe. Even the odor wasn't so overwhelming. She rode the rest of the way in his arms, surrounded and protected by his power.

Eventually, she was lying on a lounge in another luren room, the drugged fog dissipating. She wasn't sure if that had really happened. Then she overheard Elias saying to Zuchmul, "Whatever you did for her in the truck, thank you."

Idom asked, "What exactly did happen, Zuchmul? If she's having a bad reaction to the drug, we'll never succeed."

"The medics say she's doing fine."

"Even so, maybe we should set up a few trials before we go for the Pool itself," said Idom.

Kyllikki sat up. "I think I ought to be answering for myself, don't you? And I refuse to take that drug just to play around with the effect!"

"But—" protested Idom.

"You keep saying I always do the right thing. Well, I'll use the drug in the Pool, but no trials!"

Idom conceded.

They were in the citadel, in a lovely apartment that had been furnished and lighted for them. It had a kitchen in the space normally used for orl. There were several pairs of goggles hanging on one side of the apartment door, and another bunch on the other side with different kinds of lenses. One set was for them to use if they wanted to go out, and the others were for luren who came to visit them. The door itself was hidden behind a curved baffle that kept their light from spilling into the hallway beyond.

As Kyllikki rubbed crusts out of her eyes, the door signal— which made a pleasant tinkling noise—interrupted.

Zuchmul stepped behind the curved baffle to open the door. They all heard the soft murmur of the luren language. Zuchmul came back with a recording cassette in one hand and a grin on his face.

"Idom! D'sillin got *two* of your colleagues to agree with your plan. You have the complete backing of this citadel. They'll do anything you say!"

chapter **seventeen**

●●●●●●●●●●●●●●●●●●●●●●●●●●●●●●●●●

With Idom's new status among the luren, it took only a few hours to equip their sitting room with data taps into both the general Inarash system and the coded access system available only to the Families, and to hook up communications including news and entertainment, all with readable displays mounted on or around a good Teleod-designed desk unit.

Kyllikki had planned her moves carefully, and as she sat down among the screens and graphic projectors, she couldn't help grinning at the startlingly sensuous pleasure of the feel of familiar controls, of the gratification as data appeared in the right colors, expressed in the right parameters. She needed to do no mental gymnastics to extract meaning. Her spirits soared.

As she searched for a particular data table, she ran across an old serial that was still running. She paused to identify the characters and deduce what must have happened to them since she'd stopped voting on their decisions. When she noticed the men watching her, she quelled her curiosity, fetched up the table, then turned to her cohorts.

"Well, this is it. Do I try my old code to see if it still works, or do we see if that citadel tech can break into the Families' coded access files?"

Zuchmul observed, "Your code could be trapped."

They'd been over this before. "It might be worse to try to break in. And didn't you say this line can't be traced to the citadel? If I spring a trap, they can't trace me."

"That's what the technician *said*," agreed Zuchmul.

Something was bothering the luren. He was grimmer than he should be, his Influence gathered tightly. "So what harm can it do to try? If it doesn't work, then we can ask the citadel to try. It's illegal, but they said they'd risk it."

"Spring a trap," said Idom, "and Zimor will know you're on Inarash."

"Maybe. Somebody else might have my code and might want her to think so. Springing a trap might just confuse her."

Zuchmul paced away, then back to the desk and laid one naked hand on top of a display housing that was shrouded in mesh. He snatched his hand away with a grimace of distaste and stuck it behind his back. Inspecting the far corner, he admitted, "Last night, I got the citadel's data-pirating code. It's reputed to work very well in the Family files."

Kyllikki gaped at him. With all she'd learned about how luren survived in a hostile galaxy, she shouldn't have been so shocked. But she couldn't recall ever suspecting the Teleod's luren of possessing or using such information.

Zuchmul commented, "The kind of data the Families keep to themselves here is public knowledge in the Metaji. Traders can't make intelligent decisions without it."

"Traders simply ally with a Fam——" started Kyllikki. "No, luren aren't ever . . . Well." *What choice do they have?* She had to remember that Blood Law always took moral precedence for a luren. It might be easier for others to deal with them if they'd ever reveal the whole of that Law.

Elias said, "We ought to use the citadel's code first, see what's going on, then decide if we want to spring a trap as a message to Zimor."

"Sensible," said Kyllikki, and moved aside to let Zuchmul

fumble his way through entering the code sequences. He was wearing filters so he could see the screens, but the color contrast he saw wasn't too good and the controls were not Metaji standard. Eventually, though, the displays all lit up with invitations through the Family access gates.

Zuchmul got out of the chair. "I can't even read that!"

Kyllikki sat down. "I can." After only three minor mistakes, she got the feel of the board and soon had several functions going at once, saving it all into her recorders. Things had changed drastically among the Families. Zimor had attained a choke hold on the nodes of power before anyone noticed, but lately, she'd been losing ground.

"Elias," Kyllikki said, staring at graphs of financial exchanges juxtaposed against production curves. "Tell me again what you did here before she sent you to the Metaji."

He recounted what he remembered of his early training and Kyllikki threw names and places at him. Once in a while, he'd answer that he'd been to some party or function in a particular place, or had met someone, but very often his memory was hazy.

She knew she should have tried to remove Zimor's memory blocks. But it was too late now. There was enough evidence, though, to indicate that Zimor had used her Dreamspy to secure her power. Once his memory was opened, Elias' testimony would destroy Zimor. In fact, the existence of the blocks themselves was a nicely damning piece of evidence.

They might not need it, though. By following the ownership records of large companies and the alliances among decision makers, Kyllikki saw where a rebellion had started. Shortly afterward, certain key figures among the rebels had died. Zimor was just as capable of using the data access as Kyllikki was, and she wouldn't stop at sacrificing a shipload of innocents to remove one threatening person.

Since then, there had been no indication of a dissenting opinion among the Families. Zimor ran the war the way she wanted it, spent public funds as she decided, and rewarded contractors she favored. But the Family files also gave the real statistics on the war, showing a profile much closer to that visible in the Metaji. The Teleod was winning ground, but at too high a cost. The Empire's resources, however, were not as depleted. Zimor needed her one-stroke coup *soon*.

Stiff and hungry from the long session, Kyllikki was about to quit when she came to the Personal Mail lattice and saw her own name flicker across the screen. She froze the display and demanded access to her mail. Nothing happened.

The indicator showed there was material in her file. She rattled her fingernails against the desk.

Idom and Zuchmul were sprawled in lounges while Elias explored the kitchen. Idom asked, "Something wrong?"

She explained. "The citadel's code lacks something."

"Your personal mail," said Zuchmul, "is likely trapped."

"Probably. But it's time to spring it." She outlined what she'd learned. Elias came out to lean against the kitchen door-jamb and listen. "So, there's still a movement against Zimor, but they've learned to hide their activity."

"They wouldn't reveal themselves in the mail drops or gossip boards," said Idom.

Zuchmul added, "With her power, Zimor can reach anywhere, including the citadel. Luren are human. Some can be bought. There's a quarter million of us living here. We can trust those of my blood, but the others. . . ."

"True," allowed Kyllikki, "but if I spring Zimor's trap, it'll send a message to the movement. Everyone knows how I've always felt about Zimor. They'll contact me."

"How will you know it's them, not Zimor?" asked Elias.

"I don't know, but it's a risk we should take. At the very least, it will give Zimor something to think about."

At length, they all agreed, and Kyllikki backed all the way out of the Family files, then went back in using her own personal codes verified by her own living touch on the scanner pads. She rifled a few files of incriminating data, then picked up her mail, recorded it, dropped "Hello, I'm back" notes to some of her friends, along with copies of the rifled files, adding a few "What do you think of that?" notes, and copied the gossip boards. She did it all in the same unmistakable style she'd always used, and shut down.

There was no way to know if she'd sprung a trap, or if the trap had traced her to the citadel, until Zimor moved.

The next day, using her own codes again, she answered the old letters that had been sitting in her mail since she'd left, and tacked comments onto the gossip boards designed to convince everyone that she was herself, not Zimor's spy. Her work of the previous day had produced an overnight explosion on Inarash, with the main argument being whether she was alive, and if so, where had she been all this time? Had she become Zimor's pawn?

It would take days to get responses from other planets, but meanwhile, she kept working on the local nets. Within three days, the furor reached the general news with an official denial that the "culprit" was Kyllikki Lady of Laila, who was still officially presumed deceased. The prankster would be apprehended shortly and there was no truth to the rumor that the origin of the output was untraceable.

The succinct item went by so fast that Kyllikki had to back up and go over it again. Then she let out a whoop that brought Elias and Idom running. "We've got her!"

Idom wasn't as thrilled, but Elias agreed it was a good development, and Elias, after all, knew Zimor.

But later Kyllikki concluded that if they did nothing but stir up the Families, either they'd be caught or Zimor would be pushed into using her Pool. It was time to move.

Kyllikki cornered Zuchmul. "How can we get outside transport? Surface, that is, and not in an orl cage?"

Elias asked, "Into the Laila compound?"

"No. Not yet, but soon."

"How soon?" challenged Elias. "We haven't settled on how we'll get in yet or how to get at the Pool."

"There's only one viable choice," said Kyllikki. "I'll go in as your prisoner, and we'll make a lot of noise doing it. You're more dangerous to her than I am, because you're living proof of her crimes. She's never done anything to me she didn't have the right to do. After all, I'm supposed to be able to defend myself."

"She'll never believe I'd return willingly."

"But enough people will. Everyone knows a Dreamer who's tasted the Bond will do anything to get it back, even bribe her with me. Her supporters *and* her enemies will crowd into Laila, clamoring for her ear. Then it'll be easy to get Zuchmul in."

"How?" asked Zuchmul.

"Simple. We break something. The household staff will call a repair truck, and you respond. Then we improvise a way into the Pool, using the confusion generated by the return of Kyllikki from the dead, prisoner of a Dreamer. And I have an idea of how to get some help creating a diversion to give us time to work in the Pool."

It was an awfully thin plan, but they had to move fast now, and it was the best they'd come up with. Then Kyllikki had an idea of how to stir things up even more.

When she'd been provisionally declared dead, all her property had been transferred to Zimor, but until the decree became final, her credit rating was still registered. She'd borrow to the limit and invest as if certain the Teleod would lose the war. If she handled it right, Ansarios Beditzial's Pool Rim business would be threatened with ruin, and he'd demand help from Zimor. And the repercussions would spread the chaos in a ripple effect, harassing Zimor so much she'd make mistakes. It usually worked against her in battle in the realms, so it might work here, too.

Zuchmul interrupted her train of thought. "But where do you want to go, if not Laila? Under no circumstances can the citadel allow you to endanger us. With all the attention you've attracted, any hint of your presence here—"

"You're right. What if we leave here, go to Yinay, then go directly to Laila without returning here?"

"Maybe," conceded Zuchmul. "What's Yinay?"

"A Family. Their main headquarters is on the coast, half a day's drive, surface. Yinay runs the ocean farms. They're in the rebellion, if not leading it."

Mollified, Zuchmul went to summon the appropriate authorities, and within hours their plans were laid. The citadel would provide one of the large trucks that carried orl cages, and a smaller, faster vehicle that could be run up inside the truck. With a bit of gear installed, they could put the car into the truck and sleep in the truck one night.

Again, she had to swallow her shock when the citadel instantly forged identification for both vehicles and provided an expert red-and-white paint job that would get them into a corporation's parking lot for the night. They'd be lost among hundreds of other identical vehicles.

Meanwhile, Kyllikki borrowed and bought into companies that only the Families could own, selling quickly at enough of a profit to pay off her debt, borrowed again and invested, betting against the Teleod's winning the war, against the Teleod Pool industry and Ansarios Beditzial, its leader.

She wielded enough of her old power that the Families saw the effect long before news reports reflected the fall of Beditzial fortunes under Laila's ax. The next morning, she nailed home her message with a few quick moves, then thanked her luren hosts and led her friends out of the citadel.

Wearing a corporation uniform, Idom drove the truck out of the delivery-dock chute as if it had arrived that morning with a load of spare parts. When they reached a deserted stretch of coastal highway, Zuchmul helped Kyllikki maneuver the smaller vehicle, also heavily insulated, out onto the road, then retreated from the brutal afternoon sun. The truck continued to their rendezvous point while Kyllikki and Elias drove boldly onto Yinay property.

Elias, nervous though he was, drank in the scenery. They sped along the shore road, blue water visible far out beyond a white sandy beach. The sky was particularly blue today, with puffs of white cloud. Most of the traffic was in the air above them or out on the water, but the ground traffic increased as they rounded a hook of land and came up on the huge, nearly circular bay where Yinay had its base.

The Yinay Family compound sat on a rocky precipice above the bay, every bit as well fortified as Laila, but much more beautiful. As Laila had specialized in controlling the flow of manufacturing capital, Yinay had concentrated on food production. Many colonies depended on them for basic staples, and all the companies supplying meals for spaceship galleys were controlled by Yinay. Though few noticed, Yinay was more powerful than Laila and Beditzial combined.

Kyllikki drove up to one of the outbuildings surrounding Yinay's ancient walls. "This is where Esten has her office."

She parked three cars away from the door, wishing Idom were there to decide if that was significant, and led Elias to the door with a confident stride.

She had dressed carefully, wearing a coif that bound her hair back and shielded the sides of her face. With eye makeup and forehead paint, she didn't look at all like herself, and yet she resembled the typical Laila enough for any live guards to accept her forged credentials. She wore slim pants under a long, full-cut tunic with floating sleeves, the height of current fashion among the Ladies, but in garish pink and mauve, which she would never have chosen.

Elias was dressed in Laila bodyguard livery complete with the armband that certified him to carry weapons into Family compounds. It wasn't a counterfeit band, either. It had been stolen, and a luren tech had altered it to Elias' pattern as expertly as if he did it daily. Furthermore, Elias was armed with weapons he had no idea how to use. They were charged, too. She'd had some misgivings about his costume until she'd seen him march around the apartment and post himself beside the kitchen door with arms folded.

She'd laughed out loud. "You walk just like one of Zimor's uglies! Where did you ever learn that stance?"

"Watching Zimor's uglies. You're right. They're laughable."

She'd walked around him. "That's wonderful! We'll do it." The livery did fascinating things for his shoulders.

Now, with her barriers slammed tight—as any Family telepath would do approaching another Family's security—she strode right up to the building's door, pausing in apparent surprise when a live guard stopped her.

Elias took up his pose behind her as she looked the guard up and down, sighed, and presented her credentials. As the woman inserted the slender disk into her reader, Kyllikki said, "Be quick about it. I'm here to see Esten."

The woman was thorough, but exceedingly polite. "Yinay is pleased to welcome a Lady of Laila." She entered Yinay's pass signal onto Kyllikki's disk so internal surveillance wouldn't stop them, then returned it to Kyllikki. "Through the entry and to your right—"

"I know the way," snapped Kyllikki and strode off, Elias on her heels. Esten still occupied the corner suite at the end of the hall, but the number of titles on the plaque over her door had increased. When Kyllikki had run away, Esten had been fighting a reduction in rank. Apparently, she'd succeeded. *Good. We'll need every string she controls.*

They passed through another security check at the entry to the suite and finally came to the calendar desk, which was also staffed by a living person. Kyllikki had entered her appointment on Esten's calendar with an access routine they'd established years ago, before Esten had rated live staffers.

Kyllikki breezed past the man behind the desk, making straight for the private office, saying, "I'm exactly on time for a change. Don't bother to announce me."

As she neared the unmarked door, she held her breath, hoping it would still flick aside for her. It did, and Elias slid past her, weapon drawn at the regulation angle toward the ceiling, to check the room with swift, professional movements. "Lady," he invited, bowing Kyllikki in.

Kyllikki strode forward, absolutely certain that Elias would have missed even the crudest traps, but ignoring that to concentrate on the woman working at the data screens.

Esten was already glaring at them, starting to rise to throw them out when Kyllikki swept off the coif, shook her hair out and said, "Esten, that was easier than I expected!"

"Ky——" Esten absorbed the shock quickly. "But—"

"It's really me." She advanced to the desk, hands out to invite physical contact while simultaneously she evoked a key image that accessed their private communications realm.

"But even the investments this morning were said to be a hoax—no, obviously not." She put her hands in Kyllikki's.

The communion blossomed between them, deep and rich.

For a moment, Kyllikki rode with it, appalled at how overwhelming the pleasure of it was. Esten picked that up instantly, and her anguished sympathy was followed by curiosity, and then horror at the life Kyllikki had been forced into. And the reason for the exile drained all the color from the Yinay's face.

Kyllikki, too, was stricken by the grief Esten and her other friends had felt at her "death." The bleak desperation of the battles they had fought in her absence roused her sense of guilt and shame at deserting them.

Esten came around the desk and hugged Kyllikki to her, face wet with tears. "Damp it down, now. It's too much to take in all at once. Verbally, now, verbally, or we'll both cry the rest of the day away."

"Can't afford that," choked Kyllikki. "Make us private. Millions of lives depend on just how private you make us."

"My equipment's been upgraded," she said, activating snooper shields. "Zimor couldn't get through this."

"You're betting your life on it. Esten, this is Elias. Do you notice anything odd about him?"

She looked him over. "Too good-looking to be one of Zimor's—but then he can't be ''

"Come closer. Examine him carefully. Convince yourself, because the rest is even harder to believe."

After circling him, touching his face, and probing him mentally, Esten finally said, "A Dreamer. Un-Bonded. Where'd you get him? Is he one of Zimor's? Why bring him here?" Encouraging Esten to cast a verifier key over her, Kyllikki sketched the highlights of the story, from Barkyr to Veramai and her killing Grenmer Lady Beditzial, to their arrival on Inarash with a plan to use the Pool. "So I've got Guild sanction and a luren volunteer. We're going through with it, using the commotion I've stirred up as a diversion." She had minimized the luren involvement to protect the citadels, but eventually it would all come out.

When she'd finished, Esten was wide-eyed and white

around the mouth. The tips of her fingers shook, but her voice was steady as she said, "I knew that if you survived, you'd come through for us, somehow, but this is—Kyllikki, even for *you* it's—incredible."

"You don't think they'll help me? Esten, if you can't convince the rest of Zimor's opposition to help me—tell me, who should I talk to? Who can convince them?"

Half sitting on one corner of the desk, Esten folded her arms and bowed her head. Then she looked Kyllikki in the eye. "We don't have a leader. That's why we haven't tried anything since she decimated our ranks. We knew she had something planned with that giant Pool, but we didn't know what. We didn't know about the Dreamers. You'd think one of the Laila would have come to us over that one."

"I did—I have. I need your help!"

"No. We need your help. There isn't a single one of your Family who's willing to stand up to Zimor. Without someone to replace her with, there's been no point trying to get rid of her."

"They're not all as bad as Zimor!" protested Kyllikki.

"Mostly not. They're just afraid of her. You were the first to see her for what she is, and the first to stand up and defy her openly—when everyone else thought she was the best thing to happen to Laila in a thousand years. But you had the courage to defy her alone. People thought she'd murdered you for it. You've been our—well, our martyr! And now you've come back—people have been talking about making you our leader and Zimor's successor."

It was Kyllikki's turn to be stunned. She shook her head. "But I don't—I'm not—there are dozens of—"

"There's no one! And we can't start anything without a candidate to rally behind, someone we can all agree on, someone Laila would accept. Kyllikki, we all thought she had defeated you—but she didn't. You're alive. And you've come back to fight again, this time with allies, proof of worse crimes than we'd ever suspected her of, and a plan to stop this war without surrendering to the Metaji. That makes you the strongest and the smartest Laila around."

Kyllikki argued, but Esten prevailed. She could, she said, guarantee the whole movement's cooperation if Kyllikki would record her story with a statement of her intentions to wrest control of Laila from Zimor and make an equitable peace with the Empire. When Kyllikki had done that, Esten asked, "So, exactly what do you want us to do?"

"Do you have a map of the compound?"

Esten displayed one, and Kyllikki hooked a knee over the corner of the desk and pointed at the map as she spoke. "Create chaos. Stay away from here, and here. Concentrate on here, the main house, and this. A vehicle broken down here, for example, or a delivery tanker leaking something noxious into the kitchen area, or—"

"Something noxious? How about a load of rotten fish spoiled because the stasis generators on the truck failed?"

Kyllikki laughed. "With a Yinay truck!"

"Never! But I know how to arrange it. And while I'm at it, how about an invasion of armed men chasing a recently escaped, dangerous convict? They'd have to search everywhere, even the private rooms. Meanwhile, a dangerous leak might be traced to pipes that run under the compound, so the Health Department comes to tear up the paving. All night long?"

"Great! How do you think of these things?"

She rose, chuckling. "We've been working on several plans of this sort for more than a year. You want Laila agitated, we'll agitate them."

"I want them agitated, but I also want two Detention Officer uniforms so I can put two of my own men into your invasion force. Can you do that?"

"Certainly. When do you want the commotion?"

"Tomorrow afternoon, just before sundown. Possible?" She donned her coif again, tucking her hair out of sight.

"Sundown. Guaranteed. Where can I get in touch with you to give you the uniforms?"

"Can you get them for me now? One supervisor rank for an older man, and one for a luren." She told her the sizes.

"A real luren? Has his own protective gear?"

"Yes. My volunteer."

"Then—yes. I can get two plain uniforms and a bunch of insignias. It'll take a while." She sat down and issued some orders in careful code phrases. Then she asked, "How can I contact you if there's a problem?"

"I'd prefer you didn't, but if it's vital, try our private realm. I won't always be able to respond, though. I'm going to be very busy."

"Doing what?"

"Risking my fool life."

"And Elias' life, too?"

"No avoiding it."

"If he dies, how are we going to prove all this—when it's all over? We can't afford to risk him."

"I've decided," said Elias, "I'm going to do it. Our best theoretician says it has to be the three of us or it won't work. There's really no choice."

Esten stared at him aghast, and Kyllikki laughed out loud. Esten said, "I forgot he was here!"

Elias turned an offended gaze on Kyllikki and she explained, "Anyone in a banded uniform is *invisible*. They can't hear conversations among Families members unless there's a physical threat involved, and so they certainly can't insert personal comments."

Esten said, "I'm sorry, Elias. I didn't mean to be rude. But of course that's just a costume. Your mind hasn't been—altered. I could sense that, but somehow—"

Elias just laughed and accepted her apology.

She examined the armband. "It can't be a fake—you walked in here armed to the teeth—but how did you tune it?"

"Don't ask," advised Kyllikki.

Their eyes met, barriers nothing but wisps, and Esten nodded. "I won't ask. I just take it as proof that you're the right candidate to replace Zimor, and I'm sure everyone else will see it that way too. Most of them already do, considering what you've done to the Families' coded access system." She reached up to put a hand on Elias' shoulder. "Elias, if you both live through this, Yinay will see to it the law won't make you two risk your lives breaking that new Bond. One Dreambond won't hurt the Teleod, and if you pull this off, you'll deserve any reward you want to name."

Clearly skeptical, Elias nodded. "Thank you."

"Kyllikki, are you sure you weren't followed? Even by long-rangers?"

"Maybe from orbit, but I don't think—"

"I'll have your car checked and brought around. You'll go out an exit from the other side of the compound."

While Esten issued the orders, Elias whispered to Kyllikki, "Are you *sure* about her? She could be—"

"There may be traitors in the movement, but she's not one of them. I trust her with more than my life."

Esten led them out of the office by a hidden door onto a stair leading down to a secured tunnel chiseled out of solid rock. It was well lit but vaguely dank. At intervals, other stairs led up, and mazes of tunnels branched off, looking like natural caves. "This is why the compound is up here rather than down in town. It used to be a real fortress."

There were no signs, but Esten confidently chose a narrow, twisting stair up to a camouflaged exit. Elias was grinning hugely when he looked back and saw the door disappear. As their little red-and-white car rolled up, he whispered to Kyllikki, "See? I told you! Secret tunnels!"

"Laila isn't this old, and it isn't built on rock."

"The vehicle is clean," reported the guard, handing Kyllikki's disk to Esten with the uniforms in a bundle.

She gave them to Kyllikki. "Compliments of Yinay," she said formally. "Return at your pleasure."

They drove off down an unfamiliar road, and Kyllikki had to use the onboard mapper to command the car to find the rendezvous point. Unwilling to admit Elias' comment had roused her suspicions, she double-checked to be sure the mapper hadn't been tampered with. It hadn't. Then she relaxed, enjoying the scenery. "Elias, look! That's shaidberry growing there. Yinay makes the best shaid—fermented shaid, that is."

Elias seemed interested, and she continued to explain the crops Yinay cultivated here and how they fit into Yinay's overall commercial strategy. He soaked it all up eagerly and commented so intelligently that her admiration for him grew. On impulse, she asked, "Elias, you converse freely on economics, agriculture, music, psychology, military strategy, and even politics. You're obviously very well educated. Why don't you ever contribute to the discussion when Idom tries to explain his theories? He tries so hard to simplify things for us without revealing any Guild Secrets, and every time you just look at him as if he'd committed an indiscretion."

He glanced at her with a hint of that look in his eyes, but it vanished as he said, "It may be some flaw in my mastery of the languages. I know, rationally, he can't possibly be saying what it sounds like he's saying."

"Which is?"

"Oh, nonsense. Look, there's a big galaxy out there, with people going about their daily business, doing things I understand for reasons I can relate to. As weird as it may look on the surface, it's fundamentally comprehensible, even if I don't comprehend it all. I'm not going to let myself get upset if I don't follow all the technical jargon. After all, I'm a musician, not a Guild Guide!"

He put his arm around her shoulders, and she snuggled into his embrace and let herself relax. After all, in just a bit over a day, they'd be a lot closer than this.

Gradually, she became aware that they'd ceased speaking. His lips were brushing her forehead. "Do you think Esten can keep the law from separating us, if we live through this?"

"I don't want to think about it. The only way I'll have the courage to face Zimor is if I have nothing to lose."

He glanced out the windshield. "There's the truck!"

It was off the road, up a farmer's access lane, ostensibly broken down.

Elias said, "We've only got a few seconds now—not enough time to get into serious trouble. May I kiss you?"

She turned her face up to be kissed, then lost herself in it.

As their vehicle came to the end of its instructions and began to slow, a roaring filled her ears.

It was a real, physical roaring—outside the car.

She tore away from him. A squadron of vast armored units descended from the sky in perfect military formation.

Metaji invasion already? No. The largest ship, the command vessel, displayed Zimor's crest. Then a loud whumping shook the car. A dense pall of smoke blanketed the area. Kyllikki detected a familiar sweetish odor filtering into their car.

"Elias, hold your breath!" She gulped air and held it. Outside, the rear door of the truck rose. Zuchmul's masked face gleamed against the darkness behind him as he worked the control to extend the ramp for the car. Then he crumpled, his inert body rolling down the ramp. Under the mapper's control, the car homed onto the ramp and stopped when it sensed the body in the way.

Elias choked out, "Esten betrayed us!"

"More likely the citadel!" Kyllikki curled down onto the floor and searched under the driver's seat until she found a polishing rag and a bottle of window washer. She bit and tore the rag in half and dampened it. The dense fibers of the soft cloth impregnated with various chemicals plus the washer fluid smelled a lot worse than the crowd-control gas.

The chemicals might damage her lungs or her liver, whereas the gas would do her no harm, but she was determined not to surrender to Zimor without a fight. She passed a wet cloth to Elias and motioned him to feign unconsciousness.

She squirmed between the seats and into the back of the car, pulled the back of one of the rear seats down and rolled over the flat bed to where she could reach the rear loading door release. Then, breathing the noisome chemicals as sparingly as possible, she waited.

Very quickly, the gas dissipated as it was designed to, and troops closed in on the two vehicles.

As she expected, they clustered around the front of the car where Elias was slumped across the driver's seat, hiding face and cloth against the seat.

When they finally defeated the door locks and reached in to drag Elias out, he exploded into motion. Kyllikki didn't wait to see what he was doing, but slammed her exit open, rolled out and came up running—toward the command vessel that was sitting, with Zimor's crest proudly displayed on its flashing display screens, a short distance away.

The troops were deployed to prevent the occupants of the vehicles from leaving the area, but not from attacking the command vessel bare-handed.

Kyllikki's exercises had increased her running speed. She made it to the open side door of the command center and leapt through before any of the troops there could react. The automatics wouldn't respond to an unarmed person.

She took a forward roll and came up confronting a vaguely familiar woman who was about to scream. In one smooth motion, Kyllikki grabbed her arm, stepped into and around her, whipped the arm up into a painful lock, and got an elbow around the woman's neck, pulling it into a threatening angle. Pitching her voice low, she warned the armed troops, "One move, and she's dead!"

Then she saw Zimor coming toward her with a wide-nosed stunner, an often lethal weapon. "That's enough, Kyllikki. Let her go and step aside."

The woman struggled, apparently recognizing the stunner and Zimor's intent to include her in the shot in order to get Kyllikki. Kyllikki pulled her back a step and jerked the woman's head around. "Be still."

Then, glancing down at the woman, she suddenly recognized who she was. Zimor's Dreamer, the one who was scheduled to enter the Pool. Why Zimor had brought her here, Kyllikki couldn't guess, but it had been a mistake.

Zimor's hand came up to fire. In that instant, the Dreamer heaved against Kyllikki's hold, trying to turn so Kyllikki took the full brunt of the stun beam. Kyllikki resisted, and there was a sickening crack as the Dreamer's neck broke, followed by an indescribable mental scream of a Dreamer's death mounting and mounting, for the brain took a long time to die. Then the stun beam enveloped Kyllikki in oblivion.

chapter eighteen

●●●●●●●●●●●●●●●●●●●●●●●●●●●●●●●●●●●●

I killed her! I killed a Dreamer!

The thought spread through Kyllikki, bringing creeping horror in its wake. It had fully possessed her before she'd even realized she was alive and hurting from the stunner. The thought pulsed in time to her beating heart and throbbing head. *I killed a Dreamer, a helpless victim just like Elias.*

Worst of all, the woman hadn't been trying to kill her, as Grenmer Lady Beditzial had. The contrast in the sensations was a stark lesson. *Why did I hold on to her?* Instantly, she knew the answer. *Because I'm afraid of Zimor.*

As she woke, awareness spread to her barriers, locked against the outside world, confining the aching horror inside herself, cutting her off from the perspective of reality.

She heard herself moan as she struggled with her leaden arms. Her hands moved up to her head, where she encountered a single spike, a medical probe, sticking up from the shaved crown of her skull.

Korachi!

In frantic denial, she attacked her own barriers from the inside. And nothing happened. Her barriers were under control of a Monitor—as if she were a common criminal.

Kyllikki forced her gritty eyes open and saw the Monitor sitting at a desk across the hospital room, arms folded over her chest as she studied her readouts. She nodded and flipped an intercom switch. "Inform The Lady that my prisoner is awake. Then send the Attendants." She subsided into inactivity without even glancing at Kyllikki.

The grip the Monitor's mind had on Kyllikki's barriers never wavered. It was like being enclosed in a thick glass jar. She could see, hear, smell, taste—even move a little—but everything outside herself seemed totally unreal.

Zimor ordered this! Fighting panic, Kyllikki tried to force her recovering body to move despite the pain. By the time the door opened to admit two Attendants, she was convinced the stun hadn't left her paralyzed.

The Attendants' examination was impersonal, thorough, and professional until the end, when one of the men asked the other, "Should I give her something for the pain?"

"I suppose so. We weren't given any special orders."

"Could have been an oversight."

The senior Attendant's eyes rested on Kyllikki speculatively. "The Lady doesn't commit oversights. She said so herself. 'Use standard procedure as for any prisoner.'"

As the door opened silently behind him, the younger man adjusted his injector and sent relief into Kyllikki's blood.

Zimor swept into the room behind two of her guards. She was followed by two more, who posted themselves on either side of the door in the very manner Elias mimicked so well.

"What are you doing!" demanded Zimor. She gestured at the Monitor. "I didn't order this!"

The Attendants met each other's eyes across Kyllikki's supine form, and she knew without a whisper of mental contact that Zimor had ordered them to secure a Family telepath as a prisoner and they had done exactly that. Yet, as Zimor crossed the room, flashing orders at Attendants and Monitor to shut down the apparatus and come back later to remove the probe, Kyllikki studied Zimor. Either Zimor was lying better than ever, or something was wrong with her mind. *Could losing a Dreambond drive a Bonder insane, as it often did the Dreamers?*

Kyllikki shuddered, though there was little hope now she'd ever be joined to Elias, never mind severed from him.

As the Monitor and Attendants left, assuring Kyllikki that she'd regain command of her barriers soon, Zimor took up a station at the foot of the bed. She looked older, her face hardened with tension lines. And she was thinner, which made her nose more prominent, her cheeks hollow.

She was wearing a serviceable pants-and-blouse outfit under a decorative robe and cape, all of fabrics done in whorls and swirls of golds, russets, and creamy whites, the spark of a rare jewel from each of the planets of the Teleod in the center of each whorl. The sparkling gold-and-black medallion bearing the white-and-scarlet Laila coat of arms dangled between her breasts on a gold chain. It was an imposing costume that could be stripped away in a moment to leave her free to defend herself, and Kyllikki knew from experience that her elaborate hairdo and inconspicuous boots held an array of weapons.

She propped one foot on the lower rail of the hospital bed's lifting mechanism and rested her elbow on the raised knee. Kyllikki resisted the urge to be the first to speak simply because that was what Zimor wanted. Finally, The Lady of Laila observed, "You never learn, do you?"

"A Family trait." Her fear of Zimor had already taken one innocent life. She wouldn't let that happen again.

"Don't try to duel with me. I'm giving you one last chance to serve the Family—"

"You think destroying the firmament serves the Family?"

Zimor made an exasperated noise and moved around the bed to look down on her from the other side. Kyllikki found it hurt less to turn her head this time.

"Kyllikki, I don't know how you've run this rebellion of yours from out in the Metaji, but I'm putting a stop to it right now."

"Run . . ." Kyllikki started, then thought better of it. If Zimor was misinformed, it could be an advantage. If she was simply paranoid about Kyllikki, denial would only bring retribution. "Your sources are, as always, impressive."

"I have complete control, and I'm not going to allow you

and your supporters to put all the commerce of the Teleod into the hands of the Metaji Guild. Kyllikki, think for yourself for a change. The Guild has been trying to seize control of the Teleod by *claiming* that the Operators are doing the damage, and that my Pool will do even more harm. It's believing their lies that's doing the damage, and the way to stop it is to air the truth, backed by experts with unassailable credentials. Experts like you—and your Guild friend."

Idom's alive! The Monitor's blocks had barely started to wear off. Though Kyllikki couldn't get any impressions from Zimor, Zimor got nothing from her, either. "I know it's hard for you to believe, Zimor, but nothing we can say would change any minds. And we've no reason to change our minds."

"Kyllikki, you used a luren's Influence to manipulate a Dreamer."

"To sever an illegal Bond!"

"I'm covered as far as the law is concerned. Are you? I can prove what you've done under invasive scan, and yours is a far, far worse crime than accidentally acquiring a Bond. Would it do Laila any good to have one of its prime leaders executed for attempting to form a Triumvirate?"

Feigning calm, Kyllikki murmured her own threat, "N'hawatt."

"No connection to Laila. None."

"I see." Of course Zimor would be legally in the clear.

"Good. Now let's look at the other side of the ledger. You've known nothing but misery, anguish, and alienation trying to live in the Metaji. If they win the war, and find out you've not only bespoken luren, Dreamer, and human non-telepaths, but that you've used keys freely, despite all your oaths, they'll—well, it doesn't bear contemplation, does it? However, if we win the war, you'll be free to use your mind as you see fit, and"—she paused, a gleam in her eye—"to fulfill your genetic heritage as well."

"You know I unscrambled the mess you made of my memory. I remember all about the Dreamers you're keeping to reward your followers."

"Of course you do. I didn't mean it to last more than a year. It wouldn't have taken you so long had you not accepted their training restrictions. You were supposed to stay here and have the truth dawn on you gradually, so you'd come to understand that one day, a Dreamer would be yours. I intended it as a kindness."

She's trying to make me feel guilty. "Did you ever consider it from the Dreamers' point of view? Do you give them a choice—a real choice?"

"Kyllikki, Bonding a Dreamer isn't in the same class as forming a Triumvirate. The luren do quite well without us. But without the Dreambond, both Dreamer and Bonder are essentially unhealthy. What sort of law is it that would keep us apart? A Dreamer can't be unwilling, any more than a Bonder can."

Kyllikki felt the pall of the Monitor's grip lifting at last. Her barriers shimmered and vanished. Zimor *watched* with the inner eye, avidly gleaning images of Kyllikki's recent dealings, all mixed with the indignation at Zimor's attitude.

After so long under the will of the Monitor, Kyllikki couldn't control her barriers at all. Desperate, she tried the oldest ploy she'd ever learned to use on Zimor. "I'm not surprised you know everything. But it seems uncanny how you are always one step ahead of us. What I can't figure out is how you knew where we'd rendezvous with our truck."

Zimor smiled. "My people on Insarios learned who your luren had become there. When Grenmer failed to net you on Veramai, it was simple to deduce that the newly important luren had bought you sanctuary. So I watched the citadels, making sure they knew I was watching. When they finally got nervous enough and threw you out, it required no particular genius to realize you'd head straight for your old friend, Esten, though it was something of a surprise to find you on Inarash. The luren are too clever. Still, Yinay took only a bit longer than I expected to deny you sanctuary. You see, I know the whole story, Kyllikki. I have my people everywhere, even inside Yinay. I have *control* of the Teleod."

In the time it took for Zimor to explain, Kyllikki had rebuilt her barriers and could curse in private. *Korachi!* But at least Esten hadn't betrayed them. *Denied us sanctuary!* She fought not to laugh aloud. Obviously, some of the spies Zimor trusted were really double agents feeding her false information. That was an extraordinarily dangerous game, and the fact that Yinay would have their double agent feed Zimor a story about sanctuary assured Kyllikki the disturbances would be on schedule.

Watching Kyllikki, Zimor misread her silence just as she had misread earlier events. "So you see, I really can deliver on my promises. With one simple stroke, Kyllikki, we'll carve a pattern into what the Guild terms the firmament, a key-image pattern that will allow those who can use the key to travel anywhere in perfect safety. The Guild opposes this because their power will be broken, their system won't work anymore. So they tell people that *nothing* will work anymore."

"You put it very plausibly." *She is insane!*

"It's the truth, Kyllikki. But Laila does not fight for personal triumph. We do not drive toward victory and fail to think beyond it. If we win, the Guild will be broken, and the Empire will crumble. It will be up to us to save them from utter disintegration. The job is too large for me alone. I have many people I can trust, but no one of your caliber whom they'd all respect. Our generation in Laila seems to have produced people who can't think for themselves and thus do nothing but agree. What if I make a mistake? I need somebody who can argue with me—and even win sometimes. I need someone to stand beside me. The job is truly enormous. We're going to rewrite all the interstellar codes. The Teleod/Metaji Accords we've been living under are outmoded to the point of being dangerous—as the current crisis with transportation demonstrates."

"Oh, that's obvious."

"Well, the first thing we're going to change is the Accord which keeps Bonder and Dreamer separated and nearly too ill to function. You'll be able to keep a Dreamer, Kyllikki. And it won't be a guilty thing to sneak around about or an oddity to turn heads on social occasions. What do you think of that? No more sleepless nights."

"It would certainly be a fundamental change."

"Ah! You're worried I'll take Elias back from you?"

"Well—"

"If you want him that much, I'll let you have him. It's the least I can do for my own cousin. You'll need him, you know— or perhaps you don't know?" At Kyllikki's questioning look, she prompted, "The Enhancement effect."

"Enhancement?" She hoped her display of ignorance of something Zimor had assumed she knew was bolstering Zimor's sense of superiority.

"A Dreambond magnifies a Bonder's natural mastery of the realms. I thought that was why you stole Elias from me, until you turned up here without having Bonded him."

She doesn't know the real plan!

The thrill that seized Kyllikki must have seemed like power lust to Zimor, for she nodded. "Yes, we can become ten times stronger with the Bond functioning. That's why I was so surprised when you were able to cut Elias free—then I found you had help, and rather unorthodox help at that. That was very clever, Kyllikki. But I can't figure out why you didn't Bond with him immediately. He must have been begging you within three days."

Think fast! she ordered herself. *Bargain!* "He was in a pitiful state, but I needed him to get me into Laila again, so we could destroy your Pool. They convinced me we had to stop you, so I planned to have Elias bring me to you as his prisoner and beg you to take him back into the Bond instead of giving him the advertised reward for my return. Now, well, you've given me lots to think about."

"I see. Quite a plan. I might have fallen for it, too. For a while." She studied Kyllikki, rocking back and forth on the bed, the motion making Kyllikki's head throb. "Do you want him?"

"He's the only Dreamer I've ever known. I like his music."

Zimor laughed, a fulsome sound that convinced Kyllikki she was gaining the woman's trust. "That noise that's always in his head? Well, I'll make you a deal. Give me your unbarriered Word that you'll work for me, starting by helping me set the key in the firmament, and I'll let you keep Elias. You see, you have to be Bonded to the Dreamer when you take him down into the Pool to set the key. And afterward, there'll be no law that can force you to free him."

Zimor threw a key image at Kyllikki to carry the multidimensional sensory impression of taking a Dreamer into the Pool. Kyllikki couldn't help but react.

"Ah, you see how easy it would be to use him in a Pool? Just the thought has you going. And let me tell you, sex with your own Dreamer is—unique, especially when he Dreams it back to you. It's almost as good as when he has sex with someone else, and Dreams it to you."

He never mentioned that. A peculiar, curdling sensation invaded Kyllikki's stomach at the idea of Zimor being so intimate with Elias. "We don't complete the act, in the Pools."

"Not usually," agreed Zimor. "But don't worry about it. Tomorrow night, at just after midnight, the time will be right for the setting of the key. We've missed two other opportunities because of mechanical difficulties, and I'm not going to let this one slide by. Either you will take Elias down into the Pool—or I will." Her eyes met Kyllikki's and held. "You know my preferred method in the Pools."

Pain. She means she's going to arouse Elias with pain! "He wouldn't respond. He's not the type."

"Really? Are you sure?" She paused as if to plant the doubt deep in Kyllikki's thoughts. "He has to be raised quickly to peak intensity. It's critical for this. Do you think you could do it without—tools?"

"I've never had any difficulty with my Operators."

"He's not trained or conditioned."

"If I chose to, I could do it. You know how I feel on this point. Let's not quarrel so soon." She looked up at her cousin, letting her see total capitulation.

"So you'll take him down and set the key to save him from my—methods?"

"I'm not sure he's the one I want. I have to think about it. But when I give you my unbarriered Word, you can depend on me—and *my* methods."

"In any event, one or the other of us has to Bond him tonight to be ready to take him down tomorrow."

"Tonight? What time is it? What day is it?"

Zimor told her it was the day after her capture, commenting, "You weren't out very long as stuns go, but it's mid-morning now. I must have your decision by evening."

If Yinay struck at sundown as arranged, perhaps, Kyllikki thought, she could get away while she was being escorted to Elias. But how could she fake an unbarriered Word in order to get them to take her to him?

The door signal ticked politely, a sound calculated not to disturb an ill patient. "Get that," Zimor ordered one of the banded guards by the door. She rose to face the messenger, who stopped in the door, gave a formal bow, and said, "Lady of Laila, Lady Kyllikki: The Beditzial, Ansarios, has arrived seeking an emergency conference."

"Tell him to come back in three days. Extend all courtesies, but—"

"The Beditzial charged me to say he's been betrayed by Laila. If I return without The Lady of Laila, he'll see that Laila's fortunes wither forever."

Kyllikki had a hard time keeping her face straight and her barriers firm. Her buy-and-sell orders had apparently gone through as programmed and had done the damage she had hoped for. She hadn't lost her touch.

But she hadn't planned on being Zimor's prisoner when Zimor discovered the manipulations. She might have to undo it all under the observation of her cousin and Ansarios both. Then Esten and her friends might take that as a signal that she'd changed plans and no longer needed the diversion, or they might believe she'd betrayed them.

Zimor headed for the door, calling over her shoulder, "I'll be back for your decision this evening, Kyllikki."

Kyllikki was left alone for a few minutes, her mind jerking this way and that, searching for a plan. The glimpse of the inside-out way things looked through Zimor's eyes, while shocking, hadn't really changed anything. Knowing how Zimor would punish and coerce her scientists into finding facts to support her prejudices, Kyllikki didn't even consider that the setting of a gigantic key into the firmament would solve the transportation problem.

Even if it worked, it would only limit the number of people who could Operate a ship, putting more power into Family hands. There'd never be enough telepaths to handle the growing needs of commerce. The whole scheme was simply designed to destroy the Guild and the Empire, not to solve the transportation problem.

So she considered how to make an advantage out of Zimor's conviction that Kyllikki had grown into a powerful leader. She was used to Zimor's underestimating her, but she didn't know what she could do with Zimor overestimating her.

At least, she thought to herself with satisfaction, she had grown past the stage where Zimor's visions could tempt her into believing Zimor's promises. Zimor might demand an unbarriered Word, but she'd never give one.

Kyllikki was still stewing over it all when the medics came to remove the probe from her brain, and when she woke up an hour later, she was given food and a supervised shower, followed by a complete examination that revealed she could be released as soon as Zimor gave the order.

"And don't take that as license to go wandering around," said the medic. He was an elderly man who'd been serving Laila since before Kyllikki was born. "Zimor has this room protected for you, but outside you'll need your guards, and they haven't been assigned yet."

"Personal guards inside Laila?"

"There's a war on, child. Now, I know you must be curious and lonely and eager to pick up where you left off, so, since no contrary orders have been issued, I've taken the liberty of asking some of your relatives to stop by."

They brought her a lovely red-and-white sleeping gown and bed jacket, with liveried pillows and matching spread. Several sprays of flowers preceded her visitors, and then three young men burst into the room, preceded and followed by their banded guards. They came right to her to bestow welcoming hugs and kisses.

Only when the third finally stood back did she recognize them as the triplets grown to manhood. The three boys had been the bane of existence at Laila until they were sent off to school just before she'd left. They were so much younger than Kyllikki, that she'd never been friends with them, but not quite so young that she could have helped raise them.

"I don't know what to say," said Kyllikki. "Are you really that glad to see me? My reputation—"

"Your reputation has just been endorsed by Zimor herself," said one of young Lords of Laila.

The middle one continued, "—so we wanted to greet you personally and make sure you know how the *whole* family welcomes you back. Zimor says you're on her side now—"

There was something odd in the way the words meshed out of sync with the young man's thoughts. She softened her barriers as the third one picked up the sentence, "—and Zimor says that means we're all Family again. But I think I'm the only one of us who remembers you. You taught me to use the data tap because my brothers could and I couldn't, and you thought that wasn't fair. Do you remember that?"

She grinned. They were identical triplets, and Kyllikki had never gotten their names straight. She didn't try now since they still seemed to function as a unit. "Of course I remember that!"

One of the others asked, in the same tone of casual reminiscence, "Do you remember Finad's Special key?"

Finad had been one of Kyllikki's playmates who was such a distant relative that they never figured out what to call each other. But he was a Bonder and a skilled telepath as well as a genius, which made him more persecuted by the young Zimor than Kyllikki had been. As Kyllikki had retreated from her lessons, Finad had thrown himself headlong into his studies.

As the memory came back, she realized they were telling her that their conversation was being recorded. Mentally, she traced the key. Under Finad's Special, they'd brewed conspiracies right under Zimor's nose. The key acted to keep them

conversing intelligibly aloud while they communed at considerable depth. It was a technical marvel, but could be mastered in
early youth, so it had become the clandestine tool of a very
small segment of the Laila telepaths who were both precocious
enough and motivated enough to learn it.

When she had a good grip on it, Kyllikki released her barriers and let them see her building it. "No, I don't recall that
one. But I remember Finad. Where is he now?"

"Finad is running Laila operations on Bicjrack, which is
about as far as you can get from Inarash." He'd been sent away,
Kyllikki learned through the key, because he had defied Zimor
once too often. The final vitriolic banishment Zimor had pro-
nounced on Finad played through Kyllikki's mind as if she'd
been there.

They had all built Finad's key together and now experiences flowed among them, shared in full context. The story of
Finad's downfall led naturally into the history of Zimor's takeover, how people felt about it, and why they hadn't been able to
do anything. The childhood key, used by four mature adults,
created a powerful four-way commune.

It was the first time Kyllikki had reached this level since
well before she'd left Laila, and she reveled in it shamelessly.
Whole sequences of images flashed by, telling interwoven stories, not in the linear order in which they had occurred but in
the all-at-once way that a memory washes up onto the shore of
consciousness, orchestrated with emotions and linked to older
associated memories so that every image was fraught with sig-
nificances. After a few moments, it was almost as if she'd lived
through those years here at Laila.

And with that came the knowledge that Laila wasn't so
enamored with Zimor. There was no concrete evidence against
Zimor, but the list of convenient casualties among Laila's own
was already too long to be coincidence.

Though many of them could see how her ideas would lead
Laila to prosperity, they didn't like the way Zimor grasped the
reins of power. Now unable to finish the war as quickly as she'd
promised, Zimor had lost their confidence. A number had be-

gun to suspect that she wasn't quite sane anymore, and some, the few who knew about it, went so far as to claim that her plan with the ground-based Pool was based on wishful thinking, not science. There was even a faction within Laila, albeit a silent one, that claimed the Metaji was right and the Operators should be abandoned in favor of Guides.

But Laila didn't know how to get rid of Zimor. When rumors of Kyllikki's exploits with the coded access system hit Laila, the opposition had collected around the triplets to support Kyllikki as a candidate to succeed Zimor.

The last of Kyllikki's objections to this evaporated when she learned that some of the recently deceased, people who should have been ahead of her for the post, had died or been lost on ships that vanished.

The exchange worked two ways, and though Kyllikki held back the details, she let the triplets know her objective in coming here was to destroy the Pool and leave the galaxy safe for the Guides. It wasn't Idom's technical arguments that won them over. It was her conviction that it was their only chance, a conviction that remained unwavering even after Zimor's "truth." When all she'd felt and said in that confrontation with Zimor had been laid out for them, they were astonished at her optimism. There was no way Zimor would let her out until she'd given her unbarriered Word, and *that* couldn't be faked.

She couldn't argue the point, but had to assume she could handle it somehow. She needed to know how many of Laila might help her, if she could manage to get away.

There were at least twenty, perhaps thirty, of those within the compound who could be counted on.

As she was deep in their minds, she knew they were sincere. So she told them that a commotion would start within the compound that afternoon just before sundown and asked them to martial their people to magnify the disaster while keeping everyone away from the Pool building. She and her friends would do the rest.

All this while, they had been chattering aloud about *remember when* and *how long has it been since* and *whatever happened to so-and-so.* As they dismantled the Special, they chattered to a halt, unaware of what they'd been saying.

"I guess we'd better be going," said one of the triplets. "We're scheduled to play a round of nidru before sundown, and we just have time. I'm going to win today."

Nidru was an outdoor game that took about two hours per round, and commonly ran eight to ten rounds before a winner was declared. The Laila courts were the envy of the Families. "I hope you have a good-sized audience."

Another observed significantly, "Oh, I expect the usual thirty or so will show up. They've all been following the contests. We play pretty hard."

The middle triplet leaned down and confided, "Actually, he likes to talk more than to play, but we can always coax someone else onto the court while he circulates."

They left, tossing nidru jargon back and forth as if nothing more interesting could possibly be going on, and Kyllikki began to believe there was really a chance.

Shortly after that Zimor stormed into the room and inserted an activator into the data tap at the side of the bed, coding directly into the financial files, then turned to Kyllikki with a stern look. "If you expect to have any choice about Elias or how he's treated in the Pool, you will reverse your raid on Beditzial within the hour, even if it puts you back in debt!"

Before Kyllikki could answer, Zimor was again summoned to an emergency conference.

Looking more than a little harried, Zimor added over her shoulder that she expected results within the hour. "And you must drop Ansarios a note explaining that you were pointing out how vulnerable he'd left himself. But, Kyllikki, don't do anything like this again. If you need funds, come to me."

And she left to a repeat of the urgent summons, without leaving anyone to supervise Kyllikki's use of the unrestricted data tap. Kyllikki decided that either the pressure was building on Zimor, making her careless, or she had some other means of monitoring what Kyllikki was doing.

Kyllikki ran her personal security programs, not too surprised to find them still in the household files, since she'd hidden them well. She found two spy lines. With infinite care, she arranged for each of them to report that she had done as ordered. Only a sophisticated cross-check would reveal what she was actually going to do.

Once free of surveillance, she checked her investments. It was amazing. All the smartest money had followed her lead, betting the Teleod would lose the war. The gossip boards now showed a rumor that a Metaji invasion fleet had departed Veramai, heading for Inarash. The Teleod's own fleet was not ready to move yet. There were various contradictory reports on the timing of the two fleets' movements, making many people doubt all the reports. But Kyllikki believed the Imperial fleet was on the move. There had been more than enough time. The Pool had to be used and destroyed before the Imperials made their final jump into Teleod space, for in that most damaged region, the Guides would lose perhaps half the ships in their fleet.

Considering that those ships carried a full complement of Guides, and that the first report of their departure probably had taken some time to arrive, Kyllikki figured that the fleet could arrive as early as dawn.

She paid off her debts and invested the profits where they'd do the most possible damage to Zimor's personal holdings if the Teleod lost the war. If things went as planned, Zimor wouldn't have time to notice what Kyllikki had done until morning, and by then it would be all over.

It was almost sunset by the timer set into the data display. And as she leaned back, resting, alone in the room, she became aware of the faint but discernible lilt of Elias' music.

It was distinctive. There could be no mistake. Considering the kind of insulation used in Laila buildings, he had to be very close. Try as she might, though, she could only sense that hint of melody laced with anxiety, frustration, hope, and tension. *He knows the time.*

And then she heard a crash followed by a rumble that shook the walls. She leaped to her feet and began to search for her clothes. Pieces of ceiling sifted down onto her. She gave up looking for her clothes and yanked the door open, only vaguely surprised that it yielded to her touch.

chapter **nineteen**

●●

$\mathbf{A}$s she stepped out of her room, Kyllikki heard the evacuation hooters go off. A patch of lights dimmed, and fire-control sprayers erupted randomly. But the shaking had stopped. The air was humid and stale; the circulators had failed in the corridors.

The soft-floored hall stretched in a slight curve in both directions, forming a circle around the central area of Attendants' offices and emergency-equipment storage. But that area was deserted. The Attendants were all heading for the other end of the building to evacuate the helpless patients.

One Attendant raced by Kyllikki pushing an empty floater bed, and instructed, "Emergency stairs are *that* way, Lady. Take it easy. You've got plenty of time."

"What happened?" asked Kyllikki, tagging along with her for a few paces. "Can I help?"

"Something crashed into the roof. The building may collapse." She jerked her chin at a door as they passed. "There's another emergency stair you could use, Lady."

Kyllikki dropped back and turned to the stair. When the woman was out of sight, Kyllikki doubled back, following her sense of Elias' music, which was now fraught with strident alarm and helplessness. As she crossed the restricted area behind the Attendants' counter, her eye fell on a familiar bundle tucked up into a cubby: luren insulation mesh wrapped around that stiff cloth they used for outdoor clothing.

She snatched at it, and an Inhibitor necklet rolled out, followed by the case for protective eye inserts and a pair of goggles. Wherever he was, Zuchmul was trapped. Gathering the gear into her arms, she closed her eyes and sought the familiar tenor of Zuchmul's mind. //Zuchmul?//

A faint startlement registered, and Kyllikki asked, careful to stay in audio-analogue, //Are you drugged?//

//It's wearing off again,// he told her, shaking with fear. //I don't have my gear and it's daytime out—//

It felt like an exchange with someone on the farthest edge of her range, but he had to be right here in the building. //I have your things. Look on the wall above your bed and tell me the number of your room.//

//I can't read their numbers!//

Through the well-insulated walls, she could get no sense of where he might be, so she had to risk discovery by the Laila telepaths. //All right. Calm down. Focus your eyes on the number.// As she reassured him, she traced the delicate lines of the key she needed. At once, pain flashed through her eyes into her brain, carrying an impression limned in scaring light and cross-hatched with dizzying distortions, low-grade magnetic fields seen through luren eyes.

A long, jagged crack split the outer wall of his room. Raw sunlight poured into the darkness. The color seemed all wrong to her, but it had to be the setting sun.

//Shield your eyes. I got the number. I'm coming.//

//There was a guard outside my door. I think she's gone—but be careful.//

Kyllikki dodged a cluster of hurrying Attendants with a critical patient. They shouted advice as they swept by.

She called back, "I'm all right. I'm going down that way!"

She pointed at another emergency stair. They were gone and she found the door.

//No guard here. Zuchmul, I'm coming in.// If Zimor's guards were deserting her prisoners, maybe there was hope.

The door display showed it wasn't locked. But then why should it be? Without protective gear, the luren was trapped. Even at night, the environment of the building would prevent him from going more than a few steps. Knowing that, and knowing Zuchmul was throwing off the drug that prevented him from using Influence, the guard wouldn't have gone in to try to drag the luren out of the dark room. So, with Zuchmul trapped, the guard had simply left.

Without breaking stride, Kyllikki hit the door with her shoulder. It moved, then stuck. Through the crack, she saw the curtains that had been draped around the door to protect the luren from the corridor light. They had fallen along with a chunk of the ceiling, and the debris was jamming the door. She kicked at the heap, then wedged the door open and slipped through the crack.

Zuchmul had tipped the massive bed onto its side and was huddled in the shade formed by the bed. He had wrapped every scrap of material he could find around himself.

Kyllikki pressed the bundle into his arms. "Get dressed. I'm going to find Elias. He's here somewhere."

"I heard them say his room was behind heavy security. That way—end of the hall." He gestured as he fitted the goggles to his face. "I'll be right behind you."

She picked her way over the rubble out into the hall and slid on a patch of floor that had been sprayed by the fire-control nozzles. At the far end of the hall, a portable security wall still glowed brightly, cutting off access to a room at the end of a long entry hall—Zimor's private room when she needed treatment. *That's where he's got to be.*

She slid and stumbled to the transparent wall. Behind it, masonry had fallen in a pile, and there was a booted foot sticking out from under it at an odd angle. One guard hadn't had a chance to desert his post.

She studied the control panel of the security equipment while groping mentally for Elias. //Elias?//

//Kyllikki! What's happening?//

His presence was so faint, yet he had to be behind that door. //Something hit the roof. Yinay, maybe. Are you all right? Where's Idom?//

//Haven't seen Idom. I'm trapped in a medical treatment room, but I'm all right. Where's Zuchmul?//

//He's coming. I'm right outside your door.// She found the switch and deactivated the security wall. Nothing happened. Then she saw another set of controls behind the wall. Of course, the inside and outside guards had to agree to open the gate. And there was probably a code. When the inside guard died, the outside guard deserted.

"What's the problem?" asked Zuchmul behind her.

Startled, she jumped, heart leaping into her throat. She pointed silently to the tandem controls.

Snapping the Inhibitor around his neck, Zuchmul looked over the panels. "Wait." He ran back to the Attendants' station and returned with some medics' tools. It took him only a moment to break into the security mechanism, where he very selectively smashed something. The glowing wall vanished.

They had to heave the wreckage off the dead guard to get the key to the door, but then Elias was free—and uninjured. He stepped across the debris wearing standard-issue gray pajamas. That was the first time Kyllikki realized she was wearing nothing but red-and-white pajamas herself.

Elias asked, "How can we find Idom? We need him."

Kyllikki shook her head, wiping her face with a gritty hand and feeling her hair stand up in greasy spikes around the shaved crown.

Zuchmul asked, "Why don't you just ask him where he is?"

"The building's insulated. He's not near here. Come on, there's a stair over this way." She led them into the Attendants' area, then paused thoughtfully beside some gas cylinders stowed in clips on the wall. They were as long as her arm, just as slender, and color-coded. She stared at them, summoning the trained visual memory of a Teleod telepath. "These could come in handy," she said, pulling them off their moorings and handing one to each of the two men. She rummaged in a cabinet and came up with the matching valves, which she rammed into place. "Anesthetic gas."

They went down four floors but were stopped by a missing landing. They backed up one landing and went out onto a floor filled with conference rooms, offices, and labs. She knew this part of the building, for she'd often had classes here. The doors had no locks, so there wouldn't be any prisoners on this floor. "Wait!" said Kyllikki, stopping.

They stopped behind her, peering over her shoulder. The walls here showed only an occasional gaping crack with very little fallen debris. But the cracks were in load-bearing walls. The whole building might collapse at any time. She asked, "Hear anything?"

They listened, and she flattened her barriers, searching her surroundings with all her skills. Nothing.

"There're people on this floor," reported Zuchmul, flipping the Inhibitor back around his neck. Kyllikki hadn't seen him remove it. For the first time, she noticed that his skin, barely visible through the mesh, looked red and rough instead of a healthy pasty white. He'd been radiation-burned, but was healing almost as she watched.

"How many people?" asked Kyllikki.

"Maybe five or six—no fear, no panic. That way."

"Can't be Idom, then," said Elias.

"Could be," contradicted Zuchmul. "The insulation in this building is lousy. It blurs without cutting intensity."

Kyllikki shrugged that off. "Follow me." She crept in the direction Zuchmul had indicated and rounded a corner into a hall with doors that had insulated windows embedded in them—classrooms. Alert, she expected to meet another Teleod-trained telepath at any moment. And she did.

Quickly tracing the key she'd readied, she flung one arm out to stop the men from passing her. The mild curiosity of the telepath, attenuated by the heavy insulation, was a pale search-light that passed through them as if they weren't there. Kyllikki probed the telepath's barriers, a mirror wall through which she could see shadows and ghosts dancing. This was a Laila Family telepath, skilled but not greatly talented, not anyone Kyllikki had ever met.

On impulse, she brought up two more key images and, ever so delicately, lifted the visuals she needed. Holding her breath until the other telepath's curiosity waned, she retreated.

When her heart stopped pounding, she pointed and breathed, "That door. Four Operators and Idom. One's a Laila telepath, and his two guards are stationed at either side of the door. Idom's answering questions—willingly."

The two men looked to her for instructions.

"The Operators are scholars. Probably talking about the Pool experiment. They're probably the architects of Zimor's plan with the Pool." Hefting her cylinder, she aimed the nozzle away from her. "Give me time to get close enough to alert Idom. Breathe deeply, and when I give the signal, follow me in, holding your breath. Leave the guards and the Laila to me. Gas the other three Operators."

She crept forward, readying her cylinder as she crossed the corridor, then edged up to the door and peeked through its window. Idom was bent over a course-plotting bench, the Teleod kind with dozens of screens set flush to the surface. The Operators and the telepath crowded around him as he pointed at the screens. He was lecturing with a joyful enthusiasm. The Operators looked very skeptical.

With great care, she schooled herself back into the Metaji audio-analogue mode. //Idom?//

She sensed his mind, but it was highly focused and concentrated, as if he were counting into a dive.

//Idom! It's Kyllikki.//

//????//

//It's Kyllikki. Listen. Elias and Zuchmul are with me. We're going to get you out of there.//

//Kyllikki, not *now*! I've—//

JACQUELINE LICHTENBERG

//How long are we supposed to wait out here? Until we get caught? Or until the building falls down?//

//?????//

She had to explain why the building was being evacuated and remind him of their plan. At length, she felt him straightening up with a sigh, then posing his listeners a question before he told her, //The Laila over there is a telepath, and there are two guards—//

//I know, and my relative will notice you screaming at me any moment now. Start hyperventilating. When I give the signal, take a deep breath and hold it, roll under the table, count three, then go for the door, and *don't breathe* until you're out in the hall. Can you do that?//

//What if I don't?//

//You'll get a good night's sleep while the three of us work the Pool.// *He's an old man! He'll never make it.*

//Then I can and will.//

She peeked through the bottom corner of the window again to check the layout, then, shielding it from her relative inside, she flashed the picture to her companions along with a graphic sketch of what she planned for the guards. Then, as she tore the door open, she sent to all of them, //Now! Deep breath and hold it!//

Her gas jet caught the first guard on an inhalation, but the second drew his gun.

With the butt of the cylinder, she smashed his gun aside, hearing his wrist bone crack. He gasped. She sprayed him in the face. He sank to the floor, as astonished as she was that she'd bested two banded guards.

Meanwhile, the three Operators and the telepath had backed away from the advancing luren and Dreamer. As Zuchmul and Elias cleared the door, Idom scrambled out into the hall.

Crossing the room with her cylinder hissing, Kyllikki used the audio-analogue to drive a mental voice into her relative's mind, ramming the Metaji protocols into the Teleod-trained telepath. //This isn't lethal gas. Would you prefer a realm duel?//

With a grimace of pain, the man raised both hands before his face as if warding off a blow. Their eyes met, and she was instantly contrite. Her mental "voice" must have been worse for him to endure than raw sunlight was for Zuchmul. Very deliberately, the telepath drew a deep breath, then stretched out on the floor.

The other three Operators were also down. Retreating, Kyllikki snatched a black cloak from the back of a chair.

Outside, with the door closed behind them, they gathered around Idom, gulping lungfuls of clean air. She leaned on Elias, repairing her barriers, hoping that if anyone had noticed her using keys, they wouldn't be able to find her through insulation and barriers. Elias wrapped his arm around her and let his hand rest just below her waist. His mental music filled her, and he leaned down to plant a swift kiss on her lips. Comfort washed through her, as if the shattered bits of her life had reassembled into a picture.

With a squeeze, he let her go and began helping her into the black cloak. "What now?"

She twisted the material away from him and handed it to Zuchmul. "There are others outside in sleeping clothes, but I doubt there are many luren around."

As the luren swept the thing around him, flashing the red lining and raising the hood to shadow his face, Idom said, "You're right. We've got to get to the Pool." He dug a chain out of his shirt. On it was his astrogator's mnemonic medallion. The luren had carved a secret pocket for a single tablet in it, the drug Kyllikki would need. "I still have this."

Zuchmul removed his Inhibitor and checked a hidden compartment. "Mine's intact, too."

"They got mine," said Elias.

Kyllikki nodded, "Mine, too." She held out her hand to Idom. "With luck, we'll be at the Pool in a few minutes, so I'd better take it now."

She swallowed it dry and it burned all the way down as she led the way to the far corner of the building. On the way, Kyllikki gave them a mental picture of where they were on the maps they'd studied, and where they would come out at the bottom of the staircase she was heading for.

At the bottom of the stairs, they left their gas cylinders. They were much too cumbersome, and were nearly exhausted. Turning to the door, Kyllikki put her hand on the safety-latch mechanism. The seal had already been broken, so they wouldn't set off any more alarms when they exited.

One hand on the closed door, she gestured as she said, "When I open the door, you'll see the power plant to the left, and beyond that, the kitchens. Around to the right is some sort of new building, and beyond that, an environmental plant. We go straight across the open ground in front of this door, circle the big black building, the one with the white roof, and then you'll see the Pool building. Just like the map. Remember?"

They'd all studied the maps of the Laila compound until they thought their eyes would fall out. But there were more than eighty buildings scattered randomly about. Zuchmul was the first to nod his understanding, then the others agreed.

"Let's go." Kyllikki pushed the door open. A cataract of noise assaulted her. She was three steps beyond the threshold before the scene in front of her registered.

Directly before the door, a large repair truck was parked over an open hatch set into the pavement. The truck bore the logo of the company Laila retained to care for the compound's environmental plants. Uniformed workers swarmed over the area creating noise and confusion while five people in Laila livery yelled at them, their voices unheard over the pumps and motors on the truck.

Kyllikki halted, she and the three men behind her unnoticed by the frantically struggling workers.

As she stared at the churning mob cutting off her planned escape, a Lord of Laila strode into the midst of the workers and bent to yank the power supply of the noisiest equipment. Three uniformed men tried to stop him, shouting and gesticulating toward the distant kitchens. One went so far as to tap the Lord's wrist with a finger.

With a wrathful expression, the Lord silenced the pump,

and his voice was finally heard. ". . . obviously broken or it wouldn't make that much noise!"

The Lord was one of the triplets. He stared down at the uniformed worker who cringed visibly, stuttering, "B-but L-lord, the *smell*. . . !" It wasn't a very convincing cringe. *Pinda Lord Yinay!* His eyebrows were shaved, and they'd done something to his complexion, yet Kyllikki was sure the worker was Esten's cousin. But who'd ever guess in that uniform?

An odor stole into their midst. Kyllikki told her companions, //Hold your breath and follow me!//

She led them through the crowd while everyone looked about with expressions of growing disgust. Kyllikki jumped over thick hoses and piles of new pipe, the men close behind. They'd reached the other side of the work area when the first person vomited. It was contagious.

Some uniformed workers had scattered while others bravely stood their ground and succumbed to the reeking fumes that billowed back along the conduits. Rotten fish must have been dumped into the system near the kitchens.

When she finally had to breathe, Kyllikki glanced back. Both the Yinay and Laila Lords had gone, leaving the Laila bystanders to bear the brunt of it.

She fought her own rising gorge, and turned away to circle the white-roofed building, peeking around the corner before dashing across an open area. The hangar where the Pool was located was on the edge of the planned disturbances.

The pavement between them and the hangar was deserted. The evening sky was already darkening, throwing the near side of the hangar into deep shadow. "Zuchmul, see that door—the big gray one? It'll be locked. Try to get it open. The rest of us will circle the hangar looking for another way in. Tell me silently if you get it open."

"And what am I supposed to use for tools?"

"Improvise," said Elias. "I'll circle left. Kyllikki, you take Idom and circle right. Meet me halfway."

Before she could say anything to him, he was off. "Come on, Idom," she muttered. "Be careful, Zuchmul."

Ordinarily, Zimor's guards would have that open area under surveillance. She hoped their attention had been diverted, or that maybe one of the triplets was in the guard's booth. She and Idom had hardly gone a quarter of the way around the hangar when Zuchmul cried, //I got it! Kyllikki?//

//Here,// she answered and told Idom and Elias, then asked Zuchmul, //How did you do it so quickly?//

//Improvised. Hurry before somebody notices.//

They ran and came to the gaping door just as Elias arrived. When they were inside, it took all their combined strength to roll the inert door shut, and then Zuchmul used something he had in his hand to short out the lock mechanism and fuse it. "They'll never get that open from the outside." He squinted at the row of windows near the roof, several stories above them. "But they could get in that way."

"Not worth it," said Kyllikki. "There have to be doors in the back leading directly into the offices and storerooms. We can't block them all, so we have to hurry."

She turned to survey the hangar she'd seen in N'hawatt's memory. Dim lights had come on when they stepped through the door and there was still a reddish glow from the windows. The Pool itself dominated the area to the left of the huge door. Protected by a safety rail, it was sunk beneath the level of the floor. Steps led down to it. It was about five times bigger than a normal ship's Pool, circled by an enlarged version of a standard Beditzial rim.

While she and Elias skirted the Pool, Idom moved to the consoles, studying them, one hand wandering over the touch panels. "It's a good thing I had a chance to interrogate Zimor's people." He selected a control, then cautiously activated it. The displays came to life, the touchpads glowing. He sat down, rubbing his hands together. "I almost had them convinced they'd misunderstood everything. If I could have gotten to them in the beginning, we could've stopped this war before it began."

Zuchmul crossed to stand behind Idom. "Turn it on. I'm not going to get out of this gear until you've got it all activated—and maybe not even then."

Idom gave another tentative stroke to a control pad. "Can't wear that stuff into the Pool, especially not the Inhibitor—" He twisted to glance at Zuchmul, then gaped. Coming up behind them, Kyllikki, too, noticed Zuchmul no longer wore the Inhibitor—nor was it attached to his belt.

"I used it to open the door—and close it again. Not much left of it now." He held out his palm to Kyllikki. "I saved the tablet, though, in case we need it."

"No. I think I'm all right." The drug wasn't making her sick this time. "Go ahead and test me."

"See that Pool?" he asked. "Describe it."

"Well, it rises about my height above the floor, and the steps leading up are made of green—" She blinked, vaguely remembering that the Pool had been recessed into the ground. "But . . ." she muttered, starting for the Pool.

Zuchmul's hands clamped on her shoulders, and suddenly the Pool was deep in the floor again.

She wiped her face with one shaking hand. "I guess I passed the test."

"Perfectly," said Zuchmul, pulling her close. "I'm sorry if that was a shock."

"A necessary test." Then the distinctive whine of a Pool coming into function echoed off the walls. It was a lower growl of power, a more bone-shaking sensation than she'd ever felt before.

"I think it's out of tune, Idom," said Kyllikki. She twisted to look at Zuchmul. "Unless you're doing that."

He shuddered. "No."

"I told you they didn't know what they were doing," muttered Idom. "I've almost got it now, though. Listen."

The sound became more harmonious as it spread both higher and lower than the hearing thresholds of humans. The bone-aching noise stopped.

Zuchmul looked toward the immense device, his lips whiter than Kyllikki had ever seen them. "It better stop that or I'm going to be sick."

"Just a minute," said Idom, working the controls.

Elias went to peer down into the pit to watch.

"It's getting better," offered Zuchmul. "Idom, I think that's it. It's more like a ship's Pool now."

"Yes, that's the way it's supposed to work, so if you're going to do this, you'd better get going. And, Zuchmul, remember what I told you about those images."

He put one hand to the fastening of his mesh mask, then froze. "I can't even remember them!"

"Don't panic, I'll help you," said Kyllikki, each image Idom had concocted springing fresh into her mind. She traced a quick key image and gave him the designs. "Remember, first three—then one, then two, then four, then five and six? Three is the three of us together."

Tossing the cape aside, he stripped away the mask and the headpiece and began to shimmy out of the rest of the mesh garment. "I remember now. You'll have to find that place on the rim where I have to enter from." He paused with the mesh on the floor around his ankles and his hands on the fastenings of his shirt. "Idom, I can do without the goggles, but I need the insert lenses. It's horrid in here."

"They're organic. That'll be all right."

"Get undressed, Elias, and come on, I'll show you where you go down." She crossed to the stair and descended without letting herself pause to think about Elias following her.

On the narrow deck around the outside of the rim, she piled her gown and jacket in her own place, then circled, reading the incised markings to find where Zuchmul had to enter. He would need more courage than the rest of them, since no one knew what would happen when a luren descended into a Pool.

Zuchmul appeared at the top of the stair and paused. "Come on," she called. "This is your place."

At that moment, as the nude luren came toward her, Kyllikki was suddenly glad she'd seen him that way before. It would have embarrassed him if she'd been shocked into staring at his sunken abdomen, prominent ribs, and stick-thin thighs and arms covered with stark-white skin. The scorch marks from his previous exposure were now growing angrier under renewed assault. *Is Idom wrong? Will the Pool environment kill him?*

She smiled at him as if he were any handsome partner she was about to take into the Pool. Then she gestured to Elias and pointed out the rim markings and how they related to the whorls embedded in the billowing blackness. The surface had come to the consistency of viscous smoke, and she knew it would feel silky on her skin, sensuous and exciting.

The others, however, didn't know that. As they joined her, she could feel both the men shaking, and not just with the chill emanating from the Pool.

"Here," she said, stooping down. "Puddle your hand through it, like this—as if it were a swimming pool. Feel how it curls around your fingers. It's not really a substance, it's more like an energy-solution. But it feels great, doesn't it? It's not even cold. Try it."

She'd said all this before, but it had been just theoretical to them then. Now it was real.

Zuchmul bared his teeth as he knelt to scoop one hand through the nonsubstance. But the grimace turned to a smile. "It's better in there than out here."

Kneeling between them, she put an arm around each of the men and hugged them close, running her hands up and down their goose-bumpy sides. "When you step into the Pool, you won't feel like you're falling. You'll sink as if into thick oil, but it will feel like warm silk. Very sensuous."

A great echoing crash filled the air, followed by a wordless shout of dismay from Idom.

Footsteps rattled, weapons jingled, and Zimor's voice rose over it all. "Out of there, all of you! Now!"

chapter **twenty**

•••••••••••••••••••••••••••••••••••

Kyllikki's barriers materialized. With her eyes alone, she saw the cold dread on Elias' face, the shock in Zuchmul's eyes. Through both the drug and her barriers, she felt his Influence gather power like a clenched fist.

Above them, two guards appeared at the gate in the railing, motioning preemptively for the three to come up.

As Kyllikki led the way up the steps, the Pool behind them began to solidify, the hum becoming strident with unbalanced forces. She heard Zuchmul gasp, doubling over. Elias supported him, murmuring softly. When Kyllikki's head cleared the level of the floor, she saw Zimor bent over the Pool control console, holding a gun at Idom's head with one hand, poking at the controls with the other. Finally, the strident shriek abated. The hum of solidification made the stair vibrate under her bare feet.

Elias joined Kyllikki between the two guards; Zuchmul remained behind them, his head below the level of the floor. In a quick glance, Kyllikki saw that the usually pink glow of his Influence had become blue-white, throbbing with new power.

At the console, Zimor had discarded the decorative layers

of her outfit, as if ready for a martial-arts workout. There were sweat stains on the fine fabric. With the Pool and Idom under her control, she turned and snapped, "Well, kill them!"

The white-hot power of Zuchmul's Influence lanced through Kyllikki as if she were transparent. But the contained beam struck the two guards with surgical precision, sending them reeling. Without waiting to see what Zuchmul had done, Kyllikki launched herself at Zimor, hoping to get her before her reflex struck at the luren.

Behind Kyllikki, both the guards staggered, lurched into the railing, and jackknifed over it, dropping headfirst into the Pool's well. As they fell, Zimor's gun hand sagged and a look of horror petrified her face. *She's seen Zuchmul!*

Simultaneously, Kyllikki heard a skull impact on the apron around the Pool, realized that Zimor was not reacting to Zuchmul's Influence and that *that* more than anything was what scared her, and felt the Pool's hum die to silence as a warbling scream echoed from the ceiling: "My leg!"

Then she rammed her shoulder into Zimor's hip. Zimor's gun went off with a loud sizzle-crack and an odor like burning hair. Far above them, a lighting fixture exploded, showering bits down on them. Kyllikki's chin hit the floor with stunning pain, but she was on top of Zimor.

Zimor brought her gun down to bear on Kyllikki.

Idom kicked Zimor's gun from her hand, and Zimor yelled.

Kyllikki humped up to get her knees under her, trying to pin her cousin down, but Zimor squirmed, punched, kicked and twisted to land on top, one knee planted firmly in Kyllikki's stomach. Her right fist came up clenching the pommel of a forceblade. As Kyllikki's breath wheezed out of her lungs and her arms fell to her sides, the tip of the blade sang into existence not an eyelash length from her eye. Pain lanced through that eye and into her brain, but that was nothing compared to the agonized cry from Zuchmul at the unleashing of that dissonant force.

"I don't know where you got a luren who can't be controlled by the Families' reflex, but control him now and I may let you both live. Maybe even Elias, too."

Elias was trying to protect Zuchmul with his own body. Idom was frozen in place, watching the forceblade.

Flickering blackness edging her vision, Kyllikki whispered, "I don't control him." Despite hardly being able to breathe, she was maintaining her barriers.

"Don't lie to me!" grated Zimor, "or I'll crush your memory to shards and extract the controlling key."

"You couldn't!" But already she felt a sharp point of fire etching a pattern into the reflective surface of her barriers. It was an unfamiliar key, yet it woke resonances deep in Kyllikki's mind where its twin resided, hidden like a virus within the nucleus of earliest childhood memories. When Zimor had planted the false memories, she must have planted a memory pulverizer too, as insurance.

"Can't I?" muttered Zimor.

All Zimor's attention went into forming her key, an act requiring total concentration, which was why a telepathic duel couldn't be started in the midst of a physical fight. In the instant when Zimor was most vulnerable, Kyllikki stopped trying to repair the gouges in her barriers and schooled herself down to audio-analogue. As she used all her last strength to bring both her hands up and shove the forceblade aside, she unleashed a telepathic shout of raw noise focused directly into Zimor's mind on a level where she had no barriers.

Mentally and physically, Zimor recoiled, screaming. Idom and Elias lunged forward. Kyllikki rolled free of Zimor's weight and grabbed something that was lying in the dust under the console. It was cold and heavy, as big around as her fist. She smashed it into Zimor's head. Elias caught Zimor and lowered her to the floor, the forceblade rolling free, gouging furrows in the floor. Idom snatched the forceblade and shut it. A muted sob came from Zuchmul.

Still on her knees, still clutching the weapon, Kyllikki scanned the building for other guards, and gasped, "There's no one else coming." The frantic chaos outside was unabated. Her voice was thin, her lungs empty, her heart pounding.

Idom went to his knees beside Zimor as Zuchmul staggered over. Idom touched the blood on her head. "She's dead."

Kyllikki found she was holding a length of chain. She flung the bloody thing aside and knelt by her cousin, her heart in her mouth. "Oh, no! I didn't mean it."

"She's not dead," gasped Zuchmul without examining her.

Then Kyllikki saw Zimor's chest rise. The woman's brain was still active. A sharp sound escaped Kyllikki's lips, not quite a sob, not quite a groan.

Elias said, "Kyllikki, you should at least block her memories if not remove them. If she comes to while we're—"

"I won't."

Very softly, haloed by throbbing Influence, Zuchmul said, "Kyllikki, she'd have done worse to you, and even worse to me. I've never done it to a human—but I know how. I could make it temporary amnesia. Or permanent. They'd assume the blow caused it by accident. Elias is right. We can't risk her coming to and—"

"No!" Zuchmul was tense and miserable but resolute. One more unforgivable transgression wouldn't soil him any further, and by doing it for her, he'd protect her from the guilt. "No, Zuchmul. That's what Zimor would do. I won't be a party to it. Tie her up. As soon as we're done, we'll get medical treatment for her."

Zuchmul nodded. "You're right, of course. It's just that—she scares me." He rubbed absently at the skin flaking off the angry but healing burns all over his body.

Idom broke the silence. "The sooner we get this over with, the sooner we can get her to a medic." He started ripping strips off Zimor's clothes.

"Yes," said Zuchmul, bending to help. "Idom, you'll have to knock her out again if she comes to. Can you?"

While Elias joined Zuchmul in binding Zimor, Idom looked around for a softer weapon. "I can do it." He finally settled on a long strip of cloth looped around Zimor's neck, making a choke collar and leash. "This ought to keep her under control." While they finished tying Zimor up, Idom reawakened the Pool, fussing meticulously over the tuning.

Kyllikki went to the rail to judge the black medium's readiness, and suddenly Zuchmul was at her side, one hand restraining her. But it was too late. The scene below was engraved on her mind forever.

She gaped, unable to believe she had forgotten what must have occurred behind her while she was charging at Zimor.

One guard's body lay bent and broken half on the apron around the Pool, his head resting partly submerged in the solidified blackness. The other guard sprawled on top of the Pool, but one leg was sunk into it up to the knee.

As she watched, the Pool clouded and turned to mist. The body on the edge slid down into the mist with a stately grace. A vortex swallowed the other. In moments, there was no trace of them save a single blood smear on the rim.

Firmly, Zuchmul turned her away from the scene. Barriers wavering, Kyllikki couldn't help but feel the luren's hunger roused at the smell of blood, which, to him, pervaded the hangar with three distinct aromas: Zimor and the two guards. He buried his face in her hair and whispered, "I didn't want to hurt them. I couldn't think of anything else I could do without Zimor killing me instantly."

"What did you do to them?" she asked as Elias came up.

"Vertigo. It took very little and their own bodies did the rest. I meant only to bring them to their knees."

Oddly enough, there wasn't a flicker of jealousy in Elias as Zuchmul held her close. The Dreamer's eyes were on the smear of blood. "Where did they go? Why is the universe still here if entering a planet-based Pool is so dangerous?"

"Inert organic matter doesn't affect a Pool. It's mind, or mentation, that causes function."

Zuchmul said, "The bodies are consigned to oblivion."

Elias nodded, as if that satisfied him. Music began to thread through him. Dark music. "Let's get this over with."

"Yes. The Pool's ready." Kyllikki mended her barriers, groping for the images Idom had worked out so carefully. All the years of telepath's and Operator's discipline had to be good for something. "Let's go before this drug wears off."

She led the way down the steps, projecting calm, purposive discipline to the men as she brought the memorized drills back up into her mind. "All right, Zuchmul, do it."

Zuchmul's Influence spread through the Pool's well and the Pool surged with rhythmic tides in time to his power pulse. Kyllikki brought up the opening image that the luren was to project, the three of them bound together by a three-colored cord that formed a three-lobed figure. She made it real for Zuchmul, and he gave it the luminous glow of his Influence, making them *believe* it was really there.

She could feel the warmth of the cord as it tightened at the small of her back. She rested her elbows on it, feeling the vibrant tension of the binding, the faint jerk as Elias wrapped a hand around the part that encircled him.

Zuchmul had them completely in his thrall now. They'd rehearsed this part a few times, but never, of course, around a real Pool. He gave them the illusion of the cord shortening, drawing them together, forcing them to step into the Pool, to sink into the black mist.

Meanwhile, Kyllikki stretched out her hand to Elias, who reached toward her, and Zuchmul likewise held his hands out, providing them the illusion of hands clasping, though they were much too far apart to touch. From that point on, they must not lose contact with each other. Idom had been adamant on that point. The illusion allowed them to see each other, despite the black mist, and that was vital.

When the illusion was solid, Kyllikki projected the visualization of the map of the galaxy as Idom had given it to her, first as it was now, cross-hatched with scars and gouges, ruts and cracks, then fading into what they all wanted it to become, healed to a pristine loveliness where the only features were the stars, the gouts and vortices of particles, the throbbing glow of ribbons of energy, and the few natural fissures.

It took all Kyllikki's Operator's training, for the images weren't of specific places but of all places. But it got easier as Zuchmul made them feel as if they were one being smeared into three locations. The two men fed the vision back to her as if they shared one brain.

The roiling black mist caressed her skin with sensuous, soft tendrils, a familiar, comfortable sensation she'd thought never to feel again. The only thing missing was the tension of roused energies, and the focus of it on one specific partner. It lent the proceeding an air of unreality, like an altered memory.

She drew back from that thought and began to feed the men the knowledge that they had completed the establishment of their origin and destination, the way the galaxy was now, the way they wanted it to become. It was time for the next step. Using the nonsubstance of the mist, she began to weave the loops and whorls of the Dreambond pattern she and Idom had created. It would not be a screen blocking the entrance to Elias' mind, as Zimor's had been. It would be a path he could walk or not at will, a bridge supported by the pattern of girders Idom needed, surfaced with the key-image patterns of mind dictated by the natures of the two to be joined.

She felt Elias' mind as if it were her own. Here in the Pool, their very identities overlapped. As she probed the place in Elias where Zimor's Dreambond had been seated, she found a raw, oozing sore, throbbing and sensitive, the painful spot that had been there so very long, that would never let Elias rest. *The price he was willing to pay for his freedom.* The wound in him had been reopened by the conflict with Zimor, and there was now no way to heal it with the anchoring of her own Bond.

As she pondered the problem, she became aware of Zuchmul's revulsion. The Dreambond was an alien horror to him, so revolting that he almost let go of their hands.

Kyllikki tightened her clasp on his hand, hoping to reassure him by bringing up between them all that they had shared. She felt a whisper of a touch on her forehead, the shadow of a benediction carried on Influence, wakening a memory of what it had felt like to *be* luren. Zuchmul's visual evocation of the binding cord connecting them and the firmament around them stayed sharp, but gained detail as he wove a net of white threads, a veritable insect's web of connecting emotional memories anchored within each of them and spreading tautly among them. As the web built, Zuchmul was able to tolerate the gleaming ebony construct that would become the Dreambond.

//Kyllikki,// moaned Elias, //hurry, please. I can't take much more of this.//

Within herself, she could feel his wound throbbing where she'd irritated it. But she didn't know how to anchor her bridgehead there without killing him in the process.

Without warning, something blazing-hot screamed between them, a gold streak that hit the web Zuchmul had woven among them, coalescing into an image of Zimor as the web stretched and thinned to the breaking point, but it gripped and stopped her. Dangling upside down, hair flying, face twisted in rage, crusted blood mixed with fresh all over her naked body, she groped feebly about herself, stunned. The web stretched, leaving Zimor in a well in its center.

Kyllikki recognized the touch of Zimor's mind and knew she was really there in the Pool with them, focused on Elias, beginning to reweave her own Bond with him. The image of her window into his mind, seen now from inside Elias' mind, blossomed in both Kyllikki and Zuchmul. Locked into his identity as they were, when Zimor touched the raw wound, they felt Elias' involuntary flare of sexual arousal, memories kindled as strongly as if a probe had touched two brain cells at once: a savage groping with Zimor when she'd formed her Bond; the windswept precipice, billowing curtains, sweet sea air, and Kyllikki warm on top of him, soft, gentle, and melting into ultimate satisfaction.

In that same instant of searing arousal, Zimor's power withdrew and then began to build.

Family reflex! thought Kyllikki, as that bolt of mental energy focused on Zuchmul. Gripping Zuchmul's hand hard, she shoved, thrusting at him, dragging Elias behind her, forcing the circle to rotate, placing herself at Zimor's focus.

In normal space, such movement would not have mattered. Zimor's strike would have followed Zuchmul. But here, where identity itself was smeared, Kyllikki took the full brunt of her cousin's blow. It would have ripped any luren mind apart. Kyllikki reflected it back to the source.

She never knew if it arrived. The black mist heaved, the bright tricolor strand convulsed, and the stretched-tight web of memories rebounded like a tensed bowstring.

Zimor flew into the mist, becoming smaller and smaller, trailing a scream of despair and rage.

Any trained Operator, any Teleod telepath, knew that the imagery the mind produced in the Pool or the realms bore only the scantiest relationship to reality. But all three of them recognized death, final and absolute, and searingly cold.

The men drew close around Kyllikki, seeking the warmth of life, and then hands slid naturally around each other's waists and they hugged each other close fighting the searing cold flame of extinction that had brushed too near.

The tremors of reaction passed, and once again Zuchmul's visualization of the tricolor cord and the firmament waxed steadily brighter. Elias, discovering the raw wound in his mind cauterized and numbed by the cold of that dying, concluded to himself, *I wasn't Dreaming that, was I? It was real. She's really dead.*

Kyllikki wondered, *Is that what a Dream is like?*

Elias was glad that Dreams weren't always like that, especially not for the Dreambonded. Reality wasn't usually so *nightmarish*. Still, this particular *nightmare* was one he'd had before, many times, complete in every detail. He'd gotten so used to it, it hardly woke him up anymore.

Zuchmul knew it had really happened, and Kyllikki and Elias would share that Dream once they were Bonded.

Distantly, Kyllikki was aware that their minds were no longer separated. They were thinking each other's thoughts.

But Elias, knowing he was not in everyday waking consciousness, concluded that he was indeed asleep and Dreaming. He exerted a sort of control Kyllikki had never experienced before. It was a practiced control, as if un-Bonded Dreamers were accustomed to avoiding unpleasant Dreams by selecting what to Dream about.

And once again, all three of them were back in the curtained pavilion high atop a cliff, overlooking a dazzlingly blue sea.

The luren arranged the dots of white cloud overhead to form the image of the healed firmament, while the white foam on the sea below delineated the crazed and damaged firmament. The tricolor cord bound them to a wide, comfortable couch. And then he just left the images there to tend themselves as he turned his whole attention on Kyllikki, having decided that Dreaming was better than reality.

The Dreamer agreed and decided that this time, nothing would interrupt.

Kyllikki was aware of the danger in such a deep blending of minds, especially when the minds dared to surrender to the subjectivity of the Pool. But that awareness was a pale and distant thing compared to the luren touch that began to convince her of her beauty, and the Dreamer's insistent worship of that beauty. The silky ambience of the Pool's substance was deeply associated in her mind with this kind of growing tension. It was right. Oh, so right.

When they achieved that great triumphal moment, Kyllikki's barriers vanished and she stood naked before the cosmos while luren Influence wrapped them all in a primordial shout that the Dreamer gathered up into the music of more than a hundred instruments all crying out together.

Kyllikki was lying on a slick, hard surface, cold air drying the sweat on her body.

Elias groaned, curling up on his side, letting more cold air get at Kyllikki. He whispered, "I think—I think I had a—"

//How embarrassing.//

Numbly realizing she had heard Elias' voice as well as his thought, and that the searing heat flushing through her was his embarrassment, Kyllikki opened her eyes to the dim emergency lights of the hangar.

"You're not the only one," commented Zuchmul ruefully. "I told you it was real."

"That's not proof," groaned Elias, sitting up.

Zuchmul's eyes, protected only by his inserts, took on something of that wild look that Elias sometimes got when Idom explained things rationally.

They were on the hard, glassy surface of the Pool. In the back of Kyllikki's mind, like the burned-in key image, lurked the vision of the healed firmament, sky and sea blended into one. It was a place that existed in both her own mind and Elias'. And the two places were connected by the gleaming black latticework of the bridge she had built, the Dreambond.

She dragged her mind away from that marvel and found that around the railing above them, faces peered downward.

The rushing, babbling roar of hundreds of voices filled the hangar.

As someone started down the stair carrying a pile of clothes, Kyllikki gathered herself to her feet. She didn't know what disturbed her more: that she'd broken Operator's conditioning in the Pool; that she'd lived through it, which was theoretically impossible; or that she'd involved both men—at the same time! Of course, Idom would probably say that was the reason they'd all survived it. *Three again.*

But Idom had not counted Zimor into his calculations. *All of that, and maybe it didn't work.*

She gathered herself to her full height, forced her hands to stay down at her sides, and strode toward their rescuer with all the dignity of a Lady. She took a cloak off the top of the pile and found Esten Yinay behind the heap of material.

As Kyllikki swung the yellow cloak about herself, Elias and Zuchmul seized material and wrapped themselves as if in armor. The rasp of embarrassment faded somewhat, leaving her free to control her barriers again. She offered Esten a portrait of Idom and asked, "Where's this man? Have you seen him? Is he alive?"

"He's been poisoned."

Korachi! I forgot about them!

"Looks like he was stabbed with one of Zimor's needle weapons." There was an image of Idom, face covered with sweat, head tossing this way and that. "The medics are on the way. Are you all right?" She glanced at the men, obviously aware of their feelings.

Kyllikki nodded, slightly astonished at how easily her own barriers had reformed, and how efficiently they were filtering out the noise from the crowd. There was a kind of strength in her she'd never had before. *The Enhancement Zimor spoke of!* "Esten, I have to talk to him." She started for the stair, and the crowd parted to let her through.

Idom was lying beside the console, which had been properly shut down. He'd probably managed that with his last strength. She knelt beside him as a man was wiping sweat from his face with a bit of gold cloth.

"Idom." She got his attention, but it was clear he couldn't talk. In audio-analogue, she told him what had happened. //I failed you. I didn't think anything could break an Operator's conditioning, but I—I took them both into a full orgasmic experience. It even manifested physically. Did we do more damage to the firmament?//

His head tossed in a negative gesture. //It's all right. It must have worked. She stabbed me three times with two different poisoned needles hidden in her hair.//

His head drooped to one side. He was unconscious. Had that been the demented ravings of the poison? Or the studied pronouncement of the galaxy's foremost Pool theorist?

Beside her, Elias was asking Esten, "So we won?"

"Yes. And we all saw Zimor go mad and fling herself into the Pool—which we all thought was the end of everything. But the galaxy is still here. She didn't reappear, though."

"She's dead," said Kyllikki. "I'll have to stand examination for it, but I didn't kill her. At least not on purpose." She gave her a visual impression of Zimor's death.

Esten's expression ran the gamut from relief to surprise to satisfaction. "Then it is over." Spreading the news to the Yinay telepaths, she turned to gesture to the others around them, then froze.

Behind Zuchmul a cluster of armed guards pointed drawn weapons at him, waiting for an order to shoot.

He's not wearing an Inhibitor. Even in the Metaji, luren were shot on sight for that. She moved between Zuchmul and the weapons, holding her arm out to the luren. "Get close to me and they'll know you're not using Influence."

Esten finally absorbed the fact of Zuchmul's race and her eyes went wide. "You took a luren into the Pool!"

"He may have stopped the war! Come close to him, don't let them shoot him. He's not going to harm anyone. He can't use Influence in the midst of all this Family."

Esten glanced at Zuchmul, raked his mind in quick assessment, and moved up beside Kyllikki, gesturing at the guards. They promptly pointed their weapons at the ceiling.

Mentally, Kyllikki groped for contact with the triplets and summoned them to the Pool hangar while aloud she explained why Zuchmul had no Inhibitor. The triplets arrived while she was still talking and moved right up to surround the luren.

Zuchmul kept his gaze lowered, his power stilled, with hardly a hint of the pain he felt while standing unprotected in the uncontrolled environment.

At that moment, someone turned on the regular lights.

Instantly, Zuchmul curled in on himself, burying his eyes in several folds of his cape, stifling a cry of dismay.

Throwing a fold of her cape over Zuchmul, Kyllikki sent a demand to every telepath to get the lights out, fast. They died back to the dim emergency lights. Then she ordered the luren's protective gear brought to him. The moment the heap of things was handed to him, he seized his goggles and slipped them on. While Zuchmul dressed, the telepathic and verbal murmuring built as people spread the word of Zimor's death. Outside, hostility was subsiding as Laila realized it hadn't been invaded but liberated.

Kyllikki kept her barriers permeable, letting all curious telepaths gather the fragments of the story, absorb her motive for her actions, compare with what they gleaned from the men, notice the Dreambond, the explanation for it, and form their own conclusions about the effect Zimor's action might have had on the attempt to heal the firmament and stop the war and the loss of ships.

As she gave permission for the lights to come on again, she queried Esten about the scholars they'd left anesthetized in the hospital building, and was informed they'd been found.

When the medics came to carry Idom away, she fell in behind them, anxious to be sure he'd be all right. But the experts didn't seem overly concerned as they administered the antidote to Zimor's poison.

By the time they neared the hangar doors, the telepathic uproar had begun to subside, but the verbal roar was growing as the non-telepaths were filled in. Technical arguments erupted in little pockets here and there, heavily laced with Idom's name.

The crowd tightened up around them, slowing them to a stop despite the Yinay pleas to make way.

Elias and Zuchmul tensed, certain they were about to be lynched. Kyllikki didn't even have a chance to reassure them before a chant gathered in the back of the crowd.

"Kyllikki, The Lady of Laila! Kyllikki, The Lady of Laila! Kyllikki, The Lady of Laila, now!"

It spread rapidly until the consensus was clear even to the non-telepaths.

Kyllikki was about to tell them that the new head of the Family would be chosen in the usual manner, after due deliberation, when a noise overpowered the crowd's chanting.

A somewhat damaged vehicle clanked and rattled across the open space before the hangar doors, dragging a piece of its body behind it. It stopped just within the puddle of light spilling from the doors. A young man got out and clambered up onto the roof. He wasn't a telepath, but he had an amplifier and powerful lungs.

"A Metaji fleet is entering the Inarash system and our own fleet is three days away! The Metaji fleet is twenty-five hundred ships strong! The Duke of Fotel, commanding for the Metaji

Emperor, is asking to negotiate with Kyllikki Lady Laila and no other. He says that her efforts to stop the war have been made known to him, and his ships will not attack anything Teleod if he can speak with her directly."

Kyllikki looked at Elias, who said, "Twenty-five hundred. That's what was estimated as the whole fleet."

"Exactly," confirmed Zuchmul. He bent and whispered, "I bet D'sillin got to Fotel with that tape and used the Sa'ar power to get him to listen. For the first time since you talked me into this, I think there's a chance we may all survive the success of your plan."

"It worked," repeated Kyllikki blankly. A grin split her face. "It worked!" She let it out telepathically. //It was a success! It worked!// She gave everyone the vision of the firmament healing, ships passing without losses.

She let them push her to the vehicle, where Zuchmul put his hands around Kyllikki's waist to lift her onto the hood. He paused, his goggles reflecting her image back at her, and she had the oddest feeling that he was studying her with all his luren senses as if seeing her for the first time. Then, in a sudden wash of guilt, he set her up on the hood and she climbed up beside the youth with the amplifier.

Commandeering the amplifier, Kyllikki told the crowd, "You call me The Lady of Laila! Then I tell you we must not fight the Metaji fleet. We must offer truce and negotiate a peace. We need not surrender. We need not succumb to the Empire. We need only admit that we were wrong about the Pools and learn a better way to use them. Can the Teleod admit to an error?"

"Yes!"

"Do we need the Metaji to pound it into us?"

"No!"

"Do we need the Metaji to tell us how to change?"

"No!"

"Then I will speak with the Duke of Fotel, and with the Emperor himself if I must, and I will tell them the Teleod will no longer use Pool Operators. The Teleod wishes to be a good neighbor to the Empire, but will not allow the Empire to dictate policy to us. We will treat the firmament with respect not because the Empire demands it, but because it is right!"

She had to shout down the cheering crowd to finish, "As the temporary head of Laila, I order all Operator-staffed ships to proceed immediately to the nearest port and remain there until new staffing can be provided. And as the temporary head of Laila, I guarantee that such staffing will be forthcoming—from the Metaji's own Guild, if necessary—soon enough that profits will not be drastically impaired. And those same Guild Guides will train us to run our own ships."

This time the cheering didn't stop, and Kyllikki swung down into Elias' strong arms. He shouted into her ear, "Will they do that?"

"It's no more than they offered Zimor before the war broke out. Besides, I'm sure Idom can arrange it."

An older man, a Yinay whom Kyllikki finally recognized as Esten's father, The Lord of Yinay, came around the vehicle and offered her a hug, roaring into her ear to be heard: "Thank goodness you're nothing like Zimor!"

Tears leaked from Kyllikki's eyes, and her throat clenched tight. *I'm nothing like her. I never was. I never will be.*

Very silently, not a verbalized thought or even a communed evocation, but a diffuse awareness of Elias standing on the gleaming black bridge that abutted the cliff that held the curtained pavilion, crept through her. He strolled out onto the bridge, and deep inside she felt his warm strength and his knowledge of her. *No, you're not anything like her at all.*

About the Author

Jacqueline Lichtenberg was born in 1942, three months after Pearl Harbor. With a degree in chemistry from the University of California at Berkeley, she worked abroad, then married and raised two children, Gail and Debbie.

In the seventies, she won early acclaim for her *Star Trek* fan fiction, the Kraith Series, which gained her a nomination for the Best Fan Writer Hugo, and, twenty-two years after the first Kraith story was published, a feature article in *The New York Times Book Review* and the first Surak Memory Alpha Award for all-time achievement in *Star Trek* fandom. She is primary author of the Bantam paperback *Star Trek Lives!* as well as founder of the Star Trek Welcommittee.

At the same time she was selling novels in an SF universe of her own, Sime/Gen, set on the Earth of the far future and involving a kind of vampiric interdependency in which world peace depends on individuals' overcoming personal fears. The second Sime/Gen novel published, *Unto Zeor, Forever*, won the 1978 Galaxy Award for spirituality in science fiction. In addition to the four fan-originated amateur magazines dedicated to Sime/Gen, there are newsletters, single-edition fanzines, and eight novels in the universe, three co-authored with Jean Lorrah, and one Jean Lorrah original.

Between Sime/Gen novels, she wrote *Molt Brother* and *City of a Million Legends*, the tale of two galactic civilizations and crucial family bonds between human and nonhuman.

The first book in her Dushau Trilogy, *Dushau*, a fast-paced adventure in yet another universe richly populated with nonhuman species, won her the 1985 Romantic Times Award for Best Science Fiction Writer. After completing the trilogy with *Farfetch* and *Outreach*, she said, "I enjoy blending romance with a touch of the occult and a strong science motif to ask hard questions about life's most basic relationships."

Her short stories include contributions to the universes of Marion Zimmer Bradley's *Darkover* and Andre Norton's *Witch*

World, where she introduced a good vampire, as well as a story written for the anthology *Tarot Tales* involving the hero of her recent novel, the vampire love story *Those of My Blood*.

She is past Chair of the Science Fiction Writers of America Speakers' Bureau, and in her spare time she gives tarot and writing workshops, attends *Star Trek*, SF, and esoteric conventions, reviews student manuscripts for the SF&Fantasy Workshop and *Star Trek* fanzines for *Treklink*, and pursues studies such as vampires, Arthurian legend, numerology, astrology, Qabalah, the tarot's ancient history, *Blake's Seven*, and *Doctor Who*. She serves on the Board of Directors of the North American Time Festivals, Inc., which organizes *Doctor Who* conventions.